The Sharp Edge
of the Soul

The Sharp Edge of the Soul

❦

GEORGE CHOVANES

Library of Congress Number: 2001116051

ISBN #:   Hardcover   0-7388-6035-2

                   Softcover   0-7388-6036-0

This is a work of fiction. Names, characters, places and incidents either are the product of the author's imagination or are used fictitiously, and any resemblance to any actual persons, living or dead, events, or locales is entirely coincidental.

This book was printed in the United States of America.

To order additional copies of this book, contact:
Xlibris Corporation
1-888-7-XLIBRIS
www.Xlibris.com
Orders@Xlibris.com

Contents

To my wife, my parents, and my brothers

For my children, their children, and so on

In valor there is hope

Tacitus

4530-CHOV

CHAPTER 1

As long as he'd been doing this, he still regretted doing it to a little girl. Alex took the knife, held it steadily and tenderly for a moment over the prostrate child's shaved and glistening head, the curved blade gleaming a hairsbreadth from the pristine, nearly translucent pink skin. He pressed deeply through the thin flawless scalp until blocked by the skull, cutting a full thickness cleft to the pearly white bone, carving an elegant crimson curve as blood spurted from the severed arteries. The small woman standing unsteadily next to him groaned, eyes wide, then ivory as they rolled up, then fluttering closed as she crumpled to the floor.

"Why'd they let her in?" muttered Alex as he applied clips to the bleeding scalp edges, clamping and stopping the streaming flow. "Somebody help her."

Joan the circulating nurse rushed over, cradled the groggy girl in her arms, then helped her up and out of the room.

"You know we need new scrub nurses, and they have to learn sometime." Carol, the chief scrub nurse, turned to Alex sharply. She was standing next to him on his right, with Curt, the first year resident, to his left. All were gowned, gloved, and masked, arrayed around the child's head, draped and isolated at the top of the operating table. "It makes it much harder when there's a chairman like Dr. Todd. You know how it is," she said accusingly, like Alex had something to do with it. "When Dr. Todd gets in a bad mood, they scatter like flies and we lose them. Can you blame them? Who'd want to stay?" She shook her covered head, the ties to the surgical hood fluttering at her neck, and adjusted the instruments on the table next to her, then looked up at Curt, the new resident. "They call him the Antichrist."

His eyes widened over his mask.

"You'll see" she added, encouraged by the effect on him.

"Don't scare the boy, Carol."

She turned slightly to Alex, her dark eyes flashing, surrounded by the blue of her mask and hood like islands in the sea. "I'm just informing him. He should know what he's in for." She glanced at her instruments, the wrinkles around her eyes lengthening. "It wasn't this way with Dr. Henry."

"Was Dr. Henry the Chief before Dr. Todd?" Curt asked.

"Yep. He was Chief up until a couple years of ago. He was the one that accepted me into the program. Great guy."

"The man was a saint" Carol said reverently.

"Well, those times are gone. Now we have University Hospital Chief of Neurosurgery Victor Todd. And he is" Alex paused, precisely rotating the needle holder to complete a stitch, "the Boss", he put in another stitch, "and I'm only a resident."

"The Chief Resident."

"Yeah, that means I have the most to lose."

"No, that means you finish this year and you'll be gone, on your own in your own practice. We'll still be stuck here." She had a scalpel in her hand and shook it. "Don't forget us when you're out there."

He smiled under his mask. "Don't you worry. I'll hire you."

"That's what you told me before, and then I go and talk to Margie in the ICU and I find out you've promised her the same thing."

"There's room for everybody, when I'm free."

She snorted. "I'll believe it when I see it."

As they chattered, he continued the surgery, the blazing operating lights overhead focused on and vividly accentuating the intense whiteness of the skin, the flaming red of the blood, and the surrounding glowing blue drapes. Alex adeptly opened up the skull and levered out a silver dollar sized piece of bone. Underneath bulged the brain's natural covering, a grayish membrane, the dura. A loud buzzing noise started.

"Curt, get off the bipolar pedal."

"Sorry." Curt had pressed too closely to Alex's left and inadvertently stepped on the pedal for the electric cautery tool. He backed off, fascinated. Looking and wondering, with wide eyes peering above his poorly tied mask, he was only days out from completing his internship, a year after medical school. Everything interested him; the smooth teamwork, the way Carol seemed to anticipate Alex's needs, the calm as a human head was opened up, the anatomy under the scalp, what protected the brain, what the living brain looked like. All of this was new to him.

Gracefully, Carol handed Alex instruments she plucked from neat rows on a brilliantly lit table covered with blue sterile waterproof drapes. Alex worked easily, teaching Curt as his hands continually moved.

"Exposure is the key, Curt. You have to remove enough bone to see down to where the aneurysm is."

"What do you mean?"

"This poor girl had bleeding around the brain. The cause of that bleeding was an aneurysm, a weak spot on one of the major blood vessels feeding the brain. It's like a light bulb sticking out of the side of a pipe. More people than you think have one of these babies lurking up in their heads. Do you get constipated?"

Curt was taken aback. "Nope."

"Never?"

"Well, rarely."

"Good. A lot of straining, a lot of pushing can pop one of these bad boys, and then you're really in deep shit."

Curt's eyes bulged.

"Now look who's trying to scare him." Carol observed.

"Just reviewing some clinical facts. At any rate, the aneurysm is deep under the brain. In order to see it, we'll have to lift up the brain and look underneath it several inches, to the main blood vessels. You always want to minimize the pressure on the brain, though. If you remove enough bone, you don't have to lift up the brain much to get a straight view down to the problem."

Curt nodded, staring down at the pulsating cerebrum.

Alex outlined the hole in the skull with the tip of a surgical instrument. "Here's the final exposure. We'll be able to do what we need to through this."

Curt heard tension in Alex's voice, and glanced at him.

"Well Carol, I guess we're as ready as we'll ever be. Time for the Boss."

Carol turned toward Joan, the circulating nurse, who went over to the telephone embedded in the green tiled wall and quickly dialed Dr. Todd's office.

"They're ready for Dr. Todd in the OR." She listened to the reply and then hung up. Turning, she nodded to Alex, who was looking up at her, hands motionless in front of him. "He'll be down. Audrey says he's in a bad mood, though."

"Great" muttered Alex. Carol, veteran though she was, shifted uneasily. The atmosphere mutated, charged now as if with static electricity. Curt felt everyone coming to mental attention, and straightened up. The anesthesia resident bustled behind his curtain.

"Curt, here's a couple of ground rules to survive your residency with Dr. Todd. Don't speak unless spoken to, don't ask stupid questions, don't try to help unless I ask you to. Got it?"

"I thought there was no such thing as a stupid question. That's what I've been taught from kindergarten on" Curt observed politely.

He won't last long if he can't keep his mouth shut, Alex thought. "That was kindergarten. Now you're in the twenty-second grade, and I'm in the twenty-seventh grade. In this school with this teacher there are plenty of stupid questions. Do yourself a favor. Keep your mouth shut."

Curt nodded. Already nervous at starting his neurosurgical training, he became tenser. Alex's about done, thought Curt. What's he so uptight about?

"Curt, why'd you come here for residency?"

"It was the best program."

"And why was it the best?"

"Dr. Todd is a world famous brain surgeon."

"Right. That's what they told you. Only what they didn't tell you is that he's a world class pain in the ass as well." Alex stabbed a scalpel in the air, the blade for a moment flaming with reflected light. "The big boys often are. He can be mean as hell. Don't get on his bad side. Remember." He stabbed again into the air.

Curt shifted uneasily. "Sure, Alex." His mask felt tight around his face, and he wondered how long he could breathe through its constriction.

"Remember Gordon Hoeffel, the resident you met last year during your interviews?"

"Yeah."

"Well, he's gone now. Fired. Just like that. In his fourth year of neurosurgical training, fifth year after graduating medical school. Something happened to a patient in the ICU when he was on call one night. Not his fault, but on his watch. The Boss flipped out. Gordon was a marked man. Never recovered. Fired a couple of months later. Couldn't find another position."

Alex glanced at Curt. He's already a bit bug eyed, thought Alex, then realized it was a combination of wide-eyed amazement and an improperly tied mask whose edges cut into the skin below the eyes, bulging them out even more.

"In this training program, to finish is to arrive in the promised land, the end of a long and arduous road." Alex spoke as if from a distance, looked up for the briefest of moments, then resumed working. "That's what my chief resident told me."

"Be smart and don't make trouble for yourself and us, Curt" Carol added.

Curt nodded.

"Joan, fix his mask."

Joan came over in back of Curt and carefully reached around, adjusting his tangled ties. As he turned to make it easier for her to work on the mask, his eyes were drawn to a shape whose bulk suddenly blotted out the light through the window in the OR door, in the corner of the room.

The anesthesiology resident, looking over his curtain, announced, "Here's the man."

They all turned. Dr. Todd's masked face looked for a moment through the window, then the door opened and he thrust his hooded head in.

"We're ready to go, Dr. Todd" Alex said quickly.

Todd closed the door and went to the scrub sink.

"Remember what I said, Curt."

He nodded. Joan was still working on his mask.

"Finish it quick, Joan."

Todd pressed the pedal at the sink and washed his hands quickly. He thrust the door open with his foot, holding his large hands up, palms inward, and strode into the room. Curt looked at the backs of his hands, his fingers surprisingly thick, then to the massive shoulders behind the hands, then to his face. Todd stopped, his hands still up in front of him as if offering a blessing, and nodded to Carol, his stygian eyes contrasting with the pale surgical hat and mask. Curt had forgotten how dark and deep set they were, hovering above his mask like two piercing and luminous ebony crystals.

"Good morning, Dr. Todd." Carol said as she helped him on with the surgical gown.

As Joan scuttled around behind him and tied the rustling paper vestment, Alex updated him quickly.

"The exposure went well. The brain is soft and it retracts nicely."

"Did you get the lumbar drain in?" His voice was a deep rumble, and with the mask over his mouth, seemed to come from his chest.

"Yes. No problems."

"Good."

After Carol finished gowning and gloving Dr. Todd, Joan carefully moved closer to him with the headlight. She stood up on tiptoe as he leaned down slightly, gingerly placing the headband on him like an emperor being crowned. After plugging in the fiberoptic tube to the light source, Joan waited as Dr. Todd checked the aim of the light.

"Is that OK, Dr. Todd?"

He grunted assent then moved, looming over the child's head.

Alex, looking diminished, shifted to the left, pushing Curt over with his elbow. Carol stayed on Dr. Todd's right. They were arrayed around the head and prostrate body like a crescent.

Dr. Todd looked for a moment at the brightly-lit brain, framed by a series of concentric edges composed of dura, skull, scalp, white gauze and blue drapes. The successive layers looked like a divot taken out from an onion, the pulsating brain outlined by widening rings.

"Brain ribbon." Todd slipped the metal instrument under the soft, gray brain and gently lifted it up, directing his headlight down the axis of the blunt blade into the shadows under the brain.

Curt pressed against Alex's side, trying to get a better view. Alex nudged him in warning and glanced at him. Curt backed off.

"Aaah" Dr. Todd grunted in frustration.

Carol, observing the operation closely, jumped slightly. Blood suddenly started spewing from the crevice under the brain, filling the hole in the skull and flooding the drapes. Curt felt something tap his shoe, looked down, and saw blood dripping onto it. He quickly moved. This wasn't supposed to happen. The little girl's in trouble now.

Alex barked, "Large suction."

Carol quickly handed him a silver suction tube with trailing clear plastic hose. Alex smoothly brought it into the dark pool, and a red streak of blood shot through the tubing, gurgling and slurping, dumping redness into the canister mounted on the wall, spattering the clear container. Still the blood flowed, covering the brain, cascading out of the wound onto the drapes and then to the floor. Curt looked down at the spreading puddle, dark blood on the black floor. It was coming towards his shoes. He hoped somebody would do something.

"Not enough suction. Give me another sucker. Anesthesia, we're losing quite a bit of blood," Alex said briskly. "Get a towel for the floor."

A commotion was heard over the curtains as the anesthesia resident moved quickly to open up the valve on the intravenous tubing, forcing fluid and trying to buy time until the blood arrived.

Todd looked up at the anesthesia resident, his eyes glittering. "Get your boss in here. Now." His voice now had a grating rasp in the deepness, like a dull saw laboring to cut the skull open.

The resident nodded and grabbed the phone.

"Another sucker." Alex took a second suction tube in his right hand, also bringing it to bear on the bleeding. The gurgling increased. Twin contrails of blood filled the tubing and streaked to the wall. Slowly, with both suckers working, the blood level receded. Alex gradually deepened the suction tubes into the crevice as Dr. Todd held the brain up with a metal blade.

"The blood pressure's dropping" the anesthesia resident reported tensely from behind the drapes.

"Where's the attending?" Todd demanded, not looking up.

"He'll be right in."

"I said now." Todd looked up for a brief moment, locking on the anesthesia resident, clawing at him with his eyes.

Curt winced, glad of his anonymity behind the mask.

The OR door opened and the anesthesia attending hustled over to the resident. They conferred in urgent whispers, and both started working on the tubes and bags of fluid hung over the patient.

With a metal suction tube in each hand, Alex followed the bleeding to the base of the brain, finally placing both suckers next to a grape sized ballooning of a weakened main brain artery.

"Dr. Todd, here's the aneurysm. Can you get a clip on it if I keep sucking?"

Dr. Todd peered under the brain and nodded. "Good job. Straight clip."

Carol handed him a tool with a small metal clip on the end, like a tiny metal clothespin. He opened up the clip with the handle, carefully bringing it down into the abyss underneath the brain.

"Looks good, Dr. Todd. I'll move my sucker slightly so you can get in better."

Alex held the tips of both tubes right at the rent in the aneurysm, continuously sucking the high-pressure stream shooting out. The jet of blood looked deceptively solid, in constant flux but for all appearances an immobile column.

"Blood pressure still dropping" said the anesthesia attending.

"You don't need to keep announcing it." Todd snapped. He maneuvered the clip around the pulsating, gushing bag of blood and closed the clip down. The metal arms closed over the rent, sealing it off. The bleeding stopped. Alex removed the sucker tubes and Dr. Todd withdrew the metal blade, gently letting the brain down onto the floor of the skull once again.

Curt, bug eyed to Alex's left, took a deep breath. They were working in a hole about an inch wide, half an inch high and two inches deep. He wondered how he could ever be able to do anything like that.

Dr. Todd backed up slightly. "Excellent, Alex." He looked into Alex's eyes. "I guess you've learned a thing or two here. Hopefully it will stay here." The instruments clattered as he put down the clip handle on Carol's table.

"Blood pressure coming back up. Very nice, gentleman" came the announcement from behind the anesthesia curtain.

"Well, that's done with. Close up, Alex." He looked to Alex's left, noting Curt for the first time. "Who the hell are you?"

"Curt Smith, sir. First year resident."

The Boss ignored him. "How is he doing, Alex?"

"Terrific, Dr. Todd. He's keeping his mouth shut and his bowels open." Dr. Todd grunted and turned.

"Superb. This is what we are supposed to do. The direct repair of nature's error. We're getting pretty good at that."

Alex nodded, relieved at the save and pleased at the Boss's comments. "We do well with vascular problems. And with the radiosurgery we can hit tumors without opening the patient up."

Todd looked at Alex, his hooded and dark eyes focusing on him. "The only objective left is improving the brain itself, therefore improving mankind."

Alex nodded, his eyes matching with the Boss's, his exhilaration and relief now mixed with unease. He wasn't sure what the Boss meant. "You mean, fix the evil in men's souls?"

Todd snorted, his facemask rippling with his breath. "Spoken like a philosopher. Isn't that what your major was in college?"

"Moral philosophy."

"Well, I'm not a moralist. I don't know what that means. All I know is that we need to make the brain work better."

Dr. Todd abruptly backed away from the operative field, ripped off his paper gown and turned towards Alex again.

"Not bad for a philosophy major. Look what I've done with you."

"Moral philosophy."

"Whatever. Let me give you a word of advice. Don't worry about the good and evil stuff. Let's do what we're supposed to do—just make the brain work better." He turned and walked out the door. Carol took a deep breath.

"What'd he mean by that?" Curt looked at Alex.

Alex shrugged. "I have no idea." He shook his head. "He goes off on tangents sometimes. We're not God, that's for sure."

"Well, you nodded when he said it."

"I'm an agreeable sort. Especially when it comes to the Boss."

Curt sighed. "What's that radiosurgery you were talking about?"

"A way of using radiation, focusing it very precisely to any area in the brain."

"I think I've heard of it."

"Dr. Todd was a pioneer. He did much of the original research work developing it." Alex talked as he worked, feeling voluble now that the crisis was over. "A special frame is put on the patient's head. A computer is then used to plan the radiation treatment, and the patient is placed on the radiation couch, the headframe is bolted down preventing any movement, and the radiation machine gives the radiation."

"How's it different than regular radiation?"

"The computer planning and special hardware, as well as the headframe, allow the radiation to be focused with millimeter accuracy to any area in the brain, without any scar or open surgery."

"Wow. I think I've seen the frame for the head. You've got to put pins into the skull to hold it, don't you?"

"The newest development is a headframe that is placed on the head without any pins. No scars. No nothing."

"Incredible. Same day brain surgery. One chair. No waiting. No fuss, no muss."

"Yep."

Alex stopped working for a moment and looked up, straight ahead, at the green tiled wall, his hood ruffling. "Only."

"Only what?"

"I wonder what he meant about improving the brain." He lowered his gaze and continued.

Carol looked at them. "Well, whatever he meant, that was a beautiful job, Alex." She turned to rearrange her instruments on the table.

Curt nodded. "That was amazing, Alex. The Boss really liked it. And what did he mean with that stuff about staying here?"

Alex chuckled.

Carol said proudly, "What do you think it means? He wants him to stay here after he finishes training. That's high praise."

Alex, relieved at the outcome and basking in the Boss's words, felt expansive. "Someday all this will be yours" he told Curt with a giggle and wave around the operating room.

Curt shook his head once again.

They focused their attention on the brain. Alex continued squirting saline solution onto the cortex, cleaning out the clotted blood that had formed from the hemorrhage.

"It's important to close well to avoid postoperative complications."

"Can I close?" Curt blurted.

"No. Watch me carefully and you'll be able to do it some time, but you gotta walk before you can run. If you close improperly, postoperative bleeding can devastate the patient. For that matter, it can happen even if you close correctly. Just watch and learn."

Carol nodded to Curt. "Some of the residents don't close the whole first year. They just don't get it."

Alex neatly stitched together the brain's covering and then put the disc of bone he had removed earlier back into the opening in the skull. He used tiny metal plates and screws to secure the bone back on, then sewed the scalp closed.

"Four by fours." Carol handed Alex gauze pads, which he placed over the c-shaped incision. He held the pads on the wound as he and Carol carefully removed the blue paper drapes over the head.

"Okay Curt. Let's take her out of the clamp and put the dressing on. Hold the head."

Curt carefully cradled the small head, heavier than he expected. He looked at the pale, angelic little face, eyes hidden by translucent lids beautiful with a delicate filigree of tiny veins, hinting at the divinity within. He touched the child's cheek, cool as marble, and then his gaze rested on the large incision above. Amazing. "We were just into this child's soul, behind this beautiful face," he murmured.

Alex paused and silently smiled, his eyes crinkling above his mask, then removed the metal pins embedded into the skull that had immobilized the head.

"Okay, Curt. Now the sterile dressing."

"Can I do it?"

"No. This is what the patient's family sees, and more importantly what the Boss sees. It has to look perfect." Alex used several rolls of gauze, turning and flipping them over the head until the entire scalp was covered with a smooth white shell, a large helmet over the small face. "That's how it should look," he said with pride. "Now, this is the way to put the tape on."

Curt watched the precise ritual carefully.

"You do the operative note and orders. I'll see you in the ICU after that."

Curt nodded. "Yes, my liege." He bowed.

Alex stepped back, tore off his paper gown and gloves, throwing them in the trash.

The anesthesia resident nodded at Curt. "Be good and someday you'll be like him."

Alex shook his head.

The anesthesia resident continued. "He's the only one to pass the written part of the board examinations in the first year."

Curt turned to Alex. "Is that true, Alex?"

Alex nodded. "You've got the year to study for it. One thing at a time. Do the orders and the notes and I'll see you in the ICU." He turned slightly. "Thanks a lot Carol."

"Very nice job, Alex."

"Pride goeth before a fall." He smiled under his still masked face. "Thanks, anesthesia." As he reached to push open the door, he looked through the crisscrossing wires embedded in the glass window, his mind turning to Dr. Todd's words. Improving the brain? What the hell did that mean?

CHAPTER 2

Alex usually enjoyed the stroll out of the hospital, but this evening he was unsettled. Before he entered the dank parking garage, his head craned upward to catch a glimpse of the blue sky, then he lowered his gaze and found his car. Driving automatically through the sparse city traffic, down the expressway to the suburbs, he mulled over the events of the day. Taking the exit to the right, he stopped at the light and made a left to go under the expressway. The road immediately became tree lined, houses and large yards on either side, with frequent wooded patches. Motoring through, he came to the lane where he lived. Turning, he glanced at the twin stone sentinels, old remnants of some unknown estate whose former magnificence had been reduced to the containment of new houses and vast yards.

Alex pulled into the long driveway to his garage apartment. Every time he drove home, out of the noise and congestion of the city, he thought how fortunate he was to have gotten a place in the green, leafy suburbs.

He drove along the lane, passing the large stone home of his landlord, a retired anatomist at the University, then around the house to the garage in the rear. It was a detached stone structure, with bays for three cars, his apartment above. A hardwood forest abutted the back of the garage, and trees surrounded the large back and front yards of the house.

As he parked and got out, he noticed his landlord in a long brimmed white hat, white shirt and pants, bobbing up and down in his garden like a huge white stork.

On impulse he walked over. He didn't usually speak much to his landlord, Dr. Sutcliff, as they both liked their solitude, but Dr. Todd's cryptic comments weighed on his mind.

The evening was cool and clear, the sun setting with a beautiful yellow light illuminating the leaves of the oak trees and garden, making them glow a golden green. Alex walked on the trimmed grass over to the old man, who was busy pulling weeds out of the moist black soil.

"Hi, Dr. Sutcliff."

Startled, the old man turned around, still bent and reminding Alex even more of a stork looking for prey. His thinness was emphasized by the large hat and old brown leather belt pulled tight around his waist, the worn end dangling like a battered snake. As he slowly straightened up, his long, inquiring and lively face broke into a smile.

"Hello, Alex."

"How are things going?"

"Okay, I guess." Sutcliff nodded, his long brim bobbing, the shadow of the brim on the grass even longer. "I always seem to get a lot of weeds this time of year, but I know how to handle them."

Alex smiled. Sutcliff inspected him. "How are things at the University? How's Victor Todd?"

"Did you work with him much?"

"Well, as you know, my interest was in neuroanatomy. I was in the Anatomy Department, not Neurosurgery, but at one point I did regularly attend Neurosurgical Grand Rounds. I would discuss things with him from time to time. He did have a unusually keen interest in neuroanatomy, and how the brain worked."

"How was it unusual?"

Sutcliff chuckled. "Well you'd have a hard time explaining this to a layman, but you know how most neurosurgeons just want to know the important neuroanatomy, the stuff immediately relevant to surgery of the brain."

Alex nodded.

"Well, Todd was different. He wanted to know how the brain

worked, how it does what it does, how does it think, feel, reason. As you know, these were the most profound questions, for even with the most sophisticated techniques we don't and didn't know much about the brain." Sutcliff coughed. "By the way, are they starting to use MRI scans more?"

"It's the mainstay of diagnosis for brain and spine problems."

Sutcliff glanced at Alex, somewhat embarrassed. "Well, things move very quick, don't they? MRI scans have been clinically used for what, five years?"

"Oh, about ten." Alex mentally decreased the length of time to spare the old man further embarrassment. He fleetingly wondered how he himself would feel as the world accelerated around him.

Sutcliff looked at his garden. "Well, I guess I better stick to this."

"Did Dr. Todd ever mention anything about improving the brain?"

Sutcliff looked at him, still embarrassed. "No, don't think so. He was working on radiosurgery techniques at the time and that was his main research interest, as I recall."

"Well, nice talking with you, Dr. Sutcliff. I don't want to keep you from your garden. Can I help you?"

"Thanks, Alex. You were a big help moving the rocks for the Japanese garden. I'll give a yell if I need you." The old man turned and slowly, impossibly slowly, bent down again, aiming for a weed, the stork-like white figure folding down.

It's a good thing the weed doesn't have legs, Alex thought sympathetically. I guess that's all he can do at this point. He turned and walked back to his apartment, jumping up the rickety stairs to the quarters above the garage, taking them two at a time. Opening the round topped green wood screen door, he fished in his pocket, pulled out a key and unlocked the faded, flaked white inner door.

The waning light of the sun lit the cream walls of the low ceilinged apartment with a warm glow. He went to the small kitchen, made dinner, and sat down. As he quietly ate from a table which was a visual archeology of different finishes successively applied, mulling over the Boss's words, the shadows lengthened outside and night came. He heard a knocking, more like a rapping on the screen door, as he had left the inner door open. Surprised, he got up and walked through the small dining room to the living room. A whitish figure stood outside, barely visible through the screen. As he got closer, he recognized Dr. Sutcliff.

"Alex?"

"Right here. Come in, come in."

Sutcliff opened the door and stepped awkwardly in, his head bare.

"Sorry to bother you." He nodded apologetically, his white pants stained with green and brown patches around the knees.

"No problem at all. What can I do for you?"

"Well, you got me to thinking."

"About what?"

"About Todd. You know, about improving the brain."

"Oh, yes."

"As a matter of fact he did tell me once, and I had forgotten all about it until you got me thinking."

"What's that?"

"Well it was after a Grand Rounds that he gave, lecturing on the anatomic correlations of the frontal lobes of the brain." He coughed, then looked upward, stretching his wrinkled neck, eyes bulging like a turtle sticking his head out of his shell. "Now this was an area in which I had a special concern. You may have read my paper on 'Olfactory Correlates in the Brown Squirrel?'" He glanced at Alex questioningly, his white eyebrows arching spasmodically.

"As a matter of fact I hadn't, but now that you bring it to mind, I'll be sure to look it up. Sounds very interesting."

"Well, it isn't important. At any rate, after this Grand Rounds I came up to him and spoke about some anatomic points that I felt needed clarification."

Feeling fatigued after his arduous day, Alex looked at Sutcliff's wavering, rheumy eyes, a watery blue, and hoped his weariness wasn't showing.

"It was then that he said it."

"Said what?"

"He said that I didn't understand. That a new science of the brain was developing, superb and unprecedented insight into the workings of the central nervous system."

He looked at Alex for a reaction.

"A new science of the brain?"

Sutcliff nodded. "We then discussed what evidence he had for his thoughts, which were quite interesting although to tell you the truth I can't tell you exactly what the details were."

He stopped and looked at Alex, a bit embarrassed. Alex nodded again encouragingly.

"I told him he only had an animal model, no human data, and he looked at me so strangely, so strangely that I just stopped the conversation right there. I never felt like reopening the discussion." He shook his head. "I'll never forget that look." He shivered. "And he's your Chief now."

"Yep. But I wonder what it means?"

He sighed. "I can't say that I know. Well, that's it for what it's worth. The ramblings of an old man."

"Thanks very much. They were really very interesting." Alex rubbed his head, closed his eyes for a brief moment.

Sutcliff watched him. "How are you feeling?"

"OK. I get these headaches now and then."

"Are they bad?"

"Sometimes it feels like a boa constrictor is wrapped around my skull and giving it a real good squeeze."

"Sounds like you need an MRI scan."

"I got one. One night the Boss wanted to try out a new MRI technique, and I was the guinea pig."

"The other residents must have loved that."

"It was just the Boss and I. They had all gone."

"So you have a brain?" the elderly man cackled softly, pleased at his effort.

Alex smiled wanly. "I assume so. The Boss didn't show me the films. Needed them for his database. Hopefully he would have told me if there were ping pong balls there." He rubbed his head again. "But, thank God, he said the films looked OK." He shrugged. "He wants to get another one for his database in a couple months."

"Well, I'd better be going. Sorry to bother you. Hope what I told you was of interest."

"It was. That was exactly what I was wondering about."

"Well, you're very kind." He looked around the room. "You haven't done much with the place."

Alex looked around as well. "You're right. I'll have time in the spring."

"You'll be gone in June. You won't do anything." Sutcliff said softly.

"I'll see what I can do."

Dr. Sutcliff turned and walked out. Alex flipped on the outside light, the crickets chirping, the dim yellow light barely illuminating the cracked stone steps.

"Good night. Thanks for coming. And I will take a look at your paper."

"Good night."

Alex watched as the stooped white figure slowly made his way down the stone stairs, his head without the hat looking as vulnerable as a turtle out of his shell. He suddenly stumbled, and Alex leaped down the stairs to grab his arm.

"Sorry, Dr. Sutcliff. I really need to get a brighter outside bulb."

"No problem. But thanks for the assistance."

Sutcliff felt surprisingly light as Alex helped him down the remainder of the stairs, gripping his bony flexed arm. They stopped at the bottom, and Alex released his hold.

"Well, thanks again, Alex. Good night for the second time." Sutcliff shook his head like a small child, then started ambling away.

"Good night." Alex turned and trudged up the steps. As he closed his door, he saw Dr. Todd's face in front of him at the operation that day, deep dark eyes gleaming over the mask, yet with a lighter center to them. He walked around the small, silent apartment, uneasy in his fatigue, his head pounding.

New science of the brain? What did Todd mean? How can you improve the brain?

CHAPTER 3

Alex shuddered as the well-dressed assemblage of prominent and distinguished brain surgeons, without benefit of anesthesia, methodically sliced, dissected, carved and dismembered Curt, the sweating young resident physician standing before them. To distract himself from his memories, the painful situation, and the floundering trainee, who had starting gulping air like a leaky blowfish, he looked around the room. He was positioned up at the front of the old paneled amphitheater, the traditional station of the chief neurosurgical resident at Grand Rounds. They were sitting in wood seats with curved backs reminiscent of an old theatre, arranged in descending rows, facing a small elevated stage. Curt stood pale and blinking behind a battered podium, slide pictures projected next to him on the white screen. Alex felt a pang of guilt that he had assigned the first year resident, just days out of internship and a year out of medical school, the task of making a presentation, two weeks after starting neurosurgical residency. Oh well, he thought, I did it when I started out. Alex looked with clinical interest at Curt's mouth, which seemed to have dried out completely in spite of repeated efforts with flicking tongue to slather both upper and lower lips.

His mind drifted back to when he had told the young resident about doing this presentation. They were standing at a bedside, just finishing rounds. Alex, fourth year resident Dahlia Laronge, and Curt were inspecting a postoperative patient. Alex was explaining how to wrap the head to protect the large incision in the scalp above the fore-head. The reclining patient was alert enough to look suspiciously and uncomfortably upward as the surrounding doctors ignored him and concentrated on his head incision. Alex used rolls of gauze to wrap around, then overtop, the head, covering the whole cranium with a thick, fleecy white shell down to his eyes and covering his ears.

"You want it to look like half an egg on top of the head. Don't wrap it too tight. The last neurosurgery resident who did that put a big pressure sore in the middle of the forehead of one of the Boss's pa-tients." He chuckled. "You could see straight down to the bone. He didn't do that again." The patient looked even more uncomfortable. Alex finally noticed this and gave him a pat on the shoulder.

"Don't worry, Mr. Ridgewell. We won't let it happen to you."

"What happened to the resident?" asked Curt, following the story and the instructions avidly.

Dahlia looked at him. "He was fired and went into anesthesia," she said primly.

The neophyte, five years behind Alex and four behind Dahlia in training, looked at them gravely, and then looked at the egg shaped dressing on the patient's head with even more interest.

"By the way" Alex told him as they turned to go to the next patient's room, "You'll have to do Grand Rounds next week."

"I'm going to do what?" Curt licked his lips.

"You're responsible for two Grand Rounds presentations a year. As chief resident it's one of my responsibilities to assign the dates. You might as well get the first one over with, and you have a week or so to get it together. Try a topic like arachnoid cysts. We just had a patient with one of those and nobody knows too much about them."

Curt looked at him unbelievingly. "I'm supposed to lecture a bunch of brain surgeons about a topic that I know nothing about, a week into residency, with a year of internship under my belt in which I held retractors for gallbladder surgeries, tried to stay awake at night and did rectal exams on urology admissions? What am I supposed to say? Can I tell them about digitalization?" He held up his index finger, rotating it as he looked at it, than gazed at Alex questioningly.

"It's part of the educational experience. Nobody expects you to know everything." He patted Curt sympathetically on the back, then suddenly tired of the conversation. "Look, everybody does it. You have a week to search the literature, audiovisual will help you make up slides, and you can rehearse with me and Dahlia."

She nodded.

"That's the way it is. Now you've got some physical examinations to do. Beep me when you're done."

Curt continued to look gloomy. "At least I know how to do them. See you later." He turned and walked away.

Dahlia's eyes followed his dejected shuffle. "I could do Grand Rounds. Don't you think it's a little early for him?"

Alex glanced at her. She was being a pain in the ass again. "He'll be OK. I did it after my first week."

She looked doubtful but stayed silent.

Alex, irritated that Dahlia made him feel guilty, looked down the hospital hall, lined by doors to the patient's rooms, white clothed nurses darting in and out, and remembered his first Grand Rounds presentation five years before. The group of experienced brain surgeons that attended always seemed to take a savage delight in exposing the weaknesses in a neophyte's presentation. Curt's posture, straight and erect, would be taking a hit, he thought.

Alex's mind snapped back into the present when he heard his name. Dr. Victor Todd, dominating the traditional seat of the Chief of Neurosurgery at University Hospital, was staring at him from across the amphitheater. The room was silent. He was impatient with Alex's inattention and already plainly disgusted with Curt's performance in Grand Rounds.

"What was that, Dr. Todd?" Alex said smoothly.

Todd's mouth drew sharp over his teeth, showing them like a shark, his eyes cold and dark. "Did the patient have any vision abnormalities? He" with a slight nod and withering glance towards the dehydrated Curt at the podium, who gazed at Alex beseechingly "wasn't sure."

Alex also wasn't totally sure, but reflexes honed over the previous five years of grueling training swung automatically into operation. His mind raced. The patient under discussion had a cyst in the high frontal lobe of the brain, unlikely to cause any visual symptoms as the visual nerves were far underneath. He'd chance this one–the odds were in his favor. "No sir, he did not," he said authoritatively.

This seemed to satisfy the Chief. Staring at Alex for a moment, he swung around and nodded at Curt to continue.

Alex congratulated himself on escaping, but he knew how much luck played a role in the interactions with the Boss. Curt took a deep breath, changed to another slide and started haltingly and laboriously describing the various anatomic locations of arachnoid cysts in the brain.

As the resident droned on Alex's mind wandered again, and as he usually did he looked over the various persons sitting and listening. The Boss, Dr. Todd, was opposite to him in the front row on the left side. Alex, who liked to classify people according to their head shape, thought of him as a bullet head, with slicked back gray hair, wire rimmed glasses, a large forehead, deep set eyes, narrow nose and thin lips. Only his ears didn't fit, pathetically large attachments partly hidden by his carefully coifed hair. He was a tall man, with a slight forward tilt when standing and massive but rounded shoulders. On the whole, a large, elegant silver bullet on legs.

Demurely sitting next to him was Dahlia Laronge, fourth year resident, small next to the Boss's looming bulk. She was looking attentively at Curt, nodding in encouragement as he ploddingly made his points. Her delicate, well-formed features were shadowed with a grim, purposeful fatigue, and framed by a cascading mane of black hair. Leonine, he thought of her head, and feminine. She had great legs, too, but her baggy scrubs concealed them. He was told early on by another resident that when she arrived the Boss tried to make a move on her, but he hadn't heard anything more in the succeeding years. She kept to herself, with an air of serious, delicate stoicism, and rarely smiled. When she did it was a quick spasm, bereft of warmth or emotion, a smile closer to a rictus, a pure mechanical movement of facial muscles, trained perhaps by a distant and hazy memory of joy but now only a reflex. Alex learned from the other residents that she had lost her husband years before, but she never spoke of personal matters. In their high-pressure world, doing the work was the key and she pulled her weight well, with ascetic toughness.

Clark Hackman, a neurosurgeon and assistant professor in the department, was sitting in the second row, smirking slightly at Curt's situation, and looking around to see if anybody else felt the same way. Alex stared at him, trying to assess whether he was going to make trouble for the residents that evening, studying his big round head and black mustache, thinking of his matching gut. What's Mr. Melon Head up to, he wondered, trying to get a look at the eyes concealed by glinting glasses.

Paul Fox, the third year resident, sat next to Clark Hackman, like he always tried to do. These two were cut from the same cloth, thought Alex, and he had the scars to prove it. Ambitious and competitive, Paul clearly wanted to become a professor himself, and knew the best way to attain that was stay close with his teachers, Dr. Todd, Dr. Hackman, and the other attendings. The word on Paul from the other residents was that he never made a mistake, or more accurately, never appeared to make a mistake. All problems on his watch were always somebody else's fault. His head? Definitely a big rat's, with eyes darting continuously over the room, brown hair smoothed backwards with a prominent forehead. He would intermittently smile sardonically but uncomfortably, as if sharing a private joke that he vaguely suspected was on him.

Jim Dobbs sat several seats away from Fox and Hackman. An older neurosurgeon, at the University for many years, he was very competent but intermittently cranky and cantankerous. Dignified, wiry, with short cropped gray hair, '. . . and hemorrhoids for that look of concern' he liked to say when the gray hair was mentioned. The residents respected him because he was fair and treated them honestly. A stone face with big severe lips, thought Alex, like those heads on Easter Island. Just like those heads, he was a holdover from the old days, the days when Dr. Henry was Chief of Neurosurgery.

Richard Walters, the medical student, was sitting next to Alex in the front of the room. Richard was rotating with Alex, Dahlia, and Curt on the clinical neurosurgical service. It was his first experience in the hospital after being in the classroom for the initial two years of medical school. Richard was looking at Curt intently, trying to figure out what it all meant, and no doubt wondering whether he wanted to be subjected to such an ordeal. Alex glanced at him—kind of a cube head, he thought, with short bristly hair.

Movement toward the back of the room caught his eye. The head of John Parr, second year resident, was bobbing as he alternately fell asleep and then was awakened by the dim but powerful sensation of his cranium falling forward and jerking to a stop. Like a shark that has to move in the water or die, the residents were so chronically tired that they fell asleep when immobile, no matter how stimulating the presentation.

Other attendings, neurosurgeons who had finished training, sat in the second row. Further back were various other medical personnel such as operating room and floor nurses, medical students, physical therapists, and psychologists. All in all the usual suspects, thought Alex, as Curt continued to speak. He had settled into a dull monotone with frequent "uhs", and the torpid audience counted the minutes until he was done.

Alex felt sleep coming on, so he stood quietly and leaned against the wall. This usually worked, although occasionally the urge would be overpowering and the head slowly would dip, the legs suddenly buckle, and a jolt of adrenaline would spur the brain into sensibility once again.

Curt started describing a cyst next to a crucial area of the brain, the brainstem, and Clark Hackman raised his hand. Reluctantly, Curt stopped and nodded to him.

"How would you treat such a cyst in that location?"

Alex bridled. How the hell is Curt going to know that?

"Uhh." Curt looked at the slide projected on the screen, as if that would give him the answer. He finally had an inspiration. "Radiosurgery?"

Alex took a deep breath inward.

Hackman smirked. Dr. Todd shook his head. "Doctor, radiosurgery is a precision tool, but not for a lesion like this. You had better get back to the books."

Alex cut in smoothly, "While radiosurgery is not traditionally used for lesions in this area, Ivanoff et al just reported in the Journal a series of brainstem lesions treated radiosurgically. Curt was referring to that report, as we just had reviewed it."

Hackman looked stifled and impressed in spite of himself.

Curt nodded vigorously with relieved surprise, and resumed his wobbly presentation. Finally his last slide flashed up on the screen, a cartoon. In happier times while planning the talk, he had dreamed of completing his lecture on a note of collegial and triumphant jocularity. Unfortunately his universe had changed, and the picture only served to add a note of buffoonery to the effort. Curt, looking small and alone at the podium, glanced at the slide, recognized the inappropriateness of it all, and quickly concluded with a breathless "Any questions?"

Dead silence, as all eyes turned to Dr. Todd. He was looking off in the distance and clearly in deep thought. Stirring himself, he stood up, then turned and faced the audience, ignoring Curt.

"I have some exciting news. The University's two hundred-year anniversary celebration occurs next year, a very special time for our institution and city. This is still tentative, but to mark the occasion we may have as our guest here at the University the President of the United States. As you know, he was a patient of mine many years ago at Metropolitan Hospital, while he was a junior politician and I was a junior attending neurosurgeon. A little matter of some low back pain. Fortunately he recovered beautifully."

A murmur arose from the assemblage, and they spontaneously applauded.

"We'll keep you informed as the matter evolves." He paused, and looked at Alex, who took the cue.

"Thanks very much, Curt." He turned to the group. "Thank you all for coming. Next week will be a discussion of the latest treatment for intracranial aneurysms, including some interesting data of our own concerning vasospasm." The audience stood and started to depart.

As Alex started down the aisle, he passed the Boss talking with Clark Hackman. The Boss caught his eye.

"Alex, you didn't look happy at my news about the President."

"I think it will be wonderful, Dr. Todd."

"No, you didn't look happy."

"Well, I revere the institution of the Presidency, but this particular occupant, I think, leaves something to be desired."

"You don't approve of him?"

"I think it will be a great day for this University."

"No, no. You don't like him?"

"Not really."

"Why not?"

"He's a liar."

"He's a human being. And a very successful President."

"Yes."

"We can't all be perfect, Alex. We expect you to be supportive of the initiatives here."

Alex nodded. He was not going to be baited. Not with the Boss.

Todd looked at him silently for a moment, then went over to another physician.

Alex walked over to Curt, still quietly standing at the front of the room as if in shock. He looked dehydrated, tired and greasy, and gazed at him beseechingly. Dahlia was standing there as well.

"It went well, Curt" Alex said. "It really did. The professors are always tough on the new guy, and you didn't crack. As long as you finished on your feet, it went well." He slapped Curt on the shoulder.

Curt looked up at him. Alex was his chief, his lifeline to becoming a neurosurgeon. He had to be careful with what he said. "Well, at least it's over."

"One more thing, Curt."

"Yeah?"

"Do you ever wear anything but short sleeve shirts?"

"I like them. I got a good price on a bunch of them."

"Let me give you some advice. Wear long sleeve shirts. They're power shirts."

"I wear a white coat all the time."

"People can tell."

"I'd do the opposite of what he says, Curt" said Dahlia.

"What's wrong with the way I dress?"

"Nothing, nothing."

"No, I want to know."

"Don't be so sensitive."

Alex took a breath, then nodded to Curt. "Think about it, Curt."

They turned to go out of the old amphitheater, and walked up to the exit.

"Curt, don't forget your slides. We'll see you in the call room. We still need to make sign out rounds," Alex reminded him.

Curt sighed. It's been a long day, he thought, and not over yet. He disappeared into the projectionist's cubicle. Dahlia and Alex continued into the hallway and back to the call room.

Dahlia, frowning, glanced at Alex as they walked. He knew what was coming.

"Why didn't you help him more?"

He stared ahead. "I did. I answered the Boss's question."

"You know what I mean. He was floundering up there." She continued to glower.

"We all went through it. What could I have done? Given the presentation?"

"No. But you could've added some constructive comments. You looked like you were in another world."

"Sometimes I am, Dahlia. We all have to sink or swim on our own. He'll make it."

"Sink or swim? What kind of help is that? You're the chief resident. You're supposed to help him."

"Look, Dahlia. All I want to do is finish, to be a neurosurgeon. I didn't ask Curt to come here. I went through the same thing as he did, and survived. You know how easy it is to get fired here."

"I didn't get fired."

Alex was silent. Yeah, he thought. You're a good-looking babe. You're doubly protected against getting the boot.

As if reading his thoughts, she tossed her hair irritably. "I guess I want more than survival. I want to still be human, to treat other people like human beings. You could've been more supportive." She stalked off. "I'm not going to the call room. See you tomorrow."

Curt caught up with him after Dahlia walked away. He could sense something happened.

"What the matter? She looked upset."

"She has her moments. She lost her husband years ago, when she was a nurse and he was a resident here. You'll learn. She can be funny."

Curt nodded hesitantly, not understanding, but wanting to show his support for Alex.

"You did a good job tonight, Curt. They didn't get to you. You've just got to keep plugging."

Curt looked somewhat relieved at this strained encouragement.

They turned into another hallway, going towards the call room. University Hospital, like many city hospitals, was a mixture of old and new, the aged amphitheater for Grand Rounds contrasting with more recently built patient rooms. The walls changed from dingy yellow to bright azure, with darker blue carpet and soft fluorescent lighting. They kept walking in silence, then stopped and opened a door. Alex and Curt filed into the small, cinderblock lined chamber containing a bed, several old metal chairs, a bookshelf, lockers and a coat rack. At one time the walls had been white, but now were a dirty gray. John Parr and Paul Fox, second and third year residents, were already there, as was Richard Walters, the medical student.

Discouraged by the evening, and sensing a need to cluster for mutual warmth, the residents draped themselves over the furniture in the call room. Curt clicked on the TV and the President's visage appeared, talking to a crowd of supporters at a 'town meeting' staged for television. The President had a smooth unfurrowed face, capable of changing expression instantly. He was listening intently to an elderly lady, and then started speaking in reply.

Curt stared at the picture for a moment. "Look at him, snowing that old lady. We're busting our ass and that bozo's blabbing away. He's a born actor."

Alex glanced at him. Curt had now regained some color from the former cadaverous hue developed during the Grand Rounds experience. "It's more than that. It seems like he throws every fiber of his body into a statement, no matter what he says. Usually people retain some restraint even when lying, but this guy can say something, then something else one hundred and eighty degrees opposed, and sound exactly like the soul of sincerity. It's uncanny."

Richard Walters, the medical student, overwhelmed at being with residents and wanting to get into the conversation, snorted, "He has no soul."

Alex grinned. "Neither does the Boss. I bet Curt would testify to that."

Curt looked grim. "If I have to go through that again, I'll quit."

Alex laughed. "That's what I said the first week. It goes quick. Before you know you're almost finished."

They all kept looking at the television. A little old lady was gazing up adoringly into the President's face as his small mouth kept talking, endlessly enunciating.

"Why is it he has such a small mouth and so much can come out of it?" asked Alex, bemused.

"The conservation of energy" Curt observed. "He burns less fuel with a smaller mouth. It's natural selection. Somebody with a larger mouth would have died of energy failure long ago."

They all laughed, the tension of Grand Rounds broken with Curt's recovery.

"All I know is that he's inexhaustible," Alex said. "And more than that, there seems to have no connection between what he believes and what he says. He can blab on about anything, sounding totally sincere, and make some sort of emotional connection with the great unwashed that is beyond me. In a way, he has no memory. His face changes into the flavor of the day, of the minute, of the second."

Paul looked at him. "Don't you think you're getting carried away? He's a politician. They all sound like that. I actually think he's doing a not half bad job."

Alex snorted. "I'd hate to see what you would call a bad job. Sure, they all lie at times, but he's different. He does it so well you want to forgive him, to believe in him. The country is mesmerized by his voice. I'd like to see what his brain is like."

Paul looked at the TV. "He's just like the others. They all lie. They all pander. It's not the man, it's the job. He's doing okay."

Alex shook his head. "In some ways he reminds me of the Boss."

"What does that mean?"

"You know, when the Boss wants to impress someone, the charm really comes out. He's actually a very likeable guy."

Curt looked with disbelief. "That's a stretch."

Alex said, "It's true. When he wants to he can charm anyone. Remember when Mrs. Thomas was a patient? The one that went sour? Her husband came on real strong to the Boss, upset about the case. The Boss had him eating out of his hand after awhile. Why, he even made a big donation to the department."

Paul reached into his locker to get his coat as he talked. "I'm proud the Boss is such a success." He turned and looked around the room, his eyes darting. "Isn't that why we're all here?"

There was an awkward silence, and the residents shifted uneasily. Each realized that Paul might repeat their discussion to Clark Hackman, the Boss's confidant. It had happened before.

Alex looked at the TV again, remembering what the Boss had said in the OR about improving the brain. "Imagine that you really could change the brain. If we as neurosurgeons could do that. Imagine making a liar so good, you believe in him in spite of yourself." Alex cocked his head, exploring the implications. "Think of what power you would have, in this era of global communications. A superliar years ago might not have gotten very far, his magnetism diluted by distance, sapped by separation, blurred by the passage of time." He looked around at the exhausted faces, his brown eyes wide, glowing. "Imagine a superliar now, when his effect wouldn't be diluted but electronically magnified, multiplied, strengthened and transmitted. Imagine modifying the brain so that monstrous lies could be told with ease, the absolute coherence of lie and physical presentation, the face, the eyes, the mouth, the gesture, the stance, all in the direct service of a mind unfettered by any constraints, direct from conception of lie to presentation, then amplified and broadcast, a creature totally in physical harmony with any thought his brain desires to present for his own purposes." His voice dropped to a whisper. "Imagine that."

Curt piped up, entranced. "The walking dead."

Alex shook his head. "Dead indeed. But still with the semblance of life, like the hair and fingernails of a corpse that keep growing for a time."

The room was quiet. Alex occasionally veered off on tangents, but this was the first time they had heard this one.

"Alex, you've gone off the deep end. Too much night call." Paul said, smirking. "That's why the Boss isn't taking any more philosophy majors. We're all premed guys now" and he nodded at John Parr, the second year resident.

Alex didn't like the barb. "You guys could use a little intellectual breadth." He shook his head. "What do we really understand about the brain?" He took his surgical glasses out of the breast pocket of his white coat and unfolded them, pointing from earpiece to earpiece. "Look at the distance between these. In here fits the human brain, with millions of neurons, billions and billions of connections. Think of the possible combinations, the numbers of neurons, the different types and number of physical contacts, the special neurotransmitters used by each neuron, the temporal changes in signaling by each neuron, the multitude of supporting cells and their interactions." He gestured with the glasses. "A hundred million to the nth power. There's a whole universe in each of us."

Paul snorted. "It's the old mind-brain problem, Alex. Don't get mystical about it."

"Mystical? These are the facts. Who's to say what occurs with a precise and particular combination in time and space of anatomy and neurochemistry in the brain? To say nothing of the transcendent. Who's to say how we will be able to modify that?"

Their attention was drawn to the television again. The reporter was breathlessly describing a breaking presidential scandal. The picture shifted to the President commenting on the situation, looking jolly, kind, concerned, his face radiating a cheerful, chubby, harmless good fellowship. The reporter then described a tape the station had obtained of the President formally testifying in the matter. The President appeared again, but the change was riveting. The residents kept silent, captivated by what was a different man. Unguarded, he looked like a fox, inhuman and withdrawn, his eyes small and piercing, his mouth tight, his whole demeanor one of icy vigilance and fear, his face an inscrutable wall. The contrast was striking. His face was barren, necrotic, surmounted by eyes of cold darkness. Only by comparison with the bloodless face could they be considered alive. Standing alone they would be frigid mirrors, fearsome and dead themselves.

"Wow, look at him," said Curt. "He's not a Teddy Bear there."

They kept staring, fascinated at the metamorphosis.

"He reminds me of the Boss" Alex muttered, feeling a deep uneasiness.

The picture shifted to a defender of the President, and the moment changed. Move on, the talking head was saying, it's only politics.

Alex realized he had been holding his breath. "Yeah, yeah, move on, they say. Move on? Move on from the realization that the President is a liar, a cheat?"

"Lighten up, Alex" said Paul.

Alex looked at him. "That's what they want you to do. Lighten up, move on. This is the great central lie of our time. All are imperfect, therefore we simply move on. No true repentance or atonement. Instead we all swim together in the same swamp, joyfully bereft of any responsibility, no one better than another, just moving on. To do otherwise, to suggest any standard, is hypocrisy. The worst sin. Only there's no sin anymore. Hypocrisy. The final attempted coup de grace of the Platonic ideal, of Socratic virtue." He looked around at the haggard, uncomprehending faces and the gray room. "The final, pathetically lame kiss of death for the magnificent canons of western civilization. Who'd have thought it." He coughed and shook his head. "But I digress. Every once in a while the moral philosopher in me comes out."

"Every once in a while?" Paul said sourly. "What are you talking about?"

Alex ignored this. "Time to go home. Who's on call tonight?"

"I am." Curt said.

"Let's review the patients."

"Well, we're cutting out of here" Paul said, as he and Parr got their coats and left. Curt and Alex were alone.

Curt looked carefully at Alex. "I think he has it out for you."

"Who, Paul?"

"Yeah. I know it's not my place, but he does."

Alex shrugged. "He's worried that I'll be hired as an attending here and there won't be room for him. He wants to be a big boy. You be careful of him."

Curt nodded. "What did he mean about not taking any more philosophy majors?"

"Dahlia and I were chosen by Dr. Henry, the former Chief of Neurosurgery here. Dr. Todd picked Paul, John Parr and you after he became Chairman. He prefers guys who've been on the straight track, premed majors and all that. Dahlia and I have more eclectic backgrounds."

Curt stared at the wall. "I'm learning more every day. What did you do before neurosurgery, before med school? You're a little older, what with that gray at the temples."

"I knocked around. Got a little experience in life. Something you permanent students are missing."

"Yeah, yeah."

"Let's run the list so I can get out of here."

They reviewed the patients, with Alex giving Curt instructions for the night. When that was done, Alex stood up and stretched. "Time to get out of here." He yawned. "Haven't been sleeping well lately."

"What little sleep you get" said Curt.

"Been having some strange dreams." He shook his head. "Maybe I'm eating too much fruit." He stretched again. "And these damn headaches." He looked at Curt. "Have a good night. I'll be on the beeper if you need me."

Curt nodded. "Thanks."

Alex ducked into the bathroom for a moment, then came out. "Always remember—empty your bladder before driving. If you get in an accident, a full bladder can rupture, and those kind of bladder injuries are very difficult to treat."

Curt looked at him. "Where'd that come from? Don't you have enough to worry about?"

"A word to the wise." Alex was serious, then smirked. "But remember. To call me is a sign of weakness."

"Thanks a lot. That makes me feel really good."

Alex laughed. "An old joke. Just kidding. I'm around if you need me. Any questions, call. See you later." He grabbed his coat, opened the door, and left with a final nod. Curt stared at the gray cinderblock wall for a bit, wondering what was in store for him that night, wishing he could go home as well. Looking around, he picked up an old anatomy book and opened it, smelling the formaldehyde absorbed in the morgue. Spotting its once white pages were small dark clouds, remnants of cadaver fat smeared there by residents eagerly exploring the greasy recesses of the human body while paging through the classic reference.

CHAPTER 4

Four million volts into the brain, all at once. Alex was amazed each time they did it, amazed that it could be done at all, that a human actually survived, and more than that, was helped by this enormous power, this energy, beamed into a human brain. It was like harnessing the power of the heavens, bringing a lightening bolt down from the sky, fashioning it, shaping it and tempering it, then making it appear within the brain to do its job. To kill a tumor. The trick of radiosurgery was of course in aiming it properly, in making sure that the disembodied energy blast was deposited between and not in the crucial bundles of nerve cables and cell bodies that make up the endless labyrinth of the human brain.

They had finished rounds and Alex, Curt and Richard were in a procedure room on the nursing floor. A patient was sitting in a chair, with Alex standing in front of him, Curt to his left and Richard to his right.

"Mr. Owens, do you mind if I talk to the residents while I work? Dr. Curt Smith is a first year resident, which means he has had four years of college, four years of medical school, and one year internship training, and is now starting his neurosurgical residency. Richard here is a medical student in his third year."

"Do I have a choice?"

"Of course. You're the boss."

The patient, a man in his early seventies, looked up at him skeptically, his moist brow wrinkling up to a smooth scalp, beads of sweat extending up to the same line like ocean waves flattening on the beach. "Okay, it's okay. Anything for education. Just keep their hands off of me." He jerked his head towards Curt and Richard. "No offense, boys. I just have a strong survival instinct."

They nodded as if synchronized.

"Thanks."

Alex took the MR scan of the patient's brain, walked over to the lightbox and placed it under the clip with a quick, crisp flick of his wrist. "Mr. Owens has a metastases, a tumor which has spread from one area of the body to another." He pointed to one of the black and white pictures, carefully tracing out a mass, his finger dark against the light shining through the film. "Here's the lesion we're going to treat today, frontal lobe of the brain, right side."

"A silent area?"

"That's right, Curt. Richard, if you're going to have a brain tumor, this is a good spot to have it in." He patted Mr. Owens on the shoulder. "This is a silent area of the brain, because a tumor or other problem may not be detectable by any change in the patient's behavior until it is quite large and affecting other areas."

Curt and Richard nodded as Alex again traced the tumor on the scan, this time with his pen. "Mr. Owens had a choice of treatments, and he selected radiosurgery for this lesion."

"Yep. Let me see, I had a choice of having my head cut open, bone sawed off, somebody poking in my brain, no offense, Doc, or sitting here for a day and getting radiation and going home."

He lifted up both hands, palms up like he was weighing something. "Let's see, head cracked open, six week recovery, versus one day in, no scar. Hmm. It doesn't take a brain surgeon to decide."

Alex nodded. "Well, everything has its pluses and minuses."

"So we're going to treat him with radiosurgery?" said Richard eagerly.

"What do you mean we, medical student?" Mr. Owens looked at him. "I'm no guinea pig."

Alex chuckled. "He's just going to watch this time. He'll do the next one."

Richard's eyes widened.

The patient snorted. "As long as it isn't me."

Alex resumed with a pedantic tone. "Yes, we're going to treat it with radiosurgery. Curt, what is radiosurgery?"

"The use of special techniques for head immobilization, in conjunction with a frame of reference and computer planning of radiation delivery to give a large single dose of radiation precisely aimed to a specific area of the brain, in a single day."

"Good. That's right." Turning to Richard he continued, "We use multiple arcs of radiation to spread out the dose of radiation so that only in the center of the arcs is the radiation high enough to be deadly. Understand?"

Richard shook his head. "The radiation I'm familiar with involves three or four weeks of treatments."

"That's regular radiation, in which the beam is stationary, and the dose is given in a small portion every day. Over weeks it slowly adds up. It doesn't take advantage of the full capabilities of the radiation machine, which can move around the target like a machine gun on a jeep circling a bull's eye. Usually with conventional radiation you turn the radiation machine to where you want it and fire it. The dose has to be low to allow the normal tissue that is around the tumor and also getting radiation to recover. Then another treatment is given the following day, and so on. Radiosurgery is different. We use a computer to plan the dose. The radiation machine rotates around the patient so that the target, where the tumor is, doesn't move and gets most of the radiation. The rest of the brain, the normal part, only gets a small dose as the beam sweeps by."

"Like a guy on a merry-go-round shining a flashlight into the center where the organ is playing."

Alex thought for a moment. "Well, yes." He paused. "At any rate we use a special holder to fix the head securely when we do the treatment. We'll put it on now."

"Thank God, we're getting started," said Mr. Owens.

"Sorry for all the yapping." Alex glanced at the nurse. "Did he have some sedation?"

"Yes, we already gave him some Ativan."

"Good job."

Alex turned to a small table with a collection of metal parts on a blue sheet, and assembled a metal ring, larger than a human head, with four arms projecting up from the rim. "This is the head frame. We put some local anesthetic in the scalp and then secure the frame to the head with small sharp pins."

"I know. The worst part of the whole day."

"It's not so bad. I'd probably rather have this than go to the dentist."

Mr. Owens shook his head. "I'd rather be in Bermuda and forget the dentist and the neurosurgeon."

"Me too" Alex said sympathetically.

Curt chimed in. "Alex is well known as a hypochondriac. He hates any form of medical or dental care on himself. The only reason he tolerates it is his greater fear of disease eating away at him."

"How did you know that?"

"From Dahlia."

Alex was miffed. "I'm not afraid. I just know what can happen."

Curt chuckled. "She says you're a wimp."

Alex shook his head irritably, then put the ring over the patient's head and adjusted it carefully. "You can move the arms so that the pins at the end of them go into the skull at appropriate places, and miss the thin bone of the temples, for instance."

Curt nodded.

"Curt, move around and hold the frame. And don't be blabbing any more" he said in mock irritation.

Curt quickly darted to where Alex directed him, tripping over Mr. Owens legs and murmuring an apology, then eagerly reaching and holding the ring from behind the patient.

"Don't move" Alex directed.

"Yeah, you don't move," added Mr. Owens, nodding.

"Don't nod."

"Sorry."

Alex inverted a syringe with a small needle pointing upward, and expelled air.

"A little prick, then a burning." He gently injected local anesthetic into the scalp where each pin was going to go. Mr. Owens winced.

"I see a big prick."

Curt smirked.

The injections raised four bumps like huge mosquito bites, a glistening rosy sphere of blood blossoming at each hole as the needle was removed, forming a diadem of tiny rubies ringing Mr. Owens' bald pate.

"Wipe, please." Alex waited for a moment. "Steady, Curt." He then started screwing the pins through the scalp into the skull.

"Feel any pain?"

"No, only pressure."

"You'll feel pressure, but the anesthetic should take care of the pain."

Alex continued to tighten, driving the pins into the skull and securing the ring on to the patient. His fingers knew when to stop.

"Okay. That's really the worst of it."

Mr. Owens thought for a moment, tilting his head slightly and tilting the ring now fixed to his skull. "Actually, not too bad."

"I hate to say it, but usually the women are better with this." Alex patted Mr. Owen's arm. "You're a credit to the sex." The patient grunted.

The metal ring was suspended by its arms, attached to the skull with pins. It ran around Mr. Owen's head just in front of the nose to the bottom of the ears and the back of the head.

"Now we put the localizer ring on the base ring."

"What's that?" Richard looked as Alex put another cylinder-like affair over the ring already applied, and locked it down.

"This frame shows up on the CT scan and provides the computer with the three dimensional frame of reference needed to target the tumor."

"Oh."

"Richard, push Mr. Owens over. Curt, take his IV. I'll get the scans."

To an uninitiated observer, they formed an arcane and somber procession, Richard pushing the bizarrely crowned Mr. Owens in his sedan chair, accompanied by the acolyte Curt ceremoniously rolling an

IV pole with two hands, followed by Alex reverently holding the MRI scans as if they were sacred books.

The group entered the CT room, a cubicle with the large upright donut of the scanner at the end of a flat, narrow bed.

Alex yelled, "Tech, CT tech."

A short blonde woman bustled up with a walk like a sewing machine, quick and mincing. "Right here, right here."

"Here's Lee." Alex said in mock relief. "I thought I'd have to run the machine."

"Fat chance."

"Okay, Mr. Owens. Let's go over to the table and put your rear end here." Alex patted the CT couch, then gripped the patient's arm firmly and helped him carefully over to the padded surface.

"It's hard to see with this ring blocking your vision downward."

"It is, it is."

Alex held the head ring as Mr. Owens started to recline. "I've got your head, you can lay down," he said encouragingly.

The patient gradually laid back, the headring matching up with a bracket on the CT couch.

"We're just going to bolt you to the table."

Alex screwed two bolts through the bracket to the ring, immobilizing the patient's head, his body supine.

"Good. Now give us about fifteen minutes and we'll get a scan."

"Do I have a choice?"

"Not really, at this point." They laughed. "You comfortable?"

"Yep."

"Okay. Everything looks fine. Like I say, give us fifteen minutes."

They went around the observation wall to the CT scanner control console. Turning, they watched the patient through the leaded observation window as he rested quietly, hands folded on his stomach.

"He looks like one of those medieval kings in their sarcophagi," said Richard.

"Hopefully he won't end up like that, at least anytime soon" replied Alex.

Lee plopped down on her chair, sighing heavily, and rolled to the control panel. The group arrayed themselves behind her, eyeing the CT monitor.

"Now, we need to select how the scanner will take pictures of the brain. Lee, start there, thin cuts here, and five millimeter cuts there." Alex pointed with a pen at the monitor as he explained how he wanted the slices done. "The tumor is approximately here." He tapped on the glass, which showed a side view of the patient's skull. "We therefore need to view this area with thin CT slices, and use thicker ones here, away from the tumor. The software for the treatment planning computer limits us to a certain number of slices, and obviously the thinner each CT slice is the more slices there are, so we need to plan carefully."

Curt frowned. "Seems like a lot to learn."

"You haven't seen anything yet." Alex chuckled. "The technology is amazing, but you always need to be aware of what's going on. The old principle of garbage in, garbage out is still very operational."

Lee started the scanner, and the CT pictures appeared one by one.

"We're scanning from the bottom of the skull to the top. The tumor should be appearing soon."

Richard pointed eagerly to a dark area of the brain. "Is that the tumor?"

"No that's just the lateral ventricle. Everybody has those. They're fluid filled and in the center of the hemispheres."

As they watched closely, a slice appeared with a white ball embedded in the brain, the size of a grape.

Curt pointed. "Is that it?"

"That's it. That's the tumor in the frontal lobe."

"Are we finished?"

"No, we need to complete the CT scan so the computer can reconstruct the brain and the tumor fully."

They gazed silently as the slices appeared, the brain sectioned like a virtual tomato.

"It's amazing to me that we can focus radiation into the brain so precisely, without frying normal areas" Curt observed.

"Yes. As we discussed, the radiation beam is rotated around the center of the tumor, so that the tumor gets the maximum jolt and the rest of the brain gets a small dose as the beam passes through. Once one arc of radiation is finished, a different arc plane is then chosen, with the same center, the tumor, and then the process is repeated. The dose is therefore concentrated on the target and diffused through the rest of the brain."

Richard nodded. "Now I get it. You vary the size of the arc, the size of the beams, and the number and angles of arcs to treat different shaped tumors."

"Good job." He slapped them both on the back. "You two are obviously the A team." They straightened with pride.

"That's it" Lee announced as the final CT scan cut showed up on the screen.

Alex, Curt and Richard got up and went around to the patient.

"Mr. Owens." Alex gently shook him, eyes closed and head suspended in his own universe. Alex shook him again, and his eyes opened, staring straight up for a moment, then darting to Alex.

"All finished."

"I was just getting comfortable."

"Well it's back to your room for a couple of hours as we plan the treatment with the computer. We'll let you know when we're ready for you."

They helped him up after detaching him from the scanner couch, then eased him over to the wheelchair. He sat down heavily, the ring surrounding his face and head like a fallen halo.

"See you guys later." Mr. Owens waved to them with a jaunty fling of his arm as Lee wheeled him out.

"Righto. Now, boys, we go to the planning computer." Alex continued as they walked. "The CT scan information is transmitted there through the network. CT slices are then reconstructed three dimensionally and we can design the treatment."

"Amazing" said Richard. "Didn't I read that sometimes you can use a head ring that doesn't need pins in the skull?"

"Yes, a ring is available now which holds tightly to the bridge of the nose, ears and back of the head and can go on and off quickly, without any skin puncture."

"It's less accurate than this one, though" said Curt.

"That's right. You sacrifice a small amount of accuracy. Clinically insignificant."

"Not if it's my brain," said Curt.

They turned into the computer lab, a small clean room with white counters and chairs. Alex sat down in front of the keyboard and glanced at a large monitor.

"Pull up some chairs, boys."

Curt and Richard settled in back of Alex. He typed in commands and a brain image appeared on the screen.

"Here's the three dimensional view of Mr. Owens's head. We need to use the mouse to outline the important structures in each slice. Then the computer builds up a three dimensional model of these structures, and the target, the tumor."

Curt and Richard watched silently as Alex used the mouse to trace on each CT scan slice the tumor cross-section and important brain structures. Curt, to Alex's right, pushed in his chair to see more closely and knocked Alex's hand.

"Curt, watch it. Don't bang the arm. We don't want to fry the wrong part of the brain."

"Sorry."

"You did the same thing in the operating room with that aneurysm the other day. You've got to be careful. Just because there's no blood here doesn't mean we can relax. If we don't draw in the target the right way, we can miss the tumor and fry normal brain. That's four million volts right into the central processing unit. Not a good idea."

"Sorry, sorry."

"Okay, we're finished with the contouring." He clicked the mouse on a couple of commands. "The computer will reconstruct all those slices and show us the three dimensional view of the target, and also vital structures like the brain stem and optic nerves."

The computer worked for a couple of seconds, and then rendered a picture of the brain with the mass inside.

"There's the tumor, and here are the areas we have to avoid with the radiation, the optic nerves and the brain stem."

"Why do you need to dodge them?" asked Richard.

Curt answered quickly. "The optic nerves carry vision to the brain. Too high a dose will blind you. The brain stem transmits all the impulses from the spinal cord to the brain. Radiation there will disconnect your brain from your body."

Richard winced as he visualized an alert brain locked in an immobile prison of a body.

Alex added, "And it has important areas that control consciousness and nerves for the head. It's crucial that the radiation dose be minimal to the brain stem."

Richard nodded.

Alex continued clicking away at the keyboard. "Here's our radiation plan." A cloud of energy appeared around the target, like bees around a nest. "This represents the radiation dose, combining the effects of all the arcs. We can determine the dose delivered to other structures, which should be minimal."

"Temporal lobes, four hundred rads. Brainstem, two hundred rads." Curt read from the screen in his nasal voice.

Alex idly wondered for a brief moment how Curt's sinuses would look on a CT scan. "OK, Curt. I think we get the idea."

They heard a group walking down the hall, then Dr. Todd arrived with Dahlia and Paul Fox in tow.

"We've got everything ready, Dr. Todd. The plan is complete."

Todd nodded. "There's somebody in the emergency room that needs to be checked out." This was Alex's job, and he quickly got up, then turned and hesitated. A check of the machine parameters was always needed, even when the Boss set the coordinates.

"Who do you want to check the settings when you're finished, Dr. Todd?"

The Boss inclined his head slightly. "Dahlia is next in seniority, and Paul is here as well." Paul nodded and straightened slightly with the responsibility.

"Come on guys." Alex led Curt and Richard down the hall to the emergency room.

Todd eased his massive frame down into the chair in front of the computer, obscuring the seat. Paul and Dahlia stood respectfully behind him as he examined the images of the brain, the radiation plan and the target tumor. He nodded.

"Looks good. The dose can be decreased medially, and we'll change the center of the focus slightly."

A large hand closed over the mouse, completely hiding it as he moved and clicked. The computer redrew the slightly altered plan, then Todd printed it out. He took the plan and silently walked out and up the hallway to the treatment area, where the radiation was actually given. The tech at the console saw him coming, and pressed the button to open the massive, two-foot thick door. The linear accelerator, the machine that produced the radiation, and the couch where the patient reclined for treatment, were inside. The residents called it the cave.

The door opened slowly as Dr. Todd stood impatiently, then entered and went over to the headstand. He glanced at the treatment plan in his hand, and then set the parameters into the stand.

Dahlia and Paul waited and watched quietly as Todd completed the adjustments. This is the crucial time, the critical settings, they both thought. This dictates where the radiation dose is delivered. Todd grunted, then briskly got up and walked out as they followed.

The phone rang and the tech answered, listening briefly. "Dr. Todd, for you" she said, and tentatively held the phone in his direction.

He took it brusquely. "Yes?"

"It's Alex, Dr. Todd. We evaluated and discharged that patient. Simple musculoligamentous low back pain."

Todd grunted. "Look, we've set the radiosurgical stand. Come back down here and keep an eye on the treatment. I'm going back to the office."

"Yes sir."

"Dahlia is in charge." The Boss turned towards her, making sure she heard.

"I understand."

Todd hung up the phone and strode down the hall. As they watched him recede, Paul said importantly to Dahlia, "I can check the settings."

Dahlia nodded. "Do you want me to recheck them?"

"No." Paul went into the cave and came out a short time afterward. "They all look OK." He glanced at the tech. "You can call for the patient."

Alex, Curt and Richard arrived. Mr. Owens was wheeled down, his glasses perched awkwardly above the frame, the earpieces threaded inside the posts holding the head ring on.

"Hi, Mr. Owens" said Alex. "We're in the home stretch."

"Sounds good to me."

They wheeled him into the cave, next to the radiation machine.

Alex talked to him in a low, smooth voice. "Now, this will be the same as the CT scanner in terms of your position. We just need you to move to the treatment couch, lay back and we'll attach you to the headstand. Then the radiation machine will do its job. It will take about forty-five minutes for the treatment."

Mr. Owens nodded as the ring around his head accentuated the movement. They helped him onto the treatment couch, a narrow, slablike affair, then gently laid him back as Alex steadied his head, using the ring as a handle. When the patient was down, Alex guided the headring to the bracket, and bolted it to the headstand of the radiation machine. He made a brief but thorough check of the patient's position, lying on his back, head looking towards the ceiling and bolted in place, the radiation gantry ready to rotate above his head.

"In a moment we'll go out and start the treatment."

"Why is everybody but me going to leave?"

"Well, if we stayed in here we would get a dose of radiation."

"Hell, so am I."

"You'll just be getting this dose today. If we stayed here for the treatments we would be getting more and more radiation exposure every time we did a treatment. Not healthy. There's no point in blasting our DNA through carelessness–our bodies have more than enough to fight against."

Dahlia raised her eyebrows.

"But it's okay for me?" Mr. Owens snorted.

Alex patted his thin shoulder. "Yep, don't worry. You're not a regular." He turned to the tech. "Can we check the laser lights?"

"This is the final check." Alex glanced at Curt and Richard, as Dahlia and Paul listened. "The aiming lasers mounted in the walls paint lines on the patient in three planes. Where the planes join together, the intersection of those planes, indicate the target, where that extraordinary energy dose produced by the linear accelerator is focused in space, and more specifically, in the brain."

Curt said, "I just see a couple of streaks on him. How does it work?"

"You need to have a three dimensional visualization of the planes, where they join, and where the brain and tumor is in relation to the skull."

"What?"

They went over to Mr. Owens. "We're just going to be talking again, Mr. Owens. I'm still doing a little teaching."

"Okay."

"Look at these lines." Alex traced them out on Mr.Owens's head and face, the scintillating, almost alive ruby red streaks projected from lasers mounted in the walls of the room.

"Here's the first plane." Alex pointed out the gleaming line running across the patient's forehead from temple to temple. "The coronal plane is the second, from side to side over the head. The third line is in the sagittal plane, here." His finger followed a radiant filament as it ran up and over the patient's broad forehead. "Where these three lines all cross is the intersection, where the radiation is focused in space."

Curt and Richard nodded as Paul stirred impatiently.

Alex stood motionless, staring at the pulsating stripes, assembling them in his brain, calculating where they intersected.

Curt and Richard drifted out of the room, as Dahlia and Paul turned to follow. Alex stayed back, looking at the lights as if hypnotized by them, the red lasers reflected in his pupils. The tech waited quietly. Alex stared, looked up at her, and then glanced again at the patient's head.

"Just a minute, Mr. Owens. We may have to make some adjustments."

Walking out, he picked up the treatment planning clipboard, which had been leaning on the control panel. Studying it for a moment, he looked up. "We've got an error here. We need to change the settings." Quickly striding back into the cave, closely followed by Dahlia, Paul, Curt and Richard, he went over to the clamp holding Mr. Owen's head and carefully turned a knob, adjusting a vernier scale. He then re-checked the laser lights, quietly scrutinizing the tiny marks as Mr. Owens' eyes danced and eyelids fluttered, trying to get a look at what was going on though his head was immovable.

"Everything OK, Doc?" He spoke so intensely white spittle formed at the corners of his mouth.

Alex nodded warmly. "All systems go, Mr. Owens. Everything checks out right now."

"Sounds good, Doc. Thanks."

They all turned and walked out to the treatment console. Alex was going to say something to Dahlia and Paul when Dr. Todd wheeled down the hall.

"Why aren't we treating?"

Alex looked up suddenly, startled at the Boss's unannounced appearance. He swallowed, then looked quickly at Dahlia. "I made a mistake, Dr. Todd. We had to make an adjustment."

Dahlia said shrilly, "It was my job to check the settings, Dr. Todd. They were in error."

"I was the senior resident. It was my responsibility." Alex said this in such tones of deep solemnity Dahlia simply stared at him, then darted a look at Paul. Alex followed her gaze to Paul, noticing the sweat form-ing above Paul's upper lip, little beads appearing quietly. He didn't think the glands could work that quickly.

"Stay here" the Boss snarled, then strode into the cave.

The tech whispered to Alex, "Paul was the one who screwed up."

Alex looked again at Paul standing apart pale and grim, then his eyes flickered to Dahlia.

The Boss emerged from the cave like a great bear from his den. "Alex, the settings are correct now. Whatever happened, you are responsible. Any mistake would have liquefied the most important part of the brain."

Paul was silent. The other residents braced themselves. Dahlia stirred, drawing the Boss's attention.

"Quiet, Dahlia." The Boss continued grimly, "Do you understand the energies, the forces we are dealing with here? Do you?" Alex returned his stare. "This is no place for cowboys. This tool is superbly powerful and utterly unforgiving. It can destroy what millions of years of evolution painstakingly developed in an instant, or it can perfect that evolution." His gaze burned into Alex, then abruptly changed to a curious flatness of emotion, a void, which the residents found more frightening than a blast of anger. Like Moby Dick, whose whiteness passed beyond all colors, he seemed to go beyond the usual emotions into a new, unknown form of expression in which no clues were present to help interpret his thoughts. He abruptly turned and strode off.

Alex took a deep breath and turned to the monitoring screen, side by side with the tech.

Paul stayed rigid for a second, then walked away with his perpetual forward tilt. Dahlia stared at Alex, his head in profile, intently looking at the screen.

Curt and Richard, looking on in amazement, glanced at each other, then Curt nudged Dahlia. "Alex took the fall," he whispered unnecessarily, "For you."

She nodded, her lips tight, her gaze intent on Alex.

Curt whispered again, "I guess you have to be real careful of Paul around here."

She nodded again, her face red, then turned and walked away. Alex's eyes lifted from the screen to follow her.

"Arc's finished" murmured the tech, and then opened the heavy door to change the couch angle. The spell broken, Curt cautiously decided to ask a question in the hopes of changing the mood. "Alex, what did the Boss mean about radiosurgery completing the evolution of the brain?"

Alex, snapping out of his reverie, shook his head. "Don't know. Don't know what the hell he means."

CHAPTER 5

Alex always hated the way a drunk's vomit smelled when they were coding him, when they tried to bring the bloated, pungent, wet corpse back from the dead. It was just the smell that bothered him. He didn't mind when there was brain mixed with vomit, even when the brain pulsated out of a wound into the vomit. It was just the smell, the awful, sour, spoiled, rotten vapor that permeated the entire greasy body of a drunk, that reeked out from his pores, from his sweat, from his breath, from his hair, vividly bringing back memories of many such nights in an ER bay. Alex had once asked Sutcliff, the neuroanatomy professor, what was the physiologic basis for the seemingly direct connection between smell and memory, but the elderly professor seemed not to understand. 'Why, when you smell something, do the memories come flooding back in such a direct, immediate way. You can feel yourself surrounded by those memories become solid' he had asked. The professor, apparently unaccustomed to such impressionistic observations, wasn't much help, Alex recalled.

He looked at the scene in front of him, having been called down to the emergency room by Curt, standing at the patient's head with Richard Walters flanking him. Curt was still looking hurt from the discussion Alex had with him on the phone. After evaluating the patient in the ER, Curt had beeped him, and while Alex listened to his breathless description in the midst of inspecting a patient's incision, he reluctantly decided it was time for a lesson about the harsh reality of brain trauma.

"Relax, Curt. Don't spit into the phone. One thing you learn in brain surgery school. Never run to the ER. As long as the airway is secured by anesthesia, and they're keeping the blood pressure up with fluids and drugs, you don't have to rush. If you're lucky, the really bad brain injuries will have croaked by the time you get there. If you get there too soon, you're just making trouble for everybody, including the patient and the family. " A wisp of a shudder came and went through his frame. "Some things are worse than death."

There was a pause as Curt digested this cold-blooded information, uncertain as to exactly what it meant in the present circumstances.

"Well, I'm here now. What should I do?"

"What happened to this guy?"

"The usual." Curt tried to sound detached, but was too inexperienced.

"What does that mean?" His lack of information and false air of experience irritated Alex.

"Oh. Car accident. Drunk. Smashed his head. Possible hip fracture, and on the lateral cervical spine x ray he may have a broken neck." The details spilled forth in an unorganized torrent from the young physician.

"What does he do neurologically?" Like pulling teeth, thought Alex patiently.

"What do you mean?"

"What do I mean? You're going to be a neurosurgeon. You've got to think like one. It doesn't have to be complicated. Does he move anything? Does he follow commands? Do his pupils react to light?"

"Oh. He doesn't move when I ask him to. His pupils are equal and reactive."

"OK." As usual, Alex thought, I need to take a look. "I'll be right down."

Because he was the senior resident there, the other residents standing around the patient made room for Alex and awaited his advice. Conscious of the eyes on him, Alex walked up to the patient's side. The man was large, with a bulbous belly protruding out under his yellow T-shirt, covered in blood and vomit, lying on the litter in a small ER bay lined with equipment and people. Eyes closed, an endotrachial tube protruded from his mouth and a large gash in his forehead emitted pulsating red-tinged cream cheese material. Alex sadly wondered what brought the man to this condition, but he had to impress on Curt the critical importance of a concise evaluation and report.

"Curt, what kind of a description was that?"

Curt sighed. He knew he was in for some 'instruction' and while he appreciated any information he didn't particularly want his ignorance to be demonstrated in front of an audience. The other residents looked relieved that Alex wasn't directing questions at them.

"Why didn't you tell me he was smoking the big White Owl?"

"Huh?" said Curt, not understanding.

"He's got the breathing tube down. How can you tell whether he can talk? I bet he's been sedated as well." He looked for confirmation to the trauma resident standing on the other side. She nodded tentatively, not sure whether Alex would rip into her for medicating the patient.

"Curt, it's important to give me the proper information. When a trauma patient comes in, they often have to be sedated and have the endotrachial tube placed for protection of the airway. That's important because when they are drugged you can't do a proper examination, like asking the patient to move something. All we can do now is to stimulate him and see what happens."

He pinched the patient, at first gently, then harder. The patient weakly jerked one arm up.

"Real high tech medicine" said Curt.

Alex smiled faintly. The boy had spirit. "Look, he can localize. He's bringing up his arm towards the stimulus. That's important in telling us that at least some parts of the brain are working. He's potentially salvageable." Alex glanced at the trauma resident and the others gathered around.

The trauma resident was reassured. "We'll keep working on him."

"Call us when you're ready, and we'll take him to the OR and fix that." Alex inclined his head towards the split cranium.

Richard Walters couldn't take his eyes off the protruding brain, extruding out of the patient's cleaved forehead like dough rising.

"You mean, he could survive?"

"Sure, we just need to clean him up a bit. A frontal lobe is expendable. If his brain doesn't swell, he has a chance. You'd be surprised at how little brain you need to survive—some of these residents are living examples of that. "

The all laughed at the old joke.

Alex's beeper went off. He looked at the number. It was the Boss's office. Damn, Alex thought. It's time for the investiture of Curt, the new resident.

"OK, call me when he's ready" Alex nodded again to the trauma resident. He clapped Curt on the back. "Come on, we need to go to the Boss's office. Time for the review of the rules." Curt looked puzzled and uncomfortable, but Alex's suddenly grim face didn't welcome questions.

Alex looked at Richard. "Stay here with the surgical residents and watch. You'll learn something. We'll beep you shortly. Meeting with Dr. Todd." Alex and Curt turned and left the ER.

As they walked over to the Boss's office, Alex striding slightly in front of Curt, Alex explained, "Every year the Boss likes to review the rules of survival around here. It's his way of reinforcing who's top dog. All we can do is nod and agree, so whatever you do, keep quiet."

Curt, impressed by the evident gravity with which Alex viewed this meeting, nodded, but didn't say anything. Alex looked at him. Still he kept silent.

"Well" Alex said, "You understand?"

"You said keep quiet" Curt smirked.

Alex rolled his eyes. He would learn.

They turned the corner and opened the door to the offices of the Department of Neurosurgery. Alex, his head throbbing, didn't like the feeling in the pit of his gut.

In the waiting area, in front of the sliding glass window, sat the other residents. In addition to Dahlia, there was Paul Fox, the third year resident, and second year John Parr. Dahlia flashed a faint smile of encouragement at Curt. The others were in their own worlds, in various states of psychic detachment.

Alex nodded to them, and then went to the window. The secretary looked up from behind her desk.

"Here for the lovefest."

She grinned, then looked around. "Come on in. Better you than me."

Alex opened the heavy dark door next to the reception window, and they trooped in, obediently following Alex into Dr. Todd's office as the Boss talked on the phone. The square room was subdued by somber wallpaper, green carpet, dark cherry shelves and matching desk. Alex always wondered why the office never seemed to have enough light. There were two brass lamps throwing yellow puddles, one in the Boss's corner, the other at the end of the row of chairs. Books lined the walls, shadowy and indistinct, old and new neurosurgical tomes.

Curt quickly sat, excited about the first meeting with the Boss and residents as a group. Going to be a brain surgeon, he thought happily, as the other residents settled down in front of the Boss's desk. Alex stood, leaning lightly against a bookcase as the Boss continued on the phone, angled sideways to the assembled group.

He abruptly ended the conversation with a deep cackle, hung up the phone, and swung around to the silent faces observing him. At first he seemed to gaze beyond them, then he looked at each in turn, large hands resting on the arms of his chair. His strong jaw and arching mouth gave him a primeval appearance, deep-set eyes sucking in everything like twin black holes. Unnervingly primitive and intensely intelligent, Alex thought, in a small corner of his brain.

Alex knew what was coming. As Todd recited them, he recalled the words he had heard four times before. "Each year I like to make sure everybody understands the rules. Neurosurgery is a detail oriented job and it's your job to attend to those details. No mistakes are tolerated. Goethe said 'Nature never errs.'" He paused.

Alex completed the sentence. "The faults and mistakes are always those of man."

Dr. Todd looked at him. "How did you know that?"

"It's on the front cover of my soaring manual."

"You have your sailplane pilot license? Did I know that?"

Alex nodded.

"That's right. That's your only vice."

The other residents tittered, then silence. The Boss glanced at their expectant faces, and then continued. "One more thing."

Alex shifted uncomfortably, knowing what was coming.

The Boss paused for emphasis. "There are five of you in this room." He paused again. "I only need four." He looked at each resident in succession, his eyes expressionless. "That applies to everybody."

Alex stiffened imperceptibly and his eyes narrowed. He looked up at the corner of the ceiling without moving his head, which still pointed at the Boss. Only one more year, he thought, only one more year.

The Boss brought his hands and fingers together close to his face, his index fingers touching his nose as if starting a prayer, and looked again at each of them in turn. They knew he meant what he said, and silently recalled the residents that had been fired in the recent past.

"Do your job and there won't be any problem."

He looked at each of them yet again from right to left, then nodded. The discussion was over.

Alex took the cue as the senior resident. "Thank you, Dr. Todd." He wheeled around and started walking as the other residents stood up and filed out. The Boss had already turned and was gazing somberly at the wall.

They marched in single file past the Boss's secretary, Audrey, who looked at them with a mixture of pity and relief that she wasn't the target. She knew what went on at that traditional meeting. The residents always came out the same way, and made a straight line to the exit.

Only when the heavy door closed behind them did they feel free to talk.

Curt whistled, "Well, I guess he told us. Spare the rod and spoil the neurosurgeon."

Paul thrust his jaw out, barracuda-like. "He means it. No screw-ups. We all have to do the best job we can." His eyes darted at Alex.

Dahlia tossed her hair and leaned towards Curt protectively as she walked, high voice wavering. "His bark is worse than his bite."

Alex glanced over, irritated at Paul's efforts to scare Curt. "Just be careful, Curt. Do your job and you'll be all right."

They walked back to the call room, each immersed in his own thoughts. The younger residents departed after getting their coats, leaving Alex and Dahlia. Alex slumped in a chair and busied himself with his card, marking the list of patients.

Dahlia shoved over a stack of journals, perched herself on the corner of the desk, and looked at him. "Why do you let the Boss bother you?"

He rubbed his head.

"What's the matter?"

"Got another headache." He glanced at her. "Been getting more, lately."

"You worry too much."

"Worry? With what we see? We're living witnesses to how much can go wrong with the human body. Think of how many complex processes have to be done flawlessly to keep your body going. Sooner or later the law of probabilities catches up with you."

"What are you talking about?"

"Even if a physiologic system is ninety-nine point-nine-nine reliable, sooner or later, as the years go by, it's going to fumble."

She rolled her eyes.

"Go to the cellular level, the biochemical level. Think of the enormous power expenditure to keep sodium out of the cell, potassium in, the furious activity of the cell, frantically consuming energy with the threat of obliteration only a thin membrane away, like the boy with his finger in the dike."

"What are you talking about?"

"Then you go to the cellular level, the hordes of microorganisms constantly trying to penetrate the scrawny cellular wall, trying to throw a monkey wrench into our delicate and balanced machinery. At the organ level, the numerous toxins, poisons out there, the ease with which you can get fat, clogging your arteries." His hands closed into fists. "To say nothing of the present external milieu, the cacophony of onrushing images and sound that assault us, distracting, influencing, tumbling, foaming, jarring our consciousness, firing our neurons, spasmodically jamming our neuronal pacemakers, our fructifying internal rhythms."

"You didn't answer my question."

"What question?"

Dahlia studied him, noticing the little vein below Alex's left eye, in the translucent skin under the lower lash. "Why do you let the Boss bother you so?"

"He doesn't bother me."

"Yes he does. I could see it."

"Did we check the CT scan on Mrs. Moyer?"

"Why does it bother you?"

Alex put his card down. "Why does it bother me? Why do the Boss's threats to fire us bother me? Why, I don't know. Maybe it's because I worked years to get where I am today. Four years of college, four years of medical school, one year of internship, five years of residency, sweating, no sleep, hopping at a moment's notice, afraid of a mistake, afraid it will cost the patient's life and my job. I don't know why it should bother me."

"You won't get fired."

"I worked too hard and too long not to make it."

"Alex, you won't get fired."

He stared at her. "How do you know? You heard him in there. He doesn't take prisoners, Dahlia. One accident, one poor outcome, and you're a suspect in his eyes. Then that jackal Hackman gets on you, puts the pressure on, things cascade, and before you know that's it. This is no joke. You're out of a job and a life."

She stared at him in disbelief and sighed. "Look, we're all in the same boat. You can't let it get to you."

"The stakes are too high. This is what I want to be. This is what I should be."

"Never thought about anything else?"

"I thought about law school for a while."

"Law school?"

He nodded. "I was exploring alternatives. And then I thought, I want to do something truly serious and valuable with my life. You think a lawyer does what we do? No way. I realized being a doctor was for me. And when I got older I wanted to be the best kind of a doctor, a brain surgeon."

"Why a brain surgeon?" Dahlia said softly. It was rare that Alex talked like this. She supposed the Boss had really shaken him up.

He looked at her for a couple of seconds, not speaking. "We do something no businessman, no politician, no lawyer can do. We open the shell of a human being, tamper, probe, fix the brain, the most sacred repository, that which makes us different than animals, the crowning glory of evolution." He seemed to glow for a moment. "Think of it. A brain fixing another brain, a brain healing another brain." He looked at her self-consciously. "It was the right thing to do with my life."

She nodded. "How'd you get started?"

He looked at the wall. "My mother . . . died of a brain tumor. I just remember my father, as she became weaker and weaker, saying 'They'll do something, they'll do something'. I was 10 years old. She gradually went to sleep, slowly over months, in a hospital bed in the living room, and my father just kept waiting, waiting. He took good care of her."

Dahlia nodded slowly again, her thick, long, black hair shifting layer over layer as she looked at him. "It doesn't make it any easier, with a man like Dr. Todd being the Chairman."

He kept his eyes on the wall, then got up and got his coat from the rack.

"That's the thing," Alex said, putting on his coat slowly. "The Boss is so cold blooded. Don't you get that feeling? He will do anything to anybody. Under that deep voice, gray hair, and aura of concern that turns on and off as the occasion demands there is ice. I don't know where his core is, what he really believes in. His excuse for the President is, don't worry that the guy's a liar, the economy's good and besides, everybody does it." He looked around disgustedly. "The great myth of our time. Because nobody is perfect, there is no meaning or need for virtue. We can never attain perfection, so what's the use?"

"Now you're sounding like a philosopher."

He grunted and shook his head, starting for the door.

Dahlia wanted to continue. "But I know what you mean about the

Boss. I wonder what happened to Dr. Henry. Somehow it seemed like Dr. Todd took over as Chief very quickly. He was an attending for a while, then suddenly Chief of Neurosurgery."

"Yeah, things would be different with Dr. Henry. But he's gone now and we've got Todd. Him and his Ivy League boys, Fox and Parr."

"Hey, be careful. I went to Yale."

"Yeah, but you're different. Those boys, they really think they're superior."

She nodded. "I do wonder about Dr. Todd."

"There just doesn't seem to be any center to him. I've known him for five years, worked closely with him and he's still a total enigma." He walked over to the door, thinking about the Boss's assertions about improving the brain, and Dr. Sutcliff's words, when another thought struck him. "When we did that aneurysm, I shook a bit. I knew what was at stake. I know what can happen, and I care. But the Boss never shook. He just doesn't. Have you ever seen his hands tremble?"

"No."

"There's something wrong with that. I don't quite know what it is, but there's something wrong."

"Well, you're almost finished."

"If I make it."

"You and I won't be fired. You're almost there, and I'm not far behind."

Alex looked at her, thinking that was easy for her to say. She's a woman.

"I know. You think he wouldn't do it to a woman."

"You're a beautiful one, also. That makes it even more unlikely."

He walked past her and out the door. She looked after him in surprise, and wondered why he sounded so sad.

CHAPTER 6

Waiting. The residents did that a lot. Dahlia, Curt, Paul and Richard were loitering in the intensive care unit, awaiting morning rounds, monitors chirping like hyperactive crickets. Sitting at the nursing station, they watched Fran, one of the nurses, eating a piece of leftover fried chicken. Curt was fascinated by her lips, greasy and tubelike, continuously undulating like two pink snakes glued to her mouth, under a small nose and large, wide blue eyes.

Paul couldn't take it any more. "Fran, that's disgusting."

She looked at him, her chubby cheeks shiny, and smiled. "Want a piece?"

The other nurses cackled.

"No thanks."

"My chicken's not good enough for you?" Fran said in a tone of injured belligerence.

Paul shook his head.

Dahlia looked at him. "What are you doing here anyway? You're on research."

"I thought I'd tag along. I don't start in the lab until a little later."

Curt nodded. "Here comes the chief."

Alex came over to the group. "Morning, guys. We can make rounds like gentleman today. Plenty of time. No operations 'til later."

Fran smiled. "Good. I don't have to rush the chicken."

Alex looked at Paul. "What're you doing here? Not busy enough in research?"

"As I was saying, research doesn't start until a little later today. I thought I'd tag along."

Alex nodded. He knew what the game was. Paul heard there was no surgery this morning, and figured on being there with Dr. Todd. Getting a little face time in, Alex thought as he glanced at him. Then he looked around.

"Who was on last night?"

"John."

"Is he here?"

Fran angled her head towards the cubicle where the residents slept when on duty. "He's still in the call room, I think."

"We need to know what happened last night. Can you get him?"

She scuttled off, thighs audibly rubbing together and immense backside trailing her, scurrying around the nursing station to the call room door. Knocking briskly, she inclined her head up, then yelled sweetly, "Time to get up, dear. I'm sorry I tired you out last night" she giggled ferociously, "but they're making rounds. Chief Alex wants you out here."

Chuckling, she waddled back. After a moment, the door opened and second year resident John Parr came out, shaking his tousled red hair, then yawning and putting on his white coat. He ambled on over to the group, now assembled at the first patient's bedside.

Alex looked him over. "Morning, John."

Parr nodded his flushed face, his cheek creased from a blanket fold.

"How was the night?"

"Not too bad."

Alex walked over to the top of the bed and looked down at the patient, a young man with eyes closed and head wrapped in white gauze. A small plastic tube came out of the dressing and ran to a transducer.

"Richard, Mr. Bilsky is about twenty four years old. He had a tumor of the left side of the brain, operated on several days ago. We put an intracranial pressure monitor in place, to watch for any brain swelling."

"That plastic tube?"

"Yes. That tube is placed in the brain, tunneled through the skull and scalp, and hooked up through a fluid coupling and transducer to the monitor. It provides a continuous reading of pressure in the cranial cavity. The strain on the brain."

Richard nodded.

"All very high tech medicine. We can also read cerebral blood flow directly from the surface of the brain, in real time. But all of this is meaningless without a skilled and experienced nurse." He looked at Fran fondly.

She looked around in mock dismay. "Oh, she left, Doctor. I'm the only one here."

"Without an expert like Fran, all this high tech stuff is just silicon and metal."

She giggled. "With an expert like Fran, it's all silicon and silk." She made eyes at Curt.

Alex ignored her, and warmed to the topic. "Fran's the best there is. If she tells you something, you'd better listen."

Impressed, Curt and Richard pursed their lips.

Alex continued. "A little unstable, perhaps." She laughed. "But if I were sick, she'd be the one to care for me."

"Oh Doctor." Fran sidled up to him. "If you're ill, can I put your catheter in?" She chuckled throatily.

Alex looked around to make sure none of the patients were listening, and then turned to John. "How was his intracranial pressure last night?"

Parr coughed. "Mostly below twenty."

Fran raised her eyebrows in surprise, her tube lips inverting.

Alex glanced at the nursing report, which listed the hourly readings. His eye ran down the column. "Looks like it went up to thirty fairly consistently at one point."

"I guess so."

"Did you know that?"

Parr looked at Fran. "They did call me."

"What did you do about it?"

"Well, I figured since cerebral perfusion pressure wasn't affected, we'd sit tight."

Alex turned to Curt. "What's cerebral perfusion pressure?"

"Arterial pressure minus intracranial pressure."

"Right. The driving pressure for blood into the cranial cavity." He looked at the nursing log again. "Well, it's true that the perfusion pressure was not affected. But given the fact that the intracranial pressure had been stable for a while postop, then became elevated, it probably would have been a good idea to check a CT scan of the head."

Parr nodded in acknowledgment.

"But he was clinically stable" interjected Paul Fox.

"The intracranial pressure was persistently elevated, and this was a change from the postoperative baseline," said Alex evenly.

Paul shook his head. "As John said, the perfusion pressure was adequate."

"Just because the perfusion pressure was OK, the elevation of intracranial pressure several days after surgery is unexplained." Alex took out a reflex hammer from his white coat pocket and began tapping his palm with it.

"The patient was doing well."

"This patient. At that time. But things can change quickly. Medicine is a percentage game. If you miss one out of ten problems in the neurosurgical patient, that's a ten percent loss rate. Unacceptable." He waved the hammer at Paul, who was silent. "The point is to have a low threshold for getting a CT scan. The penalty for missing a problem could be death, and you should be expecting to get some normal scans as the price for not missing a problem. That's why you have a monitor in." Alex turned to the patient again.

"Mr. Bilsky."

The man stirred.

Alex reached down and shook his shoulder slightly. "Mr. Bilsky, are you in there?" He tapped his head very gently with the hammer. The man lay silent. Alex reached down and pinched his shoulder.

"Ow." The patient left arm reached up and brushed away Alex's hand, without moving his other side.

"How's his strength?"

Fran shook her head sadly. "He's still paralyzed on the one side."

The patient opened his eyes.

"Good morning, Mr. Bilsky. It's Dr. Adams and the team."

The patient looked unimpressed, one eye open more than the other like a frozen beginning of a wink.

"We're making our rounds. How are you doing?"

The patient looked steadily and silently at Alex.

"Where are you?"

"University Hospital."

"Good." He turned to Fran. "How's his speech?"

"Been OK."

"You're doing well, Mr. Bilsky. Soon we'll be able to move you out of the ICU."

The patient nodded. Curt was writing the progress note as they spoke, then closed the chart and put it back in the rack with a clatter.

Alex led the group to the next bedside, where they continued the process, checking the patients, writing notes.

At the end of the line of beds, as they were completing the last patient, the clerk answered the phone. "Dr. Todd is coming down for rounds," she announced.

Alex turned to the group. "We'll wait here for the big boy."

They broke up for a moment, Alex going back to the first bed, Curt, Richard and Dahlia clustering and talking, Paul and John Parr murmuring together.

Fran sidled up to Alex. "I don't trust those guys."

"Who do you mean?"

"You know, Parr and Fox."

"Oh well."

"They're brown nosers."

"We all are. We have to get through."

"The rest of you guys are human. They're snakes."

"Well, the Boss picked them."

"What do you mean?"

"The Chairman of the department picks the residents. Dahlia and I were picked by Dr. Henry. When he retired and Dr. Todd became Chief, he got to select the residents. That's who chose your friends. They're highly qualified. They're Ivy League."

She looked offended. "So what."

"So they're the best."

"You're the best. All the nurses here think so. We're the ones who really know."

"Well, thanks."

"It's those big brown eyes, and the little ass."

"Easy, Fran."

She giggled. "And the patients love that graying at the temples look." She inspected his hair. "You may be getting more of it lately, though."

"I wonder why." Alex looked at his reflection in the chrome paper towel dispenser, turning and inspecting his face and hair. "There's a face like a Greek god. Full, sensuous lips, sensitive chin."

"You mean weak chin."

He looked anxiously at the reflection. "I wouldn't call it weak. Sensitive is the right word. But the nose might be a little bulbous." He gave the tip of it a squeeze.

She giggled again. "You're a love god."

"The capacity for love parallels one's capacity for illusion," he said sourly, continuing to inspect himself in the mirror.

"It does not," she said indignantly, her chins quivering. "By the way, that Curt seems to be a good egg. Even if the Boss did pick him. Is he married?"

Alex looked at her speculatively. "I don't think so."

Dahlia walked up. "What's up?"

"Doctor and I were discussing relationships." Fran nodded at Alex, who was gazing out the window.

"Oh, really. And what did doctor say?"

"He doesn't believe in them."

"That's because doctor dissects relationships like he dissects the brain, like he minutely examines every bodily perturbation."

Alex raised his eyes. "You better wipe that grease off your cheek, Fran. That's no way to greet the Boss."

She looked surprised, then ran off to the utility room to get a paper towel. She reemerged seconds later, her cheeks less shiny. "Thanks."

Alex nodded. "Just in time. Here's Todd."

"He looks mad."

"He always looks that way." Alex squinted as he examined him more closely. "But you're right. He looks worse than usual."

Todd had appeared with the other attending, Clark Hackman, and stopped to talk with Paul Fox. Fox nodded towards Alex, and the Boss turned and came striding down the aisle. Hackman quickly pursued him, his bulging belly billowing over his pants like a spinnaker sail straining full with the wind, his head protruding above his narrow neck like a crow's nest atop a mast. Parr and Fox followed in their wake.

Todd abruptly stopped in front of Alex, hulking over him. Alex waited for the storm, hands jammed in the pockets of his white coat.

"Alex, do you know where I was?"

"No, Dr. Todd."

"I was down in the operating room, just like any other day."

Alex realized with a sudden sinking feeling that the Boss might not have known about the operative schedule. "We had no cases this morning" he said glumly.

Todd opened his deep-set eyes. "That's right. And I had no way of knowing that. Look, Alex. You're the chief resident. You're job is to keep me informed. If you can't do the job, I'll get someone else to do it."

The group had silently gathered round.

"I'm sorry, Dr. Todd. It won't happen again."

"It better not."

Alex waited for a moment, but nothing more was forthcoming. He turned and led the group over to Mr. Bilsky's bed, who gazed back at them from under the sheets.

"Young Mr. Bilsky had a quiet night. He continues weak on his right side."

Todd turned to Hackman. "Clark, look at this. We resected a parietal brain tumor and now look at him. Wrecked" he said disgustedly, shaking his head.

Hackman nodded, his mouth pursing under his mustache.

Mr. Bilsky's eyes bulged as he gaped at the assortment of faces somberly staring at him. Fran came over and stroked his shoulder. Todd turned abruptly and wheeled out of the room, the rest of the group following.

Alex could hear Fran soothing the patient as they continued. He hurried into the next room, and walked up to the head of the bed.

"Mrs. Lupo, frontal meningioma, craniotomy yesterday with complete resection by Dr. Hackman and me. We took off the head wrapping today. Her incision looks good."

Clark Hackman pushed up to the patient's bed, stopping next to the Boss. Alex focused on his belly for a split second, and with a corner of his mind wondered how the musculature of the abdominal wall held in the face of such tension. Hackman looked at the patient, triumph in his eyes. He had looked forward to this moment, clearly was prepared to hear her happiness, relief, and gratitude. The patient just looked tired, and gazed straight ahead.

"Mrs. Lupo, it's Dr. Hackman."

She said nothing, looking frightened, sad and dazed.

Hackman waited for a moment, but she continued silent. "She has no idea of what we did for her," he said to Alex, with the group arrayed at the bedside.

Alex frowned in thought. "I think she's a little tired. She was talking and moving fine this morning."

Hackman nodded, and looked at her. Todd brusquely spun around and the entourage headed out. Alex lingered at the bedside for a moment, looking at her, thinking. She's still scared stiff, she's been scared since she came in. She'll never be the same, she knows that, she knows she's mortal, her health is an illusion, now she knows.

He reached out and took her hand gently as she continued to stare. "Some patients are more afraid when we take off the head wrapping. They feel safer with it on."

She looked at Alex and smiled wanly. "I don't want the air coming too close to my brain."

"You'll be fine. You're doing very well. Your brain is well protected, and we'll be getting you out of here soon."

"Thanks."

"The nurses will keep a close eye on you, and we'll drop by again later." He gave her hand a squeeze, slowly dropped it to the bed, turned and walked quickly to rejoin the group.

After completing rounds in the unit, they headed towards the regular floor, the place for patients who were not as sick as those in the intensive care unit. As they went down the hallway, the elevator opened and a chubby, disheveled woman came out. It was Mrs. Bilsky, mother of the patient in the ICU. She saw the group, found Dr. Todd, and rushed up to him.

"Dr. Todd. I was trying to call you. How's my son doing?"

Todd looked down at her. "Stable. He's stable. We just saw him."

"Thank you." She lingered for a second, and then trundled off to the ICU.

The group continued, Todd and Hackman at the head of the entourage as it went from room to room. Fran was waiting as they came out of a room, her lips in a downward curve. She gestured for Alex to come over.

"Mrs. Bilsky's very upset," she whispered to Alex, glancing over as the group paused several steps away. "The kid really freaked out at Dr. Todd calling him wrecked."

"Alex, what's the problem?" Todd demanded, pacing impatiently.

"Mrs. Bilsky's very upset about her son."

"Of course it's about her son. What else would it be?"

Alex waited.

"Go talk to her after rounds." He led the group down the hall.

Alex turned to Fran. "Tell her I'll be over in a couple of minutes."

Fran nodded and started off for the ICU.

Alex walked towards the group, already filing into a patient's room. He thought of Mr. Bilsky's eyes, imploring them not to give up. Well, Todd just gave him the works.

As he turned the corner he nearly collided with John Parr, standing and looking up at the patient's TV like the others. Alex's gaze flickered around the room, at the upturned faces. Todd must've started it, he thought. Like a flock of birds. One takes the lead and the others follow.

Alex looked up as well, at the President speaking. Even the patient's eyes were drawn to the screen.

Todd smiled, lips flattening over his teeth. "He's a good public speaker, isn't he? Presents himself well."

Clark Hackman pursed his lips. "The people like him."

"He's a liar." Dahlia piped up.

Todd laughed and looked down at the supine man, resting after a spine operation. "He's a politician. They're all like that."

The patient grabbed the rails of his bed and automatically rolled on his side so the team could examine his incision. He talked over his shoulder, his face blocked by the siderails like a man in prison. "The President projects his agenda very persuasively, so everybody can understand it. So what if he stretches things a little? The job gets done."

Todd turned to Alex. "What do you think of him?"

"I agree with Dahlia."

"So the fact that the economy's blazing, the country's at peace, doesn't that matter at all?"

"He had nothing to do with that. He is a liar."

"The country's doing well." Todd shook his head. "They all bend the truth." He turned from the TV to the patient. "Youthful idealism. Only, Alex is getting a little long in the tooth to still harbor those illusions." Hackman and Fox smirked. "Well, I can see you're doing well. Home tomorrow."

The patient nodded eagerly. "Great. Thanks very much, Dr. Todd. You did a terrific job."

Alex led the group out. Heather Mackenzie, one of the floor nurses, caught his eye. "Fran called from the unit. Mrs. Bilsky is still very upset."

As Todd emerged, Alex turned to him. "I'm going over to the ICU, Dr. Todd. Fran called about Mrs. Bilsky again. I need to talk to her."

"You do that, Alex." Todd looked at Alex slowly and deliberately, then led the group to another room.

Alex walked down the hall and around the corner. Two rotund figures were outside the ICU, Fran comforting a crying Mrs. Bilsky. She greeted him with relief. "Now, here's that nice Dr. Adams."

As he walked up, the mother's corpulent body distracted him. She had on a shapeless gray sweater, with numerous folds and bulges like a stack of inner tubes. One of the inner tubes was whiter that the rest, though, and as she turned to him he cast a fleeting glance at what was actually a ringlet of fat uncovered between pants and sweater, but in the same shape and sequence as the other sweater covered bulges. Some effect, he thought. The corduroy pants were baggy, just like the rest of her, covering her shoes with multiple folds. Her knees sprung slightly backward, as though near collapse by the immense weight they were supporting.

The woman looked at him, her small brown eyes peering out through fleshy ramparts, mouth repeatedly opening and closing. Her face was kind, for all that, and love and concern for her son overwhelmingly apparent.

"What can I do for you, Mrs. Bilsky?" Alex said softly.

"What did he say to my son?"

"What do you mean, ma'am?"

"My son. He's crying in there. What did he say to him?"

"Well, I don't exactly know. Your son's doing OK."

"Doesn't he know what's he's doing? Doesn't he care about people? Does he have a soul? My son is in there" she jabbed a stubby finger towards the unit, "crying his eyes out. He thought he was getting better. Now he thinks he's had it." She started crying as Fran held her by her shoulders.

Alex looked sympathetically at her hairy, round face, multiple chins quivering. Speaking quietly, he reached out and held her upper arm gently. "He really is doing well. He just had a huge brain operation, and is recovering appropriately. He's weak, but we hope and believe the strength in his arm and leg will improve. Therapy may be needed for that. We've already made arrangements for him to be transferred to the rehabilitation hospital after his stay here. All in all, he's doing well. He's just been through about the most difficult experience a human being can have, and he's getting better." He took the tissues Fran was proffering and gave them to Mrs. Bilsky, who accepted them gratefully.

She looked at him, her sobs quieting, then buried her face in the tissues. "I guess I just needed to hear that."

"Fran will talk to him about this as well, and I'll come back after rounds. I'd be happy to answer any more questions. You have to hang in there for him."

She nodded.

"You need to get some rest yourself. We're in this for the long haul."

"Thanks, Doctor. What did you say your name was?"

"Adams, Dr. Adams."

"Well, I'm glad you're taking care of him. That other doctor, he's as cold as ice."

"We'll keep a close eye on your son."

Fran took her by the shoulders and guided her back to the ICU. Alex turned and started walking back to the nursing floor. Images of the mother's concerned face, Dr. Todd's cavalier assessment at the bedside, the son's imploring eyes, and the President's smooth and untroubled face floated in his mind.

He approached the group as they came out of one of the last rooms on the floor. Dr. Todd, at the head, saw him coming.

"Alex, did you get everything straightened out?"

"Yes, Dr. Todd."

He turned to Hackman. "Alex needs to be like the President. Smooth."

They all laughed except for Alex, as Todd prodded him again. "Still don't like the President, Alex?"

"No."

Todd waited expectantly for more.

"He's a con man. No moral fiber."

Todd nodded to Clark Hackman. "Alex is our moral philosopher."

Hackman grinned, and said to Alex, "President Davies must be a smart guy. He made it to the Oval Office."

Alex shook his head. "He's lost his way, lost track of the fundamentals."

"Seems to me he knows the fundamentals pretty well. That's what got him where he is today."

Alex shook his head again.

"And the people like him as well."

"That doesn't prove much." The other residents were looking at him, not sure why he was continuing the conversation. "Polls are artificial. Results depend on how the questions are asked, who is asked, how they are asked. And a lot of people out there have lost track of the fundamentals as well."

"How'd that happen?" Todd asked indulgently.

"TV, newspapers, books, movies, music. Part of the problem. They're all illusion, all distortion. Too many people have slipped away on the wings of their gossamer illusions, lost contact with virtue, with the direct relation between belief, thought, action, consequence."

"Virtue. Nobody talks about virtue." Hackman smiled again. "What are you, Alex, some kind of fossil? Did they find you frozen in ice in the North Pole?"

"I guess that's the moral philosophy major in me. If a civilization does not cherish and teach virtue, it will decapitate and then devour its young."

"Don't be an intellectual, Alex" snapped Hackman.

"Intellectuals have a reputation for being in a crystal tower, but now the mass media has given everybody the opportunity to be seduced, distracted, and overwhelmed with sensation and emotion." Alex nodded at the television. "Brain surgery brings you back to reality quick. A false move, a careless judgment, and somebody is hurt badly or dead. It reminds us to stay close to the basics. He's forgotten those. He's forgotten about right and wrong."

Hackman smirked. Todd rumbled. "Well, Alex, I see you have strong opinions. Right and wrong can be slippery concepts, though."

"Many times it is not exactly clear what is right, but the act of considering it, of remembering it, of acting on it, is at the core of civilization, the essence of what is means to be a human being. Without it, we're just so many chemical reactions."

"That's too simplistic, Alex. Mankind, the human brain, the mind, is much more than a single dichotomy. It's never that elementary."

"Especially in this computer age" added Hackman, looking at the Boss.

"The computer age?" frowned Alex. "Right and wrong is the digital archetype, the ancient dichotomy." His gaze flickered from Hackman to the Boss. "Interesting how that ancient dichotomy has lost its impact in this age, how a puny mechanistic copy in the form of bits and bytes has become ascendant."

The Boss stared at him for a moment, then turned and shook his head. "How'd we ever get on that? Let's get going." He led the group down the hall. Dahlia fell in alongside Alex.

"Alex, you say the oddest things sometimes. Digital archetype?"

"I've got to catch up with the Boss." He hurried and turned into the last room on the floor, just behind the Boss. The first bed was curtained and in the second was a prominent lawyer, Harold Brandt, recovering from spine surgery. He was looking up at the television, watching the President, as the Boss came up.

"Does a good job, doesn't he?" the lawyer said, reclining in his bed.

Todd nodded, then turned slightly as Alex came into the room and up to the bed, regaining his usual station. "Our chief resident doesn't think so."

Brandt turned to Alex. "What's wrong with the President? He's very media savvy."

"I don't think spinning the media is the most important requirement to be a President."

Brandt laughed. "Communication is the key to leadership, and he is a master of communication. I'm a media lawyer. I know communication."

"To truly communicate, you need a message."

"He's got a message. He's a good guy, a good, caring leader."

"The media no longer, if it ever did, communicate anything. The rules of personal behavior, the care of children and family, how to do one's job, the importance of taking care of each other, these are the key issues. This is the core of civilization no one writes about, no one talks about, but is the reality of life and of people's lives."

"The media talks about those issues."

"I don't believe virtues such as truth, sincerity, love, discipline, are shown by the modern media. There is an unspoken assumption that the media can depict all reality. Maybe part of our problem as a society is that the media is fundamentally unable to portray those values, those virtues, with any potency. It's most effective at portraying brief, impressionistic moments of violence, sensation, emotion, leading to a subtle but pervasive distortion of presentation and perception." Alex paused. "Remember Aldous Huxley's novel Brave New World?"

"A bit."

"Remember Soma?"

"Soma?"

"The all purpose drug. Available everywhere, at any time. Tranquility, placidity in a bottle."

Brandt glanced at the Boss. "Yes, I recall."

"That's the media. Soma on the screen. The nepenthe for the new age. Huxley was right. He just got the form wrong."

Todd laughed, a hint of uneasiness in his voice. "Alex was a philosophy major."

Brandt sat up, grimacing. "People use the media to obtain information. Everybody is exposed to it."

"Precisely my point. The public looks on the media as telling the truth. But by its very nature, construction and methods, it simply misses the most vital characteristics of a civilized, honorable people like a blind spot in the eye that you don't even know is present. The media has a giant blind spot for the most critical aspects of life."

Brandt smiled uncomfortably and looked at Dr. Todd. "I don't know what you're talking about. Television, cable is very successful."

"There's no relevance to life in terms of moral analysis or instruction. Example, personal choice, codes of living, how to live from second to second, minute to minute, person to person, day to day, incident to incident. How can you portray that on TV, video, movie? It cannot be distilled to the desiccated, distorted, detached, shrunken, simplified image of reality portrayed by the media. Only great artists touch on that successfully, and they are always few. Now they are hugely diluted out in the onrushing sea of images, cheap copies, reruns forming the immensity of what we call media."

Todd grunted at Brandt, "I warned you." He turned slightly, but the group gathered closer.

Brandt looked at Alex. "Talk about idealism." He put his hands in back of his head. "We started on the President, and ended up with the media."

Alex nodded. "Both are closely related. What we call the media simply cannot convey the patient, long-term accretion of actions directed by codes that constitute moral life. And this only applies to that subset which attempts to represent reality, albeit in a distorted way. It leaves out most of the media, which are just a collection of disjointed impressions and stimulating in a purely physiologic manner."

"What does this have to do with the President? Admittedly he's no moral giant, but he is effective." The patient glanced at Todd.

"Maybe this is why there seems to be fewer and fewer moral giants left at all. People are raised by the media rather than the infinitely more powerful and congruent influence of direct personal example. Maybe this is why the President can simply appear on TV, lie, and disappear and people actually believe him, or at least tolerate him. They do not know what truth is, or the importance of truth." Alex took a deep breath. "Maybe the President is the embodiment of that gigantic blind spot of the media, or more accurately the embodiment of everything the blind spot doesn't include. Maybe the President gets his power because he most directly, efficiently, and representatively reflects and radiates empty motion, emotion, and impression, that which the media presents most effectively."

"I.e. he has no soul." A new voice came from the next bed, which was curtained. Dr. Todd, surprised, whipped it open. A withered old man sat there, with lively eyes, listening intently. "But where did the President get that skill, that insight, that compatibility with the media?" he said in a hoarse voice.

Alex thought for a moment, and then answered. "Pure genetic

mutation. He was born with it. One in two hundred sixty million. Just our luck."

Alex stared as the old man shook his head, eyes glittering in their sockets. "It's too resonant, too unselfconscious." He cackled and continued. "Who's to say we're not totally misusing, misapplying, misunderstanding the media, and our assumption that there can be something edifying about it completely wrong. Exposure to it without the human mind prepared by personal instruction and example may not be" he paused and looked around like an inquisitive parrot at the group staring at him, "constructive. The unspoken assumption that the media in some way can be useful morally, philosophically, practically in the development of a codified individual spirit completely illusory, illogical and deceptive in a most profound way. Listening to the media beguiles one into believing one is making or learning moral choices when one is in fact merely deceiving oneself and making no choices at all, or merely being distracted." The skull-like head rested back as the eyes flickered closed.

Alex continued to stare at him. "You mean, the ancient Spartans may have been right?"

"Precisely."

Todd's eyes blazed deep black for a moment, then the fires were banked. He shrugged impatiently. "Whatever that means."

Alex wouldn't give up. "In ancient Sparta, no written literature was kept, as they thought virtue could only be taught by example, and books would only be a distraction."

Hackman laughed heartily. "Now the Luddite wants to get rid of the media."

Brandt chortled. "At any rate, you can't argue with success."

Todd slapped his leg and nodded. "Right. Well, you're still going home tomorrow. Try not to listen to this guy too much. Or your roommate. They'll tire you out."

Brandt nodded. "Nice talking with you all."

The group filed out. Todd wheeled on Alex. "What the hell were you doing in there?"

"What do you mean?"

"Don't be upsetting the patients. And that nut in the next bed—don't get him going with that philosophical crap. He's crazy enough with that limbic tumor."

Alex stared at him for a moment. The Boss sounded slightly uncomfortable. "Yes, sir."

"I know the President. He's a good man." He abruptly turned. "We need more like him" he turned his head and slowly brought his eyes to bear on Alex for a moment, and strode down the hall, the entourage breaking up.

Alex stared after him, cold. More like the President?

"Alex, loosen up a little," grinned Paul as he passed Alex and hurried down the hall with a loping tilt, like an upright wolf.

Alex turned to Dahlia. "That's the kind of thinking that's got us where we are today. Loosen up a little, relax a little, bit by bit forget. What bullshit incrementalism."

"Are you always this rigid?" she said, her eyes sparkling.

"Only with the big things. You have to know not to sweat the small stuff."

"Isn't that incrementalism?"

"No, but your question is." He shook his head, then started walking down the hall, the image of the skull-headed patient held in his mind, the words lingering.

CHAPTER 7

Alex hated the shrill squawk of his beeper, jolting his consciousness with a myriad of unwanted memories. The spectrum of possibilities it both announced and concealed were infinite, anything from a signature needed in medical records to an agonizingly sick patient requiring concentrated and exhausting care for hours. He read the number on the screen. The neurosurgical research lab. Like all residents with beepers, it was automatic to wonder about the purpose of a call, to anticipate the problem, to immediately react. For the last four months Paul Fox, the third year resident, was doing work with the Boss's monkeys. Alex wondered what was up, as those on research never needed to call the residents on the clinical service.

He dialed the number.

Paul answered, his voice strained. "Alex?"

"What's going on?" Traditionally research time was the easiest rotation, the one during which the stresses of taking care of patients were replaced with meandering about the various labs in the medical school, assisting one of the attendings with their project in a leisurely manner. "The lab too soft for you? You need more call time?"

Paul ignored the question. "You need to come on down right now. One of the Boss's monkeys is in trouble. He looks funny. The Boss'll have a fit if it croaks." He paused. "Can you come?"

Alex looked at his watch. OR was due to start in one hour, and to be late was unthinkable. He wondered what was going on with the monkeys. Nobody was real sure of what the Boss was doing with them, and nobody was asking. The fact that Paul was so agitated was unusual, different from his usual irritatingly self-sufficient air. He was distraught, really worried about his hide, troubled enough to show weakness to a rival.

"We'll be right over." Alex nodded to Richard Walters, standing beside him. "C'mon."

Going to the end of the hall, they took the elevator to the basement where the research labs were located.

They walked along the old corridor, lined with dusty machines, bookshelves, and other detritus of the medical school's long existence. Stopping at an aged door with a frosted glass window, they turned and opened it, entering a room crammed with dark cabinets, cages, black countertops and sinks, a foul stench everywhere. The floor was worn brown wood, here and there spotted with dark stains. Paul was bent towards one particular cage, peering into it sadly.

As he got closer, Alex saw a small brown monkey inside, on its back. The animal had its eyes closed, but would intermittently cry softly and move its arms and legs around weakly. Suddenly the left arm and leg of the monkey started twitching, faster and faster. Paul looked up, startled and panicked.

"The Boss's key experiment. I don't know what he's doing with it except he said to watch it like a hawk. If anything happens to it I'm in trouble" he moaned.

Alex said nothing. As usual Paul was worried most about his own ass, about how things looked. Alex opened the cage and looked at the animal. It had stopped twitching, and lay unresponsive. Alex gently lifted an eyelid. "Got a flashlight?"

"Sure."

Alex flashed the light into its eyes. "How long has the right pupil been dilated and unresponsive to light?"

Paul looked startled, "Looked OK to me before all this."

Alex took an opthalmoscope and examined the animal's eyes, focusing at the back of the eyeball. "There's an odd bluish tint to the retina. I wonder what that means." He looked up for a moment, and then turned to Paul.

"How's the operative suite here . . . still available?"

Paul stared at Alex. "You're not thinking of opening it up?"

Alex nodded.

Paul's voice became louder. "Are you crazy? We've not scanned it. What if you're wrong? What if there's nothing in there? The Boss'll kill us. What if he doesn't make it through the anesthesia? What if this behavior is part of the experiment?"

"Paul, it always comes down to this. Cut or no cut. We can posture, we can explain, we can theorize. But it comes down to cut or no cut."

"Yeah, so simple."

"Paul, this isn't a novel with a complex story line. This isn't a court of law with argument and sophistry. We don't have flights of fancy here. It comes down to the final common pathway, cut or no cut."

"It's not that simple. What if it just had a seizure? That would explain the blown pupil. Maybe we should just wait it out."

"I'm not saying that the decision isn't complex. We can't calculate each factor, each chance, each possibility exactly. Decisions in surgery are often shaded in gray. But in the end, it's cut or no cut. We need to cut."

Alex knew that Paul would make it Alex's fault if the monkey didn't survive. He kept looking at the monkey while he said, slowly and methodically, "It's dying now. It'll be dead soon. That's what we do, Paul. Make the best judgment with the available information. That information is incomplete. But we have to use what we have and make a rational decision. That's surgery. Second guessing is for the lawyers."

Paul looked skeptical. "Easy for you to say. You're almost done. I screw up, and I'm on the first bus out of town to a residency in anesthesia."

Alex looked steadily at Paul. "I've got a lot on the line as well. You know how it is around here. Nothing's sure until the last day."

The animal twitched again.

Paul looked at the monkey, then slowly turned to Alex. He nodded. "The instruments are sterile and ready. I'll do the anesthesia. I might as well start practicing for a new residency."

Alex gave a short bark that Paul interpreted as a laugh, then carefully picked up the monkey, holding its small limp body like a baby. He carried it into the other room, where a small operative suite was located, putting the animal down gently on a soft pad on the operating table. Paul quickly intubated the monkey, placing a small plastic breathing tube down its throat. Alex started an intravenous line, and checked the dripping fluid.

He then took a battery powered clipper and started shaving the animal's head. The instrument jammed and he shook his head in disgust. "Don't we have a better clipper?"

Paul tossed him another one. Alex continued to shave the right half of the monkey's head. "Might as well learn from this in case the scanner ever goes down. What side should we open up?"

Paul said quickly, "The side of the dilated pupil."

"Right." Alex kept working, cleaning off the shaved area. "Why is the pupil dilated, Richard?"

"Uuh, something is compressing the nerve controlling the pupil?"

"And?"

"Well, the nerve controlling the pupil runs along the bony base of the skull. A clot pressing on the brain causes the brain in turn to press on the nerve and stop it from functioning."

"Good." He nodded to Paul. "What incision should we use? What are we aiming for?"

Paul thought for a minute. "Well, we don't really know where the clot is on that side. We should make a large scalp flap, then cut a sizable bony opening to expose as much of the brain as possible." He traced the shape of the incision on the monkey's head.

Alex nodded. "Exactly. We're going to do a trauma flap here. Richard, Paul's going to do the anesthesia. You help me with the surgery."

Richard nodded eagerly. "I've operated before. One time the surgical attending let me slice off a bunion."

"Great. Just don't cut yourself, and give me a hand when I ask."

"We better get going," said Paul.

"Right."

Alex gently put a small ring pillow under the monkey's head and turned it to the left, with the clipped right side uppermost. The monkey looked peacefully asleep.

"Now, Richard. Put the gloves on and prep the head."

"Huh?"

"Here, take the gloves, put them on in a sterile fashion, dip the gauze pads into this iodine solution, start in the center of the shaved area of the head and work outward in enlarging circles." Alex spoke quickly. "Didn't they show you this when you were a master surgeon taking off bunions?"

Richard nodded, put the gloves on and started swabbing.

Alex turned and went over to the scrub sink. Taking a facemask from a box over the faucet, he tied it on after carefully bending the metal stiffener so it fit over his nose. He turned on the water with his knee, then started scrubbing his hands.

Paul looked more worried. "Come on, Alex. We've got to move."

Alex kept washing his hands. "Don't worry," he said irritably. "We're moving." He looked at Richards, still applying the iodine. "That's it. Don't see any bugs. Go scrub."

Richard quickly took off his gloves and went over to the sink, waiting respectfully for Alex to finish.

"Don't forget the mask" Alex nodded towards the shelf.

"Thanks." Richard eagerly grabbed a mask, tying it on loosely. Time was too short for Alex to correct him.

Alex rinsed his hands, turning the water off with his knee, and walked over to a flat table holding towels, gloves and gowns. He dried off his hands, put on a surgical gown and then his surgical gloves. After Richard did the same, they took paper drapes, placing them around the incision line, isolating the operative site. When they had finished, only a patch of the monkey's scalp was visible, surrounded by a sea of blue.

"Aim the light, will you Paul?"

Paul came around and moved the small overhead surgical light so it focused on the surgical field. He then resumed his position behind the drapes.

Alex expertly incised the scalp, flipped it back, and secured it.

"So that's the skull, huh?"

Alex grunted.

"How are you going to get the bone off?"

"With this." Alex took an air-powered drill, and quickly drilled several circumferential holes in the skull.

"How are you going to get in there? Or do you just do the operation through those little holes?"

"We join the holes with this." Alex showed Richard a flexible wire saw.

"Oh, just like camping trips."

"Yeah. We have a power saw for the human operating room, but this for the animals. Wasn't so long ago this used to be the way to open a human head as well."

He slid one end of the wire saw into a hole in the skull, and with a special tool guided it out of another hole. Holding the two ends in his hands, he sawed back and forth, finally cutting through the skull, popping up the sawblade. Continuing in this manner, he joined all the holes with saw cuts.

"OK, now we can remove the bone flap." He took a small metal implement and levered the disc of bone out, exposing the covering over the brain. "See how the dura is bulging?"

"Dura?"

"The brain's covering. As you can see, once you take the skull off, there's a gray membrane, looks almost plastic, covering the brain."

"Where's the clot?"

"Well, if we're right, it's under the dura."

"If we're wrong, this'll be the last operation you'll see, Richard, so concentrate" Paul chimed in somberly from behind the drapes.

"Only one way to find out." Alex took a small scalpel and sliced the dura in a swift motion. Dark currant jelly came protruding out through the rent like toothpaste. "We're right, Paul. You can breathe now."

"Yahoo" Paul said weakly, sitting and looking at the ceiling.

"We cut the dura more, like this, and then can remove the clot with gentle suction," Alex said, swiftly opening the membrane more widely, allowing more coagulum to protrude out.

"Wow, Alex. I've never seen anything like this."

"Yeah, it's a little different than bunion work."

After removing the entire clot Alex started inspecting inside the skull. "Now we're trying to locate a source of the bleeding." He looked around the cavity. "Here's the frontal lobe" pointing with an instrument, "and there's the temporal lobe. With this retractor we can lift up the frontal lobe as it sits on the skull floor and look into the depths underneath the brain."

Richard was silent as he gazed at the first living brain he had ever seen.

As Alex spoke he gently took a retractor shaped like a tongue blade, inserted it between the bottom of the brain and the bony floor of the skull, and lifted the brain up, beaming his headlight down into the deep crevices underneath the brain.

He stopped. "That's funny."

"What?" asked Richard eagerly.

Paul stirred. "What's going on?"

"There's a lot of scarring around the optic nerves and chiasm. It's quite matted down." He peered around as he lifted the brain further, then explained to Richard. "Normally the optic nerves and junction are easily freed up and separated from the brain just above. Here there's a lot of scar tissue."

"What does scar tissue here mean?"

"Inflammation."

"Infectious meningitis" said Paul.

"No, the scarring is very focal, very confined. Meningitis scars up diffusely."

"What caused it?" asked Richard.

Alex continued to peer. "I don't know. Something really inflamed this area. It looks like the basal forebrain above the optic nerves really took the hit."

"The where?" asked Richard.

Paul was eager to show his knowledge to the medical student. "The basal forebrain. One of the most important areas of the brain is here at the base of the skull–the area you're looking at. These areas have to do with memory, personality and the control of vital body functions."

Richard nodded, looking impressed underneath the surgical mask.

Alex continued to think. "Maybe this is why the retinas were bluish tinged."

"Huh?"

"The optic nerves are connected to the retina. These are the optic nerves, just below the basal forebrain." Alex pointed to the scarred area. "If they are changed in some way, it's logical that where they end in the back of the eyeball, the retina, is affected as well."

"I've never heard of that." Paul piped up from behind the drapes.

"Just speculation. Well professor, I guess we better close," said Alex. "Things are well decompressed, although I still don't know what the heck that scarring is."

Alex removed the brain retractor, letting the brain relax down to the skull floor. He patiently showed Richard how to stitch closed the membrane covering the brain. Then they took the silver dollar sized piece of skull, placed it back into the opening, drilled small holes around the edge and tied it back in place.

Alex's beeper went off just after he finished stitching the muscles under the scalp, and then the scalp itself. "I gotta go. Paul, finish up and tell the Boss what happened." Alex regretted that it was going to be Paul to break it to the Boss, but he knew he had to go to the OR to help Dr. Dobbs, one of the other attendings. "Richard, stay and help Paul take care of the monkey." Richard nodded. Alex knew he would tell him what Paul said to the Boss.

CHAPTER 8

Alex walked quickly through the old building to the hospital, going to the OR locker room where he changed clothes. He picked up the telephone and called into the operating room where Dobbs' patient was being prepared. Joan the circulating nurse answered.

"OR Three."

"Alex here. I'll be right in."

"The patient is ready on the table."

After hanging up the phone he turned quickly, and found the Boss glowering at him. He moves quietly when he wants to, Alex thought rapidly in a corner of his brain while looking up at the Boss's grim visage.

"What the hell happened in the lab?"

"Did Paul tell you about it?"

"I'm asking the questions," he thundered. "What the hell happened?" His eyes opened wildly. He was as close as Alex had ever been to him, and with a detached part of his brain Alex wondered if his dark pupils were slightly bluish in the light.

"The monkey lost consciousness and blew a pupil," said Alex, uncertain as to where this was coming from. "It was dying. We had a choice to let it die or explore. I did the best I could."

The Boss stared at Alex. Past the Boss's shoulder Alex could see another resident, Cooper, a plastic surgery trainee, looking at the scene, relieved that he wasn't the target. His head was just over the Boss's shoulder, and his small head dangled in the distance, just next to the big head that was leaning ominously towards him.

"Don't touch my experiments. Understand? You're not out of here yet."

The Boss stalked away, shoes grinding on the floor. Alex kept looking straight ahead for a moment, then at the other resident who was still staring at him. The resident nodded. "I'm glad I'm not in neurosurgery."

Alex thought yeah, you'll just fix noses the rest of your life.

Jangled by the blast, he moved slowly, wondering where the Boss's broadside came from. He reviewed in his mind what they had done at the lab. It was all reasonable judgment. As he passed the OR desk without his usual cheery hello, the nurse glanced up to see him trudge somberly by, looking straight ahead. Her eyes followed him down the hall, to the neurosurgery operating room, where he turned and entered.

Dr. Dobbs, already in the room, pivoted, his eyes questioning over his mask. "Dr. Todd got a phone call when I was up in the office. He steamed out of there like a locomotive."

Alex looked at him, silent. He knew Dobbs was waiting for some information. Shaking his head, he went over to the viewbox and placed the MRI scans up, then walked over to the operating table. Dobbs waited for a comment, but Alex kept his eyes on the incision line that was diagrammed on the patient's back.

Dobbs reached for the scalpel. "Get scrubbed and give me hand." Alex nodded.

After the surgery, Alex left the OR and paged Paul. "What did you tell the Boss?"

"What happened."

"What do you mean? You told the Boss what happened or are you asking me what happened?"

"I told him what you did in the lab."

"What I did? The monkey was your responsibility. I was trying to help you."

"Alex, it was your decision to go in," Paul said reproachfully.

"We had to do something," Alex snapped. "Have you forgotten that? We did the right thing."

"Well it's dead now."

"What?"

"The Boss came down and looked at it. It was in the cage, still breathing. He told me to leave, came out a couple of minutes later and said that it had died and he would get rid of it."

"Thanks Paul. Thanks a lot."

Alex hung up. While Paul hadn't said it explicitly, Alex knew he had blamed him for the entire episode. Opening his locker, he tossed in his sneakers, making a clang in the emptiness. Some of the other residents had pictures of families, wives and children. Alex thought of the picture in the locker next to his, a tiny child sitting in the bathtub looking up at the camera with impossibly large cheeks and a puzzled expression.

His beeper went off. Alex grabbed the wall phone and dialed the number. Richard Walter answered.

"What happened at the lab?"

Richard excitedly told him. "Paul called the Boss and said that the monkey was a little funny. He said he called you for help, and you came down and made him operate. He said he didn't want to open it up, that you forced him."

Alex hissed "What a jerk", then remembered he was talking to a medical student. "Richard, forget that."

"Sure Alex, that's nothing. When I was on general surgery the residents hated each other's guts, they just kept sniping at each other."

"Right, right. What about the lab?"

"Oh yeah. The odd thing was that Paul didn't get the response he was looking for. Things seemed calm until Paul mentioned that you had seen some scarred brain in the, what was that area?"

"Basal forebrain."

"Yeah. Paul was just gushing with details, but when he mentioned that, there seemed to be a big reaction on the other end."

"Great." Alex wondered what the hell it meant. "What about when the Boss got there?"

"Well, the monkey was actually starting to come out of anesthesia and move around. The Boss told us to leave and we did. He came out in a little while and said that it had died. Then he locked the door."

Alex gripped the phone tightly. "Okay Richard. Thanks. See you in the morning."

"Okay."

Alex hung up. He turned to his locker and continued to change, deep in thought, running through the operation in his mind as he slowly took off his blue scrubs. He mentally replayed the removal of the blood clot from the monkey, and the inspection of the brain cavity, thinking of the scarred area, trying to match it to other patterns of pathology. There was no fit. What the hell kind of experiments was the Boss doing? What did the scarring mean? Then he thought of the Boss's words about perfecting the brain, and he felt alone.

CHAPTER 9

"So, Alex, what really happened?"

Alex closed his locker with a screech. Jim Dobbs had come in and was starting to change as he casually asked the question.

Alex glanced around. The room was empty. He walked into the bathroom, bending down. No feet in the stalls. He walked back.

"The Boss's experimental monkey. It went sour on Paul, and we had to open it up. Took out a subdural hematoma." Alex stared at Dobbs. "What are the Boss's experiments about? What is he doing?"

"Don't know. He doesn't talk about it. Even at meetings, with the other big boys, he doesn't say much." Dobbs looked in his locker, reached for his shirt, and put it on carefully. He shook his head.

"You know as well as I do, Alex, you have to be careful here."

"What was I supposed to do? I'm a surgeon. I made the best judgment I could. We didn't have a CT scan. As it turns out, I did the right thing with that damn monkey."

"What happened to it?"

"Dead."

Dobbs snorted.

"It was the right thing to do. It only died after the Boss went in to see it. It was coming out of the anesthesia. At least that's what Paul said."

"Look Alex, all I'm saying is that you have to be very careful around here. You know that." He came up to Paul, his large head heavy with an expression of awkward severity, lower lip protruding, and glanced around. "It's no secret that Dr. Todd and I aren't soulmates. I'm a hold-over from Dr. Henry's era. You know that. He picked you. I want to see you finish." He looked around again, the room suddenly very quiet. "Todd's different. He's like ice."

"Can't you do anything?"

"I'm just putting in my time, waiting for retirement."

"The Boss, he's . . ." Alex hesitated. "He's not good for this place."

"Alex, you're too idealistic. I'm old. That's what getting old means. You lose that idealism."

"And that's good?"

Dobbs smiled. "You know why old people envy the young? It's not only physical. They no longer have the ideals of youth, some would call the illusions of youth."

"They're no illusions."

Dobbs nodded, his head heavy. "And they miss those illusions, be-cause they suspect they might not be." He moved slowly, looking in his locker.

"Getting old isn't a stripping of ideals, of dreams. It doesn't have to be."

Dobbs smiled faintly. "You've got your whole life ahead of you. You've got a lot of time before the point where the biggest thing in life is hoping for a good crap. Be careful of him."

Alex nodded. "Do you remember yourself as a child?" He smiled self-consciously. "When I was young, I often wondered what I would be like when I was all grown up, how I would change. I sensed people lost something as they got older." He shook his head. "I never want to disappoint that little boy."

Dobbs sat down, and looked up at Alex, not understanding. "We all change. Todd's changed a great deal over the years, and yet he hasn't. You know when he operates? There's something strange about the man. He doesn't shake. Ever."

Alex waited.

"You ever wonder why he doesn't shake?" He looked closely at Alex. "He has no ghosts."

"What?"

"Surgeons have it easy at first. No memories, no recollection of failures, no ghosts. As they get more experienced, the procedures become easier technically, yet they accumulate ghosts that haunt them. When something goes wrong during surgery, a bleeder cuts loose, the brain swells, early on you have no memory of the problems that follow, the tragedies, the maimed patients, the families shrieking, the lawsuits. You deal with the problem, unencumbered by fear. As you do more operations, get more experience, when something goes wrong the ghosts gather round, haunting you, even as you're operating, struggling with the problem. As a surgeon gets older, it's a race between his technical growth and strength and how many ghosts he accumulates."

Alex's eyes narrowed. He said nothing, then looked around quickly. Still quiet.

"The Boss has no ghosts. Or as least, they don't bother him."

"He's a man of steel."

"I've operated with Dr. Clifford Sykes, the greatest neurosurgeon in the world. One time we were clipping an aneurysm, and at first the clip wouldn't fit. He just had to do a little dissection. But his hand started shaking, shaking. I can still see it in front of me, through the microscope. I didn't see any insurmountable technical problem. But you see, the ghosts did it. Everybody has ghosts."

"Everybody except the Boss."

Dobbs nodded ponderously. "He's different. Look, Alex. You're older than the rest. That's why I'm talking to you this way. Be very careful. You're dealing with a different kind of person." He turned and put on his white coat, walking out in the stillness.

CHAPTER 10

Todd strode back to the office, oblivious to the stares of patients and the nods of security guards, stopping at his secretary's desk. "Audrey, get me Alex Adam's chart."

She jumped up and rummaged through a file cabinet as Todd went into his office. Grabbing a file, she brought it in, carefully laying it on his desk.

"Close the door, please."

She walked out quickly and closed the door quietly, both hands gently easing it shut.

Todd opened the chart, and grabbed a small dictation machine from his desk drawer. He reached down under his desk and took out a large manila envelope, sliding out a series of MRI scans. They screeched softly as he put them up under the lightbox clamps, his large hand moving to turn on the light.

He stared at the film, the lines in his face illuminated by the pale fluorescence, then started dictating.

"This is absolutely confidential, Audrey. Office note on Alex Adams. I've reviewed Alex Adams' recent MRI scan, done one month ago for headaches. The tumor is present in the deep brain nuclei. There is very little swelling associated with the lesion, and thus little functional effect at this point. However, there may be unpredictable neuropsychological consequences in the future, and we need to watch for them. We will obtain another study in several months."

He stopped his machine. Pausing for a moment, he dialed the phone. "Dr. John Allen, please."

He waited, then was connected.

"John, Victor Todd."

"Everything's well. How are you?"

"Good, good. I wanted to touch base with you and get your advice, Chief to Chief. It's about a resident, very good clinically, with an unfortunate problem. I've been following him medically for a while. He has a tumor in the thalamus. Untreatable, of course."

Todd listened. "Yes, that's my problem exactly. He's functioning well at this point, although he has some mood swings."

He looked at the films as Allen spoke, then replied. "One of Henry's boys. Older, been around a bit. A philosophy major in college. Not like my newer guys. I think Henry took a chance on him."

He listened and nodded. "He does operate very well." A pause.

"I agree. Whatever the lesion is, no need to stir anything up. It's unresectable, incurable. If it functionally declares itself, causes serious problems, that's the time to review and address the situation." His voice became soft, as if his vocal cords were suddenly wrapped with velvet, and he swallowed hard. "Although that would be most painful for me."

The Boss nodded vigorously, the telephone cord writhing.

"I have seen too many people crippled, not physically, but mentally by the burden of knowledge. I will not play God, but until there is more, I will not encumber him."

"Of course, any hint as to functional impairment, such as double vision, or blue predominant color distortion, would be definitive. We watch him carefully." He shrugged. "On the other hand, the tumor may stay utterly quiescent for years."

He listened. "Thanks very much, John. Yes, this is the most difficult part of the job."

He sighed, and then hung up. Inspecting the MRI, he then took it down, sliding it back in the envelope and replaced it under his desk. Picking up the dictation machine, he continued, "I reviewed the situation with Dr. John Allen, Chief of Neurosurgery of Metropolitan Hospital, and he is in agreement with a conservative approach at this time, as we have little choice." He put his hands down and turned to the books surrounding him, the shelves extending up to the ceiling, dwarfing even his bulk. His shoulders sagged slightly, and his mouth softened as he took out the MRI scan again and held it up to the waning light of the window. Putting it down after a time, he closed his eyes, his head bowed.

CHAPTER 11

It was evening. Alex walked out of the side door of the hospital, towards the parking garage. The long day was over, at least until he got called back for an emergency. His head was lowered and he missed his usual nod to the security guard, engrossed with the peculiar scarring of the monkey's brain. Never seen anything like that. And the Boss's tantrum. His stomach flipped as he thought of the great head leaning towards him, and he didn't like the feeling. There was something else, too. Then he stopped and remembered. It was the night of the Dean's dinner party.

All the chief residents were invited, as well as the Department Chairmen. He had to go, but he needed a sport coat. Turning, he sprinted back into the hospital, past the guard and over to the elevator, riding it up, then running over to the call room. He unlocked the door and walked in.

Curt was flossing his teeth, an anatomy book propped up at the sink.

"What are you doing here?"

"The Dean's dinner party for the chief residents. I need a sport coat."

"Oh, the big boys are getting together. You love that stuff. Sucking up and all."

"Yeah. I'll have a great time." Alex watched closely as Curt kept flossing. "Take care of your teeth. A family of four in China could live for a year on what you're getting out of there."

"Yeah, thanks."

Alex shook his head, going over to the rack where he kept one of his few sport jackets. Pushing the wrinkled white coats aside, he found it. Shapeless brown Harris tweed. Not quite seasonal, but it'll do.

Curt put the floss down. "You look a little jangled."

"Yeah, I love going to those things. Phoniness reeks from all. They remind me of those old western movies, the towns with the false fronts. Everybody has their false front, desperately staying behind it, sweating, trying to keep it propped up, so busy they don't notice everyone else doing the same thing."

Curt laughed. "I can see you're looking forward to it. Have a good time."

Alex grunted. "Call me with any problems." He walked out the door. For once he wished he were staying in that call room, dealing with familiar situations instead of a snake pit of people. He hurried down to the lobby, then ran out the door. Glancing at his watch, he noticed the skin on his arm. A little dry and wrinkled, he thought. Too much sun. Gotta watch for melanoma. Quickly walking to the parking garage, he wondered what he would look like when he was old–hopefully not like one of those old pruned ladies who had always been in the sun. He especially disliked the wrinkles around their mouths, the fine lines that radiated from their lips. After getting into his car, he momentarily wondered where he was going, then remembered the Dean's party. Stop getting distracted, he told himself. Keep on top of things.

Alex drove out of the garage into the narrow inner city streets lined with old brown row homes, glancing up at the sky. It felt good to get outside. How you get used to things. Before he started residency, when he was an intern at a new suburban hospital, he hated cities, felt hemmed in. Now he was happy for just a small blue patch of sky.

Turning through the maze of streets, he got onto the expressway and out to the suburbs. Getting off at the exit for the Dean's exclusive neighborhood, he started down the residential streets, alternately looking for the Dean's residence and glancing down at the directions on the torn seat next to him. The street appeared and he turned. Cars were parked outside the stately stone houses, the road lined with maple trees.

The Dean's house was larger than the others, its front door bordered by white columns and a white sun porch off to one side. He drove by the house, feeling more nervous, watching a fashionable couple getting out of a gleaming red BMW and walking up to the door. Hell, he thought, that's Carver, the medicine chief resident. He looked at the well-tailored suit the resident was wearing and shook his head. How'd he learn to dress so well? How'd he afford that car? Who's the babe?

Driving down the lane, he finally found a parking spot at the end of a line of shiny cars. Getting out, he glanced at his blue Chevy Nova. The driver's side rear end was mottled from an inept body job Alex had done after finding it crumpled one night. He recalled troweling on the body putty, ignoring the recommendation on the can to use at most a half-inch layer. Sighting down the line of shiny cars, their contours intact, he looked at the Nova again. Smallpox, that's what it looked like. He started down the sidewalk to the Dean's house.

As he got closer, he heard classical music, an unknown melody. Walking up the slate pavement, he looked at the elegant, lighted windows and the people within, then knocked at the elaborate door. Metal. He shuddered. Metal doors reminded him of caskets. The door opened, and the Dean of the School of Medicine stood there, a tall man dressed in lederhosen. Alex, surprised at the attire, drew back slightly.

"Hello Dr. Tripp." Alex stammered. He tried not to look at the Dean's garb, green suspenders with some sort of angular repetitive design on them and short pants trimmed with leather along the sides. The Dean looked down at him with small dark eyes. "I'm Alex Adams, the chief neurosurgical resident. Thanks very much for inviting me."

The round-faced, balding Dean looked steadily at Alex for a moment with a glint in the eye, as if he suspected Alex's thoughts on his lederhosen.

"Glad to meet you. I've seen you around."

They stood quietly for a moment, both realizing that Alex didn't want to be there, then the Dean looked startled and said, "Come in, come in. Have you met my wife, Doris?" He opened the door further.

Back slightly and to his right stood a woman who, Alex realized, was the embodiment of chronic sun overdose. She must have originally been fair skinned, but now was colored in a permanent grayish shade. Her hair was gold, in round rigid arcs around her face, hard as a helmet. She smiled at Alex, and when she talked he shivered to himself as the teeming wrinkles around her mouth came and went. "Drinks are over there" she beckoned, "and your Boss is on the patio. Have a good time." She waved her hand vaguely and went looking for somebody more important, as did the Dean.

Alex walked through the small vestibule, the inner door of which was bordered by columns. He entered the spacious foyer, twin stairways cascading down to the polished floor, turned to his right and went into the living room. It was filled with people, most of whom he recognized. Various Chairmen were standing and talking, including those of Pathology, Medicine, Obstetrics-Gynecology, and their respective chief residents.

He realized again how much he hated doing this stuff. Looking around, he went over to the hors d'oeuvres. Might as well start here.

"Hi, Alex."

Alex turned and saw Hector Harris, the Chief Pathology resident, who had come up to him.

"Hi, Hector. How ya doing?"

"OK. This is a pain in the ass, though." He nodded at the surroundings and people. "Gives me the creeps."

"Yeah, I know what you mean." Alex savored the irony. Hector himself gave many people the creeps. Wide eyed and earnest, he spoke with his head thrust forward and down slightly, so his bulging, damp eyes were closest, projecting upward. His speech, just like his eyes, was moist, his humid enunciation washing over the listener. Once he told somebody that he liked to do autopsies more than anything else in the world, which became folklore among the residents. Alex had made an offhand remark to him once about a cadaver in an anatomy book, about how beautiful the face was, and this had endeared him to Hector.

"I guess everybody's here" Alex looked around, making conversation.

"Well, the Chief Residents could hardly miss it. We're all looking for jobs, now, and it doesn't pay to honk off your boss at this stage of the game."

"Yep, I guess we all have to suffer for a while longer. Where're you looking, Hector?"

"I'd like to stay at the university, but I don't know if there's a slot for another attending. I've been looking around in the area. Like to stay in academics, but I don't know whether I'll be able to. How about you?"

"Well, assuming I finish . . ."

Hector snickered. "Don't BS me, Alex. You're the best. Everybody knows that. Besides, nobody gets fired their last year of residency."

"You know how it is. Dr. Todd is a great neurosurgeon, but he has no soul. He just as soon run over his mother if he's having a bad day."

"Yeah, that's what I hear. If anybody is safe, though, you are. Anyway, what are you going to do when you finish?"

"Well, I'd like to continue in academics, at a university center. Do some research, but take care of people as well."

Hector laughed. "Still idealistic. You mean six years of residency didn't bleach that out of you?"

"Nope. You remember your first autopsy?"

"Of course."

"I remember mine. I was a medical student, and stumbled into the morgue looking for my professor. Up on the slab was Dr. Rogers, the former Chief of Internal Medicine. He had just died of a massive MI."

"I remember."

"They had him open from stem to stern, as you boys do, splayed on the black table. He had his chest and abdomen cored out, only a brown shell of muscle and bone left. Looked like one of those old wooden salad bowls, dark, greasy and empty. I thought to myself, might as well try to do something with my life, before I ended up there. That's all I ever wanted to do, help people. That's what we're here for."

Hector nodded. "You're right. I hope everybody here feels that way, but I have my doubts. So where're you looking?"

"Here, if I'm lucky. I'm also going to interview at Metropolitan Hospital."

"Well, both good places."

The conversation died out and they both looked around the room. Hector sighed. He tilted his head further forward.

"I guess I'll start mingling. See you around."

Alex nodded. He looked down at the Oriental rug, then wandered over to the mantle, where the Dean's family pictures stood. There was one portrait of the Dean and his wife, apparently on a trip to Europe, in front of a castle.

"That was a long time ago."

Alex turned to see Mrs. Tripp next to him. In the picture she was pretty, but now her weathered, overly tanned face had turned haggish, elongating to a prominent jaw. This, her almost scaly skin, and the spaces between her jutting teeth, made her resemble an emaciated Tyrannosaurus Rex. She smiled.

"Hello, Mrs. Tripp. I'm Alex Adams, Chief Neurosurgical Resident," he reminded her, knowing she didn't remember seeing him at the door. The surrounding conversation was loud and he had to bend towards her. She leaned as well, her hard golden hair immobile, the curled tips rigid. Alex had a fleeting thought that if the sharp end of the curls touched him he'd get cut.

"Oh, Alex. I'm glad to meet you. Dr. Todd speaks very highly of you."

"Thanks. Nice party you have here. Nice for the Chief Residents" he babbled.

"Well, we have it every year. All of you work so hard."

"That's for sure." He laughed. Might as well probe a little. "Do you get together with Dr. Todd much?"

"Once in a while. He's such a brilliant man. He doesn't have a lot of free time. You're very fortunate to be working with him."

Alex nodded vigorously. "Absolutely."

"He's the most well known doctor in the medical school, I think. And" she said coyly, "he speaks very highly of you. It looks like you might have a future here at the university."

Alex smiled. "Well, I take one day at a time."

"That's wise." She smiled like she was about to ingest him. "Nice to meet you. Enjoy." She wafted away, Alex turning to look at the picture again, thinking. He wondered what the Boss was saying about him after the experience with the monkey.

"Hello, old boy."

Alex turned around. It was George Carver, the Chief Medical Resident, with Heather Mackenzie, the nurse on the neurosurgical floor. Carver had long black hair elegantly swept back, and was dressed impeccably in a three piece tailored suit, with a gold pin holding his collar together under his tie. His white teeth gleamed, contrasting with his tan.

"Hi, George. Hi Heather."

She smiled. "Hello."

Carver nodded to Heather. "Now we know we're among the cognoscenti. The brain surgeon's here." He smiled. "The guy with the Chevy Nova."

Alex smiled back. "It gets me from here to there."

"What happened to the rear end?"

"A little body work."

"Did you do it?"

Alex nodded.

"Hope you operate better than that."

"You know what they say–the fancier the car, the smaller the penis."

Carver coughed. Heather laughed. He recovered quickly. "Hear you had a bit of trouble today, though."

Alex frowned. "Where'd you get that?"

Carver smirked.

Alex nodded. "Cooper, the plastic surgery guy, must've told you."

"Todd really flipped out, huh?"

Alex stared at him. "The usual" he shrugged. "We're all big boys in neurosurgery."

Carver laughed. "Sounds like one of those days."

The conversation halted for a moment, then Alex broke the silence as he gazed over the crowd. "Where'll you be going next year?"

Carver glanced at Heather. He couldn't resist. "Well, this is confidential, but I'm staying here at the University as an attending."

Alex looked at him. Years of vigorous ass kissing paid off, he thought. "Terrific, George."

"How about you?"

"Don't know yet. I'm interviewing at a couple of places. I might even stay here."

Carver giggled. "Well, keep looking around. Dr. Todd sounded very hot."

Alex stared at him. "Maybe we'll both be here next year" he said, ignoring Carver's last remark. "See you guys later." He nodded at Heather, who smiled back.

Turning, he walked away, needing to leave the toady, feeling more jangled than ever in this abnormal atmosphere. The food table was near and he approached it, inspecting the various plates. Most were unrecognizable to him.

Motion caught his eye, and he looked up. Coming towards him was Rebecca Martin, chief resident in Obstetrics-Gynecology. She was a large, broad beamed woman, with a kind and expressive face. Navigating through the throng, she parted people like a battleship cleaving the sea with its prow as her small husband followed behind her like a tender, bobbing in her wake. As she got closer he could see the freckles scattered around her cheeks and eyes.

"Hi, Becky."

"Hi Alex. Have you met my husband Albert?"

"No. Glad to meet you." They shook hands.

"I saw you were suffering with Carver. Figured I'd come over and rescue you." She looked at him. "Rough day, huh?"

Alex shook his head. "What, is it all over the hospital?"

She smiled. "Us residents love to hear about this stuff. Even the brain surgeons are human."

"No big deal. The Boss got a little hot, that's all."

"It wasn't even about a patient, huh?"

"Nope. Don't ask me why. I had to open up an experimental monkey of the Boss's. Took out a clot, everything went OK. It must've been pretty far gone, though, because it died afterwards." He decided not to mention the scarring. "But I had Paul Fox helping me, and I'm not sure what the Boss was told, if you know what I mean." He looked at Rebecca's husband, but he looked like a stolid sort who wouldn't tell tales, staring back at him like a turtle, unblinking and secure in his shell.

Rebecca nodded. "Every residency program has one of those." She sighed. "Well, hope it works out all right. I know how much you want to stay here."

"Stay here! Hell, I just want to finish."

She laughed. "Just like the rest of us." She turned to her husband. "Alex and I started our residency at the same time. Ob-gyn is shorter, but those maternity leaves strung it out for me."

"It's all his fault." Alex chuckled, nodding at her husband.

She turned to her mate, and then looked at Alex again. "I'll always remember how proud Alex was to be in the neurosurgery program. We were at the first day orientation program, and you looked so happy. I asked you what program you were in, and if you said 'neurosurgery' with any more pride your chest would've blown apart." She laughed deeply. "And here we are. Almost done."

Alex nodded. "Well, it's not over yet."

"Oh, Alex. You don't have anything to worry about."

"Hopefully not."

"Well, we've got to mingle. Good to see you." She turned and started making her way again through the crowd, her husband obediently following her.

"Alex."

It was the Boss's voice. Alex turned.

"Hello, Dr. Todd."

Smiling, Dr. Todd looked down at Alex, glinting glasses hiding his eyes. "Good party, eh?"

Alex nodded energetically. "Very nice."

"Alex, can you do me a favor?"

"Sure."

"My car is in the shop. I got a ride over here, but I need way home."

"Glad to do it, Dr. Todd."

"Just let me know when you're ready to go."

"No problem."

Dr. Todd wheeled about.

Alex's attention was drawn to the Dean, who had walked to the center of the room and was looking around expectantly. The room fell silent as each knot of people realized he wanted to speak. Finally the Dean cleared his throat.

"Thank you all for coming. This is always an auspicious occasion, as we informally recognize another cadre of doctors who will be entering practice, assuming the ultimate responsibility of care for the sick."

He looked at Todd, who started walking towards him.

"Traditionally, a Chairman will make some remarks at this time. I've asked Dr. Victor Todd, Chairman of Neurosurgery, to say a few words as you prepare to complete your training."

Dr. Todd joined the Dean, turning to face the assemblage. Smiling warmly, he looked at the faces around him. "All of you are to be congratulated on approaching the end of a long road. But it's also a beginning, the start of your life as independent physicians. In you will be vested awesome responsibility for the care of vulnerable and sick people, who will give you their absolute trust. Such a life is arduous and demanding, and it's good to periodically remind yourself why you have chosen this path.

"For me, perhaps I can best illustrate my motivation with a story. Back in medical school, I was walking along a busy city street when I saw an elderly couple coming towards me, with their son following them. I watched, fascinated as the trio approached, then passed me and receded. The aged couple walked slowly and closely together, the venerable man supporting the bent old woman with both arms. She was stooped, her head bowed, never looking up. Her husband, in his late seventies, helped her every step of the way in an eternal embrace. It was summer, but they were both impeccably dressed in gray wool suits. The son followed vacantly behind, retarded, severely so judging from his face, eyes roving without understanding, yet he too was impeccably dressed. His age was difficult to guess, perhaps thirty-five of our years, how many of his cannot be said.

"Look at that, I thought, how many days and nights they had cared for him, knowing he would never get better, that he was, for whatever reason, a shadow of what he could have been.

"Still, as their strength departs, they tend to him, dress him, get him up in the morning, wash him, not knowing what the morrow will bring, not knowing the future, only that it will be ending. Still they fastidiously care for him, lavishing their utterly precious and rapidly vanishing hours on him. What love, what patience, what faith."

The Boss's eyes glowed as he looked around the hushed room, and he suddenly smiled joyfully and spread his arms wide, hands open.

"When I saw that, I realized I didn't know anything. Nothing about faith, patience, or love. What a lesson. And I also realized I knew nothing about the neurophysiology, the neuroanatomy, of the son's pathology. As I mulled over this scene many times during medical school and residency, I thought, maybe all the parts are intact, and just a small connection, a key transmission is bad. Maybe he is just a synapse away from a normal life. How can we rest when we know this could be possible? Like a curtain lifting he would walk into the light, and we only need to find out how to raise that curtain. Imagine how his parents feel, seeing a shadow of what might have been, knowing it never will be fulfilled, the vessel there but the navigator gone. And imagine how it could be if we fathom those depths, and heal the son."

He looked around again, with all eyes rapt on his face. "And so when you go out there, always remember you are there to help, to comfort, to learn, and to heal."

There was silence for a moment, and then the room resounded with applause.

The Dean stepped forward. "Thanks, Dr. Todd, for those insights. I'm sure we will never forget your words." He paused, then lifted both hands. "Please, everybody, enjoy. This is your evening." He turned to the Boss and, as conversation welled up, shook his hand. "Very nice, Victor. Very inspiring, indeed."

"Thank you."

Alex, absorbed in the imagery of the Boss's words, stepped out onto the deck in the back of the house, gazing at the yard containing a built-in pool and large gazebo. He looked at the beautiful scene, recalling where he had grown up and how different this was from the tiny postage stamp patch and dusty back alley of his youth.

"Hi, Alex."

He turned around. It was Heather, alone.

"Hi again. How are you doing?"

"OK. I needed to get out too."

"Yeah, it gets a little stifling in there, doesn't it?"

She nodded. "How's things going?"

"Good, good. Having a nice time?"

"It's OK. I'm not really into this stuff."

Alex shrugged. "Neither am I. But I don't have to make the rounds with George."

"Well, you never asked me."

"I didn't think you wanted to ride in my car."

"Come on."

She paused. "Why aren't you married?"

"Now you're getting personal."

She stayed quiet.

He leaned out on the railing, looking at the trees, then farther out. "People change. The person you marry doesn't stay that person, maybe never was that person. People forget. Humans are imperfect. Love can change, can mutate." He looked at the ground. "There are no guarantees."

"You can start fresh."

"I'm forty years old."

"Oooh, you're ancient."

He shook his head. "At forty, you're different than thirty. No longer intoxicated by youth, not yet mesmerized by death." He took a breath. "All your life you're climbing mountains, seeing more in the distance, the bright blue sky above, knowing there's something incredible ahead. The endless climb, the promise of infinity, the exhilaration of limitless horizons. Then you turn forty, and it's like you finally reach the top. You see beautiful vistas, white clouds, and glorious mountaintops. But you look far into the distance, and catch a glimpse of the ocean, stretching still further away. And you know, however long your trip remaining, however scintillating the experiences, you're seeing the end, the beginning of another journey, into the unknown, far, far ahead."

"People need each other."

Alex snorted. "A great myth of our time. Need is not love. Need is need. Somebody who needs somebody doesn't love them. They just need them. Most of the time, if you are needy, you can't love or be loved. You aren't developed enough to love, and go through life perpetually confused."

"So little children can't love?"

"I didn't say that."

"There are many happy married couples, married for years."

"I see the ones who lose the spark, some sooner, some later. Think how it must be for the one in whom the spark dies last, when your partner doesn't care anymore, and you still remember. Think of how painful that would be until your spark dies as well, think of how hopeless you feel, no longer with a kindred soul."

"Is that what happened to you?"

He turned to face the house, squinting in the sun. "I'm just blabbing. Not good for a cutter." He looked at her. "Where's your date?"

"Still inside."

"Be careful of him."

"Oh, really?"

"Yeah. I see his future in front of him."

"Is that so?"

"He's going to finish, buy a fancy house, a mausoleum of materialism, and marry some tightass woman who'll want horses. She'll make him think she's doing him a favor for supporting her."

She giggled.

"I've studied the phenomenon, out in the suburbs."

"You have?"

"Yep. I have an estate in horse country."

She giggled again. "I thought it was a garage apartment."

"That's the handyman's cottage. But as I was saying, what inevitably happens is that the woman quickly loses interest in her husband, immerses herself more and more in horses, because they're easier and don't require messy human interaction."

"Such as?"

"You know what I mean. At any rate, she self importantly, with an air of busy distraction quickly makes clear by her behavior the implicit assumption that her activities are far more important than the breadwinner's, and it is a distinct honor for him to provide the wherewithal so she can continue in her all important life's work."

"And if he doesn't like it?"

"It's made clear to the hapless mate that providing such support to her is certainly enough reward, and he obviously shouldn't expect anything more out of the relationship."

She laughed again. "Who would stick around under those conditions?"

"The only saps who stick around are those who pretend to be interested in horses and their wife's riding, and who can be seen at shows, pitifully wandering about, waiting to catch her eye at a rare moment when she's not absorbed in her horse's accoutrements, desperately wanting to make some human contact, hoping for a flash of communication that recognizes them for something more than a useful prop, but of little importance otherwise."

He nearly ran out of air as he finished, took a breath, then a sweeping bow. "And we come full circle to our discussion earlier of need versus love."

"Very good for just a cutter. But you don't think the analysis was a little one sided?"

"Not at all." Alex glanced around. "You'd better not keep George waiting."

She nodded. "Yeah, I guess I should be going back. The fresh air is good, though." She took a deep breath. "Sure is nice here." She looked at him, her cheerfulness gone. "What was George talking about in there? What went on with you and Dr. Todd?"

"The usual. You know what can happen when you're a resident. Nothing out of the ordinary."

"Alex, come on. Remember when we used to talk, late at night, when you were checking on patients?"

He grimaced. "I got screwed. I did what I thought was right. I opened up one of the Boss's experimental monkeys after it developed a clot. Came out OK, but the monkey died later."

"That's it?"

"Yep. You know how it is."

She inspected him for a moment, her eyes widening, then sighed. "Alex, what's going on?"

"What do you mean?"

"I've been at University Hospital for ten years. Mostly night shift for all that time."

Alex nodded.

"You know how sometimes patients will call out at night, when they get disoriented, or are just plain sick. They can be pretty wifty."

"That's for sure."

She tossed her hair. "Well, it's only happened a couple times over those ten years, but I've just been thinking about it. Every so often a patient will call out, and babble about radiation."

"So what? Many of the brain tumor patients get radiation. You know that."

"That's just it. These aren't the brain tumor patients. They might be in for a subdural hematoma, or a stroke, or something else. Whatever it was, they didn't need radiation. But they'll babble a little about radiation, and I don't know what to make of it."

Alex felt uncomfortable. "That's not much, Heather. These old people, you know how it is. They get disoriented in the hospital, their day-night patterns are disrupted, they get all kinds of meds, and they just go bonkers."

She sighed. "I know all that. But they talk about a metal frame around their head. They shouldn't know about radiosurgery."

"They probably saw somebody in the hallway with the frame on. It does shake people up when they see it for the first time, with the frame around their head, stuck to their skull."

She looked unconvinced.

"What started this off?"

"Mr. Frederick, who you're going to operate on tomorrow with the subdural. He started jabbering last night about a frame on his head. He's never had radiation."

Alex shook his head, looking out at the lawn. He didn't know what to make of it.

"Alex, who is this lovely creature?"

Alex turned. It was Dr. Todd, in full bloom, smiling and bowing to Heather. She blushed, then looked up at him. "This is Heather Mackenzie"

He took her hand. "Charmed."

She smiled and giggled.

"Now I realize why you came out here, Alex."

Alex coughed. "Just for the fresh air."

"Of course. Heather, where do you work?"

"On Six Tower. Mostly at night."

"I'll have to make it a point to keep more patients there." He turned to Alex. "Ready to go?"

"Sure, Dr. Todd." Alex turned to Heather. "See you later."

She looked as though she wanted to say more, but held back and smiled. "Bye."

Dr. Todd and Alex made their way back through the crowd, up to the Dean at the front door.

"Thanks for coming, Victor."

"Goodbye, Bob. You remember my chief resident, Alex Adams. A credit to the hospital."

Alex straightened with pleasure at the unexpected praise.

The Dean looked at him with new respect. "Of course. Nice to see you" he said warmly.

Much better than the Dean's greeting, thought Alex as he bowed slightly in acknowledgment. He followed the Boss down the walk, basking in the rare compliment.

"Nice party, don't you think?"

"Very nice. Uh, my car needs a little work" Alex said apologetically. "It runs, though."

Dr. Todd gave a deep rumble. "No problem. When you're an

attending you will be able to afford better. Much better" he added as they came up on Alex's car.

Alex unlocked the passenger side door, reached in and quickly slid the crinkled paper with directions to the Dean's house under the seat, then straightened. The Boss settled in heavily, slamming the door.

Alex quickly walked around to the driver's side, getting in and starting up. Pausing to look for any passing cars, he then drove off.

"The Dean is a good man," said the Boss, breaking the silence. "He's moving the medical center in the right direction."

Alex nodded, flattered that the Boss was sharing insights.

"He's going to expand. We'll be able to hire new faculty." He looked at Alex quickly. "It's possible we may have an opening for you."

"Thanks very much." Alex was elated. What he had worked for all these years was apparently very close.

"Now I know you want to check out a couple of other places. But keep that option in mind." The Boss looked at Alex and even in his exaltation Alex could hear the seriousness in the Boss's voice. "Confidentially, of course."

Alex nodded.

"How are the other resident's doing? How's big eyes?"

"Big eyes?"

"The new one."

"Oh, Curt. Doing well. Starting to get the hang of things."

"Good. Keep me informed about them. All of them."

"Absolutely."

They were at the Boss's house already, the same neighborhood as the Dean.

Alex stopped and the Boss got out without further comment. He strolled up his walk with firm confident steps, the soles of his shoes causing a crackling sound as they smacked and ground small stones into the slate.

Alex drove home, humming as he steered.

CHAPTER 12

Alex looked around as he and Curt entered the square operating room. As always, it was scrupulously clean, lined by green tile walls with built in metal cabinets. He nodded to the scrub nurse, already gowned and preparing the instruments on the sterile draped table, then glanced over the anesthesia machine to see who would be there, as the Boss had strong likes and dislikes when it came to putting his patients to sleep. An inept anesthesia resident made for a long day. Alex was relieved to see Hancock, a capable resident who the Boss seemed to get along with, or at least didn't bother, getting the machine ready. Alex grunted to him, and turned to the light boxes along one wall of the room.

"Where's the MRI scan?" said Donna, the circulating nurse as she bustled into the room.

"Boss just wanted a CT scan" Alex replied, bending to pick up the films leaning against the wall.

"CT scan? Why not an MRI? I thought they gave much better detail." Hancock looked over from his machine.

Alex sighed. "Everybody's an expert. The Boss snapped at Curt when he found out an MRI had been ordered. Said he just wanted at CT. Truth to tell, I have no idea why that was. Curt was right to order an MRI. Gives much better anatomic detail." He nodded to Curt as he said this. "But as a resident, I have a limited amount of input."

Hancock chuckled, "Just ask the Boss why, Alex. Just tell him I was wondering."

"Yeah, sure."

Curt put the CT films up on the lightbox as they continued to chat.

"No" said Alex, "it goes this way." He corrected the younger resident's backward placement of the pictures, then shoved the films up into the holder on the lightboxes so they stayed. "Here's the lesion we'll be operating on." His slim, strong fingers pointed out the blood clot that had developed between the inside of the skull and the brain. "We'll be doing a frontal craniotomy, frontal for the region of the skull where we'll be working, and craniotomy meaning we will remove bone to get at the clot, then put the bone back."

"Craniectomy is when the bone stays out, right?" Curt said eagerly.

"Correct." He turned to Curt, his face illuminated by the artificial light of the x-ray boxes, accentuating the shadows under his eyes. "You were right to order the MRI scan. There's a lot of anatomy that shows up better on the MRI, such as the optic nerves, chiasm, and vascular tree."

Hancock glanced at the CT and asked Alex, "What's the problem the big boy's going to fix?"

"Subdural hematoma. But you mean . . . what I'm going to fix."

Hancock chuckled. "If only they knew how much we residents do."

Alex continued in a talkative mood. "This is a patient the Boss had treated before, although I don't know the details. When I told him he was back in the hospital, he seemed very interested."

Hancock snickered, "That's odd. Usually the big boy cuts them and forgets them."

Alex said thoughtfully, "You're right." He kept looking at the films, wondering what was on the Boss's mind, but saw just hematoma. Tracing the dent in the brain with his finger, he pointed. "Here's the clot, Curt. It's large enough to compress the brain, and the patient's condition reflects that."

"That clot is causing his weakness in the opposite arm and leg?" Curt was glad to show he had some clue to what was going on.

"Exactly."

They all turned as the nurse rolled in the patient on a litter. Mr. Frederick was unresponsive but breathing. Asleep, Curt thought, then reminded himself of the large clot silently squeezing the life out of his brain. Interesting, he mused, how the brain sends out very few danger signals, but instead mimics sleep when sick. It takes the trained mind to figure out what might be happening and check it out. He hoped he would be able to do this some day. Alex's jab interrupted his reverie.

"C'mon. Help us move him."

They surrounded the patient and lifted him from the litter to the operating table.

Alex gently turned the patient's head and placed it on a round pad. "The idea is to put the area of the head with the clot uppermost. Helps when you do the surgery-makes the mass more accessible and easier to remove."

Hancock attended to the patient, checking IV lines and hooking up the anesthesia machine.

Alex put his arms down and placed all his fingertips on the patient's head. Still for a moment, his head bowed, he studied the cranium like a fortuneteller gazing into a crystal ball. Grabbing a pen, he drew the shape of the clot on the patient's scalp, ruffling the thin hair.

Just like drawing on a pumpkin, Curt thought.

"Here's where the clot is. We need to expose this area" Alex drew on the patient's scalp "and we need to be prepared for bleeding from the superior saggital sinus." His hand moved to indicate the large blood vessel under the skull, near the clot.

Curt nodded.

Alex handed him hair clippers. "Clip his hair on this side, then use thick tape to remove all the little pieces of hair on the scalp." He tapped on the still cranium for emphasis. "It must be completely clean. No bits of hair." The tapping turned to thumping. "Absolutely clean." One more thump. "I'll get scrubbed. You come out when you're finished."

Curt nodded again. He started to clip the patient's hair, and Alex went outside the OR to the sink. Peering in through the small window, he watched Curt vigilantly and then starting scrubbing his hands. After a time he pushed the door to the OR open with his foot. "Good job. That's enough. Come on and scrub."

He washed his hands and arms carefully for five minutes by the clock over the sink, making sure Curt did it properly as well. Keeping his arms raised, he backed into the OR and dried his hands with the sterile towel proffered by Carol, the scrub nurse. Curt followed, imitating him like a duckling with its mother. Alex put his arms out straight and Carol pushed the gown on him, which was then tied in back by the circulating nurse. He thrust his hands into the sterile gloves held by Carol, then grunted when she only put on one pair. "I'm a two pair man. Where's the other set?"

She giggled. "Chief of Surgery says we only need one. It's cheaper."

"Just six months ago they were telling us to wear two pair to minimize the risk of AIDS. Now managed care tells us it's too expensive. Just give me the gloves and put it on my tab." Alex made eyes at her.

She giggled again. "The Boss won't like it."

"He'll like it less when I get AIDS and he has to take night call."

They all laughed at the image of the Boss coming in at night to take care of the denizens of the streets that the residents frequently tended to.

Curt was gowned as well. When he tried to put his hand in a glove, he got mixed up and the empty latex fingers waved like a turkey's comb at the end of his arm. Carol, getting another pair, clucked and shook her head in disgust.

"You'll get the hang of it" Alex said. He started draping the patient's head, carefully demarcating the sterile zone. "Curt, this is the draping technique. Everything is hard and complicated in neurosurgery. Even positioning the patient is different for each pathology. Sometimes they're on their back, or side, or stomach. Location of the lesion and the surgical approach dictate the patient's position, and you always have to make sure all pressure points are padded and the patient is secure on the OR table. If the patient's body happens to move, it could move the head, and with you working deep in the brain, any movement would be" he paused, "catastrophic." He spoke the last word slowly, emphasizing each syllable deliberately.

Curt, watching solemnly, nodded.

After finishing the draping, Alex diagrammed out the incision on the scalp again with a sterile marker, then gave the knife to Curt.

"Here, you start. Press firmly, right down to the bone, then follow the dotted line to open."

Hancock laughed behind a sterile barrier, securely surrounded by his machines, having made a nest to while away the hours. He settled down in his chair with a contented sigh. "Try not to bother me, please."

Curt chuckled, complemented by the good-fellowship, and looked up.

Alex barked. "Watch it, Curt. Pay attention. Stick to the line. It's all fun and games until somebody slices wrong." He glared at Curt, then at Hancock over the anesthesia curtain.

Curt shuffled his feet, then with exaggerated care slowly cut the scalp. Carving awkwardly with the scalpel, he swung wide of the line.

"Remember what I said about being exact in neurosurgery."

Curt nodded again, concentrating on using the scalpel. He laboriously completed the cut, and then took the electrocautery tool that Alex handed him.

"This is the Bovie, as you know from general surgery. We use it differently than those cretins. Use the tip to cut with, and don't get too deep with it. Cut the temporalis muscle initially, then deepen the cut to the skull and dissect the muscle off the skull."

Curt used the instrument gingerly, cutting down to the skull at the side of the head, electrical current emanating from the tip of the small probe.

Alex continued. "See how we've formed a flap of scalp. We can now dissect the flap off the skull, keeping the blood supply to the flesh intact through its base."

Curt, now more confident, used the instrument in sweeping motions to separate the scalp and muscle from the skull, peeling it off and rolling it back until a hand sized area of bone was exposed. They bent the scalp and muscle flap out of the way like the tongue of a shoe, then secured it.

"Good" Alex said. "Now we drill the hole in the skull and prepare to remove the bone flap."

The scrub nurse handed him the drill, which he examined and showed to Curt. "These drill bits are supposed to stop when you go through the skull, but you always check and make sure the chuck mechanism is intact, like this." He started the drill, then grabbed the bit with a gauze pad. The bit stopped rotating, although the motor kept going.

"See, that's how it works."

"What happens to your fingers if the bit doesn't stop?"

"Don't worry. Never happen." He handed the drill to Curt, who took it gingerly.

"Balance yourself on two feet. You don't want to lean on the drill and push it into the brain when it goes through the skull. That's called plunging, when you drill into the brain. Bad form."

Curt nodded. He put the drill against the skull and started it rotating, surprised at the whine.

Alex wet the drill with irrigation fluid, and spoke loudly over the noise. "You need to irrigate just enough to keep the bone dust down. Some scrub nurses go nuts with the fluid, flooding the field, which isn't needed. You only end up getting your shoes wet, or worse yet, your pants. Always keep your underwear dry."

Curt nodded while keeping the rotating drill grinding against the patient's skull. As the bit turned and deepened it piled up bone dust, which Alex irrigated away.

"Never stop until you are through the skull. It's hard to restart the drill in the hole. You can feel each layer of the skull. Read your hands, sense the penetration."

Curt nodded again. Suddenly the bit stopped rotating.

"Good. You're through. Take it out."

Curt removed the drill and they inspected the hole, flushing saline into it to clear out the fragments. Alex used a probe to dissect the bottom. "Here's the dura, the covering around the brain. Separate it from the skull with the dissector." He demonstrated. "Once we do that we can use the drill again with the footplate attachment to turn the bone flap." After Carol changed the drill bit to a jigsaw attachment, she handed it to Alex. Starting in the hole, he cut a line into the skull, bone dust piling up around the blade. A thin plume of smoke rose from the blade, and the acrid smell of burnt bone permeated the OR.

"Irrigation, Curt. You've got to anticipate a bit. You don't want to get to the point where the bone is smoking from the friction."

Curt swung the large syringe into the field. "Sorry." He flushed saline over the wound. "I didn't realize how much air pollution there is here. The drill and saw throw bone dust all over, and the cautery makes a lot of smoke."

"Yeah. That reminds me–try not to breath the bone dust or the smoke. I don't think it's good for you."

Curt's eyes widened.

Alex continued. "Once you have a complete circle, you can reach under with the dissector, separate the dura, and lift out the bone flap."

He cautiously detached the bone from the covering over the brain, then removed the disc and handed it to Carol, leaving a hole in the skull. "Try not to drop the bone on the floor. If that happens there's a variety of thoughts as to what to do, none of them great."

Curt nodded again. They were looking through the round opening at a bulging grayish membrane.

"What's his pCO two?" Alex looked at the anesthesia resident over the drape.

Hancock stirred. "Thirty five."

"Bring it down to thirty or so." Alex looked at Curt. "By ventilating the patient more, we can bring down the carbon dioxide level, which shrinks the blood vessels in the brain, decreases the volume of blood in the cranial cavity, and relaxes the brain. Right now it's very tense."

He ran a finger softly over the smooth, tight surface of the dura. "Here, you try it."

Curt did the same, touching lightly and gingerly like he was probing the mouth of a rabid dog.

"If we didn't have a clot in there causing this pressure, we would like it to be more slack before the dura is opened. Otherwise the brain can swell and ooze like toothpaste. Quite a sight." He chuckled in a knowing way. "The CT shows, though, that this bulging is caused by the clot underneath. Let's open the dura and take it out."

Curt took some scissors from the covered tray. Alex shook his head.

"How are you going to open the dura with that? You need a knife to start the opening, then complete it with those." He took a scalpel from the scrub nurse, held it like a pencil, then made a small slit in the membrane.

"Now open the dura with the scissors."

Curt's hand shook as he put the bottom blade through the small dural opening, then cautiously squeezed and cut, enlarging the rent.

"Good. Open it this way." Alex traced a cross shaped opening on the dura, and Curt continued cutting. Purple jelly started appearing, pulsating and squeezing out the slit.

"There's the clot. Don't cut the brain. Hold the dura up away from the brain with the scissors."

Curt continued with Alex watching closely.

"Good. Now tack the dural edges back."

Curt placed a stitch into the apex of each of the triangular flaps, then pulled and attached the looped thread to the drape towels with a clamp, folding the membrane back like banana peels as the clot continued to extrude.

"Exposure is key. Make sure the dura is retracted, so we have the best possible view through the hole to see the clot."

When Curt finished, Alex continued. "Good. Now look for the brain. It's usually a little yellowish under all this."

He gently sucked out fragments of blood clot, then irrigated out more coagulum. The sunken brain gradually appeared.

"Use the irrigation carefully to wash things out. Start in the center, then gradually work out to the periphery, looking under the bone as far as possible."

Curt lightly squirted fluid over the brain, as clot fragments floated out and away.

"Good. Now let me show you something else."

Curt felt braver. "Don't steal the case from me."

Alex chuckled. "You'll have plenty of subdurals. Just pay attention." Taking a ribbon retractor, a blunt, smooth blade, he slid it under the brain and gently lifted it off the floor of the skull. He used his headlight to peer into the opening between the bony floor of the skull and the elevated brain. "It's funny. My father used a headlight as well, but he was a coal miner" Alex mused, enjoying Curt's interest. "I use it to look in different crevices." He kept his head moving, directing the light to different angles. "We need to look for any remaining clot hiding under the brain. Here we look under the frontal lobe to the optic nerves carrying vision to the brain." He gently slid the metal ribbon deeper under the brain. "Here's where the vision nerves come into the cranial cavity." He moved so Curt could look down his light beam. "See them?"

Curt nodded. He was amazed at this tour of the brain, like taking a drive through the park. This was the first exposure to the organ that would become his mission and responsibility, after years of exhausting training, and he was fascinated by everything he saw. His eyes glowed above his mask.

Alex continued to gently lift the brain and look around, peering deep under the gray pulsating structure.

Curt felt emboldened enough to ask, "Why is it moving? It shrinks and bulges with the heartbeat."

Alex nodded. "Yeah. Most people don't know that the brain moves with the heartbeat, and also with breathing. The arterial pressure pulse expands the brain, and the pressure of breathing is transmitted to the cranial cavity as well. This moves cerebrospinal fluid in and out of the cranial cavity with each breath, making the brain rise and fall." He continued to look around. "Here's the hypothalamic area, and the basal forebrain area of the frontal lobes of the brain. Personality and reasoning are here." He stopped suddenly, his eyes narrowing with surprise. "That's funny."

Curt looked at him.

"The basal forebrain area is matted down, scarred."

Hancock stirred. "What's the big deal? It's the blood clot, right?"

Alex shook his head. "No. Clot doesn't do this. This is bizarre."

Then he made the connection. "Like the monkey in the lab." He suddenly felt detached, like looking down at somebody else's hands holding the retractor, and a curious stillness overtook him. How could this be?

Immersed in the operation, Alex failed to notice Dr. Todd staring through the window over the scrub sink. His cap was loose, and as his head moved, taking in the scene, the ties hanging down the back waved. Peering intently at the tableaux, he quickly secured his mask and quietly entered the room. Engrossed, Alex kept examining the brain, as the scrub nurse, anesthesia resident and finally Curt noticed the Boss's presence. Each stiffened.

Almost casually, Todd walked over in back of Alex, looking around his bowed head at the brightly illuminated brain. "How everything going, Alex?"

Alex, surprised but unruffled, kept working. "We got the clot out no problem, Dr. Todd. His brain underneath looks good. I don't think it's going to swell. But there's something funny here, in the basal forebrain."

The Boss leaned over, oblivious to the danger of contaminating the sterile drape. "What? What are you talking about?"

Alex pointed with a small instrument. "Here in the basal forebrain. Very matted and scarred. Haven't seen anything like this before, certainly not from trauma."

The Boss leaned more, and then straightened up suddenly, hitting the patient's sterile drape with his unsterile shirt. "Look what you made me do. I don't see anything unusual in there. I'll close up with Curt."

Alex stared over his mask. It was unusual for the Boss to close, very unusual. "I'd be happy to close."

Todd looked at him coolly, looming over Alex. "This is my patient. I'm closing."

Alex stepped backwards, reached up behind his neck and pulled apart his gown. Ripping it and the gloves off, he put them in the trash, and glanced over at Hancock and the scrub nurse. Both of them silently returned his gaze, unsure as to what was going on.

Alex spoke to Curt. "When you're finished I'll meet you in the ICU."

Dr. Todd turned to Alex. "No, Alex. I'll see you in my office. Shortly."

Alex nodded, then turned and pushed the door open, walking rapidly past the OR desk.

The charge nurse there glanced at him, and decided it was safe to inquire. "What's going on in there? The Boss went past here like a fire truck. I've never seen him move that quick."

Alex paused. "He looked OK to me when he came in. A little testy, but so what." He shrugged and held his open hands up. "Well, I'm only the resident. See you later."

Alex went back to the locker room, found his locker, and opened the rusty door. He changed slowly, going over the case in his mind. What was the Boss upset about? The scarring, that was what set him off. What the hell did it mean?

He thought of the CT scan on the patient, and the fact that the Boss didn't want an MRI scan. The MRI would have likely shown the scarring, whereas the CT did not. Was that why the Boss didn't want to get one? He continued dressing, then put his white coat on and walked over to the Department offices.

Walking past the patient reception window, he opened the door into the office and nodded to the girls sitting at their desks, who smiled. He threaded his way down to the Boss's office. Audrey looked up at him.

"He'll be here in a couple of minutes."

Alex sat down heavily next to her desk. "How's the Boss's research going?"

She glanced at him. "Don't know much about it."

Alex aimlessly stared down the carpeted aisle.

Audrey continued. "He was upset about that damn monkey, though. Paul came up a couple times and talked to him about it."

Alex snorted. "I'll bet." He knew enough to be careful.

She paused. "He was a bit irked at you."

"So what else is new."

"Now Alex, you've always been the fair-haired boy."

"Well, things are changing."

He sat up as Dr. Todd came through his private door, still in scrubs.

Brushing past Alex, he motioned for him to come in. Alex jumped up and followed, closing the door and sinking in the greenish cloth chair as the Boss settled down.

Todd looked at him for a moment, his hooded eyes hidden in the dimness of the office. The puddles of yellow light only emphasized the gloom without illuminating the interior.

"Alex, did you see anything abnormal with that case?"

"Well, the scarring was unusual."

"What scarring?"

"The pathology above the optic nerves, at the basal forebrain."

Todd shook his head. "Alex, that was a straightforward subdural hematoma. At your stage you should know that."

What was going on? "There was some scar tissue there. It was just like the monkey in the lab."

Todd stared at him, his eyes starting to glow darkly, emerging from shadow. "Alex, again, that was a routine problem. Another clot. As you know, clots can distort anatomy, and the remaining blood can look like just about anything. You can never take the clot completely out, and the remaining strands can deform normal structures."

Alex sat immobile, staring back silently. He disliked being coerced.

Dr. Todd sighed. "Alex, you're forty years old, seven years older than usual, coming to the end of the residency. It's been a long road for you. You've got the Boards coming up. Are you ready?"

Alex nodded confidently. "As ready as I'll ever be, I think."

"All our graduating residents have passed the oral exam. All of them."

"I think I'm prepared."

"And a good job is hard to get if you don't pass on the first shot."

Alex nodded again.

"Well, good luck on them. When you get back, we'll have some good cases for you."

Alex stood up. "Thanks, Dr. Todd." He walked out past Audrey, who looked up as he silently went by.

CHAPTER 13

Alex got up the next morning with a vague but rapidly strengthening feeling of dread. He opened his eyes and immediately knew what the day held. "The Boards" he muttered, thinking about the Boss's boast, how every resident he had trained had passed. Getting out of bed, he rubbed his head. It was aching again. Must be the stress, he thought. Walking down the hall, he carefully avoiding the creaking floorboards in the old place as he went into the bathroom, starting up the shower.

After dressing, he packed a small suitcase and headed to his car. Driving to the airport and parking, he memorized the location, then went to the ticket counter and checked in. After walking down the corridor to the boarding gate, he sat down in a dark blue plastic seat, one of a row, each seat separated by spindly metal arms. He liked to watch the eddying stream of humanity passing endlessly by, the young thrusting forward in their ignorance, the old walking slowly in their weariness, those in the middle more young than old, or more old than young. He wondered whether anyone else there was going to the Boards.

An older man maneuvered his wife, slumped over in a wheelchair, next to Alex. His mouth drooping, he sat down heavily, wearing brown double-knit pants flapping above beige shoes closed with Velcro flaps, a dark blue nylon jacket, and a gray knit shirt. His wife's face was buried in a pillow on her lap, her pale, thin blond hair bound with an erect white bow marking her head like a tiny gravestone.

The man nudged her, and she stirred. "I'll get you some tea. Maybe you'll feel better."

Alex shifted away from them. That's all I need, he thought. To catch something now. Facing the examiner with a sickening fever, dripping nose, upset stomach, or the worst, hyperactive bowels. He turned further, then thought of what an old medical school teacher had told him. A doctor, the ancient sage said slowly to them, should never run from disease. Pondering for a moment, he moved back and said gently to the woman, "Anything I can do for you, ma'am?"

She stirred, and Alex thought she would never look up. Then the head slowly collected its strength and rose up, focusing on him. Her eyes, a dark brown, were surprisingly clear, and she stared at him for a moment. She smiled, nodded, and grasped his hand briefly. "Thank you, but no." She dropped her gaze, then her head, back to the pillow.

By force of habit, he had put his beeper on, and it suddenly chirped. Looking at the number on the screen, he realized it was the resident's call room. Smiling to himself, he got up and found a phone, dialing the number.

"Hello." It was Dahlia.

Alex said "Dr. Adams here. Anyone page me?"

Dahlia giggled. "It's Curt and me. We just wanted to wish you good luck."

"Thanks."

"We know you won't have any problem. You're the best resident the program's ever had."

"As the Bible says, pride goeth before a fall."

"You'll do fine. Good luck. Here's Curt."

"See you."

Curt came on the line. "How ya doing, Alex?"

"Good. How are you? All the patients doing OK?"

"Yeah, yeah . . . there's one thing, though. That patient, the one with the subdural blood clot we did yesterday. He died last night."

Alex was used to death, to patients dying. It happened, sometimes unpredictably. It didn't bother him, for the most part, although as he got older he wondered about it more. But this patient shouldn't have died. His brain just wasn't hurt enough. "What happened?"

Curt stuttered, feeling guilty like every first year resident did when bad things occurred, even when it wasn't their fault. "Don't know. A nurse in the ICU called me to see him. Said he was having problems, to come over. I went over and checked him out. He had been doing well, slowly becoming lighter. He was localizing to pain, but then stopped moving, and they called me. When I got there, he was limp, no brain function, no brainstem reflexes. He lost his blood pressure shortly afterward." He sighed heavily, in a portentous manner befitting a first year resident. "The worst part is that the Boss was in just before."

"The Boss?" The Boss never came in except when the chief resident called him. But there was nothing to be done about it now, except to boost Curt and help his wavering confidence. "Don't worry about it, Curt. Can't be helped. It happens. We aren't treating measles. I'll see you guys soon."

"Good luck, Alex."

"Thanks."

Alex hung up. He looked down the busy airport corridor. Why did that patient die? His brain wasn't swollen. He had retracted it without problems and the clot had come out nicely. The only unexpected finding was that peculiar scarred area frontally. That wouldn't kill him, though. He filed it away, got up and walked down the concourse to his departure gate. They announced his flight, and after getting in line he handed his boarding pass to the attendant, then walked on the plane.

He nodded to the stewardesses, and as he always did, reassured them. "I've got my pilot's license. If you guys have any problems, just give me a call." He chuckled. They smiled indulgently, then returned to their duties. Continuing to smirk, he found his seat, nodding sociably to the adjoining occupant. Putting his bag in the overhead compartment, he squeezed over to the window seat. For a moment he looked out the window at the preparations the ground crew was making, then settled in for the flight.

When the plane arrived at his destination, Alex stayed seated, as was his habit, until the cabin had emptied. Standing up, he grabbed his bag from the overhead compartment and nodded to the stewardesses as he sauntered out. Walking through the airport, he found the taxi stand and taxi.

"University Hotel?"

"OK."

He got in as the cabby walked around to the driver's side. Just before they started off, a younger man, hair already thinning in a blue sport coat and khaki pants, ran over and spoke with the cabby, who turned to Alex. "This guy's going to the same place."

Alex wanted to be alone. The guy looked pushy. "OK, I guess."

The man opened the passenger door and slid in. "Thanks a lot." He slammed the door closed and the cab started off, as he brushed back non-existent hair with the flat of one hand and turned towards Alex.

Alex inclined his head. "You going to the Boards too?"

"Yep. How'd you know?"

"You've got the neurosurgical uniform on; blue sport coat and khaki pants. Plus you're going to the University Hotel."

"Steve Little." He held out his hand, small and soft looking.

"Alex Adams."

They shook.

"Where're you from?"

"University Hospital"

"Oh, Dr. Todd's program."

"Yep. How about you?"

"Charity State."

"I've heard of the Chief there. He's got a good reputation."

"Not like Todd. He's been keeping a lower profile lately, though. At least, that's what my Chief says." He paused. "Is he really as tough as they say he is?"

Alex looked out the window. "Yep. He's a real pain in the ass."

Little shook his head. "We hear some strange stories about that program."

"The training is excellent."

"I'm sure. Well, you ready for the Boards?"

Alex shrugged. "I guess as ready as I'll ever be."

"Me too. They can't be that bad. Although there's a couple of guys in my area who had to take them several times. A real blow."

Alex snorted. "I'll say." He looked out of the window. "They say the Boards are very practical. Down to earth. Real clinical situations. That fits our training. We see a lot of cases, get a lot of experience."

"Yeah, I've heard that as well. That worries me a little. We're not a tremendously busy program and we don't do a huge amount of cases. Our clinical exposure is OK, I guess, but not overwhelming."

"You'll be alright. It's billed as a straightforward exercise in reviewing how you deal with everyday problems."

Little nodded, looking into the distance.

The cab pulled in to the hotel. Alex paid, and gripped his bag. They went over to the desk and registered, then walked over to the elevator. Little looked at Alex.

"Going to do anything tonight?"

"Just get a good sleep."

Little nodded. "That's what I had in mind. See you tomorrow."

They went up the elevator, each to his own room.

Alex opened his door and entered. A standard hotel room, two queen beds, a small desk, a TV on top of a chest of drawers. Settling in, he looked at the books he had brought. They were standard neurosurgery textbooks, weighty and voluminous, and he sat down and leafed through them. He had read them closely many times cover to cover, and had highlighted and outlined them as well. The contents were as familiar to him as his prayer book.

Satisfied, he put them down. He was ready. Looking around, he found the menu and ordered dinner. After room service he relaxed and went to sleep.

The phone rang, and Alex immediately woke up. Picking up the receiver, he listened—his wake up call. Getting up, he showered and dressed, a slight feeling of tightness growing in his gut.

Choosing a restaurant in the lobby, he forced some food down, then walked over to the neighboring university for the examination, following the map that had been sent to him. He looked for the building holding the exam, found it, and went inside the brick, ivy covered structure. Noticing a reception desk, he inquired there and was directed to an elevator, entering it with two other pale men. They were silent, and Alex inspected each of them in turn. One was tall and blond, and had missed some patches of whiskers around the back of his jaw. The other was shorter, thinner, and darker, already sweating in his three-piece suit, his hair greasy.

"Looking forward to this?"

They gave weak smiles. The perspiring one spoke, after glancing at Alex quickly. "Not really."

The door opened, and they went into a hallway, brown linoleum floor recently waxed and shined. Light poured through a cathedral window at the end of the corridor, reflecting off the burnished floor, illuminating without brightening the dark walls. They walked down to a group of softly murmuring people gathered at one office, dressed like themselves, the women in conservative dark suits as well.

Alex threaded his way inside. A blond woman of indeterminate age with a fixed smile and hard brown hairdo sat at a desk. She looked up at him.

"Alex Adams."

"Yes, Dr. Adams." She looked through a pile of papers. "Here's your packet." She handed him a folder. "Let me see. You'll be with Drs. Hatali and Johnston for the first hour. The second hour Drs. Bennington and Arnolds. The third hour Dr. Trauberg." She shuffled among the papers. "That's odd. Usually you're with two examiners. This looks like a last minute change." She looked up at him briefly and shrugged. "Oh, well. Things get very hectic here. Good luck." She pointed out where Alex would be meeting his first examiners. He thanked her, and left as the next candidate pushed up to the desk.

Finding his way out of the crowded office he walked down the hallway, then turned around and walked back. Anything was better that just standing. He looked at his watch. Ten o'clock. Time to start. Pacing some more, he heard the woman's voice.

"May I have your attention, please." The murmurs died down as people gathered around the woman, now standing in the hallway, still with the determined, rigid smile. "I'm Ellen Hilbert, from the American

Board of Neurologic Surgery. Just some points of information. You should all have your schedules. The examination is three hours long, composed of questions about various neurosurgical cases. Marked in your packet are your room assignments, and your examiners. Between each hour you have five minutes to move to the next room. At the end of the three hours, you are free to go." She looked at the anxious faces and smiled mechanically. "Traditionally, if you know someone on the Board of Examiners, you can call them this evening and find out how you did. Otherwise, your results will be mailed to you, and you should get them within the week." She looked around again. "Good luck, then, and please proceed to your first room."

The mass of closely packed people stood motionless and silent for a moment, then started chattering and turning. Alex found the way to his room, the feeling of tightness in his gut increasing, like a washcloth being twisted.

"Good luck."

He turned. A portly woman in a dark jacket and skirt looked at him in a friendly way, her dark eyes framed by wire glasses, her lips a little too red, the lipstick going over the lip to the skin in places. "I guess we'd all rather be somewhere else."

"Anywhere else." He smiled. "Even at the dentist for a root canal. Good luck to you too." At least there were still a few human beings here. He went into his classroom, looking around as he entered. It had numerous blacktopped lab stations, with four metal chairs clustered around each square table. At a station in the middle of the room sat two middle-aged men. One was small, dark and Indian, thin hair combed backwards, grouped by the tines of the comb into dark cords over the lighter scalp, dressed precisely. The other was a larger gray-haired man, with gold wire glasses, the fluorescent lights glinting on the lenses, talking energetically. They fell silent as he approached.

"Dr. Adams?"

Alex nodded and extended his hand.

"I'm Dr. Johnston. This is Dr. Hatali." They shook hands. "Please sit down." He motioned to a chair.

"Thank you."

"We have some cases here, with x-rays, CT scans and MRI scans as necessary, as well as angiograms and other tests. Please try and relax. There are no tricks here, just good medical and neurosurgical patient care."

Alex nodded.

The next hour was made up of questions, constant and detailed. Each examiner would describe a patient, a case, some with x-rays, some with CT or MRI scans to complement the story, and then start the queries. Alex sat confidently, looking at them with a steady gaze. He concentrated on what they said, replying to them evenly. They kept at it, question after question, problem after problem, patient after patient. It seemed like a long time, but finally they stopped and smiled.

"Congratulations. You've finished the first hour. On to the second session" said Dr. Hatali precisely. Alex stood and shook their hands, then turned and walked out of the room. He felt good, and went to the central lobby where the other residents were congregating. There was a full table of food, but nobody was touching it. They all looked somewhat ashen in their dark suits, and were chattering nervously, in the manner of small boys boasting about their doings. Alex moved towards the table and grabbed a sandwich, holding a soda in the other hand. He ate in careful nibbles, taking a bite, then a sip, then a chew, then a sip. The others looked at him in sidewise glances, envious of his appetite and apparent sang-froid. Alex munched and thought. Things don't change much from the first grade.

"How'd you do?" Steve Little walked up to him.

"So far, so good. Nothing too bad yet."

"I thought I was shaky on a couple things, but I pulled out of it."

Alex kept munching.

Little continued, "Well, two more hours to go. I feel good about it."

Alex nodded.

Ellen Hilbert appeared. "Time for the second hour" she said, as if instructing a group of kindergartners. Alex put down his soda carefully, looked at his schedule and the assigned classroom number, then walked down the hall to where his second session would be held. Again there was a group of blacktop lab tables. The room was empty, so he sat down at the center lab table, looking at the unattractive brown wood cabinets lining the walls. He gazed around aimlessly, and suddenly the ticking of his watch perforated his consciousness.

Finally two men came walking into the room. One was medium height and about fifty, heavyset, and the other about the same age, thinner, with a grim look to his face.

The heavyset examiner smiled. "Dr. Adams, I'm Dr. Bennington. This is Dr. Arnolds."

They shook hands. Arnolds had a white tuft of hair springing from his scalp, like a small white cloud caught while scudding across the sky. Alex's eyes darted to the small dark hairs projecting from Arnolds nose, and he quickly shifted his gaze to the doctor's eyes, fixed steadily on him.

They started the questions as the others had done in the first session. Alex continued to answer carefully but completely. His confidence had started to grow.

"Thirty five year old with memory problems."

"Does she have anything on examination?"

"Short term memory loss on mental status examination."

"I'd get an MRI scan of the brain."

"Right here." The examiner sifted through a pile of large envelopes, selected an image and placed it on the portable x-ray board.

Alex looked carefully at the series of pictures. "Looks like a intrinsic brain tumor. I would discuss my thoughts with the patient, and recommend a stereotactic biopsy."

"The result is malignant tumor."

Alex gazed at the MRI again. The tumor was small, deep in the brain, and in an area too risky to operate on.

"I'd do radiosurgery on that lesion."

The examiners exchanged glances.

"Radiosurgery?"

"Yes. We have had several lesions like this with Dr. Todd, and we treated them with radiosurgery."

"It is close to the optic chiasm and basal forebrain."

Alex nodded. "I understand. I had the same thoughts. I brought up some of these concerns with Dr. Todd when we saw these patients in clinic. He said he had done this before without problems."

The examiners looked at each other again. "To my knowledge this is an area where radiosurgery has not been tried." Dr. Bennington said. "There may be unpredictable effects on personality." He looked at Dr. Arnolds, "But if Dr. Todd has done it . . ." His voice trailed off into an enigmatic smile.

They continued to interrogate Alex, who answered readily. Finally the session came to an end. Alex stood up and held out his hand, each examiner shaking it vigorously.

"Very nice to meet you" Dr. Arnolds said. Bennington nodded.

Alex thanked the examiners and walked out of the room. He went down the hall to the lobby and reached for another sandwich as Steve Little came up to him.

"Well, how are things going?"

"Seem to be OK." Alex started munching as Little stared.

"Well, at least your appetite isn't affected."

"Have some. It's good."

"I'm not hungry."

"You'll feel better if you have something."

"You sound like my mother. No thanks. I want to be ready for the last hour."

"Suit yourself."

Little glanced at him enviously, then nodded. "Well, see you around."

Alex raised his eyebrows, continuing to eat.

Ellen Hilbert appeared once again. "Please start the last hour. Good luck. Remember, you can leave after this final review."

Alex finished his sandwich and walked down the hallway to the third session, entering the room. There was just one examiner. Alex looked around for another, then remembered Ms. Hilbert telling him about the last minute schedule change. The man was inspecting a CT scan, his blondish thinning hair grown long on one side and thrown over a bald spot, pasted across his scalp like a flattened butterfly on a windshield. Bad comb over, Alex thought, as the examiner looked up. He stood suddenly, nearly upsetting his chair as he shoved it back with a sudden thrust of his legs. He introduced himself as Dr. Brian Trauberg, and Alex vaguely recognized the name as that of a mid-level academic neurosurgeon from the Midwest. Tall and angular, Trauberg smiled without emotion, his thin lips flattening briefly, and motioned for Alex to sit. The room, like the others, was used as a teaching laboratory, and they faced each other over a black stone tabletop.

Alex listened to the first question, having to do with a blood clot in the brain. He looked at the proffered CT scan, and made some recommendations. The queries continued and he answered with confidence. Trauberg glanced briefly at him and then went on with his case descriptions, slow and deliberate. He would pause frequently, and between words and sentences his jaw would sag and his lips part. Distractingly, behind his teeth, one could see his tongue darting slowly around the inside of his mouth like an arthritic and restless snake in a cage.

As the session continued, Alex became more and more at ease. This was the last session, minutes away from freedom. He became voluble, expounding on points to intricate degrees, as the examiner returned his energy with an absent-minded gaze.

After a time Trauberg looked up at the clock and then glanced at Alex. "Well, you've made it. That's it. Good luck."

Alex thanked him, scraping the metal chair on the floor as he stood up. He waited for a brief moment, wondering whether there was more, but Trauberg was riffling through papers and scans. Alex turned and walked out, recalling that after this portion of the examination the examiners gathered in a room and reviewed the candidates, then made their decision. Nodding to other residents who were filtering out of various rooms, he listened to their chatter, and what he heard confirmed his confidence.

As Alex walked down the hall, staring at the gleaming floor, Steve Little came up.

"How'd you do?"

"I think I did OK."

Steve started talking, almost as if to himself. "I think I passed. A couple questions threw me. The one about the third ventricular tumor. What approach did you use?"

"Splitting the brain and going through the anterior corpus callosum."

"Yeah, I think that's what they were looking for. I started out wrong on that one, but I think I recovered. What about the cervical spine fracture?"

"I fused her."

"What technique?"

"Posterior plating and autograft."

Steve looked at him. "Wow. You're right on target. I told them I'd put in a halo, only they showed me a film with the plates in place. Posterior plates. You got it exactly right."

"As I said, we get experience in our program."

"I can see that." They came to the central lobby and paused awkwardly.

"Well, good luck."

"Good luck to you. See you at the meetings."

They nodded stiffly to each other, and Steve turned and left. Alex looked around at the dark suits all around, the still tense faces. Time to get out of here.

He walked out of the building and along the sidewalks. This time of year the university was beautiful, the old stone buildings covered with fluttering ivy. Living here, he thought, would have its charms. He felt expansive, relaxed, glad that the ordeal was over, generous in spirit towards the undergraduates who walked to and fro, thinking of his own college days, and what they still had ahead of them. The hotel eventually appeared ahead, and he entered, went up to his room and packed his suitcase. The airport limousine was waiting as he came back down.

Putting his suitcase in the back of the limo, crowded with chattering residents, he climbed in. As he angled himself into the second row, he saw that the woman who had wished him good luck was there as well.

"Hi, there."

"Hi."

They didn't feel the need for introduction, as sharing the experience of the examinations seemed enough.

"How'd things go?"

Alex nodded. "Seemed OK. From what I could tell, I think I made it."

"The questions weren't too bad. It was as advertised. A review of common neurosurgical problems."

Others in the limousine, relieved and eager to share their experience, chimed in and described the questions they had encountered. Alex relaxed in a comfortably taciturn mood. From what he heard, and as he knew, his answers had been correct.

CHAPTER 14

Alex was glad to get home to his apartment. As he drove up in the gathering dusk, he almost hoped he would see Dr. Sutcliff. The green trees behind the garage rustled gently in the cool evening breeze as he walked, their shadows flitting across the stairs. Opening the door, he brought in his scarred suitcase and put it down. Settling back on the couch, he continued reviewing the examination in his mind.

Recalling Ellen Hilbert's words about calling a Board member prodded him to think of Dr. Herring, who he knew from a previous rotation at another hospital. Looking up the number, he pressed the buttons of the phone as he mulled over his career in neurosurgery. He relived the work he had done so far, the hundreds of sleepless nights, the pressure and ceaseless toil. Pride welled in him as he looked forward to speaking with the prominent physician.

The phone clicked. "Hello." It was Dr. Herring.

"Dr. Herring?"

"Yes."

"This is Alex, Alex Adams."

"Alex . . . how are you?" Herring sounded somewhat strained, but Alex remembered he was a high-strung guy.

"Good, good. I just wanted to check on the Board examination results. They said we could call one of the examiners if we knew them."

Silence, then Dr. Herring coughed. "Alex, uh, sorry to tell you this. You didn't pass. I don't know what to say."

Alex seemed to hear Dr. Herring's voice from far away. Flunked? Flunked? How could this be? He stood up, then sat down. Flunked? "Oh boy . . ." Alex muttered, to himself and to Dr. Herring. "What happened?" His mind raced. What would the Boss say? What would the other residents say? What does this mean?

Dr. Herring cleared his throat again. "Alex, I tell my residents that one test doesn't mean a thing. You know that." He sounded genuinely regretful.

Alex stood up again, and then sighed. "What happened, Dr. Herring? Everything went fine with the examination. I answered all the questions. Things seemed to go well."

Dr. Herring paused. "I'm not exactly sure. I shouldn't say this, but the main problem seemed to come from one examiner. I really can't mention any more. I know you'll do well on the retest."

Alex sat down again. He knew Dr. Herring wanted to end the conversation. "Thanks very much, Dr. Herring. I'll keep plugging away."

"No problem. Good luck. Keep me informed."

Alex put the phone back on the cradle, staring at it for a while. Flunked? What happened? He looked around the room. It was spare, furnished simply with an old black plastic chair that could spin completely around, a light tan couch that gravity was getting the best of, and a round rug. College and medical school diplomas were on the shelf, the yellow wrinkled fragment of shirt that he had been wearing when he first soloed an airplane framed on the wall. His whole world seemed to have changed. Shifting on the couch, he replayed the examination in his mind. The first session was on the spine. He answered all the questions, things went smoothly. The second section was on the brain. Both examiners appeared to be satisfied. The third section was with Dr. Trauberg. That seemed to go well also. But he was the only examiner at that session. Unusual. If he had an objection, there would be no counterbalancing opinion. The other sessions really went well. I'll bet the problem was with the third examination, the single examiner, he thought.

Getting up, he walked around, stunned by the disappointment. Always he did well, ceaselessly working but invariably succeeding. He was nearing the pinnacle of his career, just about to take off, and this happened. What would they say? What would the Boss say?

Putting his leather flight jacket on, he went outside. It helped a little to move around. Very little. He walked and walked, the cool evening breeze hinting of the fall to come, until he had to go back, still engrossed and distracted. Flunked? Taking off his coat and throwing it on the couch, he turned on the TV news, distracted for a moment by the talking head with the careful coiffure. Pausing, he stared at the vapid look, the glossy nails, the shiny lips. No brains. I work my butt off and this is what I get, listening to this airhead. The picture shifted to the President. Alex wondered why he kept staring at another talking head. More banality. They sound like they all had lobotomies. He started wondering what part of their brains had been removed. That gave him a morose satisfaction, imagining what vital parts were missing under those shiny shells. Look at those bozos, he thought. Cut from the same cloth. Yapping endlessly. They probably don't have any frontal lobes, he thought. That's it. Brain damaged. Just like that poor bastard in the OR, and the monkey in the lab. Both of them, basal forebrains shot. He walked around aimlessly, feeling still colder at the thought of the scarring in the monkey's brain, and that of the patient they had operated on who died. What was going on?

He turned off the television, brooding on the Boards. What would they think? The chair creaked as he slumped down, rotating back and forth spasmodically. The first two sessions were fine, even the third. But the last was with a single doctor. Todd had told him at the hospital, and he had heard at neurosurgical meetings, that there were always two neurosurgeons per session. Why was there only one? Who really was this guy? He had vaguely heard of him. What was his problem? He needed to find out more. An idea struck him. He'd do a computer search for any scientific articles Trauberg had written.

Going over to his briefcase, he pulled out a notebook computer and turned it on. Having a purpose eased the pain, for a moment. He dialed into the hospital network and connected through it to the National Institutes of Health database. Searching the medical literature by author name, he typed in Trauberg, and a number of citations appeared. Some mentioned surgical techniques, others were reports of unusual cases. He looked farther and farther back, then changed databases to examine earlier years.

Trauberg had not written extensively, his few published articles apparently pertaining mainly to the spine. One on disc disease, another on spine fractures. Then a name caught his eye. Todd? Victor Todd and Brian Trauberg? He looked at the citation. It was years ago, on frontal brain surgery in monkeys for behavior changes. He hadn't realized the Boss had done much work in this field. The abstract reviewed the main findings.

"The function of the frontal lobe of the brain is not well understood. Pathology of the area can lead to euphoria, or a flat affect. In an effort to explore further the function of the frontal lobes, connecting nerve bundles to the basal forebrain were sectioned from the frontal lobes and the effects observed. Monkeys with such surgery seemed to lack consideration for others . . . although they seemed to be more animated and 'persuasive' to other monkeys."

Alex remembered the monkey in the lab. He had some basal forebrain damage that could not be accounted for by his hematoma. What does this mean? Was there a connection between Dr. Trauberg and the Boss?

He made a mental note to speak to the Boss about Dr. Trauberg, if the Boss would still talk to him. The crushing burden of his failure hit again, harder after the brief respite of the computer search, and his head ached. Arching his back, fatigue joined the pain, and after slumping for a time he stirred and went to the bedroom, sitting down on the bed.

The phone rang. It was Dahlia. "Hi guy. Just wanted to see how things went."

"Well" Alex said, embarrassed. "Not too well." He swallowed. "I flunked." Even the word was hard for him to say.

"Oh" Dahlia emitted a groan. "What happened?"

"I don't know. I really don't. Everything seemed to go OK. I answered all the questions well. The first two sessions were straightforward. The last one was with only one examiner, but it went well also. I just don't know," he said despondently.

"Look, things happen. You're our best resident. You'll take it again. Don't worry."

How easily she dismissed things, Alex thought. "Yeah, sure."

Dahlia felt his pain. "Look, why don't you come on over this evening. I'll make you something. We can have a drink. You do drink, right?"

"Ha, ha. Well, OK" he said, and then regretted it, but it was too late. "I'll be over in a little while."

Alex hung up the phone and lay down, after shutting off the lights. The sick feeling he had in his stomach since talking with Dr. Herring stayed with him. On his side, he stared into the darkness. He thought of his life, how he started in kindergarten, up through elementary school, junior and senior high, college, medical school, always working, always studying, always doing well. He remembered internship, how he learned quickly, staying up nights constantly, at the patient's bedside. He recalled residency, how he slowly, painfully acquired the skill to operate on the brain. Never the flashy one, never the favorite, and yet he was the one to get the job done, and they knew it. Flunked. How the hell did it happen? He turned on his back and stared at the darkness.

CHAPTER 15

The phone rang in the gloom, jolting Alex awake. He looked around at the clock—nine PM. Must've fallen asleep. He grabbed the phone.

"Hello."

"Where are you?" It was Dahlia. "What happened? Stood me up?"

"Sorry, I fell asleep." He was glad it was Dahlia. "Are we still on?"

"Sure."

"I'll be right over."

Dahlia lived in an old area of the city, once elegant but now growing decrepit. She rented a small stone house on a street lined with sagging trees and similar homes, each in its little overgrown lot a unique style of decay.

Well, thought Alex, at least my car fits right in. He pulled up to the curb and got out.

Dahlia's house was set back from the street, the unlit walk to the porch paved with battered bricks set in a basket weave pattern. Once evenly spaced, they were now irregularly sunken and chipped, and as his eyes traveled up the walk he thought of the smoothness of Dr. Todd's slate. He picked his way slowly up to the porch as he wondered why Dahlia kept it so dark, then knocked.

She opened the door quickly, studying him, her head silhouetted by the hall light. "Bad luck, huh?"

He nodded. He couldn't see her face well at all, with the brightness in back of it. Morosely wondering whether he was developing glaucoma or early retinal degeneration, he followed her in. The hall was lined with shelves holding books and pictures. They turned to the left and walked into the living room, filled with a couch and baby grand piano. No carpet, only hardwood floors, with more books and pictures on shelves. A movement on the floor caught Alex's eye, a tiny black mouse emerging from under the coach.

"Move along" Dahlia said sweetly to the creature, as it started to scuttle across the bare floor.

Alex shook his head in disgust.

Dahlia noticed. "They're a living thing."

"They carry disease."

"Name one."

Alex thought. "Hanta virus. It turns your lungs to mush in twenty-four hours, then you croak."

"Not these little ones."

Their eyes followed the diminutive creature until it disappeared under the dusty radiator.

Dahlia turned to him. "Relax and let me get you something. How about a hamburger?"

"Sounds good." Alex suddenly remembered Dahlia was a terrible cook. When she brought dishes to the residents' picnic inevitably no one knew what they were. Too late, he thought. He'd better check the glass and plate; with those mice around they could crap anywhere, and Dahlia didn't seem like the paragon of cleanliness.

As she puttered around in the kitchen Alex got up and examined the piano. "Nice piano. I didn't know you played," he called into her.

"After I finish residency I'll use it a lot more."

He inspected the books on the shelves. Some philosophy, some religious books. Others were surgical texts.

The pictures interested him. One showed a younger Dahlia with a man, both smiling, apparently out West next to a huge cactus. Even though it was framed, the photo was starting to yellow and curl. He looked at the other pictures. They were all of a younger Dahlia, alone or with the man, and all were yellowed.

Dahlia came in with a hamburger on a small round plate, and a mug of soda. Accepting the food gratefully, he sat down.

"Thanks. Looks good." He bit into the hamburger. The meat was red in the middle. Alex thought of trichinosis but decided to keep quiet. Dahlia watched him inspect the burger.

"Everything OK?"

"It's a little rare."

"Don't be such a wimp."

Alex looked around. "You've got a nice place. A lot of books and pictures."

"It's okay. Many of them were my husband's. The general surgery books were his."

"Is that him?" asked Alex nodding at the pictures.

"Yep" she said. "That was on a trip out West."

There was a silence, and Alex felt the need to talk.

"Do you really think people out there realize there's acolytes like us, working day and night, tending the weak, the sick, plugging away, oblivious to fashion and the media, burdened by the unknowable, constantly faced by paradox, distracted by uncertainty, trying to work within an impossible collection of conflicting systems, attempting to care and learn, carrying the flame? While our struggling idealism is trapped in the crucible of a crumbling system."

"Alex, you're taking profundo pills again." She smiled.

"At the moment, I don't really feel appreciated. The boards were a real kick in the pants."

"I'm so sorry."

He went on partly to himself, partly to Dahlia. "I keep going over it in my mind, replaying it, reviewing the cases they presented. They were all standard cases. I had good answers. No surprises. The first hour was spine, the second head. Two examiners each, everything went well. They had food out and I even ate something between the sessions, none of the other guys did. The last hour was with a single examiner."

"Just one?"

"Yeah, I thought they always had two."

"That's what the Boss told us."

"At any rate things went well with that session also. I answered all the questions. I had no indication of trouble."

"Who were your examiners?"

"For the first hour Johnston and Hatali. The second hour Bennington and Arnolds. The third hour Trauberg."

"I recognize all of them except Trauberg. I wonder who he is?"

"I don't know. I haven't heard of him. The others are well known."

She shook her head. "Was Dr. Herring any help?"

"Not exactly. He was obviously embarrassed for me. He was going to tell me something, then thought better of it."

"The whole thing is funny," said Dahlia. "You're the best resident we've got."

"Not by this."

"That's not the only funny thing," Dahlia continued. "What about the monkey and the patient you operated on?"

"Who told you about that?"

"Richard Walter."

"He's got a big mouth. He exaggerates like crazy. You know that."

"Why do you eat like that?"

"Like what?"

"Like that. A nibble, then a sip, then a nibble, then a sip."

He shrugged. "It's got me this far."

She was silent for a moment, looking at him. "Alex. There's something going on," she said firmly.

Now I'm in for it, he thought. I don't need this. Not now. It was a mistake to come here. "Dahlia, you're nuts. I just need to get back to work. I gotta keep plugging away. I'm on thin ice now."

"Alex" her voice rising, "there's something going on."

"Dahlia, I don't know what you're saying. I'm forty years old. Old enough to realize what's coming, young enough to remember being young. I don't want to start again. I can't. I've come too far."

"You can't deny what's happened."

Alex stood up, walked to the window. "I need to finish. I am a neurosurgeon." He suddenly held up his hands, palms out, as if in supplication, then slowly turned them so the palms were facing him, fingers still outstretched. "With these hands, with my brain, I can operate by fractions of millimeters, work among the delicate pipes and stems of the brain without disturbing them. Or with these hands I can bend steel rods to fix a fractured spine." Flexing his fingers, he slowly dropped his arms and turned to Dahlia. "This is what I do. I cut, then I build. I must finish."

"You can't build a life on sand. Something is going on. Your flunking the Boards is very odd. Then there's the brain scarring in the monkey and patient." She looked at him. "I'm telling you we have to check it out."

He looked at the floor. He didn't like arguments. "Forget it, Dahlia. I'm the one on the edge. I've got to watch my step. You're set, you've got it made. I can't get in more trouble."

"Hector Harris, the pathology resident, did the brain removal for the patient that died."

"They got an autopsy?"

"Dr. Todd didn't want one. He told Curt, when Curt called him about it, not to worry about it. The family insisted, though."

"What'd Hector say?"

"Well, he has to wait until the brain is embalmed. But he said there was scarring at the frontal base of the brain, just where Richard said you saw it."

"Richard is only a medical student. He doesn't know what he is saying." He paused. "Maybe things are a little funny. But I can't worry about it. I have to finish."

Her face reddened, then she pivoted and hurried into the kitchen. The sound of clanking plates started.

Alex watched her go, then he cast about and turned on the TV. The evening news appeared and the President's smooth face appeared. He was explaining an embarrassing mistake, and as he did so his face metamorphosed through perfect representations of sad, wistful, sly, and sympathetic. The reporters questioning him were completely outdone and had no follow-up when he finally concluded. What a liar, thought Alex. He spins the reporters like they were children. Don't they see through his lies? Why do they swallow it? The report then switched to the latest poll figures which showed the President's approval the highest of his term.

Alex looked morosely at the graphic. The whole country is swallowing this up. If any of the residents lied like this they would be out of a job in days. Yet he just keeps blabbing along.

He heard more clanking in the kitchen. Dahlia came out flushed, her eyes red. Alex knew she had been crying.

"What a jerk" he said, looking at the TV. She softly walked to the television and turned it off, then went to a picture on the shelf. Taking it carefully into her hands, she showed it to him.

"Here" she said softly and sadly. "This is my husband. Do you know how he died?"

Alex looked at the picture, then at her face, and shook his head. He had heard stories, but nothing definitive.

"He died of a brain tumor. He was under Dr. Todd's care, doing well, but suddenly went downhill. Dr. Todd felt guilty, I think. One of the reasons he gave me a residency slot." She glanced at him as if expecting a remark.

"I'm so sorry." He felt her loneliness, her tragedy, her memories preserved in yellow pictures. A position no one should be in at her age, her past already crystallized in amber, too young for that.

"When he was dying, in bed, his mind would wander. I never told this to anyone, but he babbled about radiation one night, about being in the radiation machine."

"Why is that strange? Many tumor patients have radiation. You know that."

She looked square at him. "He never got radiation. Dr. Todd said it wouldn't help. I was a nurse at the time. I was in no position to disagree."

"He was probably just out of his mind, Dahlia. I'm sure it was a very painful time for him. He had seen radiation treatments at the hospital and he must just have gotten mixed up."

She shook her head. "He spoke about radiosurgery. He talked about the headring, being put into it, not being able to move his head."

"Well, he probably saw a patient at the hospital with the headring on, and just got confused."

She shook her head. "He couldn't have."

"Why not?"

"Radiosurgery was experimental at that time. There were no patients at the hospital who ever had the frame on." She took a deep breath, expelling it urgently. "It wasn't used clinically."

Alex grimaced. The burger was making him feel queasy.

She walked around and sat at the piano. "I think he was radiated in some way" she said loudly straight ahead, then turned to stare at Alex, her eyes burning into his. "He was radiated without telling anyone and he died. He was the finest man and a great doctor."

Alex was silent. Faintly, he could hear the sound of an ambulance. Probably going to University Hospital. At first the thought of the hospital brought a feeling of warmth and familiarity to him. Then he glanced at Dahlia's face and the picture she held in her thin hands, her pale gray eyes looking back at him with hope tempered by years of solitude, fear of the future, longing for the past.

He stared at the grain of the wood floor. Something far back came to his consciousness, a memory of play with his father, after his mother had died. His father seemed to shrink rapidly after that. They were talking about school, about a project. His father, as if speaking to somebody else, told him, 'Always do your best, son. Your mother and I tell you, always do your best.'

Alex pondered. He looked again at the yellowed pictures, the silent piano, the distant siren fading. Todd's cryptic words about improving the brain, his landlord's story, Heather's concerns, all came to mind. He thought of the patient he had operated on with the peculiar scarring, and the monkey in the lab. He looked at Dahlia and finally nodded. "We need to check it out," he said quietly.

CHAPTER 16

When the alarm went off in the dark of the early morning, he immediately opened his eyes and stabbed at the clock. When the peal stopped, his brain instantly presented him with a list of problems. The Boards, the monkey, the patient, Dahlia's husband, it all came back quickly, loading him, slowing him already. Get up, he told himself, have to start rounds.

Swinging out of bed, he showered, shaved, and made a cup of tea. The tea made him vaguely nauseated, and his headache worsened. He wondered whether he had become dependent on caffeine. Getting an average of about four hours sleep a night, and drinking the stuff constantly, it was certainly possible.

He started his car and drove to the hospital. On the way he passed a mailbox, and remembered the time he fell asleep driving to work and hit it. Had a rough stretch, in the hospital all day and night for three days before. Bad enough when you fall asleep driving home, let alone going to work.

His mind kept examining each problem, each setback, like flipping over cards one by one. Walking into the hospital and passing the guard without the usual greeting, he wondered whether the word was out that he had flunked, and then chided himself for the ridiculous self-consciousness.

Taking off his jacket in the residents' room, he put on his white coat and went to the ICU. Walking down the row of partitions to the first room, he dreaded seeing the others, each door reminding him of the opening to a sarcophagus.

As he turned the corner, Curt, Dahlia, and Richard, as well as Fran, looked up from the bedside, their faces grim in anticipation, their chattering abruptly stopping. Alex knew they had been talking about him. Curt looked disappointed and Dahlia sympathetic. Fran's bright pink cheeks and red lips bulged from a mouth full of leftover sandwich, then contracted to a crimson pout as she studied Alex. She hurriedly but carefully set the sandwich aside.

Alex took a deep breath. "Hi, guys."

They nodded.

"How is Mr. Michaelson?"

Fran daintily wiped the grease off her face and hands. "He's doing better, starting to localize to pain."

There was an awkward silence as they walked over to the first patient's bed, and Alex felt the need to lecture to Richard Walters, the medical student. "There are stages of coma, Richard. How would you define coma?"

"Lying with eyes closed."

"To be more specific, a simple definition would be inability to follow commands."

Walters nodded.

"If you pinch somebody in a coma you get a different range of reactions. Some people will reach out to where you are pinching. That's called localization. Some people will flex, others extend, and others don't do anything. That's the worst, of course."

Walters nodded again. "So he still is in a coma?"

"Yes, but since he's gone from flexing to localizing we believe he is doing a bit better."

Dahlia observed dryly, "Only neurosurgeons think like that."

Alex continued, "At any rate, how is his oxygenation?"

"Good."

They evaluated each patient, going from bed to bed. After the last patient, Alex, Dahlia, Richard and Curt slowly walked out to the hallway, awkward silence enveloping them. Curt turned to Alex.

"Sorry about the news."

"That's the breaks." Alex, shrugged, his wrists protruding out of white sleeves as his shoulders moved.

Curt shook his head. "Now I know there's no hope for me."

Alex sighed. "These things happen, Curt. Keep plugging away. That's what I'm going to do."

Alex's beeper went off. As they entered the nursing floor where the more stable patients were located he went to the phone and dialed the number. Clark Hackman answered.

"Hi, Dr. Hackman."

"Alex, don't worry about working on the tumor today. Paul Fox will help me. You need a break after the Boards. Sorry about what happened."

Alex's shoulders sagged. "I guess everybody has heard." He felt the need to explain. "I just don't know what happened. The cases were standard and I gave good answers, at least what I thought were good ones."

"Right." Hackman sounded far away. "You'll bounce back. At any rate, Paul will do the case with me."

Alex set the phone down, and then turned to find Dahlia next to him, looking up at his grim face. "Hackman wants Paul to help him with the tumor."

"That's your job."

"I guess he wants Paul to do it."

"That's not right," she said shrilly.

He looked at her. "What the hell can I do about it?"

She seemed to know what he was thinking. "It's not right," she said firmly again.

"Well, we've got patients to see."

Curt and Richard were following the conversation and moved into step quickly. As they moved from room to room, Alex stopped at each patient to check them, lacking his usual flair and energy. His voice was quiet and soft, his movements slow.

At the end of rounds he turned to Curt. "Don't forget to check the labs on the patients we talked about." Curt nodded.

"Meet you guys at one o'clock and we'll review the patients then."

Dahlia peeled off and started down the hall. "I'll see you later."

Curt and Richard stood silently, reminding him of two bedraggled dogs. Alex looked at them.

"Well?"

"Alex, can we talk a moment?" Curt ventured.

Alex sighed. "Sure. Let's go to the call room." He led them through the hallway, opened the door, and they all filed in. Alex slumped down in the dilapidated easy chair as Curt and Richard perched on the desk and bed. Alex wearily wondered what it was about. It couldn't be good.

Richard waited for Curt to speak.

"Alex, I've just about had it."

"How do you mean?"

"This neurosurgery stuff. It's not quite like I thought. Look how things have been going."

"We've had some rough spots."

"Rough spots? When I started the Boss didn't even know my name. Then there was the Grand Rounds disaster. After that the meeting in the Boss's office. 'There's five here, but I only need four of you'? What kind of encouragement is that? What the hell kind of program is this?"

Richard nodded. "And look at the hard time you got when you did the right thing and opened up that monkey."

Alex looked at the earnest faces. In spite of everything, he couldn't help smiling a bit. Curt looked like either he was going to throw up or had something more to say. "C'mon, Curt, what is it?"

"And look what happened to you at the Boards."

Alex looked at them.

"You're the best resident, Alex. Everybody knows that. If this happens to you, what kind of a specialty is this?" He stood up and pushed away the air. "I should have gone into dermatology, or been a lawyer. Make a lot of money, don't get this grief."

"Or a politician" added Richard.

Alex motioned to the chairs. "Sit down, guys. Do you know what we do?"

They were silent, staring at him expectantly.

"We do something no millionaire, no businessman, no politician could ever do. We open up the most sacred area of a human, the center of consciousness. Lions have better muscles, owls better eyesight, but we've got the best brains, and to fix them we use our hands, the best extremities in the universe."

Richard shook his head as Curt opened his mouth, then shut it abruptly.

Alex held up his hand. "No bozo lawyer can do this, tinker with the brain, not just any doctor, no stinking urologist or radiologist. You've got to be a brain surgeon. Do you know how it feels when you finish an operation, when you've altered the destiny of another human being in a positive way?"

"I don't know." Curt shook his head, looking at the wall. "My mother said I could've been a good actor. Maybe a writer."

Alex took a breath. "Actor, writer? They" he paused for the right word, "conjecture. We" he jabbed his finger at them, "do." He leaned forward, his eyes intense. "Actors, writers, they imitate, no, not even imitate but vaguely posture. We use this," he pointed at his head, "and these" he looked at his hands, slim, strong fingers held straight out. "And look what the process does to us, it ennobles us."

"It hasn't ennobled the Boss." Richard said sourly.

"We've had some bad days," said Curt.

"Bad days? Bad days? You want to know about bad days? A bad day is when you operate on a brain and it uncontrollably swells out of the opening in the skull, bleeding like crazy, soaking your pants and shoes through the supposedly waterproof shoe covers, the patient destroyed from some terrible disease, the family's sorrow piercing your heart. You'll have plenty of bad days. But you'll be alive, and using your hands and brains for something transcendent."

"I don't know, Alex. There's not much glory here. Just a lot of hard work. No flash."

"Glory? Flash? You glide into the essence of the human body, the pinnacle of evolution, and sometimes are privileged to fix that magnificent creation. The handiwork of God. Think of how you use your hands. You can be manipulating the broken spine one day with tools fit for an auto body shop, levering and bending steel, straightening and correcting the vital backbone. The next day you're under the brain in a moist labyrinth, fixing a weak spot in a crucial blood vessel, working through a microscope, moving a fraction of a millimeter at a time. The day after that you're focusing immense photonic energies, crisscrossing them into the brain to kill tumors. What more could you want?"

Curt said wearily, "I'm nervous in the operating room. I'm afraid sometimes."

"Afraid? Don't you think I'm afraid too sometimes, lying awake at night, knowing someone's existence, their body, their mind, their life, their comfort, depends on me, my steadiness, my skill, my mind, my hands? There's many things we just can't do anything about, just can't help. And sometimes we don't even realize it, and blame our own inadequacies. I battle with that every day. But what a remarkable calling it is, fusing the most human of emotions, empathy, with the most analytical discipline. Combining body and mind, knowledge directing the spirit, flowing through your muscles to your hands in precise rationality, tempered by heart, fighting the vagaries of chance, jackals ready to pounce." He hit his chest with his fist, and then smiled at Curt and Richard. "No one said it was going to be easy."

Richard and Curt looked at him for a time, then they both nodded. Curt ventured, "It's a long way."

"Long way? Sure it's a long way. College, medical school, residency, they're all long. All that time error has to be avoided, guarded against, discipline sustained, alertness maintained. In some ways it's denial, endless denial." He stopped for a moment. "And in a deeper way it's cultivation of the most noble of human qualities, compassion, kindness, discipline, courage, consistency."

"I'm more tired than during internship."

"Tired? Of course you'll be tired. Last week, I was doing a case with the Boss. He was sitting at the microscope and I was looking though the assistant's eyepieces, standing next to him. I was so tired I fell asleep as I looked through the scope at him working, banging my head into the eyepieces and shaking the scope, waking me up. I just kept standing. That's all you can do. Sometimes I get so tired I see double."

Richard started in. "It just doesn't seem like we've been saving many lives lately."

"Saving lives? In the real world you don't save lives right and left, like dropping off a log. The truth is, you work like a dog, before dawn to late at night, so tired all you want to do is sleep, but you can't. You keep going. Then once in a while, when the moon is right, the stars are aligned, the dimensions are synchronized, you save someone. You give them time, you give them life, you end their pain, you see the light in their eyes again, the old walk a little better, the young bounce again. What other job is like that?"

Curt shook his head. "It's kind of a shock to be in the operating room, to really see what we do."

"Shock? Of course it's a shock. Opening up people, learning that they're like fancy dolls, with moving eyes, muscle and bone under skin, mechanical marvels. Realizing that there's got to be something more than just flesh and blood, behind all the gadgetry. Sure it's a shock."

"Well, I meant, I don't know whether I can do it."

"Curt, I've seen you work. You can do it. One foot in front of another. You get up early in the morning, do your job, watch the details, have a steady hand and cool nerves, stand up when you fall, work when you're tired, and that's it. You're a neurosurgeon. That's all there is to it."

Curt swallowed. "Well, that's the pep talk for the day. Thanks, Alex." He grimaced, then smiled. "I do feel better. I'm glad I had a philosophy major for a chief resident." He got up to leave, and Richard stood up as well.

"Yeah, Alex. You talk better than those premed biology majors."

Alex clapped Curt on the back. "I'll tell you what my chief told me when I got tired." He shook Curt's shoulder. "It goes quick."

"That's it?"

Alex nodded. "It goes quick."

Curt looked at him for a moment, and then turned. "Well, guess we had better get back to work. Thanks, Alex."

Curt and Richard filed out. As the door closed behind them, Alex heard Curt say, "Remember, Richard, it goes quick."

He smiled, but then fatigue hit him, already this early in the morning. His head was bothering him, a dull ache that seemed to start in the back of his head, where the neck muscles fuse to the skull, and travel up and through to his eyes. It seemed to be getting worse. Rubbing his scalp with his fingertips, he sat down in front of the computer, turning it on. Sitting there for a moment, he realized he wanted to find out more about Trauberg, the board examiner. He went to the Medline web page and searched again on Trauberg, finding the reference he had first discovered at home, involving Trauberg and the Boss. Printing it out, he got up and left, walking down the hall. Paul Fox, reading a patient's chart in the ICU, watched him leave, then got up and hurried into the call room.

Alex took the elevator down to the ground floor and walked over to the medical library. Referring to the printout, he found the journal listed in the citation, pulling it out of the stacks and sitting down at a quiet table, opening the mossy tome. The yellowed pages crackled and smelled of stale solitude as he flipped through them quickly, finding the proper place.

The article delineated a series of animal experiments concerning lesions of the basal forebrain and hypothalamus. There were some changes in blood pressure and other physiologic parameters in the animals with the lesions. No other quantifiable difference in behavior could be measured. In the paper, Trauberg and the Boss concluded, "There is still a mystery as to the exact functions of this area. Additional work is needed to analyze this highly complex neuroanatomic structure."

Alex looked up in the distance. His mind firing, he made a copy of the article.

He paged Dahlia. "I found something interesting."

"What?"

"It turns out that Trauberg and the Boss did work together early on and published a paper." Alex told her the title.

More silence. "Well I guess it's something," she said doubtfully.

He suddenly felt irritated. "Damn right it's something."

"I've got to go. See you at one."

"Right." He hung up the phone, alone among the silent musty forest of green bound volumes.

CHAPTER 17

Alex jumped imperceptibly when his beeper went off, while working in Mr. Musgrave's room. Dahlia and Curt saw him tighten as he looked at the number and imagined the implications.

He turned to Curt. "Please finish wrapping that head" he said quietly, then walked off to the telephone.

Dialing the number, he reluctantly held the receiver up to his ear. Audrey, the Boss's secretary, answered. She seemed to relish when the residents were in trouble, rarely smiling otherwise. "Dr. Todd wants to see you right away" she tittered.

"I'll be right up."

Dahlia stared at Alex as he hung up the phone, at his trapped look. She came over.

"What's going on?"

He looked at her with a weak smile. "The Boss wants to see me. Guess I've been on a streak lately."

"You'll be okay. You're the best one here and he knows that."

"All I want to do is finish." He looked at her. "You'll sign out to the others?"

She nodded. "See you later."

He turned around and walked toward the elevator. Curt had completed the head dressing and came out to Dahlia, whose gaze still followed Alex. Curt glanced at her and then towards Alex.

"Where's he going?"

"He has an appointment."

The elevator doors opened and several neurosurgical nurses came out. They giggled and greeted Alex, who nodded without speaking. He entered the elevator, turned around and looked at Dahlia. The elevator doors closed. Alex stared at the scratches on the elevator door.

He got off at the lobby and walked through the hall, nodding to the security guard leaning across the information desk with an air of negligent watchfulness. Going into the doctors' office building elevator, he again stared at the elevator doors as they closed, carefully examining the paint.

The doors opened and he walked out to a carpeted hallway lined with tasteful wallpaper. Walking to the end he opened the door into the neurosurgical offices. The waiting room was elegantly decorated and lined with chairs, glossy magazines on the tables. Several patients sitting there looked up as he entered, one of them a patient they had operated on for a spine problem the previous month.

"Hi, Dr. Alex" said the woman, brightly smiling.

He widened his cheeks a bit in an effort to smile. "How are you doing, Mrs. Anders?"

"Just terrific. Since you and Dr. Todd operated on me I've really felt great. The pain went right away."

"Glad to hear it." The woman's cheerfulness made him feel more morose. He went to the window where Nancy sat.

"Here to see Dr. Todd."

The girls were a sensitive barometer to the Boss's mood, and all the residents were attuned to their emanations. This morning it was clear there were problems. Nancy busied herself with paperwork, he eyes staying low. "You can go right in."

"Thanks."

Alex walked to the Boss's area. Audrey was behind her desk. She looked up at him, her narrow face and thin lips grimacing in what she thought was a sympathetic expression.

"He's ready."

Alex turned the corner and entered the Boss's office. The dark cherry desk, cherry shelves and dark green rug called a conditioned response from him, a gnawing tightness in his stomach. He pulled over a chair, the sound muffled by the heavy drapes. The yellow lamps by the desk and couch provided illumination without brightening the room. Not for the first time Alex wondered why the Boss used such low wattage bulbs, and inanely thought back to a resident telling him when he started how cheap the Boss could be.

Dr. Todd was seated at his dark and massive desk, his body turned to a side table while talking on the telephone. He signaled for Alex to sit as he continued. Sinking down, Alex examined the Boss's head in profile as it ponderously nodded.

The Boss listened and then chuckled, "I'll see you at the meeting in New York." Putting the phone down, he paused for a moment and then swung around to Alex. His cheerfulness abruptly vanished, his face a thick mask. "Close the door, please."

Alex jumped up and caught a glimpse of Audrey studiously working as he closed the door. Turning, he quickly sat down.

"Alex, you've got a problem." The Boss stared at Alex. "What's been going on with you lately? You're not yourself. First those judgment errors in the lab and in the operating room. Then the Board examination." Todd turned and looked at his bookshelves. He looked noble, professional. "We are descended from a line of neurosurgeons dating back to the beginning. We can trace our lineage directly from the first neurosurgeon. No one in this program has ever failed the Boards." He looked at Alex. His face and bullet-like head were yellowish in the light, the lines in his face emphasized by the illumination, forming daggerlike scars. "I'm concerned about you. You've got a great deal invested here in neurosurgery. You're forty years old."

"I don't know what happened with the Boards, Dr. Todd. I thought I did a good job. The questions were straightforward, my answers accurate. I just don't know what happened."

Todd stared at him. "What about the monkey in my lab? And the patient with the subdural?"

"I did what I thought was right given the circumstances, both for your patient and the monkey." Alex decided to take a chance. "I don't know what you were told but those are the facts."

Todd knew what Alex was implying. "Look Alex" he said irritably, "these are the facts. You are the chief resident and responsible for what goes on around here. If you can't handle it why should I have you? You've got another problem. We just received notification of a malpractice lawsuit over a case you participated in."

Alex looked startled, his eyes narrowed as he exhaled. More trouble. He was silent.

The Boss waited and looked at him. "You, Dahlia, and Jim Dobbs are named. It was Mrs. Hoffman, about six months ago. Do you remember her?"

"No."

"Well let me help you. She is a lady that you did a cervical laminectomy on. Says she's worse postoperatively."

"Now I remember her. An extremely tight canal. There was certainly a risk to the surgery and she understood that. We documented it well in the chart. In fact I think she mentioned to me that she was doing better."

"Well apparently her lawyer doesn't think so. She is represented by the best plaintiff malpractice law firm in the city. You've got your hands full on this one." He closed a file with a flick of his wrist as if distancing himself from it.

"Is the department named in it?" asked Alex.

"No."

"That should make it easier."

The Boss snorted. "Not for you. You better work on this one. The lawyer is a real tiger."

"The process is new to me. Who will be defending us?"

The Boss's eyes were blank. "The hospital will be getting you a lawyer. He will be in touch."

For a moment, the Boss glanced at his books. The volumes were neurosurgical classics written by pioneers in the field. His face was partly obscured by shadow and looked as if he was communing for advice with the giants of the past. He turned sorrowfully to Alex and folded his hands on the desk in the middle of the yellow puddle of light. "Alex, this really is not easy for me. I have a responsibility to the program, however. If these problems continue I will have no alternative even at your late stage of training. I know all the other program directors and you won't be able to find another training slot. I don't want to do it, but I have always been a disciple of the rules. We go by the book here."

Alex's heart thudded throughout his body. He could feel his fingertips throb with each beat, and heard the Boss from a distance, not believing the words. He had come so far with careful, constant, disciplined, dedicated work. The years of training, the years of college, medical school, internship and residency shot through his mind. The twenty-seventh grade, he thought bitterly, canned in the twenty-seventh grade. Dr. Todd looked at him mournfully. His whole countenance was one of sympathy and openness.

"It won't happen again, Dr. Todd. I've come too far."

Dr. Todd nodded sadly. The meeting was over.

"You still have interviews at Metropolitan Hospital. Good luck."

Alex got up weakly and walked out, looking sideways at the Boss, gazing sorrowfully at the bookshelves. His head pounding, ignoring Audrey as she looked up, he followed the trail of carpet between the desks to the door. The knob was steady and cool in his hand.

CHAPTER 18

The plane descended. Alex sat at the window as he usually did when on a flight, looking absently out, engrossed in the memory of the meeting with the Boss. Where was it coming from? What was going on?

The trip to investigate a potential job was a welcome respite. With the intention of continuing in an academic practice, he was visiting a university hospital in another state.

Metropolitan Hospital had an excellent reputation. It was in fact where the Boss had started out many years before, leaving to climb the academic ladder. Alex hoped that his connection with the Boss would provide him with an advantage at Metropolitan.

The plane dropped through a cloud layer and all was gray. Alex thought of one of his heroes, Charles Lindbergh, crossing the Atlantic in such weather, wondering whether his engine would hold together, calculating how many revolutions it was enduring.

They broke through the bottom of the clouds and the city below appeared. His mind turned to the upcoming interviews.

They landed at the airport and the plane taxied to the terminal. As Alex walked through the airport concourse ubiquitous televisions displayed the earnest and smooth visage of the President. People were gathered at many of the screens, and he stopped for a second.

The President looked stern and serious, then smiled with great warmth and concern. People drew up next to Alex on his right and left to watch and listen. Their uplifted faces, initially careworn, were entranced by the talking head. Alex could feel them nodding after a time.

Irritated at himself for stopping, he broke away and started walking. When he reached the end of the concourse he continued outside and hailed a taxi.

An old checkered cab the likes of which Alex had not seen for years pulled up. Big and boxy, Alex wondered whether it was the kind with extra folding seats, like the ones he had ridden in with his parents. He opened the door and with a burst of irrational pleasure saw the round little stools nestled into the floor. Throwing his suitcase in, he sat down on the smooth upholstery and stared at them, recalling how they worked.

Just as he bent to open one up, the cabby in front half turned to him. Alex studied his head, crowned with a ring of hair around the bald center, like a medieval monk. The man turned more, with effort, stretching his arm along the seatback, and Alex noticed his thumb and little finger missing, like a permanent Boy Scout salute.

Smiling, the cabby said in an Eastern European accented voice, "Where you going?"

Alex's gaze was drawn to his left eye, which kept wandering sideways. The right looked steadily at him. "Metropolitan Hospital."

"You got it."

They swung around and pulled out into the traffic. Alex was intrigued by the vehicle. "I haven't seen one of these babies around in a long time."

The cabby chuckled "You bet. This used to be my uncle's."

"How did you end up with it?"

"It's long story. I was born in southern Poland. My uncle had come to America years before and worked at different jobs, one of which was cab driver. We finally escaped and my family came here to join him."

"Wow" said Alex. "How do you like it here?"

"Great. It's a great country. Poland is beautiful place but the system stunk. Here I got my own business and making money."

"Yep" said Alex, "It's a great system."

"The only thing that's starting to bug me is bozo at the top."

"You mean the President?

"Yeah. It reminds me of good old days in communist Poland. He is all over on the TV, talking, bull-throwing, and people seem to believe him. The guy gives me the creeps."

"I know what you mean."

"Well, here you are."

Alex paid the cabby, and tipped him well.

"Thanks a lot."

Alex nodded, "Good luck." He took his suitcase and walked through the glass doors and to the reception desk.

"Department of Neurosurgery?"

"Fourth floor to your left."

"Thanks."

He took the elevator up and got out at the fourth floor. The hallway had a dingy look with yellowish wallpaper and old gray carpeting. He walked down the hall and found the door with "Department of Neurosurgery" lettered on it. Opening it, he went through the waiting room. Here also the faces of patients lifted towards him curiously and hopefully.

He went over to the sliding window behind which sat the receptionist, chattering to another worker. He finally caught her eye and smiled. She slid the window open. "Can I help you?"

"Dr. Alex Adams to see Dr. John Allen."

She looked at him. "I'll check with his secretary. Please have a seat." She walked over to another girl, who nodded as she spoke. They looked up at him and the receptionist called, "He'll be with you shortly."

He sat down, glancing around the room and quickly inspecting the other people. They returned his gaze with curiosity and then resumed their reading. The visage of the President grandly stared out at him from one newsmagazine, a serious mien with firm set of jaw. Underneath the picture was a headline entitled "Steady In The Face of Crisis." Alex opened the magazine and turned the pages, stopping at the cover story that related how the President was handling the latest imbroglio.

"He's doing a great job, ain't he?" said the man sitting two chairs to Alex's left, then his mouth twisted, emanating crunching sounds.

Alex looked up. The man had a thin, pinched face with closely cut gray hair. Alex quickly glanced at his scalp to see whether he could find a scar, to guess what the patient had. This was an old game for the residents.

The man seemed to read his thoughts, and smiled. "Yep, the doc operated on me and I'm as good as new. Here's the scar." He turned proudly and Alex could see a triangular incision at the back of his head.

Alex nodded encouragingly. "He's a good man, isn't he? The doc, not the President" he added quickly.

"Damn right."

"He'll see you now" the receptionist said through the open window.

Alex turned to the gentleman. "Good luck."

The man nodded back cheerfully and waved a tattooed forearm.

Alex walked through the waiting room, and the secretary ushered him into the Chief of Neurosurgery's office. Sitting down in a cream color leather chair, he was surprised by how light and airy the room was in comparison with Dr. Todd's space. Neurosurgical books were scattered throughout, as well as pictures of a woman and children.

Dr. Allen entered the room and Alex stood. He was a slim, short man with a thick and bushy head of brown hair, parted casually and spurting over his forehead. Smiling at Alex, he held out his hand. "John Allen."

"Alex Adams. Thanks for having me here."

"Pleased to have you. Let me just take a look at your stuff."

Dr. Allen sat down behind his desk and picked up a file, holding it like a hymnal in one hand, paging through it with the other. Alex lowered himself slowly, examining him as the doctor looked down, his hair fluttering like a mop being shaken.

"Well, you've got an interesting write-up. I'm not going to beat around the bush, I'm not that kind of guy. Dr. Todd says that you have a great deal of promise but lately you've gotten a little wobbly." He stared at Alex in an unexpectedly hard manner, his lips compressing.

Alex cleared his throat, gripping the wooden chair arms. "I've just done the best I could throughout the years. I still don't know what happened with the Board examination. You can see I passed the written part my first year."

Dr. Allen kept looking at him silently, for a long moment. "Let me give you some advice. You seem to be a good guy. Dr. Todd is a very powerful man. Just stay on his good side until you finish."

Alex nodded. "I know that he is very well thought of."

"I don't mean only neurosurgery. He's the real power behind the medical school, behind the university. They call him the shadow pope." Dr. Allen cackled. "The University is your city's pride and joy. It's the regional economic engine. He's on the board of the largest foundation in the country. He's friend with the Mayor. He's even acquainted with the President. You have no idea." He looked at Alex obliquely.

Alex nodded uncomfortably. "I just want to be the best neurosurgeon I can be."

The answer seemed to satisfy Dr. Allen. He glanced at the file again. "Let's look at your agenda for the rest of the day. You'll be meeting with Dr. Donovan. Good. He worked with Dr. Todd years ago. You'll also be meeting with the other staff members and taking a look at our operating rooms and the research labs. Talk to everybody and get a good picture of this place. Dr. Donovan is a good guy but" he lowered his voice conspiratorially, "he's getting up there in years and has his own ideas." He chuckled. "You'll find out."

Alex nodded and smiled. "Thanks very much, Dr. Allen. I'm looking forward to this visit."

They shook hands and Alex turned and left the office. The Chief looked thoughtfully out after him.

Dr. Allen's secretary met Alex at the door. She glanced at his schedule. "First stop, the operating room, then the research labs. You'll meet some of the faculty and residents there, then you'll see Dr. Donovan."

For the next several hours, Alex toured the hospital and its neurosurgical facilities. He ended up back at the Department office, where Dr. Allen's secretary greeted him again.

"I think it's time for Dr. Donovan."

She consulted his schedule. "Right you are." She took Alex down the hallway to a small office at the end. She knocked on the door and called, "Doctor?"

"Come in."

Alex walked into a cluttered small office. The Professor, a thin man wearing bifocals below a wrinkled forehead much bigger than his face, looked up curiously. Alex held out his hand.

"I'm Alex Adams."

Dr. Donovan had a strong grasp. "Glad to see you." He kept pumping Alex's hand vigorously as they both searched for something to say.

"I'll pick you up in about a half hour," said the secretary.

Alex nodded and pulled his arm away. "I'm here for a job interview."

"Oh, of course. Sit down."

Alex sat and looked around the cluttered office. Scientific papers were stacked everywhere, books jammed on shelves lining the walls. Every inch of space was taken by paper or a variety of skulls, grinning at him. A cave, he thought, a cave with ancient and new trophies, the skulls and the papers.

Dr. Donovan noticed Alex's gaze. "Quite an office, eh?" he chuckled. "They pushed me back here. I'm one of the senior faculty, i.e. on the way out" he chuckled again. "Only I'm not going yet." He looked at Alex over his bifocals, bending his head and wrinkling his broad brow.

Alex laughed.

"Now, where are you from?"

"University Hospital."

"University Hospital", he repeated, rolling his eyes. "Of course. Victor Todd is chairman there. He used to be here, you know."

"Yes. That's one of the reasons for me coming here."

"Quite, quite."

"Did you know Dr. Todd?"

"Of course. I'm the only one left from those days. That is," he became serious, "if you don't count Dr. Frey."

"Dr. Frey?"

"Very sad. He was on the faculty with Dr. Todd and myself. A good man. He and Todd didn't really get along, though, until he got sick, then Todd took care of him. Quite remarkable, really."

"How did he get sick?"

"Had a stroke, actually. Fairly sudden event. Had a gigantic row with Dr. Todd about something or other, then the next day had a terrible stroke. He couldn't communicate. Very agitated. I know Dr. Todd always felt guilty about it. He always thought that it was the argument that put him under such stress. Rubbish really, but it shows how Dr. Todd's heart works. Todd gave such a speech to the rest of us after it happened. He put his heart on his sleeve and there wasn't a dry eye in the place." His eyes narrowed, "Of course, nobody argued with Todd after that."

Alex frowned. "Is Dr. Frey still around?"

"Yes but he's a shut-in, I'm afraid."

"Could I see him, do you think?"

"He doesn't take visitors."

Alex noticed a slight edge to the doctor's voice, and his eyes seemed to harden.

"What was Dr. Todd like in those days?"

"Well, he was a pip, a real pip."

"How do you mean?"

"At first he was very quiet, you might even say mousy." Dr. Donovan settled back, sitting with his fingers opposed to each other, tapping them together.

"Dr. Todd?"

"Yes", he snickered. "Unbelievable, isn't it, what life does to people. In his first year here he was quiet. He was one of the early authorities and researchers in radiosurgery, you know. Quietly went about his work without much fuss and only one fellow to help him with the animals, kind of an odd duck."

"Odd? Was the man's name Weber?"

"Yes. Is he still with him?"

"He's devoted to him."

"Do tell. And yes, he did do a lot of work with chimps and radiation. Although what has come of it I can't say. At any rate, after a time Dr.

Todd did change. He developed a personality, one might say. Forceful, expressive, he became, and that's when he started having the difficulties with poor Frey." Falling silent, he looked at the floor.

Alex sensed it was time to leave. He arose, and then held out his hand. "Thanks very much. It was fascinating."

Dr. Donovan nodded affably, peering over his bifocals, grabbing Alex's hand with a skeletal clutch and pumping away. "Hope you come back. The place needs new blood and new brains" he chuckled, looked around and tapped his head. "All we have now are dried empty skulls."

Alex turned and left the cluttered office. He threaded his way back to the department office, going to Dr. Allen's secretary and waiting patiently until she glanced up.

"Well, that's it for me. Is Dr. Allen around?"

"No, he's not available at the moment. But he told me to say thanks for coming by."

"It was my pleasure. Please tell him I was very impressed."

She smiled. "Of course."

"Just one more thing. A long time ago you had a physician here, a Dr. Frey, I believe."

She nodded. "That was way before me" she giggled, "But I've heard of him."

"What was his first name?"

"Stephen."

"Thanks very much."

She nodded with a proforma smile.

Alex went through the waiting room and hallway, down the elevator and outside. There was a park across the street, with a fountain in the center, a gaudy affair ringed with charging stone horses. He crossed and sat down on a bench, listening to the water splashing, thinking of Dr. Allen's words. Must've talked with the Boss. Recently. What was going on? Why did things keep getting harder?

At the corner of his vision a movement startled him. A street person was plodding along, filthy gray pants with maroon stripes down the sides, old shoes, torn shirt and ancient stained overcoat. He walked leaning backwards, feet slapping on the ground after throwing them forwards, a peculiar mixture of backward and forward locomotion. Alex looked at his face, and his eyes. They vacantly roamed from side to side, and as he passed Alex idly wondered what his brain might look like.

Dahlia would say something sympathetic about the man, he thought. He recalled their conversation at her home, at the urgency in her face. They had to check things out. He had agreed to do it. Making a decision, he watched as the man wandered away.

Getting up, he went to a phone booth and called information. "Dr. Stephen Frey, please." He wrote down the number, and then dialed. A woman's voice answered.

"Hello." It was quiet, tentative.

"Mrs. Frey?"

"Yes."

"I'm Alex Adams, ma'am. I'm a neurosurgical resident interviewing for a job here at your husband's old hospital. If I could, I'd like very much to meet him. I've heard about him and read his papers."

"He's not well. He doesn't even speak. It's nice of you to call, but he doesn't see many people."

"If you think it wouldn't be too much, I would very much like to meet him."

"Well, maybe company would do him some good. He might be happy to see a resident. I suppose it would be alright."

"Thank you."

She gave him the address. He hailed a cab and rode to the house, a small home in an older suburban area. Different than the other dwellings, it was incongruously styled like a tiny castle with notches in a second story wall. Perfect for children playing knights, Alex thought.

He walked up to a brown door of an old fashioned kind, with wood framed panes behind which was a sheer curtain on rods stretched top to bottom. After knocking, he waited, and a shape came into view through the gauzy veil. The door opened and woman of about sixty appeared, thin and alert, bright eyes canvassing him, throat encased by a frilly shirt buttoned high up.

"I'm Margaret Frey."

"Alex Adams. Thanks very much for the chance to meet Dr. Frey."

"Well, like I said, he can't talk since his stroke years ago. I do think he would enjoy a visit but you can't stay long" she ended warningly.

As he stepped in, a smell of another time enveloped him, and they walked through a quiet, musty hallway lined with black-framed pictures of white-coated doctors. Alex stopped. "Who's this group?"

"That was the Metropolitan Hospital Neurosurgery Department years ago."

"Dr. Todd?" Alex pointed at a surprisingly diffident looking man, slouching and looking away from the camera.

Mrs. Frey swallowed. "Yes. How do you know him?"

"He's my Boss."

"Oh, he's a Chairman now. Funny, he didn't seem like that type of man when he started here. Stephen always thought of him as a bit mousy initially, and later on they really didn't get along at all. They had a big argument." She seemed to deflate, and it pained Alex that he had triggered this distress. "I think there was some kind of jealousy between my husband and Dr. Todd. Of course that ended when he had a stroke and Dr. Todd took care of him. He was a dedicated physician. My husband was very agitated in the early days and frequently would get most upset with Dr. Todd, although he couldn't speak. Dr. Todd said this was a common reaction to a stroke that affects communication."

Alex kept looking at the picture. "Who are these guys?"

"That's Rene, one of the radiation technicians. The other man, I don't know."

Alex looked carefully at the narrow face with its squinty look. "I think I do. That's Weber, Dr. Todd's assistant. He's been with him for many years."

Mrs. Frey led him down the carpeted hallway, and his belly tightened as he looked ahead to the dark closed door. Knocking softly, she opened the door slightly and called in.

"Dad, there's a visitor for you. A doctor. Dr. Adams, a neurosurgical resident."

She entered, and turned and beckoned to him. Following, he saw a man in bed propped up with pillows, holding his right arm stiffly in front of him with a large, veined left hand. At one time he must have been a powerful specimen, though now his skin hung in folds on face and neck, white collar buttoned to the top but loose around his wrinkled throat. The neck supported a magnificent square head, deep brown eyes, large thin nose, and wide mouth. Dr. Frey looked at him expectantly.

"Dr. Frey, I'm Dr. Alex Adams."

He stared at Alex, then blinked slowly.

"I'm interviewing at Metropolitan Hospital for a job. They mentioned that you used to work there. I thought I would drop by and say hello."

Dr. Frey continued to stare at him, his mouth turned down in sadness, then nodded.

A painful silence. Alex regretted the visit.

"Stephen, this doctor is being trained by Dr. Todd."

With that he seemed to wake up. He held up his left arm, and Alex grasped it strongly. Dr. Frey's eyes opened wider, first looking deeply into his, and then to his wife. He pointed to the closet. She sighed, "I don't know what you want."

He pointed again, his hand tremulous, each finger shaking independently like pistons firing randomly.

"Okay, I'll look."

She opened the door, and rummaged around. "I don't see much of anything."

He became more agitated.

"Okay, okay. I'll walk you over."

With tenderness she helped him up, his large hand grasping her small shoulder, and they plodded over to the closet. He looked in, bending as his wife held him, then stretching so much that Alex came over and steadied him as well. With his left hand he took a large manila envelope from deep inside the closet.

"I've never opened that," said Mrs. Frey nervously to Alex.

They helped him back, and Dr. Frey sat down heavily in bed, manipulating the envelope. He pulled out the scan and thrust it towards

Alex. Tired by this effort, the doctor laid back and closed his eyes, then opened them, slit like, and peered at Alex.

Taking the black plastic sheet out, Alex examined it. A CT scan dated ten years before, of Dr. Stephen Frey. He looked at the old doctor, who continued to squint intently at him.

"Your CT scan" said Alex unnecessarily. The doctor nodded.

Alex walked over to the window and held the scan up to the light.

Mrs. Frey looked concerned. "I didn't know he still had that. His doctors wouldn't be happy. They thought it might unnecessarily upset him."

Alex looked skeptical as he lowered the film and turned to her. "What doctor didn't want him to have this?"

"Why, your own Dr. Todd."

Alex paused, and then held the film up to the window again. The CT scan showed an area on the left side of the brain to be darker than normal.

Mrs. Frey fluttered, "How does it look? What does it show?"

Alex angled it so that she could see, then started his standard explanation. "These are slices of the brain, as if we put them in a salami slicer and sliced his head." She looked momentarily startled but he continued. "We're looking from the top down. Here is the skull, the solid white shell, and the brain, this grayish area. These dark areas in the center of the brain are ventricles, the fluid filled areas of the brain. Everybody's got them, they're normal" he nodded reassuringly to her. "But here's the stroke." He pointed to a circular area of darkness in the left brain, staring for a time. "Only."

"Only what?"

"Well it's just more well defined than the usual stroke."

"What do you mean by that?"

"Its edges are sharper than usually seen with a stroke and it's rounder, very round." He examined it, film steady in his hand, deep in thought. "An unusual configuration. Strokes don't generally look like this."

He was startled to hear a moan. Turning around, he saw that Dr. Frey had propped himself up and had been listening intently. At Alex's last words he tried to say something, but only groans came out, painfully slow. His great head bent with the effort, his eyes watered and then tears came. Mrs. Frey held his hands.

"There there, Dad. There there. I haven't seen him this upset for awhile."

"It's okay, Dr. Frey." Alex tried to comfort the agitated man, who was reaching for his CT scan. Alex put it down, wondering whether it would disturb him more to look at it again.

"Shush, Stephen. Shush." Mrs. Frey put her arm around his shoulder. "It's okay." The doctor closed his watery eyes in frustration, at his inability to communicate. He started to sob as his head bent forward, then a small, clear shaft of saliva fell to the bedcovers, continuous and unbroken. His long face became red, and he closed his eyes in a paroxysm of sadness. Tears fell, drop by drop, contrasting with the steady stream of saliva. Mrs. Frey, a paper towel apparently permanently placed in her hand, tenderly wiped the stream of saliva, then patted his eyes with the soaked towel.

Alex felt it was time to leave. Maybe that would calm the doctor down. He looked around the room, his eyes falling on some newsmagazines with the President on the cover.

"Hand me one, please" said Mrs. Frey, following his gaze. "I get them for him. He likes to page through, even though I'm not sure how much he understands. He can't even write."

"Here, Dr. Frey. I'm going now," he said as the doctor lay back in bed with his eyes closed, his wife like a lean and aging lioness perched next to him. He picked up a magazine and put it in her outstretched hand.

"Dr. Frey, I'm going," he said again. "Thanks very much."

Dr. Frey opened his eyes slowly, looked at Alex, and then at the magazine in his wife's hand. Glancing at the cover, he looked at it more closely, then glared at Alex with frightening intensity. He let out an anguished cry, swinging his good arm up and around in a huge arc. Groaning again, the loose flesh of his neck twisting and powerful mouth straining impotently, his eyes blazed at Alex as he pointed at the picture of the President.

Mrs. Frey looked at him in alarm. "I think you'd better go."

"Thanks very much Dr. Frey. Thank you ma'am." He didn't know what else to say. "I'll show myself out. Do you mind if I use your phone to call a cab?"

They both looked at him, her arms around his shoulders. She nodded wearily.

"There's one in the hallway."

Dr. Frey slumped back into bed, exhausted.

Alex walked quietly out of the room, found the phone, called and requested a cab. He could hear Mrs. Frey quietly speaking to her husband, so soft only the soothing tone was audible, the words lost. Letting himself out of the house, he blinked in the bright sunlight.

After getting back to his room, he lay down on the bed and dialed the phone.

Mrs. Frey answered. "Hello."

"Mrs. Frey, it's Alex Adams. I just wanted to know how Dr. Frey is doing."

"Oh. Much better. He's quieted down now and is resting. I still don't know what it was all about. He threw that magazine off his lap after you left like he never wanted to see it again."

"I hope you don't mind, but I took the CT scan. I just wanted a better look at it."

"Why no, I guess not, just send it back when you're finished."

"Just one more thing, ma'am. Do you know where Rene is living?"

"Rene?"

"The technician in the picture we looked at. In your hallway. "

"Oh, no."

"Do you remember his last name?"

"Rene, Rene Ralston I believe."

"Thanks very much ma'am. I'm glad the doctor is feeling better."

"Goodbye."

He hung up the phone. He paused for a moment, then set up his notebook computer.

Tapping keys, he found a locator website, entering Rene's name and approximate age, then hit the return key. No hits.

He stared at the computer. Damn high tech stuff. No use here. How could he find Rene?

Dialing information, he found the number for Metropolitan Hospital, then called and asked for the Radiation Therapy Department.

"Director, please."

"One moment."

"Hello, Judy Toms here."

"Ms. Toms, this is Dr. Alex Adams. I'm trying to locate a technician who worked in your department years ago. Rene Ralston."

"Hmm, don't remember any body by that name. Hold on and let me ask the techs"

Silence.

"Hello, Dr. Adams"

"Yes"

"I've spoken with Chris, the girl who's been here the longest. She remembers hearing the name, but they never met. Doesn't know anything about him."

"Thanks very much."

"You're welcome."

Alex hung up the phone, then lay down again and looked at the ceiling. Then he remembered. The father of a patient at University Hospital, a girl who he had operated on for a head injury, was a private detective. His last words to Alex were, 'Doc, if you ever need anything give me a call. You saved my daughter's life.'

Alex remembered the name, called information, and got the number.

"Hello, Mallow detective agency."

"Mr. Mallow, please. This is Dr. Adams."

"I'll see if he's in."

Alex waited.

"Dr. Adams?"

"Hi, Mr. Mallow. Remember me?"

"Of course, Doc. How ya doing?"

"Good. How's your daughter?"

"Great, thanks to you. What can I do for you? Wife running around on you?"

"No, no. I just need to find somebody."

"That's our specialty."

"I'm here interviewing at Metropolitan Hospital. I need to find a Rene Ralston, about forty-five, used to work there until about five years ago."

"Any other information? A description?"

"I just saw a picture of him from years ago. Medium height, build, brown hair."

"OK. That narrows it down. Heh, heh. It's good you're not a detective, doc. Let me work on this. How can I get back to you?"

"I'm at the Regency Hotel, room 2303."

"Sounds good. We're on the case."

Alex hung up the phone, his hand resting on the smooth plastic. He thought of the images he had just seen at Dr. Frey's home, the gray figures, standing, looking into the future. He thought of Dr. Todd, how different he looked back then. What changed him? What had happened to Dr. Frey? Why did he get so agitated at the magazine with the President's picture? The Boss said he had treated the President for back pain. What was the connection?

He spent the evening in his room, treating himself to room service, then turned in early.

The phone rang the following morning. Alex, thinking it was his wake up call, answered it in a perfunctory fashion.

"Hello."

"Doc?"

"Hello?"

"It's Mallow."

"Oh, thanks for getting back to me." Alex sat up in bed wide awake.

"Well, I got your information."

"Terrific."

"He still lives in the city you're at. The river district. Address is sixty-three Front Street."

"Thanks very much."

"Glad to do it for you, Doc. Call me if you need anything else."

Alex showered, dressed, packed, and went down to the lobby desk.

City maps were there; taking one, he found Front Street. Checking out, he picked up his suitcase and went outside where the doorman hailed a cab.

As they approached Rene's home, the houses, at first neat, became seedier and less well tended, with flaking paint and unkempt lawns. Finally the cab stopped and the driver nodded at a house, a small brick bungalow with a tilting antenna precariously attached to the chimney.

"There it is. That'll be six-fifty."

Alex counted out the money. "Can you wait here 'til I give you a wave? I'm not sure he's at home."

"Can't stay long."

Alex picked up his suitcase and walked up the narrow cracked walk. The tall grass was peppered with lighter patches, like vitilago. His knock on the flaking door started the sound of barking, and as the door opened cautiously a bald, potbellied man came into view, then bent to reassure a scruffy dog. As the man straightened up, cane in hand, Alex took him in. He looked like a giant, aging frog, lips protruding, bulging cheeks flaccid, head resting back on humpy shoulders, bulky shapeless torso mounted on bandy splayed legs, small eyes darting under half closed eyes. His most impressive feature, though, was a poorly fitting wig perched uncertainly on his cranium, bearing a resemblance to the threadbare pelt of an ancient chinchilla. Alex was fascinated.

"Mr. Ralston?"

"Yeah."

"I'm Dr. Adams, a neurosurgeon from Metropolitan Hospital."

"What the hell do you want?"

The cab beeped. Alex turned and waved, and it drove off.

"Well, I work with Dr. Todd. I had some questions about how they did things in those days."

"Sorry. That was a long time ago." He started to close the door.

"Mr. Ralston, I'm not trying to make trouble. You look like you've had enough."

"Yeah, I'm on disability. Back injury."

"Look, I'm just a resident. In training. I was in town for an interview. I had some extra time, and got to thinking how my boss did things in the old days, when he was here. He's the Chairman now. He's a famous guy. I was curious as to how he got started."

Rene looked at him for a time, then nodded. "OK. It's just that I have to be careful. Come on in."

Alex opened the door and walked into the small living room, a decrepit old couch along one dirty wall.

"Have a seat."

"Thanks."

Alex gingerly sat down, wondering whether any microscopic creatures were waiting to jump on him. Ralston moved slowly, leaning heavily on his cane as he shuffled to a prostrate chair opposite Alex, then lowered himself. He looked at Alex expectantly, gripping his cane with both hands, his haunches spread out like he was sitting on a lily pad.

"Did Dr. Todd use radiation much in those days?"

"He sure did. He did a helluva lot of experiments with dogs and monkeys. We must've radiated a whole zoo's worth. He'd always have another one for us to do. It was a real pain in the ass. But the doc was always very gentle and appreciative. At least in the beginning. Never demanding."

"Dr. Todd?"

"Yeah, early on he was that way. Then he changed, slowly at first, then quick. He got to be a real son of a bitch."

"How do you mean?"

"For a while he used me a lot, as the tech. Then he started getting busier off-hours, and got a helper. Nasty bugger." He scratched his head, and Alex hoped he wouldn't dislodge the toupee.

"Weber?"

"Yeah, I think that was his name. Very nasty. Tough guy. The doc and him just made themselves at home in the radiation department after hours, even though he was a neurosurgeon, not a radiation specialist. When we complained to our department head, he just shrugged. He didn't want to make waves, and Todd and Weber kept to themselves." Ralston shifted uncomfortably as he spoke, holding his hand on his head, stubby fingers splayed over his forehead like a spider starting to descend. "How'd his research turn out? Did it mean much?"

Alex looked at the man thoughtfully, then shrugged. "Like I said, he's Chairman now. I don't know how useful his research was, though."

The room was silent.

Ralston looked at his cane. "I was just wondering. Don't do much anymore. Kind of miss working, but just can't."

Alex nodded, then stood up. "Well, thanks very much."

"That's it?"

"Yep, I was just curious about the old days."

"Well, suit yourself." Rene stood up cautiously, leaning on his cane, then thought of something. "Wait a minute. I have something that might interest you." He slowly made his way out of the room, and Alex could hear him rummaging. Limping back, he held a large, dirty brown envelope.

"Here's one of our original dose plans, for the monkeys." He handed it to Alex.

"Thanks very much. This is from Dr. Todd's work?"

"Yep. I saved it. He'd probably kill me if he knew, he was so damn careful and secret about everything. Like I said, he only worked with us day people for a short time, then did everything in the evening with that guy, what was his name?"

"Weber."

"Yeah. At any rate, I was curious in those days. I picked up this dose plan one day and thought I'd get it back to him, but I never did."

"Why were you curious?"

"Well, up 'til that time I hadn't done any animals. I liked to visit them, and Weber let me for a time."

"Did they change after they were radiated?"

"Well, not in any big way. Weber claimed that the ones we buzzed seemed to be a little more pushy with the others, but I never could see it. Didn't seem to make much difference. Then Todd stopped doing the monkeys."

"What did he do after that?"

"Well, this is where it gets a little odd. He stopped doing the monkeys, and we never saw him or Weber again in the department. Once in a while, though, we just had the feeling someone was using the radiation machine at night. Nothing for sure, but just a feeling. The table would be set at a slightly different angle, the gantry slightly rotated, but nothing you could hang your hat on."

Alex waited, but Rene was finished.

"Well, thanks very much. I hope things work out with your back."

Ralston shrugged. "They want to fuse my spine, but I'm not ready for that."

They shook hands and Alex walked out of the house. Remembering, he turned halfway down the walk. Rene was still at the door, his belly protruding out from under his tee shirt, gaze unblinking as if waiting for a fly.

"Can you call me a cab? I've got to get to the airport."

"Sure."

The door closed and Alex went down the walk. He paced along the street, pondering, then opened the greasy envelope, holding the film up to the light. It was a treatment diagram of the brain, with the radiation dose placed above the optic chiasm. He stared at the film, growing cold. The basal forebrain, he thought. Why the hell was the Boss treating there? A car passed, and he looked around quickly, then felt foolish. Putting the plan back into the envelope, he slid it carefully into his suitcase and paced up and down, waiting for the cab.

CHAPTER 19

Alex wondered how Fran could move so fast, scuttling towards him with urgent energy, her face compressed with concern. She thrust her face inches from his, and Alex caught a whiff of her breath, transporting him back in time to the small mammal house at the zoo he used to visit. "The Boss has been looking for you. Didn't you answer your beeper?"

"I haven't gotten any beeps lately. Come to think of it, I haven't got any in a while." He slid the beeper from the holder on his belt and looked at the small screen, which was completely blank. "Damn. The battery's dead. I was on that job interview trip, never noticed it. Great."

He grabbed a phone and dialed the Boss's number. Audrey answered, recognizing his voice. "The Boss has been looking for you. Why haven't you answered?"

"My battery is dead."

"You're going to be dead too. Here he is." Alex felt his heart flip, wondering whether his blood pressure dropped as well. The pause seemed forever.

"Alex, get up here right away." The tone was staccato and harsh, the Boss hanging up without a reply. Alex looked at the phone's dirty buttons, then put the handpiece down slowly. He looked up and found Fran staring at him, her mouth agape.

"Fran, close your mouth. You look like a fish."

She shut her mouth quickly, hurt, but kept staring. She looked after him grimly as he reflexively started trotting up the hallway, disappearing into the elevator.

Audrey ushered him into Dr. Todd's office. The Boss was standing, holding a book open in his hands and turning a page, his thick fingers grasping the thin paper like a vise crushing a flower petal. He turned immediately, the book still open and close to his chest.

"Alex, let's get one thing straight. If you aren't going to do the work you're out of here."

Audrey backed out quickly and silently, closing the door.

"Dr. Todd, my battery was dead."

"Not good enough, Alex. Let me make it clear." He slowly set the book down on his desk as if it were volatile. "You've got one more chance. You answer your beeper within five minutes or you're out of here. Do you understand?"

Alex nodded, silent.

The Boss turned around. The interview was over.

Alex spun about, reached for the doorknob and walked out, looking straight ahead.

CHAPTER 20

Alex woke up as the alarm pealed out in the darkroom, rolling to look at the glowing numbers. Five A.M. As usual, his brain spun into action, reminding him of the maelstrom he was somehow being drawn into. His head was bothering him again, a constricting band of pain from the back of his skull to his eyes. The tea would help.

Swinging out of bed, he showered, made some tea and left. As he drove, his mind turning and his head aching, he reached down to the glove compartment, took out a baby aspirin bottle, flipped off the top and dumped out four pink tablets. Chewing them, he thought of his MR brain scan with relief. At least that was normal.

Parking the car, he trotted into the hospital. At the call room he quickly checked his slot in the residents' mailbox, expecting the usual photocopied announcements and drug company junk. A business size envelope was jammed in, though, and he drew it out with his slim, strong fingers. "Department of Neurosurgery, University Hospital" was the return address.

Staring at it for a time, he turned it in his hands, then opened the envelope quickly. Pulling out the letter, on departmental stationery, he unfolded it and looked at the signature first. "Dr. Victor Todd." He took a deep breath and started reading.

"Dear Dr. Adams,

It has come to my attention that you have not been responding to your beeper. The demands of patient care require the residents to be in constant communication with the nursing staff and other caregivers. This is truly a life and death issue. Lack of responsiveness to your beeper will not be tolerated.

If another incident occurs where you do not respond to your beeper within five minutes I will have no choice but to remove you from the program.

Sincerely,

Victor Todd, M.D., F.A.C.S."

Alex stared at the concrete block wall of the small room. What is going on? He slumped back. Why had it come to this?

His beeper went off. Jumping up, he dialed the number for the ICU. Dahlia answered.

"Hey, where are you? We should be getting started."

"Right. I'll be right over."

"Okay."

He put the letter in his white coat pocket and opened the door, walking around to the ICU and going to the bedside of the first patient.

Dahlia, Curt and Richard were already there. He barely looked at them before grabbing the patient's bedside chart and examining it.

"How's Mr. Cullen doing?" He turned to the patient's nurse. "Is he following commands?"

She looked puzzled. "Yes" she said slowly, not quite understanding why he asked.

"That's good." He absentmindedly nodded.

Dahlia broke in. "Well, he better be following commands. He's not a head case. He just had spine surgery yesterday. He's in the ICU because the internist wanted to watch his heart."

"Oh yeah, you're right."

Dahlia and Curt exchanged glances.

Alex's beeper went off again. He knew what it announced. "Time for clinic. Curt, you and Richard come with me. Dahlia, can you finish rounds?"

"What's going on?" said Dahlia, staring steadily at him.

Alex hesitated and then turned to Curt. "I'll meet you guys down there." They departed. He turned to Dahlia. "Nothing is going on."

"You're not yourself."

"I have to get down to clinic."

"Alex, please."

"I don't have time, Dahlia." He hesitated, then pulled the letter from his pocket and gave it to her. "Look at this." He shook his head. "I don't know where this stuff is coming from."

Turning, he walked quickly down the hall, taking the stairs three at a time to the clinic.

Ginny was waiting for him. A pleasant veteran of twenty years of nursing, she maintained her good cheer in the face of many obstacles. Curt and Richard were there as well.

"Good morning, doctor."

"Morning, Ginny."

"We have Mr. Merrill Darret for you in room three."

"Thanks."

He took the chart and scanned it rapidly. Mr. Darret had a tumor in the area of the brain that interpreted the emotional content of speech and facial expressions. In spite of the Boss's letter, Alex's interest stirred. This was something more than the usual run-of-the mill blood clot in the brain or pinched nerve in the spine problem.

"Curt, look at this." Curt and Richard came closer. "Here's a fifty year old gentleman with a brain tumor in an important area. Where does the brain interpret the emotional content of speech and facial expression?"

Curt looked serious for a moment, thought for a while, then shrugged.

"Sorry."

Alex sighed. "Richard?"

"The left frontal area of the brain?"

"No. The left frontal area of the brain controls speech." He thought briefly of Dr. Frey, then paused. "Prosody, or the ability to determine the emotional content of speech and human expression, is located in the right frontal area."

Curt and Richard both nodded.

"Put the MRI scan up, Curt."

Curt struggled to put the plastic sheets up in the proper order.

"No, no, Curt. Put them up so that you can read their name," Alex said irritably.

Curt made another awkward attempt, then stood back, proud of his effort.

"Where is the tumor?" Alex turned to Richard, who eagerly scrutinized the pictures. He kept staring intently but silently, imitating the clinicians he had seen, until Alex became impatient.

"Curt? Do you see the lesion?"

Curt examined the films with exaggerated care. "Here?" He pointed tentatively to one panel.

"Yep. Good job. On the right side you see signal changes in the front of the temporal area of the brain. Not much swelling and no real mass effect present. What kind of a tumor do you think it is, Curt?"

He studied the films again. "Uh, glioma?"

"Yes, that's exactly right. It's in the substance of the brain, likely coming from one of the brain's own cell types. The most common of the intrinsic brain tumors is of course . . ." He paused, hoping they would answer.

They looked helplessly at him. "Glioma" Curt blurted.

"Right."

Alex turned and knocked at the patient's room.

"Come in, it's your place."

Alex opened the door, and then walked in briskly. Mr. Darret was perched on the examining table, skinny shoulders overhanging a sunken chest, thin arms gripping the soft edge. As he looked up with a hollow cheeked gaze, his Adams apple stuck out more from his curved neck, and his dangling legs swung. A giant vulture, Alex thought, sitting like he was on a bare and lifeless branch silhouetted against a gray sky.

"Good morning, Mr. Darret. I'm Dr. Alex Adams, this is Dr. Curt Smith, and Richard Walters, a medical student."

He paused. The patient looked at him expectantly.

Alex turned to the woman sitting in the single corner chair.

"Hello." He offered his hand and bowed slightly. "Dr. Todd will be in shortly." He spoke to both of them. "I'm the chief resident. I've looked at your chart and we've reviewed your MRI scans. I've got an idea of what brings you here, but please tell me in your own words what's been going on."

Mr. Darret glanced at his wife, then cleared his throat. "Well, it started out with a headache, then I had a little weakness in my right hand." His voice was flat, mechanical, emanating from an immobile mask, but his eyes darted around hyperkinetically from face to face, like a solitary soldier defending the ramparts of a castle.

His wife nodded helpfully, "He never had any problems until a couple of weeks ago when he said his hand didn't work right. I couldn't see anything. We went to the family doctor, who got a CT scan, then an MRI, and now we're here." Alex was fascinated by her jutting teeth, sticking out so far it looked like some small but powerful oral explosion had blown them outward.

Just then the door abruptly opened and Dr. Todd strode in. He ignored Alex, Curt and Walter and offered his hand to Mr. Darret, who gazed at him curiously from his perch.

"Hello, Merrill, I'm Dr. Todd, Chairman of Neurosurgery. How are you?" Todd leaned forward, his face a picture of concentration and concern, frowning in his solicitude.

"Okay, Victor." The patient continued to stare at Todd, who paused for a moment at the use of his first name, then turned to the patient's wife and bowed. "Dr. Todd, ma'am."

She fluttered a bit and shook his hand as well.

He turned again to Mr. Darret. "I reviewed your MRI scan, Mr. Darret," he said in a deep, resonant voice. "My recommendation would be an operation, followed by possible radiation therapy" nodding with every word.

Mrs. Darret looked at Dr. Todd. "Is it cancerous?"

He patted Mrs. Darret's arm. "Too early to tell. We would take a specimen during surgery, analyze it, and would know for sure what it is after a couple of days."

"Surgery? Brain surgery? I don't like the sound of that," said Mrs. Darret. "How risky is it?"

"It's riskier not to do it. This will just keep growing, and we better deal with it now rather than wait." He brought down both large hands suddenly in front of him like two massive meat cleavers.

Mrs. Darret's eyes widened, and she gasped.

Mr. Darret stared at Todd thoughtfully. "We will think about it. Thanks very much, Dr. Todd." He pronunciation was careful and slow, like he was trying to hug each word.

The Boss looked somewhat surprised at the tone of dismissal, and the rapidity with which the patient had responded.

"Very well. Dr. Adams here" his great head inclined towards Alex, "will complete your examination and answer further questions. We're available to help at any time."

"Thanks again" nodded Mr. Darret. His wife smiled uncertainly as Dr. Todd shook her hand again, then wheeled around and left the room.

"So that's your Boss?" said Mr. Darret to Alex, flatly.

Alex nodded. He had been watching Mr. Darret's eyes as they inspected Dr. Todd.

"He's famous," said Curt eagerly.

"No doubt" said Mr. Darret. He looked at his wife. "There's something funny about him."

"Now, dear."

He looked at Alex. "There's something that doesn't fit. He's too smooth."

His wife laughed uncomfortably. "He's not himself these days, Dr. Adams. He says the oddest things. He was just saying some peculiar things about the President."

Mr. Darret nodded. "This guy reminds me of the President. Very smooth, very very smooth. Only, nothing underneath it. No substance. No heart" he said evenly and unemotionally.

"Oh dear" Mrs. Darret fluttered again and shifted in her chair.

Alex's gaze shifted from Mrs. to Mr. Darret. "Well, we better finish the exam." He quickly completed the testing, checking strength, sensation, reflexes, walk and cranial nerves. As he automatically worked, he mulled over the patient's words.

Finished, he looked into Mr. Darret's eyes. "You check out okay on examination. I think we caught this early," he said hastily, slapping him on the knee.

Mr. Darret nodded, "You mean I'll be dead in a year?" he said quietly.

Alex was startled. He had been thinking of Mr. Darret's future, that with his particular type of tumor, surgery and radiation would help, but certainly would not cure. It was as if he spoke his thoughts aloud.

Alex glanced at Mrs. Darret, who was looking at her husband with love and concern.

"Now, dear."

Mr. Darret looked at Alex. "Don't worry doc. I'll do whatever you say. You've got a soul, I can see that. That other character, he's got nothing. I can see that too. Just like that bozo the President. He's empty inside. But he talks the talk, and people follow him like the pied piper." His words came out of him slowly, in a measured cadence, as he stared at Alex and then held out his hand.

"We'll be in touch."

Alex nodded and shook his hand. "Nice to meet you. We'll stand by. If you want us to proceed with the operation, let us know."

Mr. Darret turned to his wife. "Let's go dear." They both got up, and she looked at Alex.

"Thank you."

She held her husband's elbow, and they went out of the room.

Alex turned to watch them, his head bent in thought.

"Queer bird" said Curt.

"He didn't like the Boss, that's for sure," said Richard. "And the Boss didn't like him using his first name."

"The Boss told me once, never let a patient call you by first name. The role confusion is too great. His only exceptions were those patients who have six months or less to live" Alex absently said as he replayed the man's words in his mind.

Ginny appeared at the door. "Let's go, doctors. More patients to see."

They filed out of the room. Alex grabbed another chart from the rack in the wall, and they continued in clinic for the rest of the morning.

After they had finished with the last patient, Alex walked over to the counter where he had laid down Mr. Darret's scan. He picked up the envelope, slid the film out and put it on the light box once again, looking at it, looking at the temporal lobe of the brain, wondering, thinking of the man's words. Here was a man who was not affected by any emotional message, by any emotional intonation, gesture or expression.

His beeper went off. He looked at the phone number. The call room. He dialed the number.

"Hello." It was Dahlia.

"Hi, it's me."

"That's a hell of a note."

For moment Alex couldn't fathom what she was talking about. "The what?"

"The letter you got from the Boss."

"Oh, yeah." He remembered the threatening letter, and his stomach sagged. "The noose is getting tighter."

"You're right. I just got a call from Audrey. She said there was a lawyer man there to see us. Our ace defense counsel. You remember, the malpractice lawsuit."

Alex groaned, "Great timing. I get that letter this morning, we just finished clinic, the OR starts this afternoon and we've got to talk to this guy. Great."

She chirped, "Don't worry. Audrey said he seems like a real softy."

"Terrific. Just what we needed to defend us."

"I'll meet you at the office."

Alex hung up. He turned to Curt, who was studying the films next to him.

"Curt, I've got an appointment. I'll touch base with you in a little while."

"What?"

"I have a date with a lawyer. One of the fun parts of the job."

"Now?"

"Yep."

Alex turned and left.

CHAPTER 21

They entered the Department of Neurosurgery suite, trying to avoid glancing into the Boss's office. Audrey looked up.

"Mr. Gilson is in the conference room" she snickered. "You can thank the Boss for this one. He saw him at the hospital ball. Told me he knew instantly this was the lawyer for Alex."

Alex nodded glumly.

"Then Dr. Hackman wants to talk to you."

"He'll have to get in line." Alex and Dahlia went into the conference room.

At the end of the table sat the lawyer. Mr. Gilson stood as they entered the room, rising diffidently and tentatively, a man in his early sixties of medium height, with thinning hair combed over pink scalp. His round flushed face smiled shyly, watery pale blue eyes squinting behind salmon colored plastic frame glasses. His suit was baggy, one grayish-white shirt collar sticking over the wide lapel.

"Dr. Alex Adams?" he held out his hand.

"Hello, Mr. Gilson." His grasp was boneless.

He looked at Dahlia.

"Dahlia Laronge." She held out her small, thin hand. He bowed slightly and took it. For a moment Alex thought he was going to kiss it.

"Very nice to meet you, I'm sure," he said in a delicate, precise way. They stood awkwardly for a moment and then all sat down.

"I've been asked by Dr. Todd to represent you in this matter. Have either of you been in a lawsuit before?"

They shook their heads and waited expectantly. Alex reflexively inspected the man's cranium, trying to classify the head. Finally he hit upon it. A coconut, that's right, a coconut. Thin hair stretched over a big pink coconut.

Mr. Gilson continued. "This lawsuit is a bit unusual in that the plaintiff is actually a friend of Dr. Todd's."

Alex leaned forward, then looked at Dahlia.

"Yes, apparently Dr. Todd saw her at the hospital ball. She complained to him and somehow it turned into a lawsuit." He sighed, the padded shoulders of his old fashioned suit muffling the motion. "I must confess I find it a bit unusual, but" he paused, "here we are" and smiled wanly.

He looked at each of them, but they said nothing. "The standard warnings include, of course, don't alter any record and don't discuss this with anyone."

Alex took a deep breath. He was stunned to find out how the lawsuit had apparently started. "What does the complaint allege?"

Mr. Gilson frowned, and his eyebrows looked like two commas facing each other. "Oh, the usual about incompetent care, needless pain and suffering. We'll get into that in due time. At this point I just wanted to meet with you and discuss these preliminary considerations." ·

Dahlia asked, "Has Dr. Dobbs been notified?"

"A letter has been sent to him. I haven't met with him yet."

"Should we say anything to him on this?"

"No, as I told you earlier, don't discuss this with anyone."

Silence in the room.

"Well, I'll keep you informed. Mr. Gilson arose and again faintly smiled. "Nice to meet you all." He nodded, gathered his papers into an old leather satchel, wrapping it carefully with leather straps, and left the room.

Alex looked at Dahlia. "Great. Our legal bulldog. With a World War Two era secret courier briefcase."

"He seems like a nice man."

Alex snorted, then turned in his chair as Hackman entered, his lips pursing as his head bobbed, then came to rest as he leaned against the bookshelf.

"The Boss asked me to tell you that he thinks there's negligence in this case."

"Negligence?"

"Yeah . . . he said consider settling."

"Negligence? Consider settling? What does he mean? What are the facts as he understands them?"

"I have no idea."

"Can't he even tell me? What is the problem? Why does he think negligence occurred?"

"Don't know."

"That's like me calling a family, telling them 'mom has cancer' and hanging up. We deserve better than that."

"That's all he told me."

"Negligence . . . what the hell does he mean? The case is defensible. A bad outcome doesn't mean negligence. We ain't treating measles."

"I know all the songs. I'm just passing on what the Boss told me."

"Yeah."

Alex looked at Dahlia, quietly sitting, hands folded on the shined glass tabletop.

Hackman shrugged. "I'm only the messenger." He turned and shambled out.

Dahlia raised her eyebrows. "Well, maybe we can fight it."

"Fight it. A great option. Immerse ourselves in the vague, tortured labyrinth of litigation . . . do you know what that's like?"

"No."

"You enter a grotesque shadow world of unreal characters, forever condemned to that existence, unable to get out, lawyers, court reporters, judges, groupies. You're the only one to remember authentic experience, and you desperately try to impart the urgency, the practicality, of the real world through a wall of paper, retrospection, and arcane ritual. Those people are like the specters Scrooge witnesses on Christmas night, when Marley's ghost opens the bedroom window and they behold the wailing, doomed and trapped apparitions."

"You're getting a little carried away. We've got time to deal with it."

Alex lifted his hands from the glass, their warmth leaving fading outlines of his fingers. "And why did the Boss get involved? What's going on?"

She shook her head.

CHAPTER 22

Alex thrust the heavy OR door open and poked his head into the room. The circulating nurse looked up.

"We're ready for you."

"Okay." Closing the door, he reached above the scrubsink and grabbed a mask, tying it on. He went into the operating room, glanced at the patient on the operating table, then walked over to the lightbox and examined the CT scan. A large white shadow was present within the brain, a blood clot inexorably squeezing the brain from the inside out, trapping it against the interior of the skull. It needed to come out immediately.

"When is Dr. Hackman coming down?"

"He already called. Said to get started. He'll be down shortly."

That's unusual for Hackman, Alex thought. He was insecure with the residents and usually liked to be present at the start of the case.

"Usually Dr. uptight likes to be here." Alex murmured wearily. "Guess he's busy keeping the Boss happy." The anesthesiology resident, circulating and scrub nurses giggled without comment.

Alex prepped the skin after shaving and marking the incision on the scalp, then went to the scrubsink. He finished washing, came back into the operating room and donned a gown and gloves, then helped the nurse drape the patient. They moved rapidly, the thought of the clot compressing the brain spurring them on.

The operation began. Alex cut the scalp with a knife, the incision spouting blood. He placed plastic clips along the edges of the wound, shutting off the bleeding.

"A little oozy" he muttered.

Someone poked her head into the operating room. "Sue, Dr. Todd wants to speak with you." The circulating nurse left the room.

Alex looked at the scrub nurse next to him. "Why didn't he call in?"

"The phone is broken."

He continued the operation, removing the piece of skull after drilling and cutting the bone, revealing the bulging membrane. Alex ran his finger over it, pressing down slightly, calibrating the pressure with an experienced caress. "The dura's very tight. Have you given any furosemide or mannitol?"

"Nope."

Alex was irritated by the monosyllabic reply. It reminded him that this anesthesia resident was one of the weakest and the crankiest. He would be of no help whatsoever.

"Fifty grams of mannitol and twenty milligrams of furosemide now."

"I need to wait for the circulating nurse."

Damn, Alex thought, the brain was real tight. It needed the medication to shrink it, otherwise when he opened the dura the brain would swell out of the incision like toothpaste, uncontrollably and inevitably. Yet he needed to relieve the pressure quickly.

He looked around. The room was unusually quiet, the silence punctuated by the periodic beep of the cardiac monitor and occasional rustling of the anesthesia resident hidden behind the drapes. The scrub nurse was next to him, her back turned, busying herself at the rear table instead of readying the tools he really needed on the small stand next to him. He felt very alone.

His beeper chirped. "Shoot." Always at the worst time. Reaching, he touched the dura again, his finger outstretched. The brain felt even tighter, like a drumhead stretched to the limit.

The resident behind the drape rustled, then broke into his thoughts.

"Pulse is slowing and blood pressure increasing. The intracranial pressure must be getting worse. What are you doing about it?"

"Don't worry about me. Keep passing gas and do your job. I told you to give the mannitol and diuretic. Make sure you're hyperventilating him." He quickly looked around. "My beeper. Someone get my beeper." He was sterile and could not reach it, much less call, with no phone in the room. Where was the circulating nurse, he wondered. Where had she gotten to? Then it hit him. Dr. Todd called her out. This was Hackman's patient. He was being hung out to dry. If he didn't answer the beeper within five minutes he would be history. He desperately scanned the room. The years, the years of toil, of hope.

The anesthesia resident looked anxiously at his monitor.

"Pulse is thirty, blood pressure one eighty over one ten."

Alex looked up at the scrub nurse. She couldn't leave the room. He looked at her, pleading in his eyes. "Can you get this beep for me?"

"No way doctor, you know that. I would lose my job."

He turned to the resident, looking over the drapes. "Can you get that beep for me?"

The resident laughed, a short, clipped bark. "Doc, you're patient is dying and you're worried about a beep. I can't leave. They would throw me out of the residency. What are you going to do about this?" He nodded to the monitor, showing the fateful numbers.

Alex stared at the numbers. What am I going to do? What I always do, he thought savagely. Take care of the patient. I am a surgeon.

He quickly opened the taut layer with a small sharp knife. Swollen, distended brain protruded. Taking a small suction tube, he sucked through the extruded tissue. Gently, precisely, he used his instinct and skill to guide him toward the blood clot deep within that was pressing inexorably against the vital cerebrum. He probed delicately, steadily, through the brain, following the image in his head of the brain and the clot, putting together the two dimensional slices of the CT scan into a three-dimensional model in his mind's eye.

"Where is it?" he muttered as the brain continued swelling, obscuring his view through the narrow tunnel of pulsating tissue. "Where is it?" His steady hands, encased in white gloves gleaming in the bright light, looked like they were carved from ivory, yet were as supple as young saplings.

"Heart rate twenty and dropping", the anesthesia resident fluttered with unseen activity, panic in his voice. "We're losing him."

Alex kept working, probing through the brain. A gentle push with the sucker, then purplish jelly started oozing from the pocket he had located. He widened the opening slightly, and more and more purple jelly came out.

"Another sucker."

He trained two suckers on the bulging clot, gently sucking and working. Slowly the brain relaxed, the deadly pressure released. He kept working, delicately manipulating, holding living brain aside with blunt blades while removing the lethal mass.

"Whatever you're doing, keep doing it. Pulse is up to sixty, blood pressure down to one hundred twenty systolic. Keep it up."

Alex stopped after a time, the brain relaxed, the clot removed. It looked normal again, pinkish and vibrant, after being distended and white with a fatal pressure. He felt pleased and relieved. He had done the job.

As he began preparing to close, the door swung open. It was the head nurse of the operating room. Normally effusive and jocular, she was subdued. "Dr. Adams, Dr. Todd wants to see you in his office after you're finished." She quickly withdrew, and the door silently closed.

Alex looked up, turning to the door, then froze as he remembered. The beeper. He hadn't answered. Slowly, slowly he turned back, his eyes straight ahead as his whole body rotated rigidly. The scrub nurse looked at him for a moment, her eyes softening. The anesthesiology resident busied himself with papers and intravenous lines behind the drapes.

Alex looked at the open incision for a while, thinking. This is my last operation. How can this be happening? Why? His mind whirled. With an effort of will, he collected himself. The patient, the patient comes first. He slowly started to close.

After the head was wrapped with gauze, he took the chart silently from its place on the anesthesia machine, and muttered to the anesthesia resident, "Meet you in post-op."

Alex walked through the operating room hall to the recovery unit. He sat down, wrote the postop orders and note, then left the chart with the clerk.

Languidly he put on a white coat, and then walked through the hallways to the Department of Neurosurgery offices.

As he came into the waiting room, the patients looked up at him, hopefully, as always. Staring straight ahead, he opened the door to the office.

The secretaries, chattering away, fell silent like frightened birds as Alex entered.

He walked over to Audrey. She looked up somberly. "Go on in."

He turned into the dark inner sanctum.

Dr. Todd was working at his desk. He soundlessly motioned for Alex to sit, his large hands with thick fingers spotlighted by a focal pool of light. Taking a piece of paper, he held it out.

Alex looked at it and then at Dr. Todd's face. Initially blank, with only his eyes boring into Alex's, it shaped itself into a great sadness, frowning with disappointment, mouth heavy with defeated expectation, eyes baffled with frustration.

Dr. Todd shook his head and thrust the paper at Alex.

Alex reached out, his hand veined and hard, a hand larger than the wrists were meant for. He grasped the paper and withdrew it from Dr. Todd's hand. Slowly turning it over, he read.

> "Dear Dr. Adams,
>
> A short time ago I sent you a letter indicating and listing your deficiencies in the vital area of communication. I warned you that failure to answer your beeper will not be tolerated and was grounds for dismissal.
>
> Today I personally paged you in a matter of importance to patient care. Contrary to my expectations and regulations governing this residency program I received no answer. This cannot be tolerated.
>
> Your overall level of function as a resident has declined as well.

I have no choice but to dismiss you from this residency, effective immediately.

Sincerely,

Victor Todd, M.D., F.A.C.S.,

Chairman of Neurosurgery."

Alex stared at the paper for a time. The twenty-seventh grade, he thought. Kicked out of the twenty-seventh grade.

He looked up at Dr. Todd, his eyes burning. "I've been a good resident. You know that."

Dr. Todd shook his head sadly. "Alex, it's there in black and white."

"The beeper? I was in the operating room with Dr. Hackman's patient. The circulating nurse had left. The telephone was broken." Alex paused. "It was your call, you called the circulating nurse out."

Regret and solicitous concern were on Dr. Todd's face. "Alex" he said gently, "you didn't answer the beeper. You needed to do that. When you started here, I had an understanding, a mutual understanding with you, just like I do with every resident. You would do your best to take care of the patients, and I would do my best to train you. Well" he said regretfully, "I've been disillusioned with you. You haven't kept your end of the deal. This is serious business Alex. People's lives are at stake."

Alex looked down at the letter and read it once again.

"What's this about 'overall level of functioning'?"

The mask of sorrow on Dr. Todd shifted ever so slightly, the eyes narrowed, mouth hardened.

"You've been different lately, Alex. You've changed. That monkey incident, the operation on my patient, your judgment was not good there. You've been raising questions that aren't questions."

"In both those situations there were unexpected pathologies, Dr. Todd. I discussed it, appropriately enough, with Hector Harris, the pathology resident. There were legitimate pathophysiologic questions."

"Legitimate questions?" Dr. Todd said softly, "Legitimate questions? Both had subdural hematomas, a common pathology, as you well know."

"The area of basal forebrain scarring. How did that happen?"

"I don't know what you're talking about, Alex. You've become almost delusional." Dr. Todd said, shaking his head sadly. His visage hardened then, his head rising from his neck, neck flaring like a cobra, his eyes opening wider, the pupils large and dark. "Your ridiculous speeches on rounds. What was the point?"

Alex stayed silent.

"You're visit to Metropolitan Hospital didn't go so well. You stirred up people there. They thought you were odd. Very odd."

Alex stared at Dr. Todd. What was he talking about? His visit went well. Then it hit him. Dr. Frey. The visit to Dr. Frey. Dr. Donovan must have mentioned this to Dr. Allen, the Chairman, who told Dr. Todd.

The Boss stood up, his massive bulk rising from the darkness of the desk. Expressionless, his eyes seemed to grow larger. Alex felt as if he were being drawn into the eyes, past those large, dark portals, past all recognizable surroundings, completely adrift.

CHAPTER 23

Alex trudged out of the office, past the secretaries silent as monks in chapel, each furtively looking up at him after he passed.

He stopped at Dr. Hackman's office. The door was open and Hackman was at his desk. Looking up, he paled as he saw Alex at the door, then awkwardly reached and grasped a journal on his desk, holding it like a discus, his lips pursing furiously.

"Uh, Alex, uh very sorry, old boy."

"Sorry? Where were you? It was your case. I was alone in the operating room."

"It was a standard hematoma. I knew you didn't need my help," he said defensively. Hackman stretched his neck upward, then to the side, eyes bulging spasmodically.

"That's not the issue. You're an attending. It was your patient. You should have been there."

"Alex, you're angry because you couldn't answer the beeper, not that you needed me. You dug yourself into this. Don't try to pin anything on me." His voice rose to a higher note, the strain evident on his face as his gaze flickered in the direction of Dr. Todd's office.

"You left me high and dry" Alex's gaze bored into Hackman.

"Alex, there's nothing I can do." His eyes fluttered nervously as if on the verge of a seizure, small hands staying flat on the desk, Adams apple bobbing in his skinny neck.

Alex looked at him with contempt. "By the way, your patient made it through." He turned and left, rapidly striding out. Hackman got up and went to his door, looking after Alex, then towards Dr. Todd's office.

Alex went through the waiting room, out to the hall and down the elevator to the call room. He opened the door quickly. Paul Fox was sitting at the small desk, murmuring on the telephone. Glancing at Alex, he quickly hung up.

There was an awkward silence, then Paul said, "I'm sorry, Alex."

"News travels fast around here. Was that your pal Hackman?"

Fox nodded. "Look Alex, you know better. Never question the chief. What right do you have to question him?"

"What are you talking about?"

"The monkey, you didn't know what that scarring was from and you made a federal case out of it."

"So I asked Harris. Big deal. I guess everybody knows, though."

"Alex, who knows why that scarring was there? You kept asking questions. How can you comprehend what the Boss is thinking? What do you know about his goals, his ideas? He's internationally known."

Alex snorted, "How can mere mortals stay up with him, you mean?"

"Alex, he's brilliant."

"Brilliant, yes. The most overused word in the English language. Brilliant. Human beings as light bulbs. All the elect have to do is walk around and radiate. That excuses everything. But even for the brilliant one plus one equals two. And there's something that doesn't fit here." Alex paused. He caught himself. Don't give this guy any more ammunition.

Paul looked at him. "Alex, you're getting paranoid." He stood up. "I have enjoyed working with you" he said formally and incongruously. "Good luck." He turned and walked out.

Alex sat down in the old chair in the call room, his head tilting back, legs stretched out. Throbbing pain grabbed at his neck, and then surged up and over his head, stabbing at his eyes. He closed them for a moment, then stared at the concrete block wall, at its dirty texture and pitted shadows, trying to push the pain out of his consciousness.

Flexing his legs and standing up, he gathered his jacket and a few journals in the old metal locker in the corner, then opened the door and walked out, turning around and looking at the room as the door closed. He recalled the first time he had opened the door, thrilled to be a neurosurgical resident. The room was long and narrow, like a train. When he lay on the bed, exhausted, trying to rest between phone calls, between emergencies, he would sometimes think, it's like a train and this train is taking me places. Now he knew.

He started walking towards the elevator, not wanting to see anybody, but stopped when he remembered Mr. Darret in the ICU. They had just operated on him. Alex's feeling of obligation tugged at him. He'd check one last time.

He quickly went into the Intensive Care Unit and to Mr. Darret's bed. The patient was awake, his wife sitting next to him, both staring up at the TV.

"How are you, doc?"

"Plugging away. How are you doing?"

"I feel kinda sick. But thanks for coming in" Mr. Darret said flatly, although his eyes were appreciative. His wife nodded.

"You're doing well," said Alex with difficulty, realizing this would be his last patient visit. He was glad Mr. Darret couldn't read emotions or facial expressions. He wasn't sure what he was projecting.

"Yeah, that Boss of yours was in. I still can't warm up to him. There's something real phony there. Just like that character." He nodded to the TV where a glad-handing President was joyfully grasping outstretched hands. "Oh they're noble on the outside, but it just doesn't compute" he said flatly, like a computer himself.

Alex nodded, "Well, I'm happy you're doing well."

Mr. Darret turned to Alex. "My family doctor told me I'd feel like crap someday." He shook his head. "And now, I do feel like crap."

His wife fluttered and moaned. "Is there anything you can do for him?" She rocked her bulk back and forth in the chair, then slowed and stopped.

Alex looked at them. "You're going to get better from the operation. You're doing fine. We'll see you later."

They both nodded and their eyes found the television once again.

As he drove home, Alex brooded over his disaster, probing the past like a gaping wound, feeling the great weight of his loss. He thought about Mr. Darret's words, the same assertion twice. The President and the Boss. Peas in a pod. Rene had told him that the Boss had seen the President as a patient, years before. What did that mean? He thought of the scarred brains, the vital areas of unknown possibility and function, which were affected. What did it all mean?

Following the tree-lined driveway curving around Dr. Sutcliff's house, he parked his car. Walking into the apartment, a flash caught his eye; the telephone message light. Reluctantly he pressed the button, replaying the message.

"Hi, it's Dahlia. Give me a call. I'm at home."

Pausing for a moment, he turned and went outside. The evening was beautiful, clear and calm. The trees formed a canopy over his head as he walked through them. He thought of the time he had moved in, six years before, full of optimism at being a neurosurgeon. The lead weight of his dismissal hit him again. The ache at the base of his skull grew up into his ears.

He turned and walked up into his apartment, dialing Dahlia's number. "Hello."

"Dahlia, it's me."

"Sorry to hear the news, Alex. Come on over."

"Shortly."

He left his apartment and got into his car, driving slowly.

As he pulled up to Dahlia's house, he passed a car parked in front, in line with her walk. Usually the spot was empty. Wondering who was there, he looked at the car for a moment, and then went up the pediment, knocking on the door.

Dahlia opened it, looking at him searchingly, sympathetically, her small delicate face tilted up, her slender white arms clinging to the door. "How are you doing?"

"Okay under the circumstances, I guess." He was going to say more when Richard appeared from the living room. "What are you doing here?"

Dahlia glanced at him. "We were going over some anatomy."

Alex looked at her suspiciously.

"Neuroanatomy" she glared at him.

He nodded, and went into the living room. "How are you doing, Richard?"

"Okay, Alex."

The room was awkwardly silent, then Richard blurted out, "Look Alex, it's unbelievable. How could they do that to you?"

Alex shrugged. "They did. It happens."

Dahlia put her arm around his shoulder, the first time she had ever done that. "It shouldn't happen to you. We all know that."

Alex nodded, distracted for a moment by her closeness. "There is something going on, Dahlia." He looked at Richard searchingly.

Richard understood. "Alex, I'm in. You can count on me."

Alex gave a wan smile. He could see Richard was serious, and they might need help.

"Okay."

They all sat down, and Alex began. "When I think back, it started with the monkey."

"What started?" said Richard.

"The change. My downward slide. The monkey had scar tissue in a very unusual place, unexplained by Dr. Todd. Then Paul Fox mentioned the strange behavior. According to Paul, if you can believe what he says, the Boss flipped out when he heard we operated on it."

"Then there was the operation on the patient," said Dahlia.

Alex nodded. "Right. Scarring in the same place, with a totally unrelated lesion. And the Boss closed that patient, very unusual for him." He thought for a moment. "Heather said something as well."

"Heather?" Dahlia looked grimmer.

"She mentioned how some patients were talking about the radiosurgical frame, patients who never should've known about that. Alex thought. "Then there was Dr. Frey." He jumped up. "I still have his films in my car."

He went out and returned, holding the films up against the lamp. Dahlia examined them. "That's a peculiar brain lesion."

"What would I say if I told you this was a stroke?" Alex looked at her.

"That's no stroke. Too rounded, the edges too sharp."

"Exactly, and yet that's what this man's wife was told, years ago, when he was cared for by Dr. Todd."

Dahlia looked at him, then clutched at him with her hands. She turned pale, her eyes wide.

"What's the matter?"

"That's the same lesion, the same lesion."

"What are you talking about?"

"The same lesion." She swallowed hard and put her face in her hands, her hair billowing over. "The same lesion as my husband."

The room fell silent. Finally Alex said gently, "Are you sure?"

She nodded, her face still hidden. "It wasn't in the same place, but it had the same look. It was smaller and just as round." She finally looked up and opened her eyes. "What's going on?"

"I don't know." He shook his head. "Do you have the films of your husband?"

"No, I destroyed them. Alex, we've got to go to the Dean."

"How can we do that? We don't have anything hard yet."

"There's something terrible going on."

He nodded. "We've got to get more evidence. Nothing we have is good enough. Dr. Todd has destroyed the monkey, and the patient died." He thought for a time. "I've got the treatment record that Rene gave me." He shook his head. "That's not sufficient. We need something more, something recent."

Dahlia thought. "The patient you operated on. Mr. Frederick. With the basal scarring. That man was a patient of the Boss's. Maybe there's something in his chart."

Alex shook his head. "He would be too smart to put anything there."

"It's our only chance, Alex. We've got to check his office. We all know where the patients' charts are. We've got keys. We must do it."

Richard, who had been following the conversation, eagerly said, "She's right Alex. After all, what could he do to you now?" He looked surprised. "Sorry."

Alex grimaced, looked at him irritably. "Thanks a lot." He shook his head. He was just a medical student.

He looked at Dahlia, looked at her yellow pictures lining the room. He felt almost out of his body, out of control. Something in him pushed, something hard, gathering in him, without conscious effort.

"Okay, let's check it out."

Dahlia looked at the clock. "It's nine o'clock. No one will be in the office."

Alex nodded.

They went outside and piled into Dahlia's ancient car, driving over the quiet city streets. Alex, in the front seat, held his knees to the dashboard as they careened along, passing a black Cadillac in a no-passing zone.

"Dahlia, take it easy. You're going to kill us."

"They've got more to lose than me. They'll be careful."

"In this car, you're right" chimed in Richard.

"And what's that smell? When's the last time you checked the muffler in this thing?"

"Never have."

"Great. We'll all croak from carbon monoxide poisoning even before we get there."

"Don't worry, Alex. It's odorless" Richard chimed in.

"Yeah. We'll be a bunch of cherry red corpses in the ER."

"Cherry red?"

"Yeah. Carbon monoxide binds to hemoglobin, to the place where the oxygen usually sticks. The blood's just as red as if was carrying a nice load of oxygen. Except it's poisoned."

"Oh."

"Don't worry, Richard. He's just obsessing."

Alex snorted and continued to stare out the window.

Reaching the hospital garage, they turned and parked. After getting out they looked around warily and walked quickly through the back entrance to the hospital, quiet at this hour. Taking the elevator, they hastily went to the neurosurgery office and unlocked the door.

Dahlia hurried over to the file cabinet for the Boss's patients and opened it, flipping through the files. "Frederick." She looked up. "Not here."

They paused, uncertain where to go next. The absolute quiet in the usually busy suite was unnerving.

Alex darted over to Audrey's desk and opened a small drawer. "She showed me this once." He reached under and felt. "Got it." He held up a small key. "Not to be used on pain of death, I was told." After walking over to the Boss's dark door, he stood for a moment.

"What if he's in there?" blurted Richard, his eyes bulging.

"Shush" said Dahlia.

Alex put the key in and turned. They slowly pushed the door open.

Unexpectedly the light at the desk was on. The office was dark otherwise, the rows of books, like mute guardians, watching silently. They stood inside the office for a moment, staring at the empty chair, as if Dr. Todd would materialize at any moment.

Alex shook himself. "Come on. Look around. Neatly." He darted to the chair and sat down, quickly reaching to open the desk. Locked.

Dahlia went to the file cabinets against the wall and tried the drawers. "Locked."

"We've got to find the key."

Searching frantically, they looked under the desk, on the bookshelves, under the lampshade, then sat down discouraged and unnerved. Alex's gaze fixed on the skull staring at him from the middle shelf, looking back at him, the shadowy eye sockets hiding the cranium's memories. He sat up.

"Dahlia, the skull."

"What about it?"

"Look in it."

She stared at him for a moment, then nodded. Taking it down carefully from the shelf, she unhooked clasps on either side and lifted off the top of the skull.

Sitting inside was a key. Alex looked at Dahlia, "See where it is?"

Richard looked. "What do you mean?"

"This is just under the basal forebrain. The area that was scarred in the experimental monkey and Mr. Frederick, the Boss's patient."

Dahlia took the key and opened the file drawer. She flipped through. "Frederick, Frederick. Here it is." She pulled the file out and slapped it on the desk.

"Mark the spot where it came from," said Alex.

She nodded and pulled the next file higher, then spread the contents open on the desk, paging through.

"This is a radiosurgery treatment plan," Alex cried out. "That patient never was supposed to have radiosurgery."

"Radiosurgery?" said Richard.

"You remember that radiosurgery case you saw. A tumor in any area of the brain can be targeted and destroyed."

"Or any part of the brain itself can be destroyed" said Dahlia sadly.

Alex looked at her for a moment. "We need to make a copy of this treatment plan." Dahlia took it and made a photostat on the office machine.

"Okay, let's get out of here" said Alex. They rapidly returned the file, locked the cabinet, put the key back into the skull and after a last look, closed the door and replaced the office key.

Quickly they left the building, then silently walked through the dank parking garage, pondering and absorbing the enormity of what they had learned.

The silence continued as they got into Dahlia's car and hurtled out of the garage. She was the first to speak.

"When do we go to the Dean?"

Alex looked out the window. "We need more evidence."

"Alex, people are being harmed."

"We don't know what he's planning."

"We can't just sit and wait. Look what we've found."

"I didn't mean just wait. I mean talk to more people, investigate."

"This is all we need. We must stop whatever's going on."

Alex sighed. He looked out the window past the dark river, his career destroyed.

"I'll meet you at the Dean's office after rounds tomorrow."

"I'll be there," said Richard.

Alex shook his head wearily. "You don't have to. Don't make it worse for yourself."

"I want to."

"You're in medical school."

"Alex, bad things are happening."

"Yeah, but you don't need to be involved. It's going to get real messy."

Richard shook his head. "I want to be there."

"You'll end up like me," he said softly.

Dahlia glanced at him, then fixed her eyes on the road ahead, gripping the chipped steering wheel tightly with her thin white fingers.

CHAPTER 24

Alex slept restlessly, unusual for him. The little sleep he got, he usually lost consciousness quickly and didn't awake until the morning. After showering he dressed and made tea, troubled about the upcoming meeting with the Dean. Head pounding, the pain would distract him for a moment, then the loss of his job and career would hit him again and again. His gut in turmoil, constantly glancing at the clock, he finally went down the stairs to the car.

Dr. Sutcliff was puttering in the garden. He looked up as Alex came by.

"Leaving a bit late, aren't you?" he called out.

Great, thought Alex. From the guy who hasn't worked for years.

"Yep, I'm off the clinical service," he said, continuing to walk to his car.

His landlord sauntered over as Alex got in and closed the door. Sutcliff put his hand on the doorframe and talked, oblivious to Alex's impatience.

"How's things at the university?"

"So so. That Todd, he's a pip."

The old man studied Alex's grim face for a time, his blue eyes surprisingly intense. He nodded, then backed off. "Well, have a good day."

"You too." Alex started down the lane. It was very odd to be driving at that time of day, not to be working at eight o'clock in the morning, not to be making rounds or operating. When he was small, he remembered the feeling of being staying home, sick from school, how different it felt. It was the same feeling now, even stronger, more than a score of grades later.

He reached the University Hospital parking garage, pulled in and found his space, occupied by a dirty white car. Alex stared at it, trying to figure out whose it was, then drove on. After more turns he discovered an empty spot, parked and got out, locking the car and walking across the dank concrete floor to a pay phone. After dialing the page operator, he asked for Dahlia, then listened to the static filled music for an interminable time.

"Dr. Laronge" she answered briskly.

"Dahlia, it's me."

"I've not finished rounds yet. I'll give you a page." She sounded strained, then called out "Start seeing the next patient." A pause. "Alex, I can't talk now. I'll page you."

"Okay."

He hung up the phone. Heading back to his car, he unlocked the door and sat in the driver's seat, legs splayed on the spotted pavement. Closely inspecting the oil stains, he recalled the endless hours spent on rounds; examining, checking, writing, debating. Hearing footsteps, he looked up. Walking from her car was one of the hospital administrators. She paused, glanced at him curiously as their eyes met, and then strode quickly away, her feet briskly slapping the pavement.

Seeing Sutcliff that morning brought the landlord's recollections about the Boss back to his mind. A new science of the brain? What has the Boss been doing?

His beeper went off. Grabbing it from his belt, he looked at the extension. The call room. Getting out of the car, he went over to the phone again and dialed the number.

Dahlia's voice answered. "Hi."

"Ready to go?"

"Ready. We'll meet you at the hospital entrance."

"We?"

"Richard is with me."

"Dahlia, do you really think that's a good idea?"

"He wants to do this."

"He has no idea what he's getting himself into."

"He wants to."

Alex paused. "Okay. I'll see you in a moment." He hung up and went back to the car, grabbing the treatment plan and Dr. Frey's CT scan. Gathering them up, he walked over to the elevator, taking it down and striding across the street. Deep in thought, he didn't see the resident physician coming out of the hospital.

"Hey, Alex."

He looked up and realized it was Nichols, one of the general surgery residents. Damn.

"What's going on?"

"Politics as usual."

"Some strange rumors floating around."

"You know our department, Scott, always in an uproar."

"Actually, Dr. Todd runs a very tight ship." Nichols eyed him curiously during an uncomfortable silence.

"Well gotta go."

"See you later."

Alex hurried off as Nichols looked back at him.

Dahlia and Richard were waiting in the lobby of the hospital, both rigid with a look of awkward idleness until they saw Alex, then they urgently clustered together.

The Dean's office, for reasons of inertia, sentiment, and tradition, was located in the old medical school building. They walked through the hospital, then through the connecting tunnel to the old building, constructed some one hundred years before. The transition was striking, from modern white walls and carpets to marble floor, high ceilings and paintings lining the walls. Previous leaders in the medical school looked down on them from large, dark, intricately framed oil portraits. Imperious and grave, they stared with disdain.

"Those guys give me the creeps," said Richard, glancing upward.

They took the graceful main stairway, curving upward to the first floor, flanked by ornate white banisters. Walking down the marble-floored hallway, they ignored the portraits on either side and stopped at the last door. It was large and solid wood, dominated by the inscription 'Dean' ornately placed at eye level in golden Gothic script.

Richard giggled nervously. "I feel like the cowardly lion going to see the wizard."

Alex and Dahlia said nothing, immersed in their own thoughts. Alex reached for the door and opened it, and they all filed in. The Dean's secretary looked up from behind a desk stacked and festooned with papers.

"Dr. Adams and Dr. Laronge to see the Dean."

"Do you have an appointment?"

"No, but we need to meet. We know he's in. It is a matter of the utmost importance relating to patient care."

She looked skeptically at them for a moment. "Please wait here. I'll check." Getting up, she walked down the hallway, then turned into the Dean's office. After a brief moment she came out, an artificial mask of disappointment on her face.

"I'm sorry. He is very busy. Did you see your Chairman on the matter?"

"It is about our Chairman," said Alex forcefully. "We need to see the Dean. We will not leave until we have done so." He glared at her.

Her imperturbability slipped as she glanced at Alex, Dahlia and Richard in turn.

"I'll check with him again." She scuttled back into the Dean's office. They strained to hear but only murmuring was audible. Finally she reappeared and nodded to them warily.

"He'll see you shortly. Please have a seat."

Glancing uncertainly at each other, they sat down in several colonial armchairs in an alcove next to her desk. Silently they waited, the loud clacking of a printer puncturing their thoughts. Alex looked at the pictures on the wall, an assortment of fox hunting scenes and photos of the Dean. He studied a painting, showing horses with impossibly small heads, ridden by red-jacketed riders leaping through beautiful fields.

Richard noticed Alex's focus. "My mother rode horses. Very equestrian. She had a special hunt outfit and would go out with her group after some poor fox."

Alex fingered the CT scan silently. His gaze went to the other pictures, the Dean with the Mayor, the Dean with the Governor, and the Dean with Dr. Todd, his eyes lingering. Bad sign. The Dean and Dr. Todd were shaking hands, the Dean handing Dr. Todd a scroll, the Boss looking humble and grateful. Nobody can do it like him, Alex thought.

The phone rang. Picking it up and listening, the secretary glanced at Alex, then hung up.

"He'll see you now," she said, standing. They followed her into the Dean's office, where he sat behind a large desk with spiral carved columns at each corner, more portraits lining the walls. The last time Alex saw the Dean was at the party for the residents. There in his lederhosen he was almost comical, but in his home base he exuded dignity and purpose. He continued writing, head tilted towards them.

They sat down in three chairs arrayed before the desk and waited. He finished writing, put down his black and gold pen, and looked up.

"Now, what's so urgent?" Businesslike and cold, he stared at each of them in turn, his darting dark eyes ensconced behind round gold-rimmed glasses, the old fashioned kind that needed to be wound around the ears.

"I'm Alex Adams, chief neurosurgical resident." Alex cleared his throat. "I met you at your party." He paused.

The Dean gazed at them, his eyebrows arching expectantly.

"This is Dahlia Laronge, fourth year resident, and Richard Walters, medical student on the service."

The Dean nodded impatiently.

"We appreciate your seeing us."

"I hardly had a choice. My secretary said you wouldn't leave until you saw me." His large mouth was grim, and he thrust his lower lip out as he sat forward in his chair.

Alex cleared his throat. "Dean, there are problems on the service."

The Dean sighed. These types of warnings were frequent from residents, particularly the malcontents.

"I had to do an emergency operation on one of Dr. Todd's experimental monkeys. After removing the clot it was apparent there was additional pathology present. Pathology that could not be readily explained. There was severe scarring on the basal forebrain area. When I pointed this out to Dr. Todd he became very upset and offered no explanation."

"Perhaps he was upset over the loss of a valuable laboratory animal."

"He made no explanation to me."

"Perhaps he felt he didn't need to make explanations to you."

"According to the resident on the service, the monkey had been acting in a bizarre fashion."

"These were experimental monkeys, were they not?"

"Yes."

"And Dr. Todd is a brain surgeon?"

"Yes."

"Then can it be assumed he is doing brain experiments which conceivably could affect behavior?"

"Well, yes."

The Dean frowned, numerous parallel lines appearing on his broad forehead.

Alex moved on. "I did an urgent operation on a patient of Dr. Todd's. That patient had unexplained pathology as well. Pathology again involving the basal forebrain, odd scarring in an unusual location."

"And what did Dr. Todd say?"

"He had no explanation. He was upset with me for pointing it out and closed the case himself."

"Dr. Todd is a concerned, conscientious physician. I know that first hand, as well as from reputation and report." The Dean spoke slowly. "Is it not possible he was upset at his patient's difficulty? Again, does he need to answer to you?"

Alex studied the Dean, who looked at him obliquely, without expression, except for his dark eyes. "Dean, this patient had no history of radiation treatment."

"And so?"

"Here is a record of the treatment plan done on this patient, with the radiation targeted in the same place as the scarring, done for no clinical indication, no clinical need."

Alex took the paper from Dahlia, who handed it to him from the edge of her seat. He held it over the Dean's desk, the edges of the paper vibrating, fluttering ever so slightly.

The Dean looked at him, glanced at the paper, then slowly took it, turning it around and examining it, his lips curled.

The room was quiet except for the tick of the large clock continuing inexorably. Dahlia shifted in her seat.

The Dean handed the paper back to Alex. "There's no patient's name on this plan."

Alex took it quickly and scrutinized it. The box for the patient name was blank. He looked at Dahlia.

"This was in the patient's file," she said.

"There's no name on the plan. This is meaningless." The Dean shook his head in exasperation. "Look Dr. Adams, you're in trouble. Big trouble with the program. I should say, you were in trouble. I understand your performance has not been adequate and you have been released. I can't do anything about that. Your difficulties are well documented and this erratic performance is in line with what your departmental file demonstrates. Dr. Todd indicates you need medical help. He can arrange for this. As for you" he turned his gaze to Dahlia, "You are clearly overwrought, and have issues you need to work through yourself. If you need a leave of absence, please speak to your Chairman." He paused. "You both should be ashamed of involving a medical student." He curtly nodded to Richard.

Alex clenched his fists. "There is another piece of evidence, Dean." He spoke quickly. "Dr. Frey, Dr. Todd's colleague at Metropolitan Hospital. Dr. Frey was Dr. Todd's patient. He became ill and was told he had a stroke. He cannot talk as a result. Here is his CT scan." Alex reached over with the envelope containing the scan, but the Dean made no effort to take the film, and he slowly lowered it to the desk. For a moment there was a motionless tableau, like a wax museum display of the signers of the Declaration of Independence, Alex thought in a disconnected corner of his brain.

The Dean sighed and snapped, "This is it. You must leave after I look at this."

Alex nodded.

The Dean picked up the envelope and impatiently took out the CT scan. He held it up to the light and looked at it. "I'm not a neurologist. I see an abnormal area. It looks like a stroke."

Dahlia cried out. "It's not a stroke. Look how regular it is, how round."

He turned and looked at her. "You're really getting carried away here, doctor."

"Carried away? Carried away? That's the same lesion my husband had ten years ago. Dr. Todd was his doctor."

The Dean said gently, "Do you have the CT scan, the records?"

She shook her head tearfully. "No, no. I destroyed them."

The Dean said even more gently. "Your husband is gone. We can't help that. The hospital has a counseling service, and as I said, we can also grant you a leave of absence if you desire."

She shook her head.

Alex spoke again. "Dean, there is a problem. A big problem in the department." Alex felt he was babbling. A feeling he intensely disliked.

The Dean looked at him. "You were the problem," he said with a steely gaze.

Alex stared at him. He had never been spoken to like this. His mind was blank, the Dean's intransigence immovable.

Alex glanced at Dahlia. She was staring at her hands.

"Now, if you will let me get back to work. Dr. Adams, I expect you will be off the campus except for medical care. Dr. Laronge" he turned to Dahlia and said more softly, "anything I can do please call me. Mr. Walters, do not let this affect your studies."

He turned. The interview was over.

Dahlia, Richard and Alex sat for a moment, and then got up. Leaving the office silently, they passed the secretary, who continued to type as they plodded by.

The hallway seemed to swallow the sounds of their footsteps as they passed the huge portraits once again. They walked down the marble steps, past the looming oil rendition of one of the first operations in the city. Dahlia stopped at the immense painting, looking up, her face hard and sad.

"Dr. Todd. He has no soul. The Dean has no soul. No one has a soul."

Alex stopped beside her, and looked up at the painting. "Have you ever seen it?"

She shook her head.

"I've looked for the soul. I've looked for it in the moist nooks and crannies of the brain, the spider webbed passages under and around the twisted convolutions, the fluid filled caverns. No light had ever shown in those places, until our bright beams lit those forever dark sanctuaries. I've looked for it, hopefully, curiously, and I did find it."

She turned to him, her cheek moist. "Where?"

His face lightened ever so slightly, like the earliest dawn when the mere knowledge of morning eased the night. "Not in the brain, but in the face, the eyes, the behavior of someone who faces their destiny, who has just learned that their body is not whole. I see the soul in the eyes of those who know they will be leaving, and I have seen it again and again." He stopped, embarrassed.

Dahlia looked at him, stared, then smiled ever so slightly, continuing to gaze at his face.

They quietly walked through the tunnel to the new hospital, stopping in the lobby.

"Well" said Dahlia, "back to work. What are you going to do?"

"Go home."

She shrugged. "We gave it a shot. If only these nightmares would stop."

"What?"

She glanced at Richard, then back at Alex. "I'll be talking to you."

Alex nodded, "Take care of yourself." He looked at her, into her eyes for a moment, and then turned to Richard. "See you later. Keep your nose clean."

He walked down the hallway. Dahlia and Richard went to the elevator.

CHAPTER 25

Alex drove home, replaying the Dean's refusal to see reality, his unwillingness to open his mind. The complete rejection they had just encountered stunned him, and he kept prodding the memory of the meeting, like an open wound he could not leave alone. The hostile disinterest was baffling.

After pulling into the tree-lined driveway he drove around the back of the main house and parked. Trudging up the stairs into his apartment, the feeling that he should be working, not home at this time of day felt stronger than ever. Uneasily he wandered through his rooms, restless but without purpose, then lay down on the bed.

The phone rang, awakening him. He reflexively grabbed for it, and spoke extra clearly so that whoever was on the line didn't think he had been sleeping.

"Hello."

"Hi." It was Dahlia. "Just checking in. How are you doing?"

"Just puttering."

Silence.

"What are you going to do tomorrow?"

Alex was looking out the window at the blue sky as he talked, then at the framed piece of shirt on the wall, cut from him by his flying instructor after he soloed.

"I think I'll go soaring tomorrow."

"Soaring? You haven't done that in a while."

"Well, I'll get checked out by an instructor. I better start learning how to use my free time."

"How can you be such a hypochondriac and go soaring?"

"I'm no hypochondriac. I just know what can happen to the human body."

"And when you put that body in a plane without an engine?"

"Statistically it's very safe."

"And after what you've just been through?"

"I guess I've got nowhere to go but up. I need to go. You can almost touch the sun."

"Just don't fly too high." She sighed. "You're a collection of paradoxes."

"Isn't that what life is? Isn't that what reality is? There are always opposites in our world. All existence is contrast. That's what makes it finite. The infinite is not of this world."

"Yeah, sure. Just be careful, Mr. Philosopher."

"Thanks for calling, Dahlia."

"You're welcome," she said softly.

"What was that about nightmares? Back after the Dean's office?"

Silence for a moment.

"Dahlia, you still there? I hate silence when I'm on the phone."

"Yeah. What can I say. I'm not sleeping so well. Haven't had it like this for a long time. They'll go away."

Another pause, which Alex felt compelled to break. "Well, see you later."

Alex fell back to sleep, awakening in the darkness. The clock said nine P.M. He got up and made himself something to eat. Sitting, he looked at the phone, then picked it up and called Dahlia.

She answered. "Hello."

"How are you doing? You didn't say much this afternoon. I just wanted to see how you were."

"Okay."

"How did rounds go?"

"The usual. Paul Fox asked about you."

"The weasel."

"No, the rat."

"And what did you tell him?"

"That you were doing okay. I told him you were going soaring tomorrow. That seemed to throw him for a loop. And then I saw him later on with the Boss. They quieted down when I came up, but Richard told me the Boss had been asking about you."

"Well I hope Paul told him I was going soaring. Life goes on."

"You sound pretty philosophical about it."

"Well, you never know what's going to happen. Reality is only one thread in a panoply of possibilities. Those people who are at the top of business, government, academia, they may be there because of ability, but more likely they've just been lucky, in the right place at the right time, know the right people. There's plenty who could do the job as well or better, only they didn't get the same lucky breaks."

"They just get screwed."

"I guess so." He took a deep breath. "Richard's not there now studying anatomy, is he?"

"What's it to you?"

"Nothing."

She giggled. "Nope. Just me and my lonesome. But I'm on call tonight and there may be a case."

"I never thought I would miss call."

"Poor baby."

"Well I'll talk to you tomorrow."

"Okay. Have a good day."

He hung up the phone and looked around. She hadn't mentioned the nightmares again.

Getting up, he took a book from the shelf, a book on soaring, sat down and reviewed the numbers for the sailplane he would be flying.

CHAPTER 26

The next morning Alex awoke automatically. For a brief couple seconds he looked outside, noticed the sunshine and thought of soaring, moving around the clouds. Then, like a physical blow, he remembered. "The job" he muttered to himself. It all came back to him very quickly. He laid in bed, looked at the small spots on the ceiling he knew so well, the mottled painted wallpaper, and his mind spun. The odd pathologies in the monkey and patient, the warning by the Boss, the boards, the setup in the operating room, his firing, the meeting with the Dean. It all went by in a flash, staring at the ceiling. His headache came back, like the memories, painful and pounding.

It helped a little to get out of bed, get started with the daily routine.

After making a cup of tea, he got into his car and drove over to the airport. The sun was shining, and the day was glorious, with puffy cumulus clouds dotting the blue sky.

It was a small grass strip, with a yellow metal hanger and office. The corrugated metal had been painted yellow years ago, but now the yellow had faded and the building was rusting along the bottom, like it had caught a disease from the ground. Sailplanes were parked on the grass, wingtip to wingtip, tied down with rope and stakes. He turned into the airport, pulling his car up against the old telephone pole laid down as a parking stop. Opening the door, he got out and looked up, gazing at the graceful sailplanes wheeling impossibly slowly high in the air. There were three, following the invisible but unbreakable traffic pattern for the airport.

He never tired of looking at sailplanes, at their thin, long wings, narrow fuselage and Plexiglas bubble over the cockpit. It always amazed him that a hunk of metal could fly in the air without an engine. He forgot everything when he was soaring, his only purpose was to stay up, to search for the invisible currents of climbing air that would kick him in the seat of the pants, signaling him to quickly bank the sailplane as he tried to stay in the mass of rising air, riding it up.

Alex looked down as he strode towards the office, across the ancient blacktop, pitted like terrible acne. Stepping into the building, he walked over the old linoleum floor, and stood at the metal counter. "Anybody home?"

A rustling started from the room behind the counter, then a man appeared, tattoos on his forearms, fluorescent light glinting on his glasses. Alex didn't recognize him, but he hadn't flown in months.

"My name is Alex Adams. I called yesterday. I need a check ride and then I'll be taking a sailplane out solo."

"Sure, sure. I'm the new instructor. Just joined this outfit. Name's Jake. I'll take you up for a workout." Jake smacked his lips several times and then grinned, a tooth missing along the side of his mouth. "Why don't you get the glider set up? I'll be right out."

"What about the tow plane?"

"He's out there." He grinned again. "Just tell him what we need."

"How high we going?"

"How high do you wanna go?"

"Three thousand feet is the usual I go to start."

"Sounds good to me."

Alex nodded and went out the back door to the disintegrating tarmac. The towplane was parked, a greasy man with a big gut in dirty khakis and yellow T-shirt fueling it up. Alex approached him but was studiously ignored.

"Looks like a beautiful day."

"You goin' up?"

"Yeah. How about to three thousand feet."

"Sounds good."

The man finished fueling and put the gas hose away. He climbed into his plane and started it, taxiing over to just in front of the glider, parked at the end of the runway.

Alex walked out over the pock-marked macadam, then onto the neatly cut grass where the sailplanes lay, wingtip to wingtip, resting, gracefully tilted with one wing touching the ground, the other wing high up in the air, like giant dragonflies. Grabbing the small handle at the nose of the plane, he put his weight down on it and gradually forced it onto its mainwheel, pivoting the craft around, pulling it to the grass runway. Starting the airworthiness inspection, he leaned in, grasped the control stick, and moved it side to side, lifting his head up to observe the ailerons and the response to his movements. Pulling the stick front to back he watched the elevators at the tail of the plane angle, and then reaching down inside the sailplane he grabbed the cable to the rudder pedal, drawing it back and forth, the vertical fin reacting. Flexing the dive brake handle backward, he looked as small hinged metal panels on the top and bottom of the wings swung out, spoiling the airflow of the moving wing and letting the glider descend quicker. These also worked well.

Walking around the sailplane, he checked the control surface hinges, landing wheels and exterior. When he had completed the circuit, ending in front of the cockpit, he leaned down and inspected the release hook, where the towrope would be attached. Taking the end of the rope, he clipped its metal ring to the hook and pulled it several times. It was secure. Reaching around to the release handle on the instrument panel he grasped it and pulled. The release hook opened up, freeing the towrope. He reattached the towrope and pulled the rope again. It was secure.

Turning around, he noticed Jake next to him, looking at him blankly behind sunglasses.

Jake nodded. "Ready to go?"

Alex gave him thumbs up.

"You first" grinned Jake.

Alex pushed down the nose of the sailplane, then climbed into the front seat, putting the safety harness on over his shoulders, snapping it in place over his chest. He had the uncomfortable feeling Jake was taking in every move, even to the way he did his harness. Jake climbed into the rear seat, right behind Alex, and strapped himself in as well. Alex closed the Plexiglas bubble over their heads, securing the latch. When he looked side to side, the wings extending out, he could see a hint of Jake's shape in his peripheral vision, sitting in back of him. Sounds in the small, enclosed space were magnified, and Jake's heavy breathing reverberated like they were sharing a gas mask.

Alex looked straight ahead through the crystalline dome, sparkling with sunlight, following the line of the rope as it lay in a gentle curve on the ground. It ended at the tail of the towplane, now with its propeller spinning. Alex looked at each wing and then stepped on the rudder pedals, first left, then right, then left, wagging the rudder in a signal for the tow to start. The pilot moved his rudder in reply and then speeded his engine, slowly rolling forward, gently straightening out the towrope. The rope tightened, then Alex felt the tug as it tensed and then started pulling them. The sailplane seemed to come alive, pivoting slightly to line up with the rope and then starting to careen down the grass. As the speed picked up, Alex started flying while still on the ground, wielding the control stick to keep the wings level and the sailplane rolling straight, gaining momentum. As the ground blurred and the jarring increased, he eased back and they rose, the ride suddenly velvet smooth. Alex pushed the stick to keep them low, so as not to pull the towplane's tail up as it gained speed. It finally lumbered into the air, and Alex lined up the towplane with the horizon to keep proper position, brandishing the stick back and forwards, side to side, keeping them right behind. As they climbed, Alex kept the towplane right on the horizon, all attention focused on stick and rudder, position and airspace. The roaring of the wind brought back memories of past flights.

"Doin' good." Jake croaked above the roar of the wind flowing by, craning his head around.

"Thanks." Alex could hear and feel Jake continually pivoting around, more than any other instructor he had flown with.

"Any problems?"

"Uhh, no. Just enjoying the view. When you goin' to fly this baby?"

"You mean release?"

"Yeah."

"We said three thousand feet." Alex said, puzzled. He tapped the altimeter. "We're just at a thousand."

"Righto."

The tiny sailplane continued its steady ascent, Alex responding to the bobbing with quick counter moves on the stick and rudder pedals. Still had the old magic, he thought with satisfaction. He waited for Jake to ask him to do the usual exercises, moving the sailplane up and down through the towplane's slipstream, but Jake was silent, occasionally humming a snippet of unrecognizable song.

On the lookout for other aircraft, Alex constantly searched from side to side, up and down, his gaze also flickering to the towplane, the top of its broad wing fiery in the morning sun. They were rising toward the cloud bases hanging like huge white dirigibles above them. As they climbed, they could see farther and farther in the hazy distance, and the airport receded below. The towplane maneuvered them into a position upwind from the airport as the altimeter needle showed three thousand feet, and Alex reached for the large red knob in the center of the instrument panel.

"Time to release" he called out.

"Please release me," Jake sang hoarsely.

Alex pulled the knob, and the sailplane shuddered slightly. With a loud twang the rope shot ahead of them, springing back. The towplane banked down and to the left, and Alex gently pulled back and to the right, working stick and rudder, trading the sailplane's speed for altitude, maximizing the separation.

The thunder of the airstream quickly faded to a soft murmur as they slowed. In the quiet he could once again hear Jake breathing behind him.

"Mighty quiet up here" said Jake.

Alex nodded as the sailplane arced around, slowly turning and displaying the land underneath them.

"Anything in particular you want me to do?" asked Alex.

"Nope. Just fly around a little and then I'll take over." He chuckled.

This was certainly the easiest check ride he had ever been on, Alex thought. He shrugged and flew, turning in the clear air, gradually descending, looking for lift.

Alex loved soaring, loved the feeling of flying, wheeling in the brilliant sunlight, looking for the invisible lift, navigating the immense and turbulent ocean of air. The sunlight bathed him in its rays, changing appearance and angle constantly as the plane turned. The cockpit gradually warmed, and Alex opened the ventilation tube in the instrument panel. The air washed over him.

"Sprang a leak," giggled Jake as he felt the breeze as well.

Alex felt a boost in his seat, like a giant had put its hand under them and was lifting up. He checked the rate of climb indicator, the needle springing upward, confirming good lift.

"A thermal."

"Whoop-de-do."

"I'm going to try to ride it up." Alex banked the plane sharply, staying in the column of rising air. He flew the glider in a tight circle, one eye on the gauge. It continued positive as they rode up with the air column, and the altimeter confirmed their ascent.

He was exhilarated by the thermal, by riding it up. They continued in tight circles until the lift petered out, then Alex straightened. He wondered when Jake would start checking him, and then the thought was crowded out of his mind by the beauty of soaring. Looking straight up, past the sun directly overhead, he saw into the mystery of space.

Jake stirred, and then giggled incongruously. "My turn now."

"It's all yours." Alex removed his hands and feet from stick and pedals so Jake could use his set of controls in the back seat.

Jake suddenly bellowed, "pull and push."

Alex looked down at his control stick, which came directly back to the stop as the right pedal mashed down to the floor. Both motions were gross and heavy handed, the sailplane bounding upward and to the right as its speed dissipated.

Alex was uneasy. I guess he's trying to do stall and spin training, he said to himself.

Jake just giggled. He kept the controls unchanged as the sailplane slowed, then as the speed decayed to a point where the wings could not support their mass, the nose fell forward and the plane started to rotate.

"Pull and push" Jake giggled again.

Alex never liked spins, although they were a necessary part of training and testing. The sailplane rotated faster and faster, falling downward. The ground spun as Alex pressed against his seat belt, his belly tightening. When does he want us to recover? Trees and buildings became closer as they rapidly plunged. Alex's stomach churned. What the hell was going on?

"Jake, what are you doing?" he screamed.

No answer. Pressed into the seat, he forced his head around and glimpsed Jake's face twisted in a maniacal grin, dirty foam at the corner of his mouth. Sunlight caught his wide eyes, and reflected deep blue from his pupils, an unnatural, utterly startling deep blue. Alex turned back, his brain gyrating, then stomped down on the left rudder pedal, but it felt fixed in concrete. He grabbed the stick with both hands and tried to push forward but it was futile.

"Jake" he screamed. "Let go."

The air roar was deafening as the plane continued to whirl. Alex frantically lunged behind him but clutched air, his arms flailing, his body tethered. Loosening the harness he tried again, grasping for Jake's throat. His strong hands closed over Jake's neck, but it slipped away. Alex desperately grabbed Jake's throat again and squeezed down, hands crunching the windpipe like oyster shells cracking. Jake gasped, choked and pulled his hands off the control stick, rasping, coughing, holding his throat.

Alex quickly turned and pulled himself back into the seat. He forced the stick forward, straightening his left leg and pushing down the left rudder pedal, neutralizing the controls. The sailplane, still pointing steeply down, stopped rotating. Alex gently and desperately pulled back on the stick, bringing the sailplane out of the dive. As it responded, crushing him into the seat, he looked up into a wall of trees.

CHAPTER 27

Alex was in a submarine, the ping . . . ping of sonar reverberating throughout the ship. He was sitting on the bridge, his sonar man to his right, the steering guys in front of him, the executive officer to his left. They were navigating through an ocean forest, a beautiful coral grove, and the pinging got louder. The executive officer bent down, and to his surprise he was a she, and she smelled nice. With a start he realized it was Dahlia, who put her hand on his shoulder. Mighty familiar for an executive officer, thought Alex, I wonder what the men will think.

The pinging became even louder and he opened his eyes. Dahlia was bending over him, Richard next to her. He was in a familiar room in the ICU, only now he was in the bed. Most peculiar. Trying to talk, he realized there was a tube down his throat, and suddenly it became very uncomfortable. He tried to cough, but his throat wouldn't work, wouldn't close, and he just blew air.

Settling down, his eyes darted around the room, then at Dahlia. Her hair framed her face, concerned but now smiling as he looked at her.

"Take it easy, Alex" she said. "They'll get the tube out." Turning her head, she called out the door, "Gail, he's awake."

Alex realized he couldn't move his legs, and for a terrifying moment thought they were paralyzed. Wiggling his toes with relief, he realized both legs were encased in full-length casts. Reaching down, he tapped them with each hand.

Dahlia saw him do this. "You broke your legs," she said slowly. Alex wondered why she was talking to him like an idiot, but he nodded. There was a deep frightening pain enveloping both legs.

Dahlia glanced at the nurse who had come in. "Gail, can we extubate him? He's alert."

The nurse looked somewhat doubtfully at Dahlia. "He's on the Trauma Service."

"Oh, don't worry. They always take three days to extubate their patients. We can't do that to Alex."

Alex shook his head, wiggling the corrugated tube from mouth to ventilator and rattling the humid droplets perched inside the hose.

"Come on, Gail, it's okay to take it out."

Alex nodded yes.

Gail looked at him, and then sighed. "Okay, okay. Let me suction him out first. But it's your fault if Trauma gets upset."

Alex gave her the okay sign. She snaked a small plastic suction catheter down his breathing tube, making Alex gasp. Deftly deflating the cuff, she said, "Take a breath, one, two, three", and then pulled the tube out. After a paroxysm of coughing, Alex quieted down. He looked around again.

"What happened? I believe is the usual question."

Dahlia and Richard excitedly moved closer to the bed.

"You crashed," they both said.

Dahlia laughed. "But you're okay now. You're going to be alright." She sat down on the side of the bed. "That damn glider, it crashed. I knew you shouldn't have gone."

It started coming back to Alex. The sickening feeling of plummeting, the ground rushing up to meet him, the maniacal Jake in the back seat.

"The instructor tried to kill me," he said weakly, closing his eyes.

"That wasn't an instructor. They found the real instructor tied up in a shed nearby" said Richard eagerly. "That guy with you croaked."

"Dead?" said Alex.

"Yes" said Dahlia.

Alex settled back. "The guy was very weird, very weird, and the strangest thing was his eyes. They were blue."

"What's so funny about that?" asked Richard. "There are plenty of blue eyes around."

"Not the iris, you idiot" Alex said weakly. "The pupils were blue. That means the retina was blue."

Dahlia gasped. "If the retinas were blue, then something damaged the optic nerves in back of the retinas, where the optic nerves come together." She didn't finish, lost in thought.

"Exactly. Damage in the basal forebrain. Just like the other brains" said Alex. "Where's his body?"

"Well, I assume it's a coroner's case," said Dahlia.

"Can you find out about it?" asked Alex.

"Sure, I'll make some calls today, but the coroner can really clam up sometimes."

"Use your charms." Alex turned his head to Richard. "Would you check out a couple of things for me?"

"Sure."

"Can you get me my notebook computer? I'm going to go nuts if I don't have something to do."

Richard nodded.

Alex closed his eyes for a moment. "My eyes want to see double sometimes, now." He shook his head. "I gave my head a good bang, I guess."

Dahlia frowned. "We've got to do something."

"Yeah, remember how it turned out with the Dean?"

She shook her head.

Alex continued. "We need to get a smoking gun." He lay back. "Richard can you tap into the video line at the radiation treatment linear accelerator? Maybe we can record one of the Boss's treatments. Joe Marr at Biomedical Engineering can help you. I took care of his pinched nerve a while ago. Tell him it's for student education."

"I can try, Alex."

"Dahlia, you'll check out that idiot Jake's body with the coroner?"

"Right."

He suddenly felt tired. His head was bothering him again. "What time is it?"

"Ten o'clock in the morning."

"If I could only get rid of this headache. What did my CT scan show?"

"The Boss didn't want to get one."

"Why the hell didn't he get one? We always get one with any loss of consciousness, especially traumatic."

"Don't want to miss a clot in the brain, huh?" said Richard.

Alex glared at him. "Yeah, right."

"He said you'd be OK. Didn't need one. He was right."

Alex shook his head. "Why didn't he get one on me? What doesn't he want to find?"

"Alex, relax. You're doing well. No one will bother you. We've got alot of friends here and they'll keep an eye on you. Rest." said Dahlia.

Alex looked at Dahlia for a moment, and then nodded.

"Alright. I gotta heal up" he said, closing his eyes. "Let's touch base later today."

Richard and Dahlia exchanged glances, and walked quietly out of the room. Dahlia left instructions for Alex not to be disturbed until they had returned.

Alex awoke several hours later, feeling refreshed. It was very odd to be lying there, surrounded by the daily bustle of the unit.

He yelled "Nurse, nurse."

Fran stuck her head in. "What's the matter? Bladder full? Need a catheter? Need a cathartic?" She chuckled heartily. "You're my patient now."

Alex made a face. "I always get mixed up about cathartics. Do they make you barf or poop?"

Fran giggled. "I hope your patients don't hear you say that. Poop is the therapeutic effect."

"I just need a phone. Can you get me one?"

"For you, anything."

She disappeared for a moment, then came in with a portable phone.

"That will do for now."

"Yes your highness."

"But Fran, when Richard gets me my computer I'll need one with a regular cord."

"Yes your lordship."

"Thanks." He took the phone from her. She stayed in the room, staring at him for a time. Then, as he stared back and made a face, she smiled and left.

He dialed the phone and asked for telephone information for Washington, District of Columbia.

"Robert Oshinski, U.S. Army."

"One moment please."

The operator came back with a number that Alex wrote down.

He dialed it, and waited while the phone rang. "Washington Military Hospital."

"Radiology Department."

The departmental secretary answered. "Radiology."

"Dr. Oshinski, please."

"One moment." A stirring military march played tinnily on the phone, then a click.

"Dr. Oshinski speaking."

"Big Bob, how are you?"

"Who's this?"

"Alex, Alex Adams, old buddy."

"Alex." Bob was glad to hear from him. "How are things going? You still stuck at University Hospital?"

"Yep." Alex felt a pang of guilt. He was stuck there, but not a resident anymore.

"See, that's why you should have gone into radiology like I told you. Remember what I said?"

"While I was taking care of the dregs, you'd be out enjoying the world."

Bob laughed. "That's right. Now what can I do for you?"

Alex paused. "Bob, I'm talking to you from a hospital ICU bed, with two broken legs, just off the ventilator."

Oshinski's voice deepened. "Sorry to hear that. What happened?"

"I had a bad accident, and it may have been intentional."

"Oh boy."

"I need help, Bob."

"Anything, buddy."

So far, so good. "Bob do you remember when we were interns and you came into work dehydrated with a terrible hangover?"

"Yep."

"I plugged an IV into you, got you hydrated, stayed around and covered for you while you got better."

"You saved me, Alex. I told you that."

Alex paused. "I risked my residency."

"I know. I owe you my job."

"I need help Bob. I need an answer to this question. Has the President ever had an MRI?"

Silence. The beeping of the monitors seemed louder as Alex waited. "I need help, Bob, like you did."

"You know Alex, this could be my job."

"I need help."

The silence continued, then Oshinski sighed. "The President did have an MRI. He got a CT scan a while ago and the docs noticed something that raised questions. The Pres refused an MRI until the docs insisted, and then he had it. Nothing came of it."

Alex sensed there was more to the story. "Bob, it's me. I need the info."

Silence.

"Bob, I'm in a hospital bed. I'm asking you because of what I did for you."

Silence. Outside his room Alex could hear the nurse's aides chattering.

"Okay, Alex. This evens us out. Rumor has it the President's MRI did show an odd area of signal change. I don't know where."

"The basal forebrain?"

"I honestly don't know. At any rate, the President told them it runs in his family. He told them an autopsy on his grandfather years ago showed a small cyst in the exact same location, case closed."

Alex lay back. That guy can talk his way out of anything.

"Bob, I need to see that scan."

"Forget it."

"Bob, I have to have it." Alex sat up, his legs aching. "Have I ever lied to you?"

"No."

"This is a matter of national security."

"Don't make me laugh."

"I'm lying in an ICU bed, nearly dead, and I'm telling you I need to see that scan."

Silence.

"Bob, I could have lost my future when I helped you out."

Bob answered slowly. "The MRI scans are kept in a data warehouse on the network server, Armymed images.org. The password to get in from the Internet is inornate."

"I didn't even know there was a word like that."

"The President's alias is Milton Munger." A pause. "Alex, I never talked to you."

"Some day I'll tell you what this is all about."

Oshinski hung up.

Alex put the phone down, then eased his head back on the bed and took a deep, painful breath. He was right. Grimacing, he closed his eyes. He was on the right track.

He awoke to Richard shaking him. "Alex, Alex, wake up. I've got your computer."

Alex opened his eyes, the square, earnest face uncomfortably close. He stretched his arms, pain reverberating through his legs. "Thanks a lot, Richard."

The student nodded and looked at him expectantly.

"Anything else going on?"

"Dahlia is trying to get hold of the coroner. Nothing else at the moment."

"Okay."

"I'm going to try to do some of that work we talked about, over at Radiation Therapy, this evening."

Alex nodded. "Good job. Don't get caught."

Richard patted Alex awkwardly on the shoulder. "I'll see you later."

"Tell Fran to bring in a real phone line, will you? I gotta go surfing."

Richard smiled and nodded. He walked out of the room and Alex heard him murmuring to Fran.

After a couple of minutes Fran came in, muttering to herself, carrying a phone attached to a long cord. She put it next to his bedside on the table. "Here it is, your nibs," she said in a tone of aggrieved petulance.

"Thanks a lot, Fran."

She walked out of the room grumbling, her knock-kneed thighs rustling together. "I'll see you later. Change of shift, but I'll be back tonight."

"Thanks."

Alex plugged the phone jack into the laptop computer and dialed up the Internet. Connecting, he located the network server that Bob had told him about. Giving the password when requested, he opened into the images database.

Scrolling through names, he located the President's alias and selected it. The next screen was a warning concerning the confidentiality of the information, which Alex ignored. He clicked on the MRI study.

As the pictures were being loaded, he was distracted by a figure blocking the light at the door. He looked up to see Clark Hackman plodding in, flashing him a sharp stare before glancing down importantly at the floor, then stopping at the bedside as Alex scrutinized him.

"Hi, Alex."

"Dr. Hackman."

"How are you doing?"

"Okay, okay."

Hackman's small eyes shifted uncomfortably. "You've had a hell of a time, haven't you?"

"Yep."

"It all started with all that talk about virtue, on rounds. Remember?" Hackman smiled awkwardly, and Alex felt cold.

"Like I said, a civilization which does not prize virtue and teach it to its children will devour them."

"Right." The word loitered in his vocal cords as Hackman glanced at the monitor aimlessly for a moment. "Well, just wanted to see how you're doing. Call if you need anything. I see you got your computer quick." He nodded at the laptop, lingering to see what Alex was doing. Alex shifted in the bed as if uncomfortable, but maneuvered the screen away from Hackman's darting eyes.

"Thanks. Thanks a lot for coming by."

"See you later."

Hackman raised up his hand stiffly, dropped it awkwardly, nodded, and turned. Alex took a deep breath, watched him as he ambled out, then looked at the screen again. He groaned in disappointment as he read the message.

"Your request will be processed in the order it was received. Please enter the email address to which the file is to be sent." He punched in his address, then closed down the computer. Sinking back in the bed, he closed his eyes, his head throbbing. The pain rammed into his thoughts, pulsing with his heartbeat. It started at the base of his skull, behind his ears, then traveled up, like someone had sunk ice tongs there and was trying to pull off his head. It was bad before, Alex thought, now it was much worse. Why didn't the Boss get a CT scan on him?

There was a sudden flurry of activity outside the room, then Dr. Todd strode in, his immaculately coifed head leaning forward with concern. Alex recognized the familiar look of compassion.

"Alex, very, very sorry" said Dr. Todd as he came around the bed. "How are you doing?"

"Okay, Dr. Todd. Other than the broken flippers." Alex pointed to his legs.

"Well, you're all in one piece. That's the important thing."

They both fell silent for a moment.

For the first time Alex had ever seen, the Boss looked ill at ease, older, as he hesitated for a moment. "May I sit down?"

"Of course."

"Thank you." He settled down into the sterile chair, then edged forward with both elbows resting on his knees, hands clasped together. He swallowed and cleared his throat with a deep rumble. "It's not the best time to discuss this, but I want to get it off my chest. I do have a heavy responsibility, Alex, for patient care, for teaching, and I take that responsibility very seriously. Very seriously indeed. I do not tolerate error well." He paused and raised his great head to look out the window for a moment. "I am hard on myself, as well as those I am entrusted to teach. Most importantly, however, I am always on guard against jumping to conclusions." His dark eyes focused on Alex, as if trying to soundlessly transmit the message he was implying.

Alex shifted slightly in the bed.

"I'm as human as the next man, fallible, with feet of clay. There's a saying about teaching doctors, however, that I've always kept in mind. 'Those who fail to teach their successors well commit a crime against humanity.' I will never be accused of that."

Alex looked past the Boss to the figures moving at the nursing station. "You always have had the highest standards of instruction."

The Boss was silent for a time, looking over to the window again. "We miss you on the clinical service."

"Thanks."

The Boss coughed. "I know you and Dahlia went to the Dean. You must realize, Alex, that Dahlia had a very hard time when her husband died. She had to be hospitalized herself. She had terrible nightmares, and her hold on reality at the time was tenuous at best. She feels very deeply, and that's what makes her such a superb physician, but that can be a double edged sword."

"She was very upset over Dr. Frey's CT scan. She thought it looked like her husband's."

"Dr. Frey was an old and dear friend. As you grow old, you learn that friends can differ, sometimes strongly, and our relationship had its ups and downs. Mrs. Frey felt very guilty about her husband's illness, because she made decisions about treatment which did not work out. As a result, I know she is very unhappy."

Alex's head ached terribly, and some of the Boss's words seemed like they were coming from a distance, as fatigue crept up on him. What did Dahlia say about nightmares? As the Boss spoke, Alex's eyes roamed about the room and would sometimes float apart, forming a double image, then snap back into focus as he willed them together.

"You also had concerns about the monkey and Mr. Frederick."

"Yes. We had discussed it in your office." Alex precisely forced the words out, trying to conceal his fatigue and pounding head.

"At that time I forgot to bring it up, but I had written a brief paper some time ago about the complications of subdural hematomas, identifying the various scars that could form." The Boss glanced at him, saw his exhaustion, drew a folded, stapled sheet of paper out of his pocket, and laid it on the bedside table. "Look at this when you get a chance. It may explain your concern."

Alex nodded, fatigue overwhelming him.

The Boss stood. "Well, I'm glad you're on the mend."

Alex closed his eyes. "One more thing, Dr. Todd." He swallowed, and whispered, "Why didn't you get a CT scan on me? On my brain?"

"I need to talk to you about that, Alex, that and the MRI scan you had a while ago."

Alex felt himself drifting away. He wanted to listen, but Dr. Todd's words seemed to come from far away. Death must be like this, he thought, an overwhelming warm fatigue that envelops you like the softest of down comforters.

The Boss looked at Alex as his breathing became regular, his face relaxed. "Another time" he said softly, then turned and left the room.

A nurse looked up as he left. "How's he doing?"

"Just needs some rest."

The unit was quiet as the evening wore on. At the change of shift, eleven P.M., the only patient was Alex, with Fran at the nursing station. She peered into the room. He was sleeping peacefully.

She sat down. The phone rang.

"Hi, Fran." It was Dahlia.

"Hi."

"How is Alex?"

"Sleeping like a baby."

"Listen, Fran. Don't let anyone in to see him, okay? Even Dr. Todd."

"What?"

"Please do as I say. I'm on my beeper, but I've been called to the emergency room by Dr. Hackman and I'll have to stay for a while. Please, please watch him and don't let anybody in. Promise?"

"You sound kind of crazy, Dahlia. What's going on?"

"Just listen to me."

"OK, OK." Fran hung up the phone and shook her head, wondering what was going on. She picked up a magazine. It was mighty quiet with only one patient.

Alex opened his eyes. For a moment he wondered where he was, then remembered. The windows were dark. What did the Boss say? He couldn't recall. He lay in the hospital bed, thinking, remembering, wondering. I've come so far, he thought. Surely it wasn't over. It can't end now. He thought of his parents, his father so proud, knowing that he would be a doctor.

"Fran?" He called out of the room.

"What?" She was sitting at the nurses' station, eating a fried chicken drumstick.

"Can you help me out of bed? I'm tired of lying in here."

"You've got to take it easy. You were just extubated this morning."

"I heal quick. I'm tired of lying here. I'll get a pulmonary embolus. Can you help me into a chair?"

"Well, okay." She came into the room.

"You're greasy again."

"So what."

"How about a wheelchair?"

"Are you nuts? You can't go anywhere."

"It'll support my shanks better. They've got those leg holder things." She snorted. "I guess so. Just don't be falling out of it."

"Thanks."

She waddled out of the room and returned, pushing a wheelchair. Placing it carefully next to his bed, she locked the wheels and laboriously bent down, breathing heavily, then adjusted the leg supports. She stood up, then noticed him staring at it.

"What's the matter?"

He looked at her and smiled weakly. "I never liked those things."

She smiled softly. "I remember. You won't even sit in them. That time we had the wheelchair races. You wouldn't sit in it. Said you were afraid you'd end up in one."

He nodded. "Well, I guess I've got to now."

"You don't have to."

"Yes I do."

Alex sat up, wincing from the pain in his legs. Fran came around and tenderly held him under his arms.

"One, two, three." She eased him over onto the chair, his casts still on the bed, then came around and slid his legs onto the wheelchair supports.

"Ow" he moaned.

"Be quiet, you big baby. This was your idea."

"It hurts."

She made a face at him. "Plenty of people hurt worse than you, they keep quiet."

Embarrassed, he was silent for a moment. "Well, thanks a lot. I feel better now."

"Just relax there. I'll get you back into bed in about an hour."

She waddled out, and sat heavily down into the chair at the nurses' station.

Alex rested in the wheelchair, thinking. What was the Boss doing? He barely remembered the Boss visiting him. Fired. The shame hit him hard. I'll never be a neurosurgeon while Dr. Todd is around. But I am a physician. And the Code says, above all, do no harm. Todd must be stopped. They must get the smoking gun. He thought again. The lab. It has to be in his lab.

After pondering, he picked up the phone and called the local pizza parlor, whose proprietor he knew. "Marie?"

"Yes."

"It's Alex. How are you doing?"

"Good doc, good. What can I do for you?"

"The girls in Special Care deserve a couple of pizzas. Can you send up three of them? One plain, one with onions and one with pepperoni?" Fran especially liked pepperoni on her pizza.

"Sure."

"Just tell them it's from a grateful patient."

She chuckled. "Don't want to take the credit, hey?"

"Tell them it's for the Special Care nurses and Fran. Make sure you mention Fran."

"Okay, doc. It will be up in twenty minutes."

Hanging up the phone, he rested his head on the back of the wheelchair, shifting his body until it cried out the least. Dozing, he woke up abruptly when the phone rang at the nurses' station. Fran grabbed it. "Neurologic Intensive Care Unit." She listened for a time. "Great, I'll be right over."

Getting up with a sigh, she went over to Alex's door and looked in.

"I'm just going next door to the Special Care Unit. We'll put you in bed when I get back."

"Okay."

She gave him a smile, and then went out and up the hall, through the double doors.

He waited for a time, then unlocked the wheelchair and started rolling. Cautiously going through the door, he looked around the unit. No one there. Turning to the left, he spun the right wheel while holding the other still. Pretty good for a neophyte.

He wheeled down the hallway and out the back door of the ICU. There were no patient rooms in this part of the hospital, and all was quiet. Stopping at the elevator, he pressed the down button and waited. The elevator door opened. Empty. Good. After rolling in he spun around, pressing the button for the basement.

The door closed, the elevator hummed and descended, his legs aching more with the heaviness as the elevator stopped. Wheeling forward as the door opened, he went into the hallway and turned right, rolling down the dimly lit corridor.

Lining the passageway was the detritus of the hospital, the equipment, the beds, all at one time thought advanced but now obsolete, standing mute, their tasks done. Alex passed by a bed mounted inside a huge circle, remembering how a comatose patient would be secured inside and then spun to help blood circulate. Alex grimaced and kept rolling.

He passed by a heavy chair looking like a medieval torture device, and stopped when he realized what it was. The air encephalography chair. He had read about that old diagnostic method, predating the MRI and CT scan. In order to get a picture of the brain, air was injected into the spine. The patient was then strapped to the chair and twirled around, head over heels, to make the air float to the nooks and crannies of the brain. X rays were then taken, the air outlining the brain and any tumors present. It was said no patient who went through the test would permit another, so sick would it make them.

He started rolling again, his arms pumping, and the hallway changed to worn, dark brick walls and rough floor. The old medical school building. His arms burning, he finally saw the laboratory door, Dr. Todd's lab. Turning, he tried the battered knob. Locked. Looking around, he tried it again. The glass clattered as he shook the door. Locked. He backed up, searching for a hidden key. No mat. Glancing up at the doorframe, he remembered a broom down the hallway. Turning around, he rolled and got it. Bringing it back on his lap, he carefully swept it along the top of the door. No key. He slumped back, and then examined the door carefully. It was old and heavy, with two locks, one in the doorplate and one above it, looking like a dead bolt. Even if he broke the glass, and opened the lower lock, the upper deadbolt would still need a key.

I need to get in there, he thought. I've come too far.

He looked around. No crowbars. Then he remembered the air encephalography chair. That was real heavy.

Rolling back down the hallway he found the chair, mounted on small wheels. Taking off his gown, he twisted it and tied one end to the encephalography chair, the other to the wheelchair. Pushing the wheelchair backwards, he towed the heavy chair back.

Untying the chair, he swung it in front of him. Locking his wheels, he took a deep breath, leaned forward and pushed the air encephalography chair into the lab door. It cracked against the door, the door rattling but holding. Startled at the noise, Alex looked around. A security guard, or the Boss's creepy assistant Weber, could be close by. The tunnel was quiet. He was very much alone.

Grabbing the chair again, he held onto it tightly, then heaved it into the door. With a loud crash it opened, tearing the doorjamb. The noise resounded through the empty halls. Somebody must have heard it. He froze and listened. All quiet.

Pushing the heavy chair before him, he rolled in and shoved it aside. Again he paused. The stillness was complete. He looked around. Things were the same as when the monkey went sour. The far wall was lined with dark windows, opening to the blank side of a newer building. He wheeled around, checking the blacktopped counters. An occasional large roach scuttled around. Alex shook his head. Couldn't stomp on them now. Continuing to roll around, he saw plastic buckets under one counter, transparent and filled with fluid. Alex bent down and pulled one out. Yanking off the top, he gazed down onto a dark black hairy ball, bobbing in the greasy liquid. Staring, he realized it was a severed human head. He looked for a time, then snapped the lid back on. Moving to other buckets, he opened one. A human brain, floating upside down. Alex examined the bottom surface carefully, following the olfactory nerves to the basal forebrain. It looked a bit scarred. Then he noticed the abrasions over the rest of the bottom of the brain. Somebody was rough with this one. It seemed to be worst, though, at the basal forebrain, he told himself.

Alex's eyes narrowed. He replaced the top of the bucket, then continued to prowl. Rolling down the aisle, he pulled open drawer after drawer. No luck. Then a small, chipped, green metal file cabinet caught his eye. He pulled at its handle. Locked. He yanked harder and harder, and gave it a jerk. Suddenly the door opened with a screech. Alex stopped, looked around and listened, and heard nothing. Glancing at the files, he saw titles on brain function and anatomy. He quickly scanned through the other drawers. Nothing informative.

Shoving the cabinet back, he spun around the lab again, thinking furiously. Fran would be back to the ICU shortly. She could only eat so much pizza.

His gaze rested on the grimy plastic pails holding the heads, reminding him of the Boss's office, where the key to the files was in the skull.

Rolling over, he slid some containers out. Far back behind the stacked buckets, he spied a small file case. He reached under, moved another bucket, then tipped it, spilling the fluid and a head out onto the floor.

Cursing, he righted the bucket and gingerly grabbed the head by its bristly hair. The skin was wrinkled like hard parchment. His eyes were drawn to the dead mouth, desiccated and shrunken, with large yellow front teeth. Like beaver teeth, he thought, then noticed the small tooth right in the middle of the two larger ones. Fascinated for a moment, he then eased it back into the bucket and snapped the top. Maneuvering the wheelchair, he reached under the counter, grabbed the file case and slid it out.

It was a small, locked metal box. Opening drawers, he looked for a hammer. No luck. He slammed down the locked side of the box on the edge of the lab table. It held firm. He tried again, then again. The clasp ripped open.

Flipping the top up, he saw a neat row of manila folders. As he reached for them, he heard footsteps coming down the hall. He froze, then grabbed the files, putting them underneath the cushion in the air encephalography chair. Carefully, he slid the filing case back into position, then replaced the bucket.

He listened. Quiet. He started to roll around, looking and listening, then stopped. Nothing. He rolled through the lab door, leaning to look up and down the tunnel. No movement. He furiously spun the wheelchair around, tipped it over, and saw the sharp, black tabletop edge coming toward him. In the corner of his eye stood Weber, reaching out from too far away. It's going to hurt, thought Alex in a flash. My headaches are going to get worse. He tried to get his arms up in time.

CHAPTER 28

D ahlia finally broke loose from the emergency room and grabbed a phone. Punching in the number of the ICU, she waited as it rang, tapping the table. Listening to ring after ring without an answer, she quickly hung up. Where was Fran? Dashing to the elevator, she went up to the critical care floor, running through the half open doors down the hall into the Neurologic Intensive Care Unit. Quiet as a mausoleum at midnight. She raced to Alex's room. Empty. Turning, she ran next door to the Special Care Unit, bursting into the room where Fran was eating pizza with several other nurses.

"Where's Alex?"

Fran looked up, her mouth open and full of pizza. She swallowed, her neck jiggling, and turned pale under her pink makeup. "He's not in his bed?"

"He's gone."

She stood up quickly. "I just came in here for a minute. Somebody sent us pizza."

"Has anyone gone through here?"

The nurses shook their heads.

That left only the back way. Dahlia turned and darted out. She ran through the rear door and down the dark hallway, stopping at the elevator.

Where could they go from here? she desperately thought. What was down below? She reviewed the floors in her mind, all patient care areas, and then the MRI scanner. That's it. Todd has taken him to the MRI scan. He's going to treat him tonight.

Finding a stairwell, she jumped down the stairs three at a time, her sneakers slapping the steps. Thrusting the radiology door open, she ran to the MRI machine. It was dark, the door locked. She looked through the window. All was quiet.

Please, please, she thought, where are they? If they had finished the MRI scan, they would be taking him to the radiation area. But what if she was wrong? What if they were doing something else? Going somewhere else?

Radiation therapy. Making a decision, she spun around. She ran down the corridor, then rapidly descended the stairs to the Radiation Department, at the furthest reaches of the hospital complex. The door was locked. She looked in the window. Far down the hall, where the radiation machines were located, she saw a man flit back and forth. The walk was familiar. Then it hit her. Weber. She pounded on the door, screaming, but the door held. She looked around for a phone, saw one on the wall and lunged for it. Dead. No tone.

She thought of Alex in the radiation machine, his brain immobilized, taking jolt after jolt of energy. Banging on the door again, she pushed at it frantically. There was no other way in.

Still for a moment, her mind raced. Hospital security can get in. She turned around and ran back to the main hospital, running up the stairs and over to the nursing floor. Going to a nursing station, she surprised two sleepy nurse's aides talking slowly to each other, reclining squatly in their chairs.

"Call Security" she yelled.

One put a hand to her chest, the other jumped out of the chair and stared at her.

Dahlia grabbed the phone and dialed.

A bored voice answered. "Hello, Security."

Breathing heavily, she could hardly talk. "This is Dr. Laronge."

"Dr. Who?"

"Dr. Laronge, neurosurgery" she shrieked. "Meet me down in Radiation Therapy."

"Yes ma'am."

She slammed the phone down and raced back the way she had come, her white coat flying behind her. The aide slowly sat down, looking at her and shaking her head.

Dahlia ran down the stairs again and down the distant hallway. Images of her husband as he lay dying came into her mind, then a picture of Alex, his head in the radiosurgery frame.

Turning a corner, she ran up to the radiation department door. It was quiet. She looked in through the window. Dark, completely dark. Rattling the heavy door, she backed up against it and closed her eyes, the metal cool on her heaving back.

Footsteps broke into her desperation. "Here, here" she called out. Two guards trotted up.

"What's the problem, Doctor?"

Dahlia moved away from the door, turned and pointed. "In there, get me in there" she said between gasps.

They eyed her curiously but opened the door. Racing down the long hallway to the dark treatment area, she stopped and looked around. The guards, breathing hard, came up. "Dr. Laronge, what's the problem?"

"There was an unauthorized use of this facility."

They exchanged glances, still puffing. "When?"

"Just a short time ago."

"We'll take a look around, doctor. You better calm down."

Dahlia ignored them and darted around, checking the treatment vaults. The guards followed her until they had covered the area.

"Everything looks okay, Doctor."

She shook her head. "I saw them down here."

"Who?" They looked at her curiously.

She paused for a moment, her breathing slowing, then shook her head. Looking up, she took a deep breath. "Thanks very much."

"We better get you out of here."

She nodded slowly and pulled herself together. They walked down the hallway, then out the door. The guards turned to lock it, but Dahlia continued as her beeper went off. She checked the number. The ICU. Breaking into a run, she sprinted away, her white sneakers pumping.

Reaching a phone, she called. Fran answered quickly. "He's here."

"How is he?"

"I don't know, I don't know. It's the funniest thing. We got a call from Radiology. They said they found him there in a litter, and then they brought him up. He's sleeping."

"What do you mean, sleeping?"

"Well, he's sleeping. I mean, he's not awake. If you pinch him he moves, but doesn't wake up. Like he got clunked on the head or something."

"I'll be right there."

Dahlia hit the elevator button and paced. The door opened and she stepped in, then turned as it closed. As soon as the door opened again, she sped down the hall, through the doors to the ICU. Fran was waiting in Alex's room, the lights off, her face round and pale as she turned to Dahlia. He was there, eyes closed.

Dahlia, icy fear in her heart, walked up to him. She opened his eyes with thin trembling fingers. Pupils reactive. Gently she let the eyelids close, then pinched him, and he stirred slightly. She thought furiously. What did they do to him? She shook her head. How much radiation did they give him? It was too early for radiation effect. Though nothing is impossible for that man. If only she hadn't left. She was down in the emergency room for too long, thanks to Hackman.

Turning slowly, she pulled up a chair to the bedside. Sitting down, she started her vigil.

Fran looked at her face, gaunt and drawn in the dark. "Here for the duration, huh?"

Dahlia nodded. "Yeah, he'd do the same for me."

She came closer. "What's really going on around here? He's the best resident, and they say he's been fired. And what went on tonight?"

Dahlia shook her head wearily. "I don't know, I honestly don't know. I'm just going to stay here, no matter what."

"Paul told me Alex is going off the deep end, just like his father."

"His father?"

"Yeah, his father was institutionalized after his mother died. Paul says it runs in the family."

"How the hell does Paul know?"

Fran shook her head, her lips pursed and cheeks sagging with uncertainty. They both glanced at Alex, then Fran's eyes moved to Dahlia. "Can I get you anything?"

"No thanks." She gazed out the window into the darkness, noticing her reflection in the glass. Then she turned and put her head down on the bed, her hair falling over her face like a monk's hood. She hoped the nightmares wouldn't come that night.

Dahlia's beeper went off and she lifted her head. It was seven A.M. and the morning shift was coming in. They cast curious looks into the room, as Dahlia shook her hair. She looked at Alex, who still was unconscious. Carefully lifting up his eyelids, she again looked into his eyes. Pupils still reactive. Pinching him, he only stirred. Sick with fear, remembering the events of last night, she brushed back his hair. Please wake up. Then she remembered the beep. Going out to the nursing station, she dialed the phone. It was Curt.

"Dahlia, where are you?"

Patient rounds, she suddenly remembered. "Sorry, sorry, I'll be right there." Hanging up the phone, she slowly walked over to Alex's room, and looked in at him sleeping. Turning to the nurses at the station, she caught the eye of a small Filipino nurse, one of the best.

"Teddy, keep an eye on him."

"Sure."

"Don't let anyone near him."

He laughed, "Only the doctors."

"Not Dr. Todd."

He looked at her, impressed at the near hysteria in her voice. "No, okay."

"Call me if Dr. Todd comes up here."

"Sure. Right away."

She looked around. He didn't understand. "Beep me if anybody comes." He nodded. She left the unit and went over to the patient floor where Curt was waiting.

"You look terrible."

"Thanks." She shook her head. "Let's get started. I've got a case soon."

They went from patient to patient, Dahlia examining them as Curt wrote the notes. She sighed as her beeper went off. Grimacing, she grabbed it from her waist. "The OR. I've got that long operation, the tumor, with Hackman."

Curt nodded.

"Curt, do me a favor. Keep your eye on Alex. Don't let anyone close to him."

He shook his head, puzzled. "I won't, I'll watch him."

"Thanks."

"Don't forget we have Grand Rounds tonight."

She thought. "Grand Rounds. Yeah, we'll give them a show."

Dahlia went down to the O.R. locker room and changed, then trotted into the operating room, the patient asleep in the center like a display on a pedestal. Ignoring the circulator, scrub nurse and anesthesia resident, she proceeded to expertly clip and shave the patient's head, then positioned it carefully, impaling the headholder pins into his skull to secure the cranium.

"Prep tray."

The circulating nurse wheeled the small metal table over, its top covered with sterile towels. The iodine solution was poured into carefully positioned silver pans, like a religious ceremony.

Dahlia donned sterile gloves, her small slim fingers leaving wrinkles in the fingertips. She prepped, then scrubbed and gowned as the nurse draped the patient.

"Knife."

"Don't you think we should call Dr. Hackman?" said Carol.

"Okay. But we'll keep rolling."

The circulating nurse called Dr. Hackman's office, murmuring in a low voice, then hung up.

Dahlia held her palm out and Carol snapped the scalpel into it, her gaze first on the diminutive hand, then traveling to Dahlia's eyes as the surgeon worked, silent and preoccupied.

"How are things going?"

"Okay." She started to cut.

"How's Alex?"

Dahlia's scalpel swung wide of the purple line on the scalp. "Damn" she muttered in frustration. "Okay I guess."

They continued to work in silence, punctuated only by brisk requests for instruments. The door opened and Dr. Hackman came in, his head enveloped in surgical hat and mask. Walking over to the operative field, he looked over Dahlia's shoulder and nodded.

"It looks good, Dahlia. I'll scrub now."

She continued working.

Hackman joined her and they operated through the day, slowly whittling down the tumor embedded in the brain.

Late in the afternoon, Dahlia's beeper went off. The circulating nurse looked at the number and dialed it, listened and then spoke to Dahlia.

"It's the medical student. He's got to talk to you."

Her head fleetingly vibrated, with a transient shudder, as she continued concentrating, wielding instruments deep in the patient's cerebrum. "I can't. He'll just have to wait."

The nurse spoke in the phone briefly. "He says to call him as soon as you get out."

"Okay" she said wearily. "Hold on. Tell him to collect the stuff we presented to the Dean for Grand Rounds tonight."

Hackman looked up at her, raised eyebrows hidden under his hood. "Something special for Grand Rounds?"

"Yep. A special case presentation" she said gravely, then glanced at the circulating nurse, her gown rustling. "Did you tell him?"

The nurse nodded. "He says okay. Don't forget to call him." She hung up the phone.

Dahlia turned to the patient once again, willing herself to concentrate on the task at hand.

Finally, at six in the evening, Hackman stepped away and grunted in satisfaction. "Nice job, Dahlia. We've really helped this patient."

She nodded. "Hopefully so. Thanks."

"I'll see you at Grand Rounds." Snorting involuntarily, he ripped off his gown and rolled it up, missing the trashcan with a careless throw. Ignoring the crumpled garment on the floor, he left the room.

Dahlia's heart sank at the thought of what she must present at Grand Rounds. Sighing, she systematically stitched the patient's bone in place, then his scalp, while visualizing Alex lying in a hospital bed, just like her husband. After finishing the suturing, she took the patient out of the clamp, adroitly wrapping the head.

Carol smiled under her mask. "That's much nicer than Alex's. It takes a woman's touch, I guess."

Dahlia looked up at her sadly for a moment. She grabbed the patient's chart and murmured, "Meet you in the Recovery Room." The anesthesia resident nodded, and Dahlia spun and went out of the room.

Carol looked at the anesthesia resident. "She's real quiet. Seems depressed."

"Naw, she's just tired. They're all shaken up about what happened to Alex."

"That's a heck of a thing."

Dahlia walked down the OR hall to the Recovery Room, her baggy scrub shirt fluttering around her small arms. She walked slowly, numbly, the maroon plastic patient binder at her side. Entering the Recovery Room, she slumped at the counter. Slapping down the chart with a clatter, she scrawled the operative note and orders, then picked up the phone and dictated the operative report in a flat monotone.

Dougherty, the urology resident, sat down beside her with a grin. "You sound like a robot. Long case, huh?"

She finished dictating and slammed the phone down. He jumped a bit at the crash. She nodded slowly, looking straight ahead.

"What's been going on in the neurosurgery program?"

She stopped breathing for a moment. "Why don't you leave me alone?"

Shrugging, he pulled back. "Yeah, sure." He hastily stood and strode away.

She glanced at the clock. Seven o'clock. Getting up, she walked down the hall towards Grand Rounds.

CHAPTER 29

Dahlia turned the corner to the old amphitheater. Thing seemed quiet. She slowed, and walked purposefully into the back of the large crowded room. As she came forward, faces glanced at her expectantly.

She passed by the chair where Alex usually sat, looking down for a moment, then continued to the front of the room where Curt had placed a pile of films to be presented. The overhead projector stood nearby.

Dr. Todd rose from his customary spot. "Due to Alex's unfortunate accident, and other circumstances, Dahlia Laronge has taken over as Acting Chief Resident and will supervise Grand Rounds the rest of the academic year, as well as next year." Smiling warmly at Dahlia, he slowly lowered himself to his seat. For a moment, his vitality and physical splendor awed her, reminding her of a magnificent lion surveying his domain. She banished the thought quickly, her face tightening. He had made no mention of firing Alex.

Turning her gaze to the assemblage, she noticed with surprise that the Dean was present, watching her warily. Also unexpected was Mr. Gilson, watery eyes framed with pinkish plastic rimmed glasses. Still for a moment, then a crescendo of blinks started, climaxed by a cacophony of facial movement. Beside Mr. Gilson were several other men and women, unknown to her.

She nodded to Curt, who sprang up and started arranging the

films of the patients to be presented, interesting cases treated recently. As she looked past him, her eyes lingered on Alex's chair.

Chief Resident, she thought, I am now Chief Resident. She took a deep breath and walked over to Curt.

"That's OK, Curt. I won't be using those," she whispered to him.

He looked at her questioningly, but her firm tone told him she had made up her mind.

"But these are the cases we reviewed, that I'm ready for" he hissed at her.

"I know. We won't need them."

"What are you doing?"

"The right thing."

"Don't do something stupid." Curt was fried from his recent Grand Rounds presentation and wanted no surprises. He well knew he would be the first target for any questions from the attendings, and had prepared by reading up on the cases they had planned to present.

"I know what I'm doing."

Curt shook his head and reluctantly sat down.

Dahlia turned to the quieting audience.

"Welcome to Neurosurgery Grand Rounds. Tonight I have decided to present certain interesting cases, some of whom may be familiar to you, Dean Tripp."

He stirred in his chair, eyes narrowing ever so slightly.

"First, some anatomy. Can I have the slides, please?"

She grabbed the slide projector controller and flashed a slide up on the screen as the lights dimmed. Bringing out her laser pointer, she raised her head and started in a loud, thin voice. "To refresh the students' and residents' memory, here are some anatomic points relevant to the cases we will be presenting. This is a low axial brain slice showing the thalamus, temporal lobes, frontal lobe, and here, the basal forebrain." She jabbed at the areas with her laser pointer, the scintillating dot dancing. "The function of this area of the brain is not well understood. It lies just above the optic nerves, which run, of course, to the back of the eyes and end in the retina. Any pathology in the basal forebrain can affect the optic nerve and hence the retina due to the proximity of these structures."

"We already know this" Dr. Todd interrupted. "What's the relevance?"

"The relevance will become clear." Her voice trembled for a moment. "The first case to be presented is that of my husband, who died of a brain tumor."

Dr. Todd exchanged glances with the Dean.

"He spoke of radiation treatments, radiosurgery, babbling as he was deteriorating, even though he never had those treatments. But I should say, we never gave permission for those treatments." She ended with a sibilant, cutting cry.

The room was absolutely silent, uncertain as to what to make of this. Dahlia took a deep breath.

"The second case is that of an experimental monkey in Dr. Todd's lab. The animal abruptly deteriorated, and examination of the pupils showed a bluish tint to the retina. Intra-operative observation showed scarring in the basal forebrain area. Isn't that right, Dr. Fox?"

Paul looked acutely uncomfortable. He said slowly, "This was an experimental monkey with a spontaneous subdural hematoma. The large clot made it difficult to ascertain any underlying pathology. After the clot was removed, normal structures were so distorted that no accurate statement could be made about that area, or any other area." Paul looked over at Dr. Todd in supplication.

Dahlia stared down at him with contempt. "Alex noted the scarring of the basal forebrain." She spat out the words, looking at Paul.

He shrugged. "I have answered you, Dahlia," he said in a gently chiding tone.

"Case three is Mr. Frederick, with an acute subdural hematoma operated on by Dr. Adams and Dr. Todd. This patient was noted to have a bluish tint to his retinas on his admission examination. Intra-operative observation showed unexplained scarring in the basal forebrain. Subsequently, it was discovered this patient had radiosurgery. Here is the treatment plan." She flashed up another slide, and outlined the area of radiation dose. "As you can see, such a dose would produce a lesion in the basal forebrain exactly where my husband had pathology and where it was present in the experimental monkey and Mr. Frederick."

The Dean and Dr. Todd were whispering, their heads together. Suddenly the Dean stood up. "Dr. Laronge, as you know, we have already been through this. We have discussed your feelings and responded to your issues," he said, turning as he spoke to the audience. "Do you have any further points to make?"

Dahlia's eyes swept over the room as she spoke to the audience. "Dr. Todd cared for all three cases. He is the common factor. These radiosurgical treatments I have mentioned are not medically justifiable, and have not been done under proper rules of medical care or experimentation."

The Dean, still standing, sighed. "Dr. Laronge, that will be enough. We have been over this before, and I have done my best to address your" he paused, "concerns. When it comes to you blackening the reputation of Dr. Todd, this Department, and this institution with wild speculation we must halt. I need to see you in my office at seven o'clock tomorrow morning." He glanced at Dr. Todd.

The room was silent. They had never seen anything like this, an accusation directed publicly against the Chief of Neurosurgery by a resident.

Dr. Todd stood up, and with a respectful bow, walked a couple paces towards Dahlia. He spoke in a low, sympathetic voice. "We appreciate your patience, Dean. I take no offense. Dr. Laronge has done exceptional work, and I think is simply overwrought with her personal tragedy, the unfortunate accident and situation with Dr. Adams, and the new and heavy responsibilities suddenly thrust upon her. Dr. Laronge is very concerned about Alex, as we all are. I think it wise and appropriate that we conclude Grand Rounds at this point." The Dean nodded, and turned to leave his seat. Several of the spectators shifted awkwardly.

Dahlia glared at Dr. Todd with a blazing fury in her eyes. She raised up her head and was about to speak, when the side door of the amphitheater opened. She turned in surprise, as did everybody in the room. Richard Walters wheeled Alex in, then angled and pushed him to the front. Alex looked straight ahead, pale and strained, then glanced at Dahlia. Hope arose in her eyes like the morning sun as she inspected Alex, noticing his veined hands, clenching and unclenching in his lap, too large for his thin wrists, reminding her of a scarecrow.

Todd's eyebrows rose for a moment, his mouth slightly open, as he watched Alex closely. Richard turned Alex to face the audience.

Alex cleared his throat. "I apologize for being late, but there are several cases to discuss this evening."

"We are overjoyed at your improvement, Alex." Dr. Todd began warmly, "but Grand Rounds have concluded." The last word altered sharply from warmth to steel, like a gate clanging shut.

"We have cases to discuss."

"You will exhaust yourself."

"I feel fine."

"You are no longer a resident. You cannot participate."

Alex paused. "I have invited guests to this meeting, and they would be very disappointed not to hear the presentations."

Dr. Todd looked around, as did the Dean. "What guests?"

"Mr. Edward Gilson."

Dr. Todd's contempt was palpable, his lips pressed together, his mouth rigid, but he waited.

"Mr. Gilson's friend, Mr. Robert McGovern, Assistant District Attorney."

Dr. Todd's eyes narrowed. "What is the reason for this?" he said softly, in a wounded tone. "This is a medical meeting."

Edward Gilson's series of spasmodic eye closures reached a climax as he held up his arm like a child in school. "Dr. Todd, Dean" he began, nodding to Dean Tripp. "May I make a suggestion? I propose we continue as scheduled with the session. Both Mr. McGovern and I are very anxious to hear the presentation."

The Dean looked at him for a moment, weighing the situation and the various responses possible. Finally, he nodded. "Very well. We have until seven o'clock as scheduled." He and Dr. Todd slowly sat down, as did others in the room.

Edward Gilson nodded, at least it appeared so, although it might simply have been a paroxysm of blinking.

Alex spoke. "Thank you for the time, Dean. We need to review matters of compelling urgency, and new evidence has come to light concerning the situations we had earlier spoke about." He stared at the Dean, then turned and smiled wanly at Dahlia.

She slowly sunk into a chair in the front of the room. "We reviewed my husband's case, the monkey, and Mr. Frederick."

He nodded in acknowledgment. "We use the great tradition of Grand Rounds to emphasize the oath we took as physicians, to above all do no harm. You have reviewed the circumstances of the treatment of Dahlia's husband, which I name Case One. Case Two is that of the experimental monkey."

"Dean, we have been over this time and time again," said Dr. Todd. "The fact is, Dr. Laronge's husband had an incurable tumor. There is no answer, no meaning to such a tragic event." He turned to Dahlia and said gently, "I understand your pain, still there after all these years."

Dahlia's face hardened.

The Dean stayed silent.

Alex took a folder from his lap. "Here is the record of radiosurgical treatment of the experimental monkey, with the radiation placed directly where I noticed the scarring during the emergency surgery." He put the transparency up on the overhead projector, and then traced the lines indicating where the deadly radiation had been targeted.

"What area is this, Dr. Fox?"

Reluctantly Fox answered, startled at being singled out once again. "Basal forebrain."

"Exactly."

"Here is an MRI scan of the monkey. Dr. Fox, where is the lesion?"

"Basal forebrain."

"Exactly. Remember that lesion," he said to the silent onlookers.

"Where did you get these films, Dr. Adams?" Dr. Todd demanded. "These were in my personal research file in my laboratory, under lock and key."

The room was silent.

"I removed them from your laboratory."

"This is an outrage."

The Dean shifted in his seat. "Am I to understand, Dr. Adams, that you broke into Dr. Todd's laboratory?"

Alex nodded. "The reasons for doing so will become clear, Dean."

Dr. Todd shook his head. "An outrage. As far as this lesion goes, I do not understand. That monkey is by definition an experimental animal. It is supposed to have lesions."

Alex continued. "Case Three is that of the unfortunate Mr. Frederick."

"Dean, I must protest. This is a ridiculous circus."

The Dean looked at Mr. McGovern, sitting stolidly in his chair, arms tightly at this side, and nodded. "We will continue until seven o'clock, as agreed, then conclude."

"Mr. Frederick was a patient of Dr. Todd's."

"Is this your proof of malfeasance, that they were my patients?"

Alex ignored him. "Mr. Frederick, like Dahlia's husband, was noted to be babbling about radiosurgery while in the hospital. However, he never had or needed radiosurgery. Yet scarring in the basal forebrain was present and observed by me during a craniotomy for subdural evacuation. Pre-operatively, he was noted to have bluish retinas on examination. The radiation treatment plan for this man was found in Dr. Todd's research records."

Dahlia nodded, "We already reviewed that."

"At any rate, these cases, the monkey, Mr. Frederick, Dahlia's husband, started me . . ."

"Us" said Dahlia.

Alex corrected himself, "started us thinking." He paused, taking a breath. "I then went to take the part two of the Neurosurgical Board Examination, the oral test. Surprisingly, though, I did not pass."

"It is not surprising in retrospect, given your situation at present," observed Dr. Todd. "Do you not remember the discussion I had with you in the hospital, the paper I showed you about scarring after subdural hematomas?"

Alex paused. There was something he couldn't quite remember, but then he surged on. "I had passed part one of the Boards, the written component, at the end of my first year in neurosurgery, which is very unusual. Before taking part two, I had much clinical experience and was confident. As you know, the oral Board examinations are made up of three one-hour segments. Each segment has different examiners. My first two sessions, two examiners per session, went well. The last hour had a single examiner, which is unheard of. It seemed to go well, but when I called an acquaintance that evening for my results, I learned the rejection came from one neurosurgeon. I think that was the examiner for the third hour, Dr. Trauberg."

"And do you think I radiated him as well?" There were some titters from the audience.

"No, but when I ran a literature search on him, I found that he had done some research with you in the past. It wouldn't take much for him to get a call from you informing him on a colleague-to-colleague basis that I simply didn't pass muster as a resident and irrespective of my performance during the oral examination, should not pass."

"Do you have proof of that accusation?"

"As you know, the notes are destroyed after the examination."

"Well, I never made such a call, but I now wish I had, given your present conduct. Certainly any concerns about your performance have been vindicated tonight."

Alex paused. "I then went on an interview to Metropolitan Hospital, Dr. Todd's previous institution. I met Dr. Frey, an old colleague of Dr. Todd's. Dr. Todd cared for Dr. Frey after his stroke, although there had been friction between them. All this is a matter of public record, but one thing bothered me. This CT scan."

He placed the scan on the overhead projector, removed the cap from his pen, and outlined the abnormality with the point. "Here is the so-called stroke. However, as you can see, the borders of the stroke are too round, too well defined, and do not match any actual arterial territory. This was not a stroke, at least not the spontaneous kind."

He stopped and picked up a file from his lap. "Then I found this file in Dr. Todd's laboratory, marked Stephen Frey." He drew out a transparency. "This is a radiation treatment plan from this file." Putting the fluttering plastic on the overhead projector, he outlined where the radiation dose hit the brain. There was a murmur from the onlookers. "As you can see, the radiation dose and the abnormality on CT scan match each other. Conclusion–Dr. Todd had administered radiation to Dr. Frey's speech area to prevent communication. Logic says that Dr. Frey found out about Dr. Todd's unauthorized experimentation and confronted him."

He looked up. "This cruel scheme has worked for years. Imagine this happening to you, finding a renegade colleague, then losing the ability to write, speak, or communicate in any way about it. Imagine how Dr. Frey felt, as the dying embers of his brain cooled, his speech disintegrating and then vanishing." He took a breath. "Today, we shine light on that dark perversion." Haggard, he looked at Dr. Todd, who stared back unbelievingly.

"Dr. Adams, have you no shame? Can't you leave even the crippled alone? Do you know what happened with this dear colleague? This is confidential patient information, but under these circumstances, I have to divulge it. Dr. Frey was hale and hearty until undergoing a sudden, spontaneous cerebral arterial thrombosis and stroke. He and his wife were desperate. At the time, I was working on an experimental protocol to improve blood flow to the brain using low doses of radiation. They begged me to try it on him. Unfortunately, it was ultimately shown not to be successful, but that is the origin of his radiation dose plan. Mrs. Frey was devastated, and unfortunately carries a great deal of guilt that she allowed the attempt." Several of the physicians were nodding.

Alex looked at Dahlia, took a deep breath, then proceeded.

"These events, then, gave us pause. There were simply too many unusual incidents. When I went to Metropolitan Hospital, I tracked down that hospital's original radiation therapist, Rene Ralston. Rene told me about Dr. Todd's early experiments, on monkeys."

"Everybody knows I pioneered these neurosurgical techniques."

"Rene gave me a copy of a dose plan he had saved, all these years." Alex pivoted the wheelchair slightly, and placed another transparency on the overhead projector. "As can be seen, the dosage is concentrated in the basal forebrain, exactly similar to the doses seen with Dahlia's husband, Mr. Frederick, and the experimental monkey. Rene told me that the monkeys didn't change much after the treatment. The relevance of this will be seen shortly."

"As I said and as is well known, I pioneered the use of radiosurgery."

"After I returned from this trip, I was in the operating room and was unable to leave to answer my beeper. I was left alone with the patient, and the phone in the OR was broken. I could not leave, and there was no one to answer the page. As a result of that inability to leave, I was fired." Alex stopped for a moment and looked at the floor. Dahlia kept her eyes on him.

"This is going from the irrational to the maudlin" Todd exclaimed. "Dean, can't we end this charade?"

Alex nodded, "These gentleman, Mr. Gilson and Mr. McGovern, are very interested in the circumstances of my accident."

As Mr. Gilson kept blinking, it was difficult to know his emotional state. Mr. McGovern, next to him, was impassive.

Alex plunged on. "After being fired, I went soaring with a quote instructor unquote. The results you see before you." He gestured at his legs. "It turned out the real instructor had been tied up behind the hanger. I went up with somebody, now dead, who giggled inappropriately, and had no idea what he was doing except carry out his last words, 'push and pull, shake him up.'"

Alex grimaced as he shifted in the wheelchair. "I've thought a lot about those words. What if he didn't know anything about flying and simply wanted to crash with me? He could force the stick down, but the sailplane might reach terminal velocity and give me time to wrestle the controls back. What if someone told him to simply hold the stick back and push the rudder pedal to the right, 'push and pull.' Does anybody know what that does?"

"Spin the glider?" timidly ventured a pimply medical student, eyes bulging, in the dim recesses of the rear seats.

"Sailplane, it's a sailplane. But you're right. Such movements reliably produce a tight spiral downward, a spin, unstoppable unless you control both stick and rudder pedal."

"But that would be suicide" observed Mr. Gilson, winking and blinking.

"Only to those who care about their life. What if you had no sense of danger?"

The DA spoke for the first time. "What are you saying, doc?"

"Suppose the patient had received radiation to his brain removing normal judgment?" Alex silently took a film out of the file and placed it on the overhead projector.

"Paul, what do you see?"

Paul Fox, miserable with all attention focused on him, reluctantly inspected the film. He scowled, "there is an area of increased signal in the deep frontal lobe."

"The basal forebrain."

Paul nodded.

"What else?"

Paul inspected the film. After a time he shook his head.

"Where is his neck? He has been traumatically decapitated. There is no neck. This is the MRI scan of the head of my so-called instructor."

The room was silent. Alex continued. "As you can see, this lesion is exactly the same as those we have previously seen, except this patient tried to kill me."

Dr. Todd said quietly, "This charade proves nothing. I see a cyst in the basal forebrain, nothing more. Fluid filled cysts can occur throughout the brain. The rest, is, I am afraid, wild and pathopsychologic ramblings."

"Allow me to complete my Grand Rounds presentation. While lying in the hospital bed, I thought about patterns. Patterns of behavior so monstrous, so barbaric, as to be utterly outside the known range of human experience, of human imagination. And yet so well hidden, I dare say, that even after this presentation, most people here are in disbelief." He paused. "What could account for such behavior? Suppose after the original radiosurgical brain experiments on the monkeys, which seemed inconclusive, the brave experimenter remembers his medical forefathers, Haffkine inoculating himself with cholera vaccine, Moniz injecting his carotid artery with dye to examine the vessels of the brain.

He felt himself on the verge of a new world much as those pioneering medical explorers had done before him. The monkeys were not harmed, they seemed enhanced, in some undefinable way by the carefully targeted radiation. He would never be able to get permission to experiment on a human, so he considered, and took the plunge. He experiments on himself, subjecting himself to careful, focused, planned radiation to the basal forebrain, and he notices no effect. But his colleagues note him to be more persuasive, louder, more, as some charitably put, of a personality." Alex looked around the room. He seemed paler, smaller, his eyes wide. "But why? Why this change? Suppose that what he has killed in his brain is the seat of choices, the neuroanatomic equivalent of a conscience, where we balance our desires and actions. That's why the animals had no obvious reaction. They have no conscience, no moral sense. They are not human. But the doctor is, or was. Now, this crippled physician is free to continue, to expand his efforts, aided by his new vigor and unencumbered by ethical dilemmas. Suppose then, he looked about for additional experimental material, eager to continue. He sees many patients for various problems, and one day evaluates a patient with back pain. The man is without parents, siblings, or children. It is a simple matter to tell him that he needs to be sedated for a diagnostic test, and instead, while the patient is asleep, do radiosurgery on the hapless patient to radiate and kill the basal forebrain in a further attempt to fathom the functions of this enigmatic area."

The room was totally silent.

Todd suddenly shifted in his seat, breaking the silence. "Have we lost our minds, sitting here listening to this? This is the ultimate flight of fancy, of irrationality." He paused, then flattened out his broad hands. "Where is the proof?"

"The proof is in three parts," said Alex gravely. "The first part is the pattern of behavior and results we have reviewed. The next part of the proof has to do with that second man who was treated with radiosurgery. The man without family, who came to Dr. Todd for treatment of simple back pain. Instead, and most horribly unbeknownst to him, his brain was violated. His chart is here. The dose treatment plan is here, and we have become familiar with it since." Reaching out, he put the transparency on the overhead, tracing out with his finger the deadly radiation dose to the basal forebrain. "I draw your attention to the initials on this plan, T.D. This is a man who was Dr. Todd's patient years ago, who started from humble beginnings, an unknown when he saw Dr. Todd for back pain. Who now occupies the most powerful office in the world." Alex paused. "President Thomas Lincoln Davies."

Attention was rapt. "While in my hospital bed, I downloaded the President's MRI scan. Here are some representative views." Alex placed the film on the projector. "Paul, what do you see?"

Paul swallowed hard. He looked like a whipped dog hit too many times, a little dog that keeps hiding its rear end, endlessly maneuvering so it can't be struck again, twisting and turning. With a jerky motion he put his hand to the side of his face, then to his forehead. "Increased signal in the basal forebrain."

There was a pause. Dr. Todd arose slowly and said gently, carefully, "Alex, I do know the story of that lesion. The President has a family history of brain cysts. The White House physician consulted me on this, and this clearly is a cyst consistent with the family history. It is seven o'clock now, and we must draw this to an end."

Alex stared back. "The President and his family grew up in Olmsted County, Minnesota. This is the county that has the finest medical records in the nation, dating back many years. There is no record of a CT scan, MRI scan, or autopsy of any of the President's relatives. There can be no evidence of a familial cyst."

Dr. Todd smiled. "The President's medical records and those of his family are a matter of national security and are protected as such. Of course, there is no public record."

Alex looked exhausted, pale. He put his hand to his forehead for a moment. The audience shifted. "My final contribution to Grand Rounds is a video tape."

Dr. Todd shrugged then turned, whispered to Paul Fox and sat down. Paul left the room quickly. Alex nodded to Curt, who started the video projector as the lights dimmed. The crowd gasped at the screen. Alex, eyes closed and head frame on, was being loaded into the radiosurgical unit and undergoing radiosurgery.

The lights went on. "That was a record from last night, when, after finding me in the laboratory, Weber, Dr. Todd's assistant, knocked me out. I underwent an MRI scan." Alex touched his head gingerly. "After that I was taken to radiation therapy and underwent radiosurgery. That is, I would have if medical student and former electrical engineer Richard Walters hadn't been working on the video camera in secret and had the presence of mind to cut the current to the radiation generator. It went through the motions, but no radiation was delivered."

Dr. Todd stood up, his face flushed and nostrils flared. "I don't know where you got that tape, Alex, but I must protest. I must break patient confidentiality. Alex, you forced me to do so. I have no choice." The room was silent, then Paul Fox returned with an MRI film flapping in his hand. He gave it to Dr. Todd.

Todd got up and walked to the other side of the projector, towering over Alex. "It was not known until today, but I have been treating Dr. Adams for a brain tumor, one which clearly and unfortunately has affected his judgment and personality to the tragic degree visible here." He looked at Alex, who stared up at him in amazement, his face lit and shadowed by the light from the overhead projector next to him. Dahlia thought for a moment Alex was winking, but then saw his lower eyelid twitch involuntarily again, repeated spasms, accentuated by the bright illumination. "It is my fault, that through my own concern and emotional attachment to Alex, I relaxed my vigilance and inadvertently allowed this sad and unfortunate spectacle." Dr. Todd took a deep breath, brought a huge hand to his face, rubbing his closed eyes, then grimaced sadly. "I will live with this for the rest of my life. Here is a copy of my office notes." He turned and placed a transparency on the projector. "As can been seen, I have been following Dr. Adams, and even have consulted with Dr. Allen, Chief of Neurosurgery at Metropolitan Hospital, about this most difficult situation." The room was dead silent as everybody read the projected text. Dr. Todd recited it in a strong but tortured voice.

"Office note on Alex Adams. I've reviewed Alex Adams' recent MRI scan, done one month ago. The lesion is small and deep. There is very little swelling associated with the lesion, and thus little functional effect at this point. However, there may be unpredictable neuropsychological consequences in the future, and we need to watch for them. We will obtain another study in several months. I reviewed the situation with Dr. John Allen, Chief of Neurosurgery of Metropolitan Hospital, and he is in agreement with a conservative approach at this time, as the lesion is incurable and unresectable." He paused, then with quick, sure movements, removed the text and placed a film on the projector. "Here is Dr. Adams' MRI scan."

Alex looked at Dahlia, and then at the name on the projected film. "Alex Adams" he read aloud. He shook his head. "That's not my scan."

"With all the confusion and falsehoods you have spewed, you're hardly in a condition to judge what is and is not accurate," said Dr. Todd sadly and regretfully. He turned to the scan. "Here is the tumor, apparent in the deep thalamus." Tracing the area with a pen, the tumor was obvious. "We have the explanation here for this sad and misguided behavior. There are no villains here." He shook his head sorrowfully, and slowly looked up at Alex, his head moving first, his eyes following. "Alex, I wanted to spare you, but you gave me absolutely no choice." He turned to the Dean, and quietly spoke to him and to the lawyers. "Now, gentleman, if we can conclude this. I think we have all had enough."

Alex turned slowly, not believing what was happening. He looked down, seemingly inward, his eyes narrowing, staring at nothing. His fixed smile, a frozen, forced rictus, lost its strength and his mouth dropped open, fishlike, hollowing his cheeks. The muscles around his eyes tightened. He looked at Dahlia for a long moment, and then took a breath.

"I said there were three parts to my proof" he said quietly, almost to himself, "and we have not heard the third part" he cried out, clenching his fists, his voice loud and firm. "I will be heard."

"Please, Alex, no more of your pathologic theories" Dr. Todd said wearily. "Dean, for his own good, we must bring this to an end."

"The test of a theory is how well it predicts reality," said Alex, his eyes jumping from face to face. "My theory predicts that if all that I said is correct, an MRI scan will show my brain to be normal and yours to have the burn in your basal frontal brain, one you made on yourself so many years ago."

Dr. Todd stopped. He shook his head.

Dahlia stood up and turned. "We must do this. We will not be silent until the matter is settled."

Richard, perched on the side of the stage, slid off, shoes slapping the floor. "Get the MRI scans."

The Dean closed his eyes.

"Dean, if I may suggest, the simplest way to settle this issue is to get the MRI scans," quavered Mr. Gilson. The Dean shook his head.

"Given what we have witnessed tonight, Dr. Tripp, I agree" said Mr. McGovern.

Dr. Todd turned to the Dean in anger, "Have we forgotten what is right and wrong? Is this some sort of joke? You're paying attention to these pathologic fantasies?"

The room was silent and the clock could be heard ticking. "Questions have been raised, Victor. We must settle them" the Dean said wearily, then nodded slowly. "This won't take long. Let's go to the MRI scanner."

Todd looked around for a moment at the silent faces.

They all arose as if church were over, and en masse walked quietly over to the MRI scanner, Dahlia rolling Alex. He was breathing heavily.

"Dahlia, my headaches are getting worse" he looked up and whispered to her.

She gripped his shoulder like the talons of a hawk, and continued to push the wheelchair with the other arm.

The MRI technician looked up, amazed and dismayed, as the horde of people came in. They walked over to the reading room, where several radiologists were clustered, murmuring in front of a backlit film like impotent solons, medieval alchemists puzzling over meaningless fluids, gravely pondering the slightest of inconsequential changes on the scan. One radiologist, with pointed goatee and a tower of hair, looked up with annoyance and then recognized the Dean.

"What can we do for you, Dean Tripp?"

"We need two MRI scans done right away."

"Of course, Dean." He looked at the technician.

"We're booked up for tonight," she said helplessly.

"This is obviously extremely important. You'll just have to bump someone."

The tech nodded and looked at the throng. "Okay. We'll get the patient off the table."

She scuttled back to the gantry and alerted another technician. They hustled the protesting patient off the MRI couch, and then came back, waiting expectantly.

Alex spoke first, "I'll go, Dean."

The Dean nodded. The technicians wheeled Alex over to the MRI couch, carefully lifting him up. He reclined slowly, his eyes darting, and then clamping shut as he was left alone before the tube. The techs scurried out to the control panel, the door quietly closing behind them. Glancing through the glass where their faint images mirrored their movement, they manipulated the controls and sent the couch into the MRI tunnel.

Alex felt the closeness of the bore, realizing he couldn't get his arms up above his head. His legs were aching.

"How long will this take?"

The answer seemed to come from a long way away, the small speaker rasping. "You'll be done soon."

Dahlia anxiously looked at the screen after forcing her way to the front of the group clustered about the console. She leaned over and called into the speaker "Don't move."

Alex's tinny voice came back, "It's a little tight in here."

Dahlia groaned inwardly as she stared at the screen imbedded in the control panel, along with all the other eyes in the room.

Pictures appeared, slice by slice, starting at the skull base. The assemblage watched and waited.

"There's the thalamus," she pointed. The images continued. Normal. She breathed again. "It's normal, Dean."

"Let's get the complete study."

They were quiet as normal scan after normal scan appeared. As the last picture formed, she edged toward the MRI door.

"Can I go in?" The tech nodded. Dahlia burst in and went over to the machine. Only Alex's feet were protruding.

His small voice came through the tunnel, "Is it over yet?"

"Hurry" she called to the tech, turning around. The tech lumbered up, pressed a button and slid Alex out.

He was sweaty and white. "It's a little tight in there."

"Alex, it's normal."

"No, not everybody gets claustrophobic."

"Your brain is normal. It's normal."

"Well, did you have any doubts?" He grimaced, then shot a look at her. "It hurts like hell, though."

Outside, the Dean turned to Dr. Todd, raising his eyebrows. Silently, Dr. Todd went in, the tech helping him onto the MRI couch and then maneuvering him into the scanning tunnel.

Dahlia pushed Alex to the console as the tech closed the door, then started up the machine once again and began scanning. All eyes were on the monitor screen as each slice appeared. Normal, normal, normal slices.

Alex shifted his weight. Then an image came on the screen, and Alex jabbed his finger excitedly. "There it is. Basal forebrain–increased signal." He looked up at the Dean, then glanced at Mr. Gilson. "As predicted."

The Dean stared, then nodded slowly. He looked at Alex and Dahlia steadily for a moment, and then said quietly as he held out his hand, "I guess I owe you an apology."

He shook each of their hands.

Alex pointed to the bright spot in Todd's brain, and said softly, "One shot and it was destroyed . . . . the truly perfect murder, or suicide, because all externals are kept intact. Only the essence of an individual is gone. What is that essence? What truly distinguishes one person from another? Their sense of right and wrong, their internal compass, what they believe to be important enough to change their behavior, to keep that internal voice, belief, conscience satisfied. What makes someone truly an individual is what he will do to do 'the right thing'. That and only that is what distinguishes us. This" he paused while he formed the word, "treatment . . . as it was obscenely described, destroyed that, destroyed the essence of the person, the transcendent contained in each of us. What is left is pure animal. Perhaps, perhaps that's why others responded so strongly to Todd, to the President. Because their animal natures responded powerfully as well, without being aware of the cause. Without a conscience, the full emotional power of the human brain is released indiscriminately, without focus, without meaning." He looked up, embarrassed, but Dahlia kept staring at him.

"How do you account for Mr. Frederick?"

"What do you mean?"

"Todd treated him, and yet he was a pillar of the community, a true good guy. I had a long talk with his family when he died, and the visitors that night all told the same story. He was a force for good."

Alex thought for a moment, and then nodded. "We don't know it all. Our science only takes us so far. What do we really know about the glory of man, of free will and imagination? Clearly, some are more vulnerable to this lesion than others." He paused and shrugged.

The silent throng suddenly started talking, then thinned out to excitedly depart, while Alex, Dahlia, the Dean, Mr. Gilson, and Mr. McGovern stayed.

Dr. Todd was slid out of the MRI tunnel. He sat up, and his face rippled with rage. At first Alex thought he was having seizures, the spasmodic jerks of his facial muscles, his lips, his cheeks, were so prominent, hideously deforming his face for brief instants. A fleeting, fragment of rage in the right jaw, shifting to the left cheek, then more anger in the lips. Alex finally realized as he stared, transfixed, that this was the direct output of the emotional centers of the brain, without coordination, without conscious direction. There was something animalistic in the display, the uncontrollable jerks forming a cacophony of expression, an atavistic window into the human brain. The tech stopped, frightened and fascinated, until the Boss's face settled into a composed mask. He walked through the door into the control room, over to the Dean, who glanced at him and nodded at the screen.

"Dr. Todd, you do have a lesion."

Todd slowly turned and looked at the screen, then at Alex. His mouth looked old, sagging like a tired shark. He smiled warmly and said, "Alex, what has been destroyed? There's nothing in me that has been obliterated. Look around you. I just accelerated a process that has been going on throughout human society. There are many people like me. This is the way of the world."

Alex looked at him steadily. "You will never acknowledge this." He thought of his college days. "Socrates said that 'No man seeks evil in his own mind—he always works towards what he perceives is the good.'" He stared at Todd for an eternal moment, and then turned to the Dean. "The President?"

The Dean nodded. "I know his personal physician. I will call him."

Alex looked at Dahlia, their eyes blazing. Exultation gripped their souls.

EPILOGUE

The twenty-fifth Amendment to the Constitution of the United States was invoked for the first time in the case of Thomas Lincoln Davies. It was publicly announced that the President had a brain tumor, very slowly growing, impeding the conduct of his official duties.

Privately it was known that the President was recalcitrant to the end, unwilling to resign, and only doing so with his physicians' signed statement that he was unfit for duty placed on his desk. His brave and eloquent attempts to ignore his disability and address public issues were dutifully and periodically recorded in the press, and ignored by most everybody.

The President's legacy proved as ephemeral as his smile. For all the poll results and uplifted faces, he vanished from the national stage quickly.

In reflecting on his public career, it was clear in retrospect that the underlying strength of the American people and their system of government, as well as the President's good luck, had been the main operative factors in his administration.

After his trial, Dr. Victor Todd was placed in a secluded hospital for the criminally insane, where other inmates avoided him. Scattered around his small room were a few artifacts from a lifetime of medicine.

Frequently the Boss moved around his chamber, prowling, looking at pictures, handling them, always ending his roaming at the same gold framed photograph of the President, his wife, and a group of high government officials. He would pick it up, eagerly at first, then speculatively, his eyes first focusing on President Davies, wistful in his longing and sadness. After a time, his gaze would shift to another face, his eyes becoming even darker, and his deeply lined face softening with the shadow of joy.